DAUGHTER
OF LIR

DAUGHTER OF LIR

·····························◆◆···························

JUDITH TARR

A TOM DOHERTY ASSOCIATES BOOK

NEW YORK

DAUGHTER OF LIR

Copyright © 2001 by Judith Tarr

This book is printed on acid-free paper.

A Forge Book
Published by Tom Doherty Associates, LLC
175 Fifth Avenue
New York, NY 10010

www.tor.com

Forge® is a registered trademark of Tom Doherty Associates, LLC.

Library of Congress Cataloging-in-Publication Data

Tarr, Judith.
    Daughter of Lir / Judith Tarr.–1st ed.
      p. cm.
    "A Tom Doherty Associates Book."
    ISBN 0-312-87616-5 (acid-free paper)
    1. Women Prophets–Fiction. 2. Goddess religion–Fiction.
  3. Prehistoric peoples–Fiction. I. Title.

PS3570.A655 D38 1998
813'.54–dc21

                         2001023178

First Edition: June 2001

Printed in the United States of America

0 9 8 7 6 5 4 3 2 1

DAUGHTER
OF LIR

THE LASTBORN

O N THE DAY the Mother's daughter was born, a storm battered the city of Lir. Winds tore at its walls and towers. Thunder cracked. Rain lashed the streets.

She was very young to be the Mother of a city, though not so young to bear a child. This was her third, and the first that was not a son: a blessing, and great joy, for a daughter would be Mother in her place, when she was old and august and had lived the full count of her years. She came to the birthing knowing she bore a daughter. She sang through the pains, though her dreams of late had all been dark.

Just as her daughter leaped into the world, the world itself split asunder. Lightning struck the topmost tower of the temple and cast it down in ruins. The Mother, secure in the sanctuary below, loosed a great cry, fierce and shrill above the tumult of heaven.

They laid the child on her hollowed belly, all bloodied and newborn as it was. In the ringing silence after her cry, the Mother bit through the cord and bound it with her own hands. But she did not take the small wriggling creature in her arms. When she reached to do it, the last strength poured out of her, a gout of blood that wrung a cry from the midwives. She fell back with a soft sound, neither a gasp nor quite a cry.

The child began to slip from her belly. One of the priestesses caught it: the youngest, standing startled as if she had not known what she would do until she had done it.

A murmur passed among the attendants. The young priestess should not have been there. She was new come to childbed herself, but her son had scarcely opened his eyes on the world before he shivered and died.

She clutched the baby to her breast, which was full and aching with new milk. The child nosed, seeking; found the nipple; began to nurse. She stood transfixed. She made no move to thrust the child away, nor did anyone move to take it from her.

⇒ ⇐

The Mother lived, if barely. They had entrusted her life and spirit to the Goddess whose living image she was. Healer-priestesses tended her. Even a man had come, one of the sacred dancers, who had a great gift of making and healing.

The rest of the Goddess' servants gathered in the heart of the temple, in the shrine that was as old, some said, as the world. It was round like the curve of the Goddess' arms, and full of lamplight. But the shadows crowded and whispered.

Before the image of the Goddess, squat and holy, the priestesses knelt in a circle. Chill as it was without, it was warm here, warm as their bodies. The dim light flickered on bare white shoulders, heavy breasts, rich swells of haunches.

As close as they seemed, linked arm in arm in their circle, their eyes on its center were hard and cold. The child lay there in the youngest priestess' lap, washed clean of blood and birthing. She was awake; her eyes were open, dark and oddly focused. She did not cry.

They had taken the omens. They had sung the words, danced the dance. They had drawn the pattern of the child's life on the floor, painting it in red ocher and blue woad and the sweetness of green herbs. Yet stronger than all that brightness was black earth, earth charred in fire. The scars of it swept across the rest, overwhelmed it, obliterated it.

"This cannot be Mother," said the eldest priestess as she knelt by the broken pattern. "This should not even live."

"This is the Lastborn, the Stormborn," said her sister, like an antiphon in the Goddess' rite. "This brings the world's end."

Voices took up the litany, murmuring round the circle. "We cannot let this—thing—see the sunlight. It carries our destruction."

"Sacrifice it here? Expose it on a hillside? Feed it to the dogs?"

"No." That voice was clear and strong, though the one who spoke had seen years enough in both sun and shadow. She was highest of the priestesses but for the Mother. In the Mother's incapacity she spoke for the Goddess, as her living Voice.

She put on no airs. She was a plain woman, thick-legged, sturdy. She had borne a dozen children, and all of them had lived. Her body showed the marks of them, on the belly, on the soft heavy breasts.

When she spoke, they all listened. She was the Goddess' own, her beloved child. "No," she said again. "This child will not die. The Goddess has no thirst for blood."

"This is bloodthirst incarnate," the eldest priestess said. "It clutches death in its hand. Let us give it what belongs to it. Let us end it now, before it ends us all."

"No," the Goddess' Voice said again. "However ill the omens, however dark the path ahead of her, the Goddess bids her live."

"She cannot be Mother," the eldest priestess said, flat and hard. "Her heart is darkness. She will destroy us."

"The Goddess will protect us," said the Voice. She sighed and sagged briefly, as if beset with weariness.

The youngest priestess spoke as the Voice paused to gather strength. Her voice was soft and shy, but the words were clear enough. "I will take her."

They had all been ignoring her—deliberately, since she took the child from its mother's slackened arms, then compounded the fault by suffering it to drink life from her breast. She would atone for that. She knew it as well as any. And yet she spoke.

"My son died this morning," she said. "My heart is empty. My breasts ache. My man is far away, trading in the southlands, and will not return until the winter. No one outside the temple knows what has passed here. If I take her and raise her as my own, and tell her nothing of the truth—might not the ill things pass us by?"

"The gods know," said the eldest priestess.

But the youngest had drawn strength and fire from her own words, and from the small warm creature in her lap. "The Goddess knows. But the gods and spirits—I took her up in my arms. I gave her her first milk. Let us cleanse her here, purify her, make her new again. I will name her and hold her up in front of the people, and she will be my child. We will weave a new fate for her."

The priestesses shifted uneasily. "That has never been done before," the eldest said. "To lie to the gods—it could bring on us the very thing we fear."

"The Goddess wishes her to live," said the Voice.

"Does the Goddess wish us to die?"

"I only speak for her," the Voice said. "I don't pretend to understand her."

"I will take the child," the youngest priestess said again. "She need not die in the world—only to what she was to have been. She will be my daughter before the gods and their servants."

The elder priestesses shook their heads. But the Voice nodded slowly. "Let it be so," she said. "Let it be done. Let this child of blood and war be raised in peace. Let her grow up in gentleness. Let her never know the darkness that would have claimed her."

"No more let her know the Goddess' service," the eldest priestess said. "Let her be a child among the Goddess' lesser children. Let no choosing of the temple fall upon her, nor great arts be taught her. Let her know nothing of power or magic. Let her be a simple woman, plain, unremarkable. Let her live and die in obscurity."

The youngest priestess bowed her head. She was the first of her family to be chosen for the temple. She had hoped not to be the last.

Surely there would be daughters of her body. One of them would go as her mother had gone—and this one, meanwhile, would live. She who had been born to be Mother and queen would be a simple village child; but better that than dead upon the altar of sacrifice.

"So let it be," she said, "in the Goddess' name."

I

THE POTTER'S CHILD

.... 1 ....

THE GODDESS' SERVANT came to Long Ford in the spring of the year, not long after the snows had melted. The river was still running high, but boats could ride down from the city, and horsemen and lumbering oxcarts venture the road.

The priestess came in a boat, sitting erect and still with her acolytes about her. She was not terribly old, but neither was she young. Her body was heavy with years and childbearing. There was silver in her hair, but her broad face was smooth. It had no beauty, but it was splendid with power.

She was one of the great ones, one whose name was taken away, who spoke and acted for the Goddess in all things. It was a very great thing to see such a one under the common sky, sailing down the river in the morning.

Her escort rode just ahead of her on the road by the river. They were haughty warriors of Lir, mounted on fine horses. Their armor was hardened leather, their ornaments clashing copper. Each wore a wolfskin for a cloak. Their commander gleamed in gold and bronze, and his mantle was a lionskin. He was highest and most haughty of them all, and his stallion was magnificent: dappled silver-grey, with a mane like a fall of water, and a dark brilliant eye.

They looked very much alike, the horse and the rider. Rhian, watching from the hill above the village, spared a long moment for the priestess in the boat, but the man on horseback kept catching her eye. He was young; he carried himself very high, but the nearer he came, the clearer it was that he was hardly older than she was herself.

This must be a prince of the city. People rode or sailed to and from Lir in every clear season, but princes did not come this way often. Not much more often, indeed, than priestesses from the temple.

They were going on past Long Ford, she supposed, on some embassy of great importance. Nobody ever stopped here. It was a small village, not poor at all, but not rich, either. There was nothing of note in it, except a smith who knew how to forge bronze, and once a daughter who had been chosen to be a priestess in Lir.

She was dead years since. The temple had not summoned another in her place, not even Rhian who had been her daughter.

A shadow on the spirit had brought Rhian to the hilltop, to the old fort that was long broken and abandoned, in time to see the priestess and the prince and the rest. She had dreamed again last night. In the dream she was a bird, a wonderful bird, a bird with feathers of flame. Her wings were wide. Her voice was as sweet as all heaven.

But she could not sing. A collar of bronze bound her throat, crushing the voice from her. The bars of a cage closed about her. She was trammeled, silent, bound till she could not move.

That dream had haunted her all her life. She had thought herself inured to it, until she woke gasping, her heart hammering, and no thought in her but flight.

She was calmer now. The wind was whispering in her ear, cajoling her, telling her its secrets. Sarai the weaver was with child again, and this time it would live. The brindled cow had delivered twin calves in the night. The hunters had found a fine stag and would bring him back come evening. Bran the smith was thinking of Rhian, and of what they would do in his bed tonight.

She blushed all over at that. The wind laughed and danced in the new spring grass. It had better secrets than that. Strong secrets, wonderful secrets. What the priestesses said in the shrine of the Goddess. What the warlords said in their hall of weapons in Lir. What the king, the great warleader, said to the Mother of Lir when they lay together in the long murmuring nights.

Not, said the wind, stilling for a moment, that they had said anything for long and long. The Mother was sick. She was dying. They were all very sad in Lir.

"Is that why the priestess is coming down the river?" Rhian asked the wind. The chill that shivered across her skin did not come from that little bit of breeze. This was an older, stronger, colder thing.

The wind wandered for a while through the grass. It came round at length to Rhian and played with the loose strands of hair that were always escaping from her plait. The priestess was looking for new priestesses, it said. It was a Ninth Year. The priestesses always went questing then. And maybe this year, it conceded, one of the young women chosen would be Mother when the Mother died—since she had no daughter, only sons; and the Goddess had not given her blessing to any priestess in Lir.

These were high matters, too high for a potter's child. But the wind had always expected her to understand things both lofty and strange. Rhian was like a goddess sitting above the world, knowing what went on in it, but having no part of it.

That was a dangerous thought. She lay down on the breast of the earth and whispered her apology. Then she leaped up. She would go to her work, bury herself in her duty. She would tend the kiln and keep the house and forget it all: The wind's gossip. The dream that had driven her out into the sun. The priestess, the prince, everything that was higher or stronger or less perfectly ordinary than Long Ford.

But as she paused, with the wind teasing her, plucking at her gown and blowing her hair in her eyes, she saw through the dark curling veil that the priestess' boat had turned toward the bank. The horsemen were pausing below the village. They were stopping after all. They were coming to Long Ford.

Her heart hammered till surely it would leap from her breast. Had they come for her, then? Would they make her a priestess in Lir? She was a priestess' daughter. She dreamed dreams. The wind told her secrets. Surely they would take her. They would shatter the collar, break down the cage. They would let her fly free.

She danced down the hill, but she was walking sedately by the time she passed the outermost houses of the village. If she would be a priestess, she must learn to walk with dignity, not run about like a hoyden child.

But oh, it was difficult. If she could go to Lir—if—if—

All her life, when she was not dreaming of cages, she had dreamed of Lir. City of bronze and gold. City of proud warrior princes. City of the Goddess, the Lady of the Birds, and of her high and holy temple, and her blessed priestesses.

Maybe now she would see it. Maybe she would be a priestess in it, as her mother had been. Maybe even the dreams would stop, and she could sleep in peace.

⇒ ⇐

The priestess and her following stayed the night in Long Ford. There was a feast, for the hunters had come back with their stag. The village elders kept the guests to themselves, as was proper, but Rhian was a bold bad creature when she wanted to be. She plucked a platter of venison from the hands of the headwoman's youngest daughter, smiled with utter sweetness, and said, "You go and play. I'll take your place for tonight."

Kimi was none too reluctant to be freed of her duties. Her eyes had already slid toward one of the younger and more toothsome of the priestess' warriors. She was gone almost before Rhian had finished speaking.

Rhian smiled to herself. Her own eyes were sliding, too, but not toward any downy-cheeked boy.

The prince from Lir sat near the priestess at the feast. He was even lovelier in the late sunlight than he had been in the morning by the river. With his armor and his lionskin laid aside, he was still a fine figure of a man. His shoulders were broad. His arms were strong. His hair was black and thick and plaited behind him. It was like her own: it seemed determined to burst out of its bonds and run riot down his back.

She made sure to serve him and the warriors and lesser priestesses nearest to him. She did not quite dare to thrust herself in front of the elders and the priestess, but she was close enough to hear what they said, and to watch their faces as they spoke.

The wind told better secrets. This talk was all of food and drink, the weather, the crops, the state of the river-trade. No one was speaking of the Mother, of her living or dying.

The warriors and the acolytes were even less interesting. They ate, mostly; eyed the young folk of the village, both male and female; and, as the ale went round, boasted mightily of their wars and hunts. To this the acolytes added tales of their journey downriver, gossip from the city, and a long giggle over the prowess of certain young men of the city.

One of them was the prince. His name, Rhian had already discovered, was Emry. He was the king's son, and the Mother's eldest child. He ignored the banter—resolute, maybe, or simply oblivious to it. He had said very little since he came to the village, only enough to assure Rhian that he was not mute. His voice fit the rest of him, deep and sweet.

She picked out the choicest bits of venison from her platter and set them in his bowl. He barely touched them. His eyes did not see anything in that place. They were dark; it was not until he raised them by chance to hers, that she realized they were not brown but deep blue.

He took no notice of her. That piqued her. She had had to fend off a dozen half-drunken advances already. Men liked her; she had always had her pick of them. They said she was beautiful. But this man, who was as beautiful as she, seemed hardly to be aware that she existed.

Maybe he grieved for his mother. When he rose to go to the privies, she followed.

He went on past the privies, as she had suspected he would, and wandered up the hill. The sun was setting. It cast a light like blood across the tumbled and broken stones.

He stood in the midst of them, wide shoulders hunched, glowering at nothing. Rhian settled not far from him, squatting on her heels. Gathering stalks of grass and a handful of pebbles, she began to build a fort with them, no higher than her hand.

When the tower and the wall were laid out in stones and the palisade of grass-stems had begun to go up, his shadow fell across her. He straightened a corner of the wall, and braced it with a bit of twig. "Your gate should face east," he said. "That's where the enemy will come from."

"More likely they'll come from the south or the north, along the road by the river," she said.

He squatted beside her. He was not offended to be so contradicted, which surprised her. "You think about war?" he asked.

"Why, shouldn't we all?"

His eyes glinted on her. "Most villagers think about nothing but the planting or the harvest. War is an intrusion—and a useless one at that."

"Some people would tell you there's no such thing; it's been driven right out of the world."

"Well," said the prince, "we've been free of it for a hundred years and more. Maybe it will never come again."

"You believe that?"

He shrugged and did not answer. The setting sun was in his face. He was the most beautiful man she had ever seen. She wanted to touch him, to see if he was real. But she kept her hands to herself.

"Are you a lover of men?" she asked him.

He looked somewhat startled. "Why do you ask that?"

"Men notice me," she said.

His eyes widened even further. He looked very young indeed then, for all his height and his breadth and his black curly beard. "Would you want me if I had?"

"Would I have had to ask?"

He looked her up and down. He did admire her then, but not as she would have liked. "Tell me what you really want," he said.

You, she meant to say. But while that was true, it was not all of the truth. "I want to go to Lir," she said.

He nodded as if he had expected that answer. But he said, "I'm not going there. We're traveling down the river, seeking out priestesses for the temple."

"That will do," Rhian said. "Take me with you when you go."

"Why? What can you do? Can you ride? Fight? Sail a boat?"

"I can stay on a horse," she said. "I can throw a pot and shear a sheep and hunt deer in the woods. I can cook. I can brew ale. I know a little of smelting, and a little more of woodworking. I can make toys for children. And," she said last of all, "I can please a man greatly."

"Toys," he said, "for children."

He was mocking her. She flashed back at him. "What can you do besides ride and fight?"

"I can dance the warriors' dances. I can sing. I can hunt boar in the woods. And," he said, "I can please a woman greatly. But I am not going to do that tonight."

"Are you grieving for your mother?"

She had surprised him again, but briefly this time. "So. Word travels fast."

It did, if one could speak with the wind. Rhian did not say that. She had learned long ago that a potter's child, even a potter's child whose mother had been a priestess, was not expected to hear more than the simplest ears could hear.

"I'm sorry that she's ill," she said.

"She's dying." His voice was soft and seemed calm, but it was deeply bitter. "She'll be dead before this journey is over."

"And you would have stayed at home if you could."

"I have my duty," he said. "I'm needed here."

"More than there?"

"More than you can imagine."

Maybe that was true. Maybe he was merely being a prince, and indulging in arrogance. That was his right. Was he not the king's son of Lir?

A proper villager would have bowed and effaced herself. Rhian had never had much propriety in her. She narrowed her eyes. "The young women your priestess chooses. Will they go with you? Or back to the city?"

"Back to the city," he said.

"So," said Rhian. "Who goes with them?"

"Not I," he said. "Why don't you simply go? Are you bound here? Is there a geas on you?"

She shivered. The wind, that had been so still, had risen to stroke her with cold fingers. "I want to go," she heard herself say, "not as a beggar at the door, but as a ruler in the house. I want my name to matter."

"You are ambitious," he said. She could not tell whether he was mocking or admiring her.

"May not even a potter's child dream of being more than she is?" Rhian demanded.

"Anyone may dream," said the prince of Lir.

Rhian shut her mouth with a snap. The wind had risen to a keen. She refused to listen to it. She spun and stalked away from him, half-running down the long hill.

2

Bran the smith would never need to know why Rhian pulled him out of the dance round the fire, kissed him till he staggered, and dragged him off to his house. He was not a prince from Lir, but he was hers. He was nigh as big as Emry and fully as broad, and he knew her body as only a lover could.

He was happy to let her eat him alive. But though he was a complaisant lover, he was not a stupid man. When they had worn each other out, when she had cradled herself in his arms, he said, "You're going to run off with the prince."

She blinked. She did not know why her eyes were pricking with tears. "Not if he has anything to say about it."

"Does he? The priestess will choose you. Everybody knows that."

"Nobody knows it," she said testily, though her heart was begging it to be true.

"I do." He ran his hand down her back, waking little shivers of pleasure. His fingers were big but delicate in their touch.

She lifted her head, peering at him in the light of the lamp. He was not the beauty that the prince was, but he was a well-made man. His face was pleasant to look at, his brown eyes quiet, resting on her with a kind of patient sadness.

He looked like one of the sheep. She pulled him down and kissed him hard. They were both gasping for breath when she let him go. "You won't forget me," she said, "but you won't sleep alone, either. I've seen how Cara looks at you."

"Maybe Cara will go, too," he said.

"Not that one," Rhian said with a curl of the lip. "She has her feet sunk firmly in earth."

"And isn't that the breast of the Goddess?"

"Maybe they'll pick *you*," Rhian said.

That made him laugh, though she had not meant it to. "And wouldn't I make a lovely woman," said that bear of a man. "No, I'm a lesser being. I'm content with it. I'll watch you soar against the sun."

"If I fly too high, I'll singe my wings." The words had slipped out before she thought. They brought back the dream, so vivid and so sudden that she caught her breath. She clung to Bran, to his solid and familiar bulk. "What if I'm not meant—what if I'm not permitted—"

"There," he said, rocking her. "There."

But she was not to be comforted. He gave it up—too easily, she thought crossly, but if he had not, that would have pricked her temper, too. He slept. She lay awake far into the night, holding sleep at bay. In sleep were dreams. And if she dreamed the cage again, she knew that she would die.

⇒ ⇐

She was up at dawn, catching the first light in Bran's workshop where she kept a bench and tools and the toys that she made for the children. She was making something new, something that she had seen in another dream than the one that so tormented her. It began as a wagon such as oxen drew, but smaller and lighter. There were two wheels instead of four, and their shape and fashion had defeated her. In the end she had carved them like cartwheels, but drawn on them the image of her dream: four spokes that would turn and spin as the cart rolled onward. She had been painting it red and gold, drawing shapes on it such as suited her fancy: wheels and spirals and the rayed disk of the sun.

The sun rose as she surveyed her handiwork. The cart rolled easily on its wheels, but teetered and tipped when she let go the pole. She frowned. It needed horses to pull it—not oxen, of that she was sure. She would carve those, but later. In Lir, if she was chosen, and if she went there.

A large and breathing presence came to stand behind her. She looked up over her shoulder, expecting Bran. Her eyes widened.

The prince from Lir seemed hardly aware of her. He was staring at her bit of nonsense with such a mingling of shock and—horror?—that she caught herself gaping at him in her own turn.

His voice came rough, as if half-strangled. "What is this? Where did you find it?"

"I made it," she said.

"From what? Who taught you?"

She was not one to be afraid of anything, least of all a man, but this man almost frightened her. She answered altogether unwisely, "I saw it in a dream."

"A dream awake? Were you wandering off to the eastward? Have you been riding with the traders?"

"I've never been more than a day's journey from this village," she said with some heat. "I've not even been to Lir. I dreamed this thing. I dream dreams, prince. Is that unheard of where you come from?"

"You dreamed *this*?"

"I dreamed this," she said.

He scowled terribly. His glare was directed not at her but at the child's toy on the table. "Did you dream it so? As a plaything for children?"

She found that her hands were fists. Her back was stiff. "I dreamed," she said, "that horses drew it and men rode in it. I tried to make the wheels as I saw them, but I don't have the skill for that. And how does one teach a horse to pull such a thing?"

"How—" He shook himself suddenly, as if his wits had recovered from a shock. "Have you spoken to anyone of this?"

She shrugged, a twitch of the shoulders. He was very high-handed. She supposed a prince was permitted, but he had begun to annoy her. When she was annoyed, she went silent.

She should not have told him about the dream. It had escaped before she could stop it. It had never profited her to speak of the things that she could do that others could not, or would not admit to.

This man had startled the truth out of her. She could not even escape him: he barred the way to the door. She sat mute and sullen, waiting for him to tire of her silence and go.

He did tire of silence, but not to the extent of leaving her in peace. "Tell me what else you saw," he said.

She blinked slowly. "Tell me why it matters."

He sucked in a breath. "Because it matters."

"Why?"

"You are—" He shut his mouth with a snap. "Maybe it matters nothing. It drove you to make a toy for a child."

"Because I wanted to know how it worked." Again she had spoken without thinking. "There was a wide field—very wide. It was full of these things, rolling like a storm over the plain. The horses were galloping. Men were shouting. They had spears and axes. They were laughing. Some were singing. The wheels made a terrible noise."

He sank down while she spoke, first to his knees, then to sit on his heels. His face had gone perfectly white. "Did you see—were there people on foot?"

Rhian had been trying not to remember that. "The wheels . . . made a terrible noise."

"Yes." His eyes were wide, blind, seeing nothing in that plain and pleasant place. Where he was, there was blood and screaming, and wheels crushing bone into earth.

She could go there, if she would let herself. She refused. She turned her back on it. She said to him, "If I make it small enough, maybe no war will come."

"The world is going to end," he said. He said it perfectly calmly. "My mother is dying, and she has no heir. The Goddess has turned away from us."

"She has not." Rhian spoke with certainty so deep she could not find the source of it. It simply was.

He was a priestess' son. He must have drunk such surety with his

mother's milk. He did not scoff as a man from Long Ford might. He
sighed heavily, shook his head, but held his peace.

⇒ ⇐

The day had begun in odd and unsettling fashion. It went on like a
song sung out of tune. Bran was unwontedly surly when he woke—
unwontedly late—and shambled to his work. The prince by then had
gone. Rhian had wrapped the thing that she had made, that had so dis-
turbed him, and laid it deep in the box of scraps and half-finished work-
ings. There was nothing for Bran to see, except Rhian stirring a pot over
the cooking fire.

Bran would not eat. She had no appetite. She left him to his smelting
and went where she should have gone hours since. She had promised to
help her aunt with the kiln that morning. She had pursued the shape of
her dream instead, and appalled a prince.

Dura was at the kiln, hair drawn back and wrapped in a bit of scarf,
broad face red and streaming with the heat. A glance was all the rebuke
she offered. Rhian bit her lip and lent a hand with the fire.

The priestess and her acolytes were shut away in the headwoman's
house. The guards kept to their own camp in the field by the river, except
two who stood at the headwoman's door. Neither of those was the prince
Emry.

As the sun rose toward noon, the cry of a ram's horn sounded through
the village, calling them all to the gathering place.

Rhian had been waiting for it. She was washed clean of soot, her damp
hair plaited tight. She had on her best gown, that had been her mother's,
with flowers embroidered on the hem; she was wearing her necklace of
shells, her armlets of amber and carved bone, and the earrings of bronze
that Bran had made for her. They were bells, and they rang softly as she
walked.

She was as beautiful as she could be, and that, she knew, was very
beautiful indeed. People stared as she passed through the village. None
of them spoke to her. They all knew. They were drawing away already.

That hurt, but she put the pain aside. If she would be a priestess in
Lir, she must rise above everything that she had been. Even her name;
even that would fall away.

The gathering-field was full already. Everyone had come, men and
women, old and young, toothless elder and babe at the breast. The sun
was direct overhead, the sky a cloudless vault. The heat was breathless,
the wind utterly still.

Rhian slipped through the crowded bodies. The priestess was standing
on the gathering-stone, her acolytes in a circle about her. They were all clad
as priestesses in a sacred rite: bare but for a kilt of woven cords dyed the

color of blood. Their free hair curled exuberantly down their backs. Sweat sheened their bodies, plump or slender, richly female or angular as a boy's.

They had no faces. Each wore a mask, blank, mouthless, noseless. Their eyes were slits of darkness.

They were mortal women, living and breathing, flawed and foolish. They stood in the open air, under the clear eye of heaven. And yet Rhian's hackles rose.

The girls and young women of Long Ford had found their way to the open space between the gathering and the stone. Rhian took a place at the farthest end, the eastward end. As she stood there, for a moment she swayed, dizzy. The earth shook as if with the rolling of countless wheels, the pounding of hooves, the onslaught of red war.

She gasped and steadied. There were no terrible battle-cars. There was only the sun and the grass, the river, the sky; and the gathered people of Long Ford, waiting for the priestess to choose a new servant for the Goddess.

The priestess came down from the stone. Two of her acolytes bowed before her. One set a shallow bowl in her hands, a bowl as plain as the earth underfoot. The other poured clear water from a jar as plain as the bowl, filling it to the brim.

The priestess trod slowly down the line of girls and women. Her mask revealed no expression. There was no sound. No chanting, no sacred words. Only the silence.

Her coming was like a fire on the skin, like a drumbeat in the earth. It was not the same as the dream of war, and yet in its way it was as terrible. Here was power. Rhian had never known its like.

Never, in the waking world.

She wanted—she felt—she could—

The priestess' advance slowed. Rhian forgot to breathe. The earth thrummed beneath her. She saw the water in the bowl, how it stirred and shimmered. She met the eyes behind the mask.

They were dark. They glittered. They saw her—knew her. Read her soul. She laid it bare to them. She gave it the dreams, the wind. She gave it all her secrets that she had kept since she was small. All the strangenesses. All the things that her kin had taught her to hide. They filled her as water filled the bowl. They brimmed over as the water surged and spilled, pouring out at the priestess' feet.

She turned away, turned her back on Rhian. She walked again down the line of young women, then paused once more. She poured out what little water was left in the bowl, a thin stream upon Cara's elaborately braided head.

⇨ ⇦

Rhian did not remember leaving the field. She did not know if she walked
or ran; if anyone spoke to her, or if she fled in silence. One moment she
was standing in blank astonishment, knowing surely, to the very bone,
that the priestess had betrayed the choosing. Cara had nothing about her
that befit a priestess. She dreamed no dreams. She knew nothing but the
world that simple eyes could see.

There was no one in Dura's house when she came to it. She took off
her beautiful dress. She put away her ornaments. She put on her plain
and work-scarred trousers, that she had almost outgrown: they strained
across her hips. But they were of good leather, and they were not quite
threadbare.

She was not thinking at all. She had had no clear thought since the
priestess turned away from her—deliberately, coldly refused the Goddess'
own choosing. She gathered certain things from Dura's house, and certain
others from Bran's. She made a pack out of them, as a hunter would. She
had her bow, and a filled quiver.

They were celebrating on the field by the river. There was music, laughter. She fancied she heard Cara's high sweet giggle.

She turned her back on them, just as the priestess had done to her.
She left them to their falsehood of a choosing.

3

Emry's world had always been a bright and splendid place. He was a
prince in Lir. His father was the king, the warleader of the city. His
mother was the Mother, Goddess incarnate. His brothers were tolerable,
and some he even liked. He did not want to kill any of them. The people
loved him. And everyone knew that when the time came, Emry would
be king in Lir.

Then came this terrible year. The wasting sickness began to eat at the
Mother from within. A sickness very like it ate at Lir. There was confusion
in the temple, dissension among the warriors. Emry dreamed of war.

Men were not the firstborn of the Goddess, nor had she blessed them
as she had her daughters. And yet Emry dreamed as a woman might, saw
visions as if he had been a priestess in the temple. Had he been born a
daughter, he would have been the Mother's heir.

But he was a son, and would be king instead. Though king of what,
he had begun to wonder.

In this village among so many, on this journey that his mother
had laid on him with the force of a geas, he watched yet another thread
of the world unravel. First he had seen a young woman's insolence,
then he had known her prescience: dreaming the war that would come

and the terrible engines it would bring, and making of them a toy for children.

The temple would take her, he thought. Simple rustic she might be, without great wit or wisdom, but she was as full of the Goddess' power as a summer cloud with lightnings. She crackled and blazed with it. Maybe she was the one, the Mother who would be.

He stood at the choosing with the rest of the priestess' guard. He saw when she came. Her gown was long out of fashion, but the blue on blue of it caught the deep and dreaming blue of her eyes. Her ornaments were poor enough, except for the bronze bells in her ears, but she wore them proudly. She was beautiful. She shone like a pearl in a field of common clay. Surely even a blind man could see that this one was blessed of the Goddess.

The priestess was worse than blind. She turned away from that shining splendor, turned her back on the Goddess' own choosing, and laid the blessing on a coarse and common creature whose only distinction was the excess of copper and shells and river pearls that she wore about her person. If that one was blessed of the Goddess, then Emry had lost all power to see.

The one who should have been chosen was nowhere in evidence. No one would admit to knowing where she could have gone, or seemed to care. They were all caught up in celebrating the false chosen.

The priestess, mercifully, was not minded to linger for the festival. She left an acolyte in the village to look after her new sister and conduct her to Lir, then took her boat and her escort, though the sun was already sinking, and sailed away down the river.

Emry was glad enough to leave that village behind, nor did he object to camping on the riverbank between towns, as they had to do when darkness caught them. A camp was simple; it was, in its way, a clean thing. And there were no strangers in it.

The priestess had not spoken a word since before the rite of choosing. She took no nightmeal, nor did she sit with the rest or share their wine and ale. She hid herself away in her tent.

In his right mind Emry would never have done what he did that night. But he had been brooding on the day's ill fortune until he was lost to all good sense. He waited till the camp had quieted, till most of the escort were asleep, all but the sentries and an acolyte or two who had drawn some of the guards into the bushes. He slipped into the priestess' tent, unannounced and uninvited.

She was waiting for him. She sat upright as she did in her boat, legs folded, hands on knees. A lamp flickered beside her. It smoothed the lines of her body and masked her face in shadow, so that she was the living image of the Goddess in the temple.

Emry had no shame of what he was. He was as the Goddess had made him. And yet in front of this most powerful of women, he was all too keenly aware of his lesser nature. Heavy bones, heavy limbs, heavy dangling thing between his thighs. He shuffled. He shambled. His voice was a beast's growl.

He shook off the spell that she had laid on him, and knelt in front of her, because he could not stand inside the tent. "You chose a lie today," he said.

Her eyes came to rest on his face. They were as expressionless as black stones. "And how may you know that?"

"I can see," he said.

"You see what a man sees."

He lowered his eyes as if in submission, but he said, "I see the truth. You chose in defiance of the Goddess."

"I chose as I had no choice but to do."

There was no yielding in her at all. If Emry had been wise he would have let be, but tonight he had no wisdom in him. "Why? What made you do it? Why did you turn away from the one whom the Goddess would have blessed?"

"A man's mind is a simple thing," the priestess said. "You believe you understand truth. You understand only the outermost face of it. When you enter the innermost sanctuary of the temple, when you stand before the Goddess as her best-loved servant, then you will be fit to judge what I have done."

And that, Emry thought without great bitterness, would be never in this life. A man did not walk in the inner shrine. He would have to die and be reborn a woman, to gain that grace.

"Go," said the priestess, not too unkindly. "Rest; be at ease. Whatever price is to be paid, I will pay it. It will not fall upon you or any of the warriors who ride with you."

Emry had had no thought of prices or punishments. She was sending him away like an impertinent child.

Maybe he was no more than that. He let himself be dismissed, and went in silence, as one who had submitted to her will.

⇨ ⇦

They passed through a hand of villages in the next pair of days. The priestess was not inclined to tarry in any of them. She chose a young woman from one, a little round dumpling of a child who was, at least, honestly blessed of the Goddess. There was nothing in any of the villages to match what she had found and discarded at Long Ford.

On the third day he was sure of what he had suspected before. Something was following them. It was skillful. If he had not happened to be riding in the rear the day after they left Long Ford, and lagging a bit as he gnawed over his troubles, he might not have caught the soft sound that brought his stallion's head about. Thereafter he had kept his eyes and ears alert.

It was human, not animal. It was a hunter: it knew how to follow softly and not alarm the horses. But it was not perfect in its silence.

Emry should have sent one of his company to capture the hunter. But he had had his fill of riding on guard against nothing at all. He left Mabon in command of the guard, shed his princely finery, left his grey stallion behind and set off afoot, swift and silent as a hunter should be.

He had not hunted alone in a long while. Princes were always escorted, and warleaders had their warbands. It might not be wise for him to do it now—what if he walked into an ambush?

This was the Goddess' country. If there was war, it rumbled still beyond the borders. Peace ruled here, for a while at least.

He ghosted through the thickets of reeds by the river. His heart was surprisingly light. He was alone; he was free. For a moment he even thought, if he tarried, if he let the riders go on, if he needed a day or two or three to find this lurker in the shadows . . .

Almost regretfully he thrust the thought aside. He had marked the last rustle in the reeds, and judged how closely it would follow the riders. When he had left them, the hunter had been, he hoped, out of sight round a bend of the river. It would see Mabon riding in the lionskin, and perhaps not find it suspicious that the commander had changed mounts to a sturdy dun.

He found the track he was looking for. It was subtle, but clear enough. The hunter had passed by not long ago. He quickened his pace.

The riders paused as Emry had commanded, where the river's bank rose up into a long hill. The road divided there, where was a ruin like the one above Long Ford. Part ascended steeply to follow the summit of the ridge. Part ran along the bottom of the hill, alongside the river. This was passable, though a day or two before it would not have been.

Emry's following halted as if to debate their course. The horses straggled somewhat, grazing the new spring grass. The priestess' boat curved in toward the bank. They would all rest, eat if they were minded, let the horses eat and drink.

Emry tracked the spy to the wall that straggled, broken, along the edge of the ridge. There the track ended, and a figure lay on its face in the bracken, peering down at the riders by the river.

The watcher was not at all aware of being watched. Emry barely breathed. It was a young spy, dressed in worn leather breeches that strained across well-rounded hips. The feet were bare and callused. The hair was black, long, and rebelling against its single plait. There was a bow slung across the bare brown shoulders, and a quiver with it. A pack lay beside the watcher's hand.

It was a very patient watcher. She—for there was no doubt of that— never moved, barely breathed, for as long as the riders paused by the river. When they mounted and the boat thrust off from the bank, she lay still, but her breathing had quickened a fraction.

She waited till they had gone out of sight before she gathered herself and rose. Emry's noose fell neatly round her shoulders. Her startled leap pulled it tight.

She was wiser than to fight. She stood still, breathing hard. Emry circled her lightly, warily, but she offered no threat.

He looked without great surprise into the face of the young woman from Long Ford: the dreamer, the toymaker, the one who should have gone to Lir. She glowered at him through a tangle of loosened hair. "You had better kill me," she said.

His brows rose. "And why should I do that?"

"Because," she said, "as long as I live, I'll follow this riding. You can drive me away. I'll come back. You can set dogs on me. I'll fight them off. You can—"

"Why?"

That stopped her. She blinked, swallowed hard. "Did you think I could stay, after that?"

"Because everyone saw?"

She shook her head furiously. "Because *she* saw. I felt the Goddess' hand on me. And the priestess turned away."

"You won't force her to change her mind," Emry said.

"Stop taking me for a fool!" she snapped. "I know that. Just as I know that you aren't simply playing guardsman. You ride with her for convenience. But when she turns back, you'll go on. Won't you? You'll ride eastward. You'll take me with you."

A woman's mind was a swift and incalculable thing, but this was even swifter and less comprehensible than most. Emry's head ached with trying to follow the leaps of her logic. "I can't take you—"

"You'll take me or I'll follow."

"On foot? Once I leave the Goddess' lands, I'll ride as swift as horse can go."

"I'll make do," she said grimly.

"If you are wise," he said, "you'll go back where you belong. Your people will forget, if any of them ever knew or cared. You'll be safe. And if the war does come so far—"

"It will," she said. "Oh, it will."

"All the more reason to turn back. What use will you be to your kin if you're killed on the wild plains?"

"I might ask the same of you," she said. "Why aren't you at home, building forts like the one here, and filling them with fighters?"

His teeth clicked together. This was no simple village child; she saw what princes and priestesses barely had wits to see. "My father and brothers are doing that. I have . . . another duty to my city."

She narrowed her eyes. Chill walked down his spine. That was a Mother's expression, a Mother's intensity, seeing clear through to the heart of him—and not greatly approving what she saw there, either. "You need me," she said.

"What for? We're not children. We need no toys."

Her jaw set, but she kept her temper. "You need a maker, one who can see how the terrible cars are made."

"We'll steal one and bring it back. Our makers in Lir can make others like it."

"Will you have as much time as that? Isn't it better to have a maker with you? And," she said, "a trader's child."

"Your mother is a potter."

"My mother was a priestess. Her sister is a potter. The father of my body was a trader. He traveled up and down the river, and into the east, and far to the west. He went everywhere. He taught me things, prince. Things that I doubt a warrior of the city would know."

Oh, she was clever with her tongue, and headstrong, and wickedly persuasive. He had to force himself to remember that she was his captive, with his noose about her body and his knife at her throat.

She met his eyes boldly, as if the keen bronze blade had never threatened her life. "You will need me," she said.

"I can't take you with us," he said in a kind of despair. "If the priestess sees you, she'll have you driven out or killed."

Rhian blinked, the only sign of dismay that he had yet seen in her. Or maybe it was anger. "Her journey is nearly done," she said. "I'll meet with you after you've parted from her. Don't think you can evade me, either. I'll be waiting for you."

It was as much a threat as a promise. Emry pondered the usefulness of binding and gagging her and flinging her at the priestess' feet. But he was too soft for that, or too much under her spell. He lowered the knife. She twitched the noose from his hand with ease that was close to contempt, flashed a grin at him, and vanished over the wall.

4

When Rhian had escaped from the prince, her knees gave way. She sank into the bracken below the old wall, gasping as if she had run a race. She lay for a long while before a stab of panic brought her to her feet. The rope about her—it bound her like—

She slipped out of it. She might have left it where it lay, but she had not grown up in a wealthy house. She coiled it and tucked it tidily in her pack.

When she had done that, she was calm. Her thoughts were clear. The priestess would go on down the chain of towns and villages. The mounted troop would follow her. Rhian could not lose them. Even if they turned back or turned aside, the wind would tell her where they were.

The wind had led her to this. It had given her the words to speak. It played about her now, plucking at her, blowing warm breath on her back.

She started and spun. There was a horse behind her, standing just above her on the hillside. She had not heard it come, not even a rustle in the bracken. And yet there, inescapably, it was.

At first she thought it was the prince's stallion. But this was a mare, dappled like the moon. She glowed like the moon, too, shimmering against the green of the grass, which in that instant seemed too bright, too clear to be mortal. She was more real, more solid than anything about her. The world seemed a dim and shadowy thing, like a reflection in water.

Rhian blinked, shivered. The mare snorted wetly and tossed her head. The vision was gone, if it had ever been more than the eyes' confusion. The mare stood above her, as mortal as any other daughter of her kind, with a dark bright eye and an air of conspicuous patience with human follies. The wind danced in her mane. It seemed to fancy that it had brought her here, and that Rhian should be delighted beyond measure.

Rhian eyed the mare sidelong. The mare nibbled a bit of alder-twig. There were burrs in her tail and grass-stains on her pale coat. And yet she was no wild thing. That coat had been tended not so long ago, those hooves trimmed. When Rhian raised a hand, she did not shy away.

The prince's rope, that she had so thriftily kept, knotted into a serviceable headstall and a loop of rein. The mare accepted it as one who had been trained to it: thrusting her nose into it, sighing as if in contentment.

Some signs were as clear as the sun overhead. Rhian bowed to it and to the Goddess who had sent this mount to carry her. Now she need have no doubt. This course was ordained. She was meant to continue upon it.

She scrambled and clambered until she sat panting on the mare's back. The mare stood motionless through her struggles. Once she was settled, the mare began to move.

It had been a long while since Rhian pressed the village pony into service. Her body remembered, vaguely. How to balance. How not to clamp and cling. How to ride the surge and sway of a horse's stride—longer, this, than the pony's had ever been, but like enough.

There was the matter of direction. The mare happened to take the path Rhian would have taken, following the track of the riders from Lir. When Rhian tried to turn her aside, she would not go.

And was this mare, maybe . . . ?

There was only one grey in the priestess' escort, and that was Emry's stallion. This one had come from elsewhere.

The wind hissed in Rhian's ears. Elsewhere indeed, far elsewhere, and such a gift as queens would die to win. Whatever priestess or temple might say, Rhian was chosen. This was a choosing. Let her be properly glad of it.

Her will had not truly been her own since she stood in the field and saw the priestess mark another for the temple. At night she would lie awake and yearn for Bran's arms about her. But she was never moved to run back. Not even for him. That cage was open. Her wings had caught the air. She had flown high and would fly far.

She had given her word to Emry. She would leave the Goddess' country altogether and go—wherever he meant to go. Out on the sea of grass, among the wild tribes.

The mare carried her swifter than she could walk. When the pain of sore-taxed muscles and raw skin muted to less than agony, riding was somewhat pleasant. Maybe someday it would be more than that.

She had run ahead of the priestess, skirting towns in which the riding paused for a day or a night. She was long out of her reckoning, long departed from any lands or people that she had known. The world was all strange. The wind and the mare between them guided her through it. She hunted to eat; she drank from streams or from the river. When she rested, she rested under stars or moon, or sheltered from rain in deep thickets.

She was nine days on that road. She never saw the priestess or the escort. She saw people on the roads, often enough, or sailing on the river. There was a caravan once, a company of traders with laden donkeys. She rode with them for a day, by the mare's choice, until the caravan turned westward away from the river.

As she drew closer to the border, the hill-forts began to be whole again, or nearly whole. She saw people in them, setting stone on age-worn stone, or raising palisades, making them anew as they had been in the days of war long ago.

The sight of them did not comfort her. Surely they were a great bulwark against invasion. Their ascents were too steep for chariots and nearly too steep for horses, and narrow so that horsemen could only come up one by one. And yet as she looked up at them, she saw smoke and flame, and such a war as even the legends of the Mothers had never told of.

The farthest town of the Goddess' country was also the highest and strongest of the forts that she had seen. It reared up above the river, perched on a sheer crag, with a road winding down from it to a second town, a traders' town, protected with walls and running along the banks of the river. This was a stopping place for caravans and a haven for travelers. It had a temple, even, though very small, with only one priestess to tend it. A garrison guarded it, lodged above and standing guard below in the traders' town.

Rhian, whose village had known only peace for time out of mind, found this fortress of World's End to be a grim and narrow place. The sunlight came in grudgingly, and there was a reek about it like an animal's lair.

There were people of the tall grass living there. These were a little like some of the families of her own country, particularly in Lir: tall pale-skinned people with hair as often brown as black, and eyes that sometimes were grey or even blue. But many of these were fair and one or two were even red, with hair the color of copper. Those seemed to be the wildest, the rankest and wariest. They looked as if they had not seen a bath since the midwife washed them in mares' milk.

They were all men. When they met a woman, they did not know how to act. Either they stared past the point of rudeness, or they kept their eyes fixed on their boots. A woman such as Rhian, armed and mounted, confused them beyond measure.

Nor was it only the weapons and the mare. It dawned on her, somewhat into the first day, that they were staring at her. At her body in its nigh-outgrown trousers. At her breasts.

They were lovely breasts, and worth staring at, but not with such raw hunger. Surely even these outlanders had seen a woman's body before?

One was so hungry that he could not help himself. He lunged at her. That was not wise at all. Even before Rhian's knife slashed at his hand, the mare had wheeled and struck him down.

He would live. He was coming to his senses even as the mare danced onward down the narrow street.

→ ←

Rhian had meant to lodge in the town for once, but the mare greatly disliked this place of close walls and manifold stenches. They camped on the riverbank upstream of the traders' town instead, near the ferry.

The mare found ample grazing. Rhian had traded a brace of rabbits for bread and strong cheese and a jar of sour ale. It was not an ill dinner, with young greens and a handful of mussels from the river. She ate it from the shelter of a sprawling willow-tree, perched on the knotted roots, dangling her feet over the water.

Fish danced and darted in the sunset gleam. Breakfast, she thought. She leaned against the bole, pressing her back to its cracks and furrows. Her stomach purred with contentment.

The boat that made the crossing had carried a company of tribesmen across while Rhian ate her dinner. The boatman had drawn his boat up on the nearer shore and gone to his own dinner and his night's sleep.

As Rhian sat half in a drowse, thinking that sleep would be a very useful thing, movement caught her eye. A lone horseman paused on the farther bank. He was dressed as a tribesman, but his hair was black. His horse was ribby and lean, the rider nigh as much so, as if they had traveled far on poor rations.

He paused, the pale blur of his face turned toward the boat and, no doubt, the boatman's absence. He swayed for a moment as if in exhaustion or disappointment. Then, with an air of one who can see no other way, he urged his mount into the water.

The current was strong. Even when the rider slipped from its back, staying upstream of it, the horse struggled against the force of the water. It carried them both inexorably downstream.

Rhian was on her feet, balanced on the willow's roots. She felt as much as heard the mare move down toward the water.

Rhian had grown up swimming in this river, breasting the strong currents of spring and the slower but sometimes more treacherous ones of summer and autumn. She had no fear of the river as it was now. A man who was not a strong swimmer, worn and ill-fed, clinging to a weakened horse, was no match for it at all.

She dived into the water, even as the mare leaped from the bank. They entered the river nearly side by side, stroking keenly across the current.

They caught the traveler and his mount somewhat downstream of the ferry and somewhat east of the river's middle. The man was faltering. The horse wheezed with strain. The mare set her shoulder to its shoulder. Rhian caught the man as he began to sink. His fist, flailing, caught her beneath the ear. She reeled, but held on somehow, before the river swallowed her.

She had no breath to curse him. His blind thrashing had carried them downstream. She got a grip on him—mercifully unimpeded; maybe he was dead—and cut across the current once more. Her lungs were burning. Her arms and legs were beyond aching. Her skull throbbed where he had struck it.

None of that mattered. The whole world was the western bank, the dying flame of sunset, the river's strength unwavering while hers drained away in the chill embrace of the water.

She came bruisingly to land, up against a tangle of flotsam. She dragged her burden up over it, hardly aware by then that it was human, only that she was bound to it.

It thrashed, heaved, vomited great gouts of water. She stared into dark eyes hazed with confusion and near-drowning. She blinked. That face— if it were younger, fuller, less greenish-pale; if there had been no grey in the beard—

He regarded her without recognition. Of course he would not know her. When he had last seen her, she had been a young child.

It was the light, fading fast, and her own watery confusion. This was not her mother's lover, her body's father. He had gone away from Long Ford after his beloved died, gone trading in a caravan that had been lost, destroyed in a storm that had swept the southlands. He could not be alive, lying on the bank of the river, looking as if he had been wandering for all those years in the wilds of the east.

Whoever he was, whatever he might be doing there, he could not spend the night on the riverbank. She heaved him up, pulled his arm across her shoulders, and half-carried, half-dragged him toward the place where she had camped. It was dark long before she came there, but there was starlight, and a pale glimmer of moon.

It seemed the moon had come down to earth. The mare stood in the clearing where Rhian had camped, glowing softly in the darkness. A shadow beside her stirred and snorted: the traveler's horse, grazing hungrily in the good green grass.

Rhian let her burden slip to the ground. He sighed and muttered, words she did not know. Maybe they were eastern words. Then he spoke a name. *Anansi.*

Her mother's name. She blinked hard against a sudden stinging in her eyes.

She dried him as she could, wrapped him closely in her blanket and her mantle, built a fire and set to brewing a tisane of herbs and the last of the honey. When it was hot and fragrant, she fed it to him, sip by sip.

He was coming to himself. The mingling of herbs and sweetness made him gasp and splutter. He struggled upright, eyes glittering in the firelight. "Tell me where I am. Tell me I'm on the western side."

"You are in the Goddess' country," she said.

He sagged. She caught at him, thinking he had slid into dream again, but he was awake. He was weak with relief. "Goddess be thanked," he said, hardly more than a whisper.

Rhian lowered him back into the blankets. He was all bones, like a bird. In memory he was a giant, a big hearty man with a splendid smile. This gaunt shadow could not be he. He was not greatly taller than she, nor very much broader.

She did not speak his name. Her heart was full of it. *Conn.* That was his name. Conn.

She sat over him all that night and watched him sleep. The stars wheeled overhead. The horses grazed and slept, slept and grazed. The fire died to embers. His breathing deepened and slowed. There was no sleep in her at all. She was full of the wind's song, sweet and high and, for once, without words.

Conn was up before the sun, trying to free himself from Rhian's blankets, to mount and ride. He could barely walk, but he insisted that his horse could carry him.

"Nonsense," Rhian said. "He's a rack of bones, and so are you. Tell me where you need to go. I'll take your message there—whatever it is that's so urgent you're near to killing yourself with it."

He set his lips together and shook his head.

He still did not know her. She opened her mouth to tell him, but the wind snatched the words away. When she tried to find them again, they were gone beyond recall. *Silence,* the wind bade her. *Spare him pain.* She heard herself say instead, "It's war, isn't it? War in the sea of grass. Chariots—"

"What do you know of chariots?"

Rhian lay gasping for breath. He had flung her down. His fingers clamped about her throat.

He loosed them a little. Oddly, she was not afraid. He had killed: the wind was sure of it. But he would not kill her. "There is a prince," she said, "coming from Lir. Were you meeting him here?"

He blinked down at her. He was coming to his senses. "Prince? Lir?"

"The king's son," Rhian said. "He's riding to World's End. He'll cross the river and enter the sea of grass. He's seeking chariots."

"He'll find them." Conn let her go. He sank down trembling. "He'll find them beyond counting."

"He wants to steal one," Rhian said.

"Then he's mad."

"Maybe they're all mad in Lir." Rhian sat up. Her throat ached. His hands had not been gentle. "Are they so terrible? The wild tribes?"

"They brew a strong drink from mares' milk. They drink it from cups made of skulls."

"Men's skulls?"

"Skulls of their enemies."

Rhian shivered. "That won't stop him. I don't think anything can."

"He should be fortifying Lir. Walls can stop them. Nothing else. Only walls."

His face was white. His eyes did not see her then, nor the brightening morning. But he saw the mare in the first long shaft of sunlight. He fixed on her. Something in him eased, that had been taut for long and long.

"Maybe," he said, "after all. Maybe not only walls."

5

A day's journey short of World's End, the priestess turned back toward Lir. She said no word to Emry before she embarked on her boat with the last of the young women that she had chosen for the temple. There was no farewell. She turned about under sail and oar, and left them standing on the shore, Emry and a dozen of his warriors. All of them were men, young and strong and wild. The women and the rest of the men rode back as escort to the priestess.

With her departure, Emry and his men were no longer princely guards. Their finery returned to Lir with the priestess. They rode from the town of Oakwood as men of much lesser eminence, garrison-troops sent out to World's End.

They were like colts let loose in a spring pasture. They whooped and shouted. They ran breakneck races. They fought mock battles on the road, to the terror of any who passed by.

Emry wondered why he felt so old. He was not the eldest of them, at all, but he was the gravest by far. Maybe it was what the priestess had not said before she left—or the dream he had had in the night. That the Mother was dead.

He supposed he was not to know. Whether it was mercy or expedience he could not tell. Lir needed what he had been ordered to do. He could not abandon it for any cause, even the death of a living goddess who happened also, and incidentally, to be the mother of his body.

He was obedient to his duty. He took no such joy in it as his young hellions did. He mourned when he could, as he could. He rode in sunlight that he barely saw.

⇒ ⇐

He had all but forgotten the odd woman from Long Ford, until he rode up the winding track to World's End, and saw her on it, barring his way. She was dressed in the same disgraceful trousers as before, her hair just as unruly, the set of her jaw not a whit less stubborn. She was a wild and striking beauty, and everything about her declared that she cared not at all.

She had a companion, a gaunt man on a rough-coated bay horse. She was mounted — on —

He heard a gasp behind him. He was less openly shocked, he hoped. It should hardly have surprised him, after what he had seen and heard from this woman.

Did she know what she had done, or what had taken her for its servant? The mare seemed earthly enough, standing there in the sunlight, hipshot like an ancient nag. Rhian sat not too badly on her back, no fleece or saddlecloth, and for bridle a rope that Emry knew rather well. He had plaited it himself.

He could not burst out laughing. They would all think him reft of his wits. He fixed her with a flat stare instead, and waited for her to speak.

She obliged him. "Prince," she said. "You come in good time."

"But not before you," he said. His voice was as flat as his eyes.

Her own were dancing. She took a peculiar pleasure in tormenting him. And he — his grief was no less. But he was aware of the sun again.

He had meant to send her away without compunction. But she was mounted on this of all horses. That gave him pause.

"Prince," she said, "here is a messenger. His name is Conn. He was a trader, wandering in the east."

The trader from the east looked as if he had traveled hard and long. The cut of his leather tunic, the devices branded and embroidered on it, marked a tribe not remarkably far from the river. And the look in his eyes — this man had seen terrible things.

Emry glanced about. The road was not greatly crowded, but there were ears enough to hear whatever he said. "Come," he said. "Come to World's End."

→ ←

The garrison at World's End was prepared for Emry's coming. The commander had set aside her own house for the guests, and furnished it with aught that they might be expected to need.

When they were all settled, she took them out of the fortress to a place some distance up the river. It was a sacred place, a grove that had belonged to the Goddess since the dawn time: a smaller image of the great grove in Lir, that most ancient and most hallowed of her holy places. Here as there, the trees were gnarled and twisted, but leaves still showed green on the branches. Flowers grew about their feet, and a spring bubbled into a basin in the grove's heart. It seemed a fitting place for such a gathering as this.

Emry had brought all his men there. They were much subdued by the sanctity of the grove. It was not a men's place. They were there on sufferance, by the Goddess' goodwill.

Conn the trader sat on the grass. He had revived visibly since he had rested and eaten and been brought to this sunlit place.

Rhian had begun beside him, but she seemed beset by a spirit of restlessness. She prowled among the trees, treading lightly on the flowers. Emry's eyes kept straying toward her while Conn told his tale.

"I was a trader," he said, "among the sunrise tribes. For some years I had lived most often with the people of the High Tor, as blood brother to one of its warleaders and consort to his sister."

Rhian stiffened at that, but she did not pause in her rambling.

Conn went on, unaware of her, for she was behind him. "There were rumors from farther east, tales that came westward with the traders and wanderers and the young men of the tribes. A god had risen, they said, among the eastern tribes. He was a great god, a strong god. He had brought a gift from beyond the horizon. That gift was a terrible thing, a mighty power in war.

"Chariots," said Conn, making of the word a curse. "We reckoned the tales but rumors, the babbling of fear before, at most, a new tribe with a new and potent leader. But as the seasons went their round, the rumors grew to a roar. Then came tribes into our hunting runs, fleeing some horror in the east. A god, they said; war as swift as fire in the grass. Battle-cars advancing with irresistible force, overwhelming any who ventured in their path." He stopped. His face was pale. His eyes were staring at a vision none of the rest could see; though Emry wondered if Rhian might have the power.

When Conn spoke again, it was with the air of one who has gathered the last of his strength. "Yes. Yes, they came at last—did you doubt they would? All of us did. Surely they would stop, we had said. Invaders always stop when they find wealth enough—and the tribes to the east of us were rich in furs and copper, and much blessed in the fighting prowess of their young men.

"But a man on a horse is no match for two warriors in a chariot. They overran the east in a short season. Then before the winter came, they came to us.

"We heard them long before we saw them. It was like thunder, a long rolling beneath our feet. The hooves of their horses, the wheels of their chariots, shook the very breast of Mother Earth. She cried aloud under the weight of them.

"They swept over us like a storm in the grass. They mowed us down as if we had been a field of grain. They trampled our men, our women, our children.

"I had gone wandering that dark of the moon, trading the spotted hides of the High Tor cattle for the marten and ermine of the northern forests. I came back as the battle was ending. I saw the chariots. I saw their men making cups of High Tor skulls. I saw—I saw—" He broke off. He was rocking where he sat, tears streaming down his face.

Rhian was there, though Emry had not seen her come. Conn wept in her arms, clinging like a child.

The others waited. Some of Emry's young men were inclined to fidget, but his glare held them still. Britta the garrison commander frowned. She could not be liking her thoughts any more than Emry liked his own.

At length Conn mastered himself. He sat up and drew a shuddering breath. He said, "I saw too much. I wanted to fall on them and kill them all—I, who grew up in the Goddess' country. But my heart was too wise. I knew that I had to ride with all the speed I could, to warn my blood kin. Because rivers won't stop them. The boldest of the tribes will barely slow them. Only—only walls can stand against them."

Britta's glance crossed Emry's. Neither said it. Walls could be broken or passed by. Warriors would still have to ride out, still have to fight.

After a moment Emry said, "Go now. Rest. Find what peace you can."

"And you will do what?" Conn was fiercely, furiously awake, freed from his dream of horror. "You should be building forts, not riding across the river. What do you fancy you can do? Raid those kings of raiders? Steal the thing they guard above all?"

"The Goddess will guard us," Emry said.

"Not even she can guard you," said Conn. That was a terrible thing to say here, in her own place, but he was beyond any simple fear.

"We are sent," said Emry, "by the Mother and the king of Lir. They know what comes. They move to protect the Goddess' country. And I," he said steadily, "I and my hellions here, am the vanguard of that defense."

"You'll die," Conn said.

"That may be the Goddess' will," said Emry. "You are safe. When you've rested and healed a little, Britta will see that you are taken to Lir. My father should hear the tale you told us, and every other thing that you can or will remember."

"And you go to your death."

Emry lifted a shoulder in a shrug. His glance caught the most restless of his men. Young Dal leaped up eagerly. "Come, sir," he said with his quick light courtesy. "Come back to the fort and rest. I saw a very nice bed in the commander's house, and a jar of wine, too. And I'm very good at coaxing dainties out of cooks."

He had the trader well in hand. Emry dismissed the rest of his men. Britta followed, still deeply preoccupied. But Emry lingered. He needed the sun and the scent of the flowers and the whisper of wind in the leaves. The Goddess' voice spoke there. He had never quite understood it, but that it was hers, he had no doubt.

He had thought Rhian gone with the rest, until she planted her feet in the grass in front of him and glared down. He frowned up at her. "You need new trousers," he said.

That caught her beautifully off balance. He watched her grope for words, caught between bafflement and temper.

After a while he took pity on her—after a fashion. He said, "I'll see that you have a pair that fits. A coat, too. And—"

"I have a coat! My trousers fit. I—"

His glance took in the worn leather that strained across her hips; the sprung seams; and the threadbare knees. He watched the blush spread. It began with the sweet swell of her breasts and climbed swiftly to her forehead. It made him think of the flush of dawn coming up over the river.

Such a song that would make.

"Stop grinning at me," she snapped.

"Grinning? I?" He stretched out in the grass, propped on his elbow. She was still standing over him. He struck another blow. "Do you know where the grey mare comes from?"

She dropped down, boneless as a child. "I didn't steal her. She came to me."

Emry laughed. "Oh, certainly you never stole her! No one can steal that one. No, not even a god."

Her eyes were wide. She did not understand. Not yet. Was she so poorly taught, then?

"This is the White Mare," Emry said to her. "The living goddess."

Rhian gulped air. "But isn't she—doesn't she have—"

"This is a black year," he said. "Both the mare's servant and the Mother of Lir have died without heirs."

She did not start at the word of the Mother's death. He had not thought she would. She knew, he thought. She would have dreamed it.

"Then I have no right to her at all," she said. "I was supposed to go to Lir. But not—to—"

"Were you, then? Are you sure of it? She came to you. She brought you here."

Rhian knotted tight, but her eyes were bold still. If she was afraid, she was not giving in to it. "So she did. She must want me to get killed."

"Or to carry the Goddess' power across the river."

"She is the Goddess," Rhian said. "And I didn't know. I didn't see—"

"She didn't mean you to see."

"I should have," said Rhian.

Emry was silent.

After a while Rhian said, "I won't take her away from her own place. I'll go afoot, or borrow a horse."

"There is no taking the White Mare," Emry said. "She'll go if she's minded to go. And if not, no force in heaven or earth will compel her."

"Can she make me go with her?" Rhian demanded.

"Would you resist her?"

"If I had to."

Emry lay on his back, laced his fingers beneath his head and rested his eyes on the dance of sun and cloud. Leaves whispered. Bees hummed in the flowers. They were building a hive in one of the dying trees. There was a great army of them, warriors innumerable.

His spine prickled. Bees were a good omen in Lir. They brought blessing to the place where they built their stronghold. They fed their hosts with honey, and lulled them with their droning song.

And yet the dying tree, the swarm of bees, the sun's burning eye, roused Emry to something like alarm. In war, omens could have two edges, like a well-forged dagger.

He said nothing of that to Rhian. When he looked, she was gone. He was alone with the sun and the bees and the buzzing of his fears.

6

Rhian had never been in a temple. Long Ford had none. Other, larger towns did, but she had never been in those, either. She had traveled very little before she walked out of Long Ford.

She could, out of spite, have spat on the doorstep and shown this temple her back, but it was not the fault of this place that a priestess from Lir had scorned her. She went inside instead, because she was curious, and because maybe, a little, she wanted to see what had been denied her.

It was dark. It smelled of old stone and sweet herbs and the faint pungency of lamp-oil. Slowly her eyes focused. A lamp burned not far from her. It illumined a shape of stone, which must be the Goddess. Walls curved behind it. Except for the Goddess and her lamp and a garland of herbs and flowers, the sanctuary was empty.

Rhian stood in front of the stone image. It looked remarkably like the priestess from Lir: squat, ugly-beautiful, and strong in power. It had no face. It wore the mask that she had seen in the choosing, blank, without living features. The eyes were mere hollows in the stone.

She looked into the darkness there.

It stared back. Her hackles rose, but she stood her ground.

"So," said the voice of the priestess from Lir. It echoed faintly, as if it came from a great distance, but she heard it clearly. "You have as much power as that. I knew; I told them. But they let you live. They thought they could keep you caged. Fools that they were. As soon cage the fiery bird of heaven as keep the likes of you in bonds."

Rhian did not understand her at all. Except for the last of it. The bird of fire. The cage. "How do you know—" Rhian broke off. "I'm dreaming you."

"You drew me into your dream," the priestess said. "That takes great strength. But you don't know what you have, do you?"

Odd: the prince had said something similar. Out of that memory, Rhian said, "I have the White Mare."

She felt the priestess' shock as a blow to her own body. The Goddess' image swayed in its place. "You cannot!" the priestess cried.

"I am told," said Rhian, "that it's never a matter of can or will or should, with that of all mares."

"This should never have happened," the priestess said. "You should never have lived."

"Why?" Rhian said. "Because I'm nobody? Because I come from a village so small it doesn't even have a priestess? Because you turned away from me when the Goddess chose me?"

"You were not chosen."

Rhian's lips drew back from her teeth. "Don't lie to me. I may be nobody, but I know what you did. I felt it in my bones."

"You could not be chosen," the priestess said. "For the sake of the city, for the sake of our world—you could not."

"But I was," said Rhian. She was not listening to the priestess' ravings, which meant nothing to her. She heard only the simplest fact. "You couldn't stop the mare, could you? She came in spite of you."

"The mare's servant has never been a priestess of our order," the priestess said.

"Well, then," said Rhian. "You're safe from me, aren't you? Isn't the mare's servant a solitary creature? She goes her own way, does as the Goddess pleases. She's a leaf on the wind. You are stones in the earth."

"You are fire in dry grass," the priestess said.

"Maybe I'll burn the enemy's chariots," said Rhian.

The priestess shuddered. The lamp flared. In the sudden light, it was indeed a living woman who sat in the Goddess' place, wrapped in a woven mantle as if against winter's cold. "Go," she said. "Go into the east. And may the gods of the tribes devour your bones."

"You hate me," Rhian said slowly. "You truly do. What have I ever done to you? What threat can I be? I'm a village woman. I make toys for children. There's no demon in me, no spirit from the dark places."

"No?" The priestess laughed, a hollow sound in that empty space. "I would have laid you on the altar. I would have slit your throat. I would have poured out your blood in the Goddess' name. But I was not permitted. You were let live. We will all pay for that. All of us. Unless you have the grace to die beneath he chariots."

"I am no one," Rhian said. "I have no demon in me."

But the priestess was gone. The fog of her hate lingered, the living stench of fear. The Goddess' garland struggled to overcome it.

Rhian lay on the pounded earth of the floor. It was battered, beaten down, but it was still Earth Mother's breast. She drew a little comfort from it.

No one had ever wanted her dead before. No one had ever hated her. Dislike, yes. Jealousy—she had seen enough of that; men liked her very well, which had never pleased the other women. But never hate. Hate was ugly, black and reeking of old bones.

And for nothing. There was no ill spirit in her. She would have known. The mare would have known. Was not the mare a living goddess?

There was no wind here, to tell her secrets. There was only darkness and silence. She fled into the sunlight.

⇒ ⇐

The prince and his men were tarrying, she thought, unconscionably long. They were waiting for traveling companions, the youngest said: traders who traded often in the east, with a caravan which they could pretend to guard.

None of them was sworn to secrecy, and any one of them would talk if Rhian slid eyes at him, but Dal was most free of what he knew. He was awkward in her bed, clumsy and inclined to spend himself too quickly. She did not mind: he had lovely cream-brown skin and a sweet smile, and he babbled happily of anything and everything.

"There is a story," he said when they had been a hand of days in World's End. "It's told in whispers. I overheard my sisters telling it—and if they'd known I was listening, they would have flayed my hide. It's a thing the women keep among themselves. A thing from the temple.

"You know how they say the Mother had no daughters? Seven sons, she had, and they all lived; but no daughter to be Mother after her. That's a lie, my sisters were telling one another. She conceived and carried a womanchild. Her brooding-dreams were full of ill omens, but she refused to give in to them. Her child would live, she told the priestesses, and would grow strong.

"When the daughter was born, lightning struck the top of the temple and brought it down. That was the first omen, but not the last. Every foretelling, every casting, told them the same. This was the Lastborn. This was the child of the world's end."

He was remarkably unfrightened by the tale he told. He was a man, and he had Rhian in his arms, and she knew what he thought of that: she had heard him crowing to his fellows. He did not understand women's things.

"Did they say when she was born?" Rhian asked. She felt odd and cold and remote.

Dal shrugged. "Seasons ago. The Mother had sons already. Two, I think. Maybe three. I wasn't born yet."

Two elder sons, thought Rhian. Emry and another. And Emry was— and she was—

Dal fell asleep as men did, all at once and to Rhian's relief. She slipped away from him, out of the room she had been given in the garrison-commander's house, up to the top of the tower. From there she could see the whole world, as it seemed: the tamed lands on this side of the river, the Goddess' grove to the north, the traders' town and the ferry below, and across the expanse of water, the wide and empty plain, the sea of grass.

The moon was high. The fort, the tower, were full of silver light. There was a second moon: the eye of heaven reflected in a cistern by the wall.

Rhian stooped over the water. Her shadow was dark against the moon. She passed her hand over it. The shape of her face came clear.

It had changed since she last troubled to look at it. The lines were purer, the eyes larger, wide and dark in the pale oval of her face.

She had not come here to sigh over her own beauty. She was looking for something else. The curve of a cheek. The straight long line of a nose. The set of brows over the eyes. Which were not dark as they seemed in the moonlight; they were deep blue, like the sky after sunset.

The woman she had called her mother had been pleasant enough to look at, but no one had reckoned her a beauty. The man who had thought himself her father was a blunt-featured man, comfortable to look at; but again, beauty had never been one of his gifts. Rhian looked like neither of them.

She looked like the prince from Lir.

Dreams and madness. Dal had been telling stories, women's gossip from the city. Rhian was the potter's child from Long Ford. She might dream of cages and yearn for escape, but that did not make her a Mother's daughter. It made her a rebel, no more, and a fool for indulging in it.

Maybe after all, she thought, she was a prince's child. Her mother had been in the temple in Lir. Maybe she had drawn a lordly eye. Maybe her daughter was of that blood and breeding.

She could not be the Mother's own child. Not the doomed one, the lost one, the one they called the Lastborn: last child of the Mothers, last daughter of the Goddess.

7

Emry opened his eyes on moonlight. A shaft of it slanted through the high window of the room. It was cool and bright and strangely substantial, as if he could stretch out a hand to grasp it.

She was sitting in the pale light, dressed in her disgraceful trousers, knees drawn up and arms clasped about them. She was very real, very solid, like the moonlight itself.

He knew he was dreaming. She had chosen Dal for a bedmate, which baffled the others, but Emry thought he understood. Dal was young and eager to please, and his temper was famously equable. Rhian, who was a spirit of fire, well might find him restful.

And yet she seemed so very clearly here. There was some great trouble on her, or on her spirit that had wandered in on the moon's road.

He rose softly. His nose caught the faint scent of her: herbs and honey, musk and leather, and a memory of horses.

He squatted beside her. She was truly there, huddled on his floor, in body as in spirit.

"Did you know," she said after a while, light and calm and seeming heedless, "that your guards are sound asleep outside your door?"

"Did you put them to sleep?" he asked her.

She shrugged. "Maybe I asked the moon to help."

"Why, did you wear out poor Dal?"

She did not respond to the jest, either to laugh or to snarl. "I don't want to bed you," she said. "I only . . ."

She did not go on. She was deeply troubled, but he knew better than to force words out of her. He had a jar of wine, a gift from Britta the commander. He poured a cup, unwatered, and fed it to her till she gasped and spluttered and fought.

Now she was annoyed. Her glare was baleful. He grinned at it. "That's better," he said. "Now tell me what's so desperate that you'd bring it to me."

"I'm bringing nothing to you," she said. "I just wanted—I needed to look at you. You snore," she added.

"I do not!"

She bared her teeth. "Do you look like your brothers?" she asked.

By now he was accustomed to her sudden shifts. This, he thought, must be what it was like to ride in a chariot. "There is a certain resemblance," he said. "Is one of them here? Does he have a message for me?"

"They're all safe in Lir," she said, "or wherever else your father has sent them. Are they all beautiful?"

"Some more than others," he said.

She took the cup from his hand and drank it down. It seemed to steady her. She said, "If you don't leave tomorrow, I'm going without you."

"I'm waiting for the caravan."

"It will come in the morning," she said.

He did not doubt that it would. "And why should it leave as soon as it arrives?"

"Because war is coming," she said, "and the sooner we're gone, the farther we can go before we find it."

"And the deeper in the tribes' lands we are, the longer it will take us to escape."

"Not so long, with chariots," she said.

He granted the logic of that. And because she belonged to the White Mare, he granted the rest of it as well. "You'll lead us," he said. "Or the mare will."

Her brows leaped up. "You trust me that much?"

"I trust the mare," he said.

He might have regretted that, but she took no offense. She nodded slowly. "She knows where she wants to go. She doesn't care overmuch if you follow."

"Goddesses never do." Emry fetched the wine and the cup and poured himself a head-spinning draft. She made much more sense in the haze of the wine, though her face wavered and blurred. "The caravan won't be pleased to leave so soon."

"The caravan is a pretense. We can take their donkeys and their trade-goods and leave them here, if they complain too loudly."

"I don't suppose," he said, "that you know the ways of caravans."

"No," she said, "but Conn does."

"Conn is going to Lir, to carry his message and be healed in the temple."

"Another messenger can go," Rhian said.

"You would force him to go back? That will kill him."

She regarded him steadily. "Ask him. Give him a choice. Let him decide."

"He's not fit to—"

"Ask him," she repeated.

Women, Emry thought sourly, were harder-hearted than any man could hope to be.

⇥ ⇤

Emry was properly trained. He obeyed her. By the time the moon had set and the sun come up, he had his men up and fed and preparing to ride.

Rhian sat with Conn when he came to the room in which the trader had slept. She was feeding him something pungently herbal, sweetened with the last of Emry's wine. Conn was taking it better than she had taken the wine.

The man had begun to mend a little. His cheeks were less gaunt. He was much cleaner, and dressed in fine new clothes. He was not an ill-made man, nor a weak one, either.

Emry waited till the potion was gone, till Conn fixed him with a stare that drew the words out of him. "This one," he said, tilting his head toward Rhian, "compels me to ask a thing that I have no right to ask."

"Yes," Conn said. "The caravan. She told me." He did not seem angry, nor did he seem greatly resigned. There was a light in his eye, and a fierce edge in the words he spoke. "Yes, I'll go. Give me a horse that can carry me—my poor bay will never survive another crossing of the river. Give me weapons. Give me provisions. Then trust the Goddess to keep me alive until I've won payment for the slaughter of my tribe."

Emry shut his mouth, which had fallen open. Rhian was keeping her smile at bay.

"I think," he said after a while, "that we are softer than we like to imagine, we in Lir."

"The sea of grass will teach you to be hard," said Conn.

⇒ ⇐

Hoel the caravan-master was polite because Emry was a prince, but he was no more willing to depart that very day than Emry had expected. "We can leave in a hand of days," he said. "No sooner. My people are weary. They need to rest. And we have trading to do here."

"The Goddess commands you," Emry said.

"Surely," said Hoel, "she can wait a little while."

"She says not," said Emry.

"Then let your men stay," Rhian said from the door of the commander's workroom, "and we will take your donkeys and your trade-goods and go. The king in Lir will recompense you, I'm sure. Or the temple, since it's the Goddess who commands this."

Hoel gaped at her.

"This is the White Mare's servant," Emry said, taking pity on the man. "She speaks for the Goddess."

Hoel was never so bold before this woman as he had been before the prince of Lir. "Lady," he said. "I didn't mean—"

"Of course you meant it," she said. "You will stay here. This prince and his hellions can play at being traders. They've a master to teach them. They'll do well enough."

"Lady, they know nothing of trading. The arts, the sleights, the skills—"

"They will learn," she said sweetly. "You go, sir, and rest. Prince, see to it that he's paid suitably for the use of his animals. We'll bring him back a share of the profits."

She smiled, dazzling even Emry, and left him to contend with a caravan-master who had, for once in his life, been outmaneuvered.

But being a trader, he had still a few wits left, and a core of plain courage. "I'll leave my men," he said, "but I'll come with you. You'll be needing me."

"We could all be going to our deaths," Emry said.

"That I knew," said Hoel, "when I agreed to this venture."

Emry inclined his head in respect. "Go," he said to Hoel. "The ferry takes the first of us when the sun touches the height of noon. If you're not there then, we'll not wait for you."

⇥ ⇤

It was not a large caravan—it needed speed more than strength of numbers. The things it took to trade were small things, but of great value among the tribes: bolts of woven cloth, well-thrown pots, ornaments of shell and bone and stone, and in the care of the master himself, a small hoard of gold and copper and bronze.

There was, with that, the true treasure, well hidden and not spoken of, but Emry had assured himself that it was there: tools for working wood and metal, and the makings of a forge. The one who knew how to work it had come in with the caravan.

He had the pleasure of seeing Rhian flat astonished, gaping at the man who stood beside Hoel's donkey. It was revenge, rich and sweet.

There were other men he could have summoned for this: masters of the art, great artisans of Lir. But on this venture that was perhaps worse than futile, that could end in death for them all, Emry had been most carefully instructed. "Let it be a good craftsman," his father had said, "strong of mind and body, and skilled in the working of metal. But choose one whom we can afford to lose."

This man of Long Ford had come to Emry the day after the priestess had left that village, and offered himself for whatever service Emry might ask of him—quite like Rhian, if she had but known it. Emry had reckoned him a gift of the Goddess. He had gone where Emry bade him, gathered the things that he needed, and joined the caravan as it passed through the cities of the river.

Now they were all together on the eastward road. For well or ill, Emry thought. For death or life. And maybe, after all, they could stop this war.

8

The sea of grass stretched away into a blue distance. There were mountains on the far rim of it, like a mist on the edge of the world. All between was long rolling plain, windswept grass, and sometimes, if they were fortunate, the trickle of a stream.

Rhian rode well ahead of the caravan—safe enough this close to the river. She would have left her companions behind completely if the mare had let her.

She had said no word to Bran. When they ferried across the river, she traveled in the last boat and he in the first. He did not try to speak to her. He barely looked at her. He was angry, she thought. No wonder, either: she had left without farewell, abandoned him as if he mattered nothing to her at all.

He mattered a great deal, or she would have been able to take proper leave of him. But a man did not understand such things.

The Goddess had her own antic humor. To bring them all together: one who might be brother, one who might be father, one who had been lover.

She had said nothing to Conn of who she was. At first she had kept silent because he was too weak and too preoccupied to hear her. Later, when he should have known her by her name at least, and by what the men of the caravan said of her, he had shown no sign at all of remembrance. She was silent then because she was angry. How could he forget her? How could he have abandoned her? Did he hate her so much, because she was no blood of his at all, nor of Anansi's, either? Maybe he had gone because he could not bear to look at her, and once he was gone, he had burned her out of his memory.

She had not told Emry the secrets that the priestess had told her in the temple, either. She had gone to him, intending to tell him, but as with Conn, the words would not come. She had baffled him instead, and convinced him that she was at least half mad.

Maybe she was. She was either Emry's sister or Conn's daughter. She could not be both. Bran's lover . . .

Poor man. He had lost her to her own pique, and Cara to the temple in Lir. What had been left for him but a venture that could kill him?

From where she rode, if she angled somewhat from the straight track, she could look back at the caravan plodding under the impossible width of the sky. Emry's hellions, even in the plain gear of caravan guards, had a look about them that spoke of princely indulgence. They could not help but betray a glint of copper at ear or throat, or the tinkle of a bridle-bell.

Bran walked beside Hoel on his donkey. Even from so far away, she could see how broad his shoulders were. He was almost as broad if never as tall as the prince on the handsome grey that, like his men's bits of gaud and frippery, he had been unable to let go.

She had yearned for so many nights to lie again in Bran's familiar arms—and now he was within her reach, she wanted only to see him gone. He did not belong here. He belonged in Long Ford, grieving maybe, but safe.

She belonged here. It had startled her when she crossed the river, when she set foot on the farther bank. There where the grass began, where the world rolled forever toward the horizon, where the sky was so deep one could drown in it, for the first time in all her life, she felt as if she had come home.

She had never expected that. Long Ford had been a cage. Lir was a dream, too vague to touch. She had never even dreamed of this, unless her dreams of flying free had meant that she would, and should, come here.

She was laden with secrets. Who she was, what she was, the truth of her kin and birth, filled her till she ached. But she could not speak of any of those who traveled with her. Even the thought of it locked her throat shut and drained her heart of words.

⇀ ↼

As late as they had begun the journey, they were barely out of sight of the river before it was time to camp for the night. Already the whole world seemed made of grass and sky. There were trees in little copses, but those were thinning.

They camped by one such, where there was a stream and a little shelter against the immensity of the sky. In the end, nearly half of the caravan's people had come with the master, refusing to let him go on without them. They made camp with the ease of long practice. Emry's men were less skilled, but made up for that in eagerness to learn. The caravaneers regarded them as men might regard a pack of hound puppies: half in indulgence, half in scorn.

Bran had acquired a surprising array of skills since he left Long Ford. He could raise a tent with admirable dispatch. A fire he had always been able to build—he was a smith, after all—but he had never made bread before.

Rhian squatted beside him as he waited for his bread to bake. He hunched his shoulders but did not move away. "I didn't know you could cook," she said.

"I can't," he said. "Unless it's bread. Bread is like metal. Simple, if you have the trick of it."

It was baking well: its fragrance made her mouth water. "You can go back tomorrow," she said.

His eyes were fixed on the campfire. She willed him to turn, to look at her, to be lost—because he never had been able to resist her beauty.

He knew that too well. She wondered if it cost him anything to turn so resolutely away from her. "Back?" he asked. "Why should I go back?"

"Because it's dangerous," she said. "You could be killed."

"I didn't do this because of you," he said.

"No?"

"No." He slipped the first of his loaves from the coals, shaking off the film of ash. His hands, long inured to heat, made easy work of the hot loaf, breaking it in two, laying one half in front of her. "You're not the only creature who ever dreamed of flight."

"You wouldn't have left, if I hadn't gone before you."

"Maybe not," he said. "But I'm not turning back because you ask. I want this. Maybe not as much as you, but I do want it."

"Even if it kills you?"

"Does that matter to you?"

She set her lips together. She had known this man—well, she thought. Now she began to wonder if she had known him at all. "You seemed content," she said. "More than content. Happy. Is it because Cara left, too?"

"Rhian," he said, and she had never heard him so close to losing his patience, "I never left because of a woman. I left because these princes needed a smith, and—yes—because I had nothing to keep me in Long Ford. I want to see the wild tribes. I want to learn what a chariot is, and if I may, to make one."

"If you stay," she said, "you'll not be invited to my bed."

He rose. His cheeks were flushed above the heavy shadow of his beard. "If you invited me, I would decline to go."

He left her sitting by his fire, with the broken halves of his loaf cooling at her feet. Her heart was still and cold. She had not meant to say what she had said. It had escaped her in the heat of temper. How dared he want anything apart from her? How dared he be his own man?

Half of her wanted to laugh, and half to weep. She lifted the portion of the loaf that he had broken for her. It was still warm. It was fragrant; its flour was well ground, its flavor rich and a little sweet, as if he had mixed it with honey.

She ate it all, and eyed the other half. But he might come back.

She would not be there when he came. Dal was waiting for her. He would give her pleasure without pain. He had little enough conversation, but she did not care for that. Not tonight.

But instead of Dal, when she went to her sleeping place, there was

Emry tending her fire. Emry who, she knew then to the core of her bones, was her brother, her mother's son. It was the last of the light on his hair that was so much like her own, fighting any restraint he tried to lay on it, and his hand on his knee, broad in the palm but long in the fingers, and the smallest finger somewhat crooked. Her hair, her hands.

She clenched her fists and thrust them behind her. "Where is Dal?" she demanded.

He looked up from prodding at the coals. "I'm very well, I give you thanks. And you?"

"I'm not bedding you tonight," she said.

He mimed massive shock. "What! Are you suggesting that I would dare ask a woman to—"

"Then why are you here?"

"To make you angry, it seems," he said. The fire was burning to his satisfaction; he raised the tripod over it—her tripod, no less—and hung her pot from the hook. Something was in it. Rabbit, she supposed, and herbs—she caught the scent of them.

People were watching. Her bit of tent was pitched somewhat apart, under clear sky, but they could all see. Dal must be standing guard: he was not among those who stared. Nor was she about to ask Emry again what had become of him.

"If you didn't come to my bed," she said, "did you come to order me back across the river?"

"I have no more right to do that than to demand that you lie with me." His antic mood was gone. His eyes were level on her, their blue as deep and clear as the sky over him. "No. I came to ask you another thing. The traders' speech—you know it?"

"A little," she said.

"I should like you to learn more than a little. And the language of the wild tribes—Conn says he knows it. Will you learn it from him?"

"Gladly," she said, and she meant it. But she asked, "Why do you ask me? Why not one of the others?"

"The smith will learn. And I. And anyone else with the will or the wit. Them I can command. You," he said, "I have to ask."

She looked him up and down, not meaning to be insolent, but wanting to consider what he had said. She had never been a personage before, someone who was asked rather than ordered. She was not entirely sure what she thought of that. It was exhilarating, and frightening. It was like all her secrets.

"Why?" she asked him. "Because of the mare?"

He nodded. "Will you?"

"Of course I will." She watched his shoulders sag in relief. That too was strange.

"We have to be able to talk to them," he said. "To their makers if we can, to know how a chariot is made. To their leaders certainly, in our guise as traders. You they'll see as a prodigy. Their women don't walk under the sun, don't show their faces, don't speak before the men. You do all of that. We're going to tell the truth of you, that you serve a living goddess."

"Yes," she said. "And that the mare brings me there, returning to the lands from which her ancestors came. We were those people once. We were wild tribes. We kept our women shut in tents, and forbade them the horses—to ride or even to touch or see them. Then the White Mare led us to the cities, and taught us the ways of the Goddess."

"You understand," he said.

She flashed a grin at him. "Think of it," she said. "If we could win them as the cities won us once—maybe the war won't come at all."

"Maybe not," he said, not as glad of the thought as she, but not excessively somber, either.

It could happen, she thought. They could do it. With the mare, with her secrets—with the young lords of Lir, and the caravaneers, and Bran and Conn. All of them. They could do it. The Goddess would help them.

II

RIDERS OF THE WIND

·································· 9 ··································

"**B**Y ALL THE gods of the blue heaven," said Dias, stretching till his bones cracked. He winced, clutched his head, dropped down with a groan. "*Ai!* That wasn't kumiss, that was poison."

"That was mares' milk brewed into fire," Minas said.

"Same thing," said his brother. Dias rolled over and buried his face in the tumbled furs. "Wake me when the world ends."

Minas tipped him out on the tent's floor and held him down when he fought. He was strong, but Minas was both larger and stronger. It was no effort to wait him out.

He lay still at last, panting, wincing at the pain in his head. Minas smiled down at him. "The world ends now," he said, "unless we push the sun into the sky. Come out and help me."

"You're mad."

"Perfectly," Minas said. "Are you coming?"

He did not wait to see if Dias would come. The young men's tent was full of snoring bodies. Minas stepped lightly over them. He heard Dias behind, marked by a trail of grunts and curses. He grinned to himself as he stepped out into the chill of the morning.

The sun was not yet up, but the sky was brightening. The steppe rolled away before him, patched still with the last of the late-spring snow. The camp of the Windriders stretched behind. The flocks were bleating, the cattle lowing. Away to the north where the horse-herds had grazed in the night, one of the stallions screamed a challenge.

Minas stretched as Dias had done, but with far more fortunate consequences. He had drunk less than most of the others, not so much out of caution as out of desire for a certain pair of grey eyes, and a certain lovely mouth and a certain ripe young body. She had been waiting for him outside her father's tent, and very willing indeed, too.

He smiled at the memory. Women were better than kumiss, by far.

He said as much to Dias, who had come out behind him, blinking and holding his head. Dias snarled in response.

Minas walked out of camp by the path that he had made, up the long roll of land to the eastward, till he stood at the top of the world. It dropped away before him, steeply down and down to the eastern plains. Their plains—their world, that they had taken in force of arms, driving forever toward the setting sun.

He laughed and spread his arms. The wind was keen, cutting through his thin leather shirt, but it was his brother, his lover. None but he had tasted it yet this morning. No lungs but his had drawn it in, no body felt its clean cold touch. He was the first, the blessed one. He was the king's heir of the People, prince and chosen, beloved of the gods.

He sang the long clear note. The wind sustained it. The sun rose on the strength of it.

Warmth wrapped him about. Dias grumbled and squinted, but he had brought a mantle to wrap his brother in. "One of these mornings," Dias muttered, "you'll catch your death."

"Not I," Minas said. "The gods love me." He let his head fall back. The wind caught his long loose hair and sent it streaming behind him. He laughed and turned slowly about, making a dance of it, welcoming the sun back to the camp of his people.

⇒ ⇐

Aera heard that clear sustained note from the depths of the king's tent. It was a defiance so subtle and so exquisite that she paused in her overseeing of the king's youngest wives and let herself dream for a moment that she stood on the world's edge beside her son.

The king should have been there. He should have raised the sun. Not a prince, not even the one whom he had named his heir.

But the king no longer performed that duty of his office. There were many things that he no longer did. Rites of the sun and air, celebrations of the daylight, daily judgments and smaller justice. When he hunted, he hunted only lion and boar. He troubled himself with nothing that was not, in his reckoning, kingly.

He was still abed with the newest of his wives. Her weeping had stopped some while since. His grunting had paused; as Minas' song died away, Aera caught the soft rasp of the royal snore.

Her charges had fallen into disarray during her moment of inattention. She brought them back to order with a sharp word. None of them was weeping, at least. Even the twins, noted for their sullenness, were mending tunics with reasonable application.

Aera's jaw was aching again. Of all these children, every one of them beautiful and every one of them the child of a man of influence among the conquered tribes, not one went willingly to the king's bed. Time was when that had not been so; there were still a few who had come here in great hopes of royal favor, dreaming of the power that a king's wife could claim for herself.

But all the power was in one woman's hands, these days. That woman was not Aera. And as for being wife to the king . . .

Some of them were whispering, off in the corner, but Aera's ears were keen. All their voices were muted to sameness, so that she could not tell who spoke. Still the words were clear, their tone unmistakable. They were speaking in trader-speech, which was all most of them had in common.

"I made myself a necklace of wild garlic," one said, "and said a spell over it, to keep him from me."

"I'm going to provoke one of the older wives into beating me, if he asks for me again," said another. "I'll make sure my lip is split. Maybe, if she breaks my nose—"

"You'd go that far?" breathed a third.

"Wouldn't you?"

There was a pause. Eyes gleamed, darting back and forth. After a while the first said, "He smells like dead things. His rod is cold. It's like a stone inside me. Even the seed he spends—it's like ice."

"Maybe," said the third hesitantly, "that's what it's supposed to be like."

The first scoffed. "What, are you an idiot? Haven't you ever played with the young men behind your father's tent at night?"

"My father would never let me out of his sight."

"Poor thing," said the second. "Believe us, men are warm, sometimes as warm as a good fire. And they may smell of many things, but death is seldom one of them."

"Sometimes," said the first, "when he takes me, his eyes go empty. There's no man in there. There is . . . something else."

"It's that bitch Etena," the second said, spitting out the name. "I've seen her in the night sometimes, when the moon is dark. She dances naked, and things dance with her. Dark things. She embraces them. She— does things with them."

"You think the king is—" the third began, but she could not go on.

"We know the king is not as he used to be," said the first. "I forget, you come from the High River people. You never knew him before. He was beautiful. He was a golden king, a sun-king."

"Like his heir?"

"Very like. Though that one is a summer prince, all red and gold. His father was paler, like winter sun, but warm. He used to laugh, and some-times he'd sing. He'd even be caught playing with children."

"I can't imagine that," the third wife said.

"It was a long time ago," said the first. "Before the king conquered

Etena's people. Her father was a shaman, did you know that? Her mother was a witch from the northern fells. She learned things from them, you can lay wagers on it. Dark things. Terrible things."

"Now she rules the king," said the second, "and through him the tribe. She has him thinking of nothing but the dark."

"And war," the first said. "Always war."

"War is not so bad," the third murmured. "Women stay home then. Men ride out. Sometimes they're even killed."

Neither of the others hushed her as wives should do, protecting their husband from the ill omen. Nor did Aera make a sign against evil. Evil was already in this place, laired in the king.

She called Maia to take her place, which did not displease that daughter of a war-chieftain. Maia was ambitious. She was eyeing Aera's position among the wives; but that, however fondly she might dream, was unassailable. A woman needed sons in order to be mother to the king's heir—and Maia had only a pair of sickly daughters.

Aera slipped through the whispering dimness of the king's tent, past women who slept and women who tended children, past women and girls chewing hides to soften them, or piecing them together into gowns or tunics or leggings. There were women spinning wool into thread, and weaving that thread on looms, and sewing the cloth into garments for the king and his favored sons—all in the dimness of the tent. Some of them had not seen the sun in time out of mind.

Aera could not live so trammeled. She passed the women's door, the flap that hid in a corner of the great tent. The sun was dazzling even so early.

When her sight cleared, she made her way to the eastward side. The cooks were tending the fires, grinding flour, baking bread, roasting a newborn calf for the king's breakfast. Its mother was lowing piteously in the king's herd, mourning her lost child.

Aera took little notice of them. Her eyes were on the two figures that walked down from the world's edge. The taller walked light and free, wrapped in a bearskin, with his bright hair falling in tangles against the black fur. The other, shorter by half a head, darker, broader, sturdier, trod gingerly as if to keep his head from shattering.

Aera smiled, watching them. Minas and Dias, brothers of the same father, one born in the morning, one born in the dark of the night, had been inseparable from that first day. They had not shared a womb, but they had shared Aera's breast, for Dias' mother Etena had had no milk, but Minas' mother Aera had had ample for both.

They never quarreled, those two, past the small squabbles of brothers. In everything that mattered, they were as one heart. They fought in battle together, sharing the same chariot, taking turn and turn about, now as warrior, now as charioteer.

The sight of them warmed Aera's spirit. It had been a long night, full of shadows and whispers, and dim cold things creeping round the edges of the light.

She hated to turn back into the tent's darkness, but she had duties, which she was shirking. As she steeled herself to abandon the sun, a shadow crossed her path.

It was Etena, swathed in black, but she had not drawn the veil over her face. Time had been less kind to her than to Aera. It had turned her dark hair to ashes and stripped her skin of its youth, softening and slackening it over the sturdy bones. But she was strong, and her eyes were as grey as flint. They cut like edged blades.

Aera chose the same weapon as her son: the sweet brilliance of a smile. It had no power to warm that bitter heart, nor had she expected such a thing. But it bolstered her courage.

"You will undertake," said Etena, "to restrain those puppies. The king objects to being roused at dawn by the howling of wolf-cubs."

Aera bit her tongue. She had learned long ago that argument with Etena only ended in confusion. She bowed her head as if in submission.

"There will be no more of that caterwauling," said Etena, "by order of the king. Go, tell them. And bid them know that if they refuse, the king will demand an accounting."

Aera's fists clenched. She was the Great Wife, mother to the king's heir. It was far beneath her to run errands for a mere royal favorite.

Still worse than that was the import of the errand. The dawn-rite had sustained the world for time beyond reckoning. The king's defiance of it would have consequences. The gods were not mocked.

"I will go," she said, soft and cool. "I will tell them. I will make certain that the gods know who has commanded this."

"The gods know," Etena said. She turned her back on Aera—rudeness heaped on insult—and disappeared into the shadows of the tent.

When she was gone, Aera drew a deep breath. The morning was clear—splendid. She was briefly free. But she could take no joy in it. Not when the tribe was ruled by such a creature.

10

The chariotmakers' camp stood somewhat apart from the main runs, a broad circle of tents on a rise to the north. The horse-herds grazed beyond it, and sometimes round about it.

The others were there already, had been there, Minas did not doubt, since it was light enough to see. They had three great war-cars begun, and three more on their way to completion. The seventh stood whole on the far edge of the circle, where it opened onto the horse-herds. It was one of the new cars, broader and longer, so that two men could ride in it.

Minas' grandfather knelt beside it, making a last adjustment to the new yoke that he had made. He was all but bare in the morning's chill. His lean corded body was as strong as a young man's. His eyes were as keen as a falcon's, his face sharp, his nose long and fiercely hooked.

As Minas paused, he sat back on his haunches, rubbing his hand distractedly through his cropped ash-and-copper hair. "That should do," he said in his harsh-sweet voice. "Will you be trying it for me?"

Minas bit back a grin. There were people who said Metos was a god, or at least the son of one. He had eyes in the back of his head, they said. He knew everything that anyone thought or did.

Minas was hardly inclined to dispute them. "Will you be riding with me?" he asked.

His mother's father did not dignify that with an answer.

One of the boys who looked after the herd was coming up from the war-stallions' pasture with Minas' best pair, the golden duns who were so swift and yet so light in the traces. At sight of Minas they pulled away from the boy and ran to him, thrusting imperious noses into his hands, searching the folds of his tunic. He brought out bits of sweet cake for them, and the last of the honeycomb that he had found on a hunt the day before. They devoured it all greedily. But when he called them to order, they turned smartly and took their places on either side of the chariot-pole.

Metos' eyes were glinting. He lent a hand with yoke and harness, adept as few others were. He had made the first chariot and wrought the first harness: a madman, people had thought him then, when he was young, before he was reckoned a god. Now he was old, as old as mountains, some said, but he could still smile at a pair of good horses, and strap on their harness, and spring into the car.

Minas was close on his heels, moving to the front of the car, taking up the reins. The left-hand stallion tossed his head, uneasy, a little, with the way the yoke sat on his neck. He on the right flattened ears and nipped. A twitch of the fingers brought them both to order. "Now," he said, purring it. "Now, my beauties."

He took them out past the edges of the herd, striking for the open plain. The wind caught him there, stronger than it had been at sunrise. The dun stallions snorted at it.

Horses never did like to run into the wind. Minas sent them in a long arc round the herds of mares and the new foals. The chariot rocked smoothly underfoot. It was balanced well, riding light on its wheels that Metos had changed as he wrought them, making them larger, stronger, and yet less heavy. The yoke was marvelous. Once the horses had grown accustomed to its feel, they liked the weight of it: they were lighter on their feet, pulling more easily. Their turns were quicker, too, and their changes of pace less harried.

When he was sure of the weight and balance, he gave them what they begged for: freedom to run as they would. They lifted up and flew.

Metos rode easily in the car behind Minas, barely holding to the sides, face to the wind, eyes shut, lost in the glory of their speed. The ground was a blur beneath. The herds skimmed past. For a while they matched pace with a hawk flying overhead, until with a leap that was like laughter, the horses passed him.

This was joy, pure and unsullied. No blood, no fear, no hate. No shadowed king, no dread of what he in his darkness would do.

But horses could only run so far, and the sun was rising toward the zenith. Minas had still his morning's labors amid the chariots, then must sit in judgment where his father would not. He chose not to be bitter when he thought of that. Bitterness fed the thing that had taken his father's spirit.

He brought the horses back slowly, till they were walking long and free, still with the chariot light behind them. He smiled at his mother's father. "This is the best of all," he said.

"The yoke could balance lighter," said Metos, "and there is a bobble in the right wheel."

"A very small one," Minas said, but he brought the chariot back to the makers' circle, unharnessed the stallions and saw them led away. His grandfather had already forgotten him.

It was not until he had stripped to his own loincloth and knotted up his hair and turned to the wheel that he had been crafting, that he saw the shadow that sat by the half-shaped curve of it. Even through swaths of veils he knew her.

Her eyes smiled at him. They were clear green, warm as if lit from within by the sun.

A man should not lower himself to acknowledge a woman in the light of day. But this was Aera, Metos' daughter. Minas smiled at her with neither shame nor fear for his honor, took her hand in his and said, "Mother. Have you come to see the new chariot?"

"I saw it indeed," she said. "How it flies!"

"Swifter than a hawk's flight," he said. "Lighter than the wind of heaven. We'll make a hundred like it, and sweep across the world."

"That will be splendid," she said.

He peered at her. Her brightness had dimmed. Her eyes were lowered as if she had been a woman like any other, submissive before the prince her son. "Mother," he said. "Tell me."

She said it directly, without shrinking from it. "Your father bids you cease the morning song."

Minas' back stiffened. "Does he indeed?"

"So says the favored wife Etena."

"Etena." Minas unclenched his teeth. "Then we may know whose will this truly is."

"I don't think it's wise to challenge her," Aera said. "Yet."

"But the morning song," he said in dismay. "The raising of the sun. Our kings and princes have done it since the dawn of the world. If we fail in it now, the gods will turn away from us."

"Child," she said. She lowered her veil for him, even there under the eye of heaven. He looked into her face that was still beautiful, as if carved in ivory. The red-gold of her hair had darkened to the color of moors in autumn, but there was no frost in it yet, no pitiless winter.

"Child," she said again, "the gods hear the heart's song even more clearly than that of the tongue."

His eyes widened. She smiled at him. "Mother," he said after a moment, "you are a woman of terrible wisdom."

"I would hope so," she said. "We do need it."

"Is it bad?" he asked.

She shrugged, sighed. "No worse than ever."

"They still don't see," he said. "Any of the men. Do you know what Nus the Hunter said to me yesterday? 'At last, a king who acts like a king. A king who kills only what is most worth killing. A king whose whole heart is set on war.' Nus was never like that, Mother. He never killed for the love of blood. He never prayed for war."

"Don't all men do that?"

He hissed at her. "Not like that! War is sacred. War is terrible, but all honor is in it. No one makes light of it. But Nus—Nus was dreaming of red slaughter."

"Are you?"

Minas shivered. "You know what I dream of. I don't hunger after it as he does. True hunger, and thirst—to drink the blood of destruction."

Aera's face was somber. "Is he the only one?"

"It is spreading," said Minas, "like a winter sickness. My battle-brothers have escaped it, so far."

"And your milkbrother?"

Minas could not help a smile. "Dias' only nightmare is a morning after too much kumiss."

"Dias," said Aera, "is Etena's son."

"Not in the spirit," Minas said with pure certainty. "The gods gave her dry breasts to match her barren soul—and gave her son to you to suckle and raise. He'll never give way to his mother's demons."

"I do hope so," Aera said.

"I know so," said Minas.

⇨ ⇦

She did not linger long after that. Minas threw himself into his work. He did not want to think the thoughts she had roused in him. Thoughts born half of dreams, half of whispers among the people. Rites of the moonless night, conquered children offered to the gods below, drinking of blood and binding of souls.

He was a creature of the sunlight. He had no fear of the dark, but he did not serve it, either. What had been done to his father . . .

He had to stop then, or the planing blade would slip and sever a finger. He turned his face to the sun. It stroked his cheeks with warmth. His father had been like the sun once, great tall golden man whose laughter could fill the camp.

But then he had turned away from the light and sought out the secrets and the silences. Little by little he had abandoned the gods of the heavens and sought the gods below.

"Etena," Minas whispered. Etena the shaman's child, the witch's daughter, the captive who had conquered a king's spirit. Preposterous, almost, that she had given birth to so cleanly simple a spirit as Dias. Aera might doubt Dias' simplicity, but Minas never would. Dias was all as he seemed. There was no darkness in him.

Minas thrust himself to his feet. He could do no useful work today. He gathered his garments, nodded to the artisan or two who glanced up at him, and left them to their labor.

⇨ ⇦

Minas judged such matters as the king reckoned too trivial for his royal attention — not many this day: a squabble or two, a handfasting, a newborn manchild welcomed into the tribe. None of the petitioners seemed disgruntled to face the king's son rather than the king himself. Indeed the new father was visibly relieved.

Minas remembered again the tales of blood and sacrifice. The children had never been Windrider children. But it had been a long winter. The spring was barely begun. The gods below would be thirsty for new blood.

When the judging was done, Minas turned toward his father's tent. It was not a thing he had done of late; he had been inclined to avoid what he could not bear to think of. That this darkness had been growing for long and long, but that this season, this chill spring and late-departing winter, it had grown measurably greater.

The king's tent had always been the largest, the richest, the most imposing. In his life he had taken a hundred wives and concubines innumerable, prizes of his conquests. Many of those were dispersed among the tribes, given as gifts to vassal chieftains. But the newest and the loftiest, and those whom he most favored, traveled with him across the plains.

They filled his tent with rustlings and murmurs, wafts of scent and a babble of high voices. But on the men's side there was none to be seen, except the three who were blessed to attend the royal person. Three, and the one who was always in his shadow, a shadow herself, but for the gleam of eyes.

Apart from these, the king was alone. He sat cross-legged on a heap of carpets, while one of his attendants combed his hair and wove it into plaits, and another shaved his cheeks and chin and combed out the long thick mustaches. The third sat at his feet and sang a soft wavering song.

His hair had been pale gold once. It was ashen now, and growing thin. His eyes, once clear pale blue, were as colorless as water.

He was still strong. His shoulders were wide, his arms thick with muscle. His face was carved in lines as stern as stone.

Minas knelt in front of him as a good son should do. Out under the sun he felt quite sufficiently a man, but here he dwindled to an awkward stripling. He felt unduly gaudy in the princely finery he had put on to sit in judgment: the armlets and collar of heavy river-gold, the circlet of hammered gold about his brows, the strings of shells and stones woven into his hair. A plait of it straggled over his shoulder, turned in lamplight from bright copper to a raw and unlovely red.

He straightened with an effort and met the eyes that gleamed in shadow. He smiled—more baring of teeth than offering of warmth or welcome. He spoke, but not to Etena. She was, after all, only a woman.

"My lord," he said. "Father. I trust I find you well."

The king lowered his gaze from unimaginable distances. For the first time he seemed to see his son. He blinked. His shoulders twitched. He frowned as if in puzzlement. "Minas? Minas, are you truly here?"

"In the flesh, Father," Minas said lightly, though his heart twisted.

"Good," said the king. "Good. And you're well, then?"

"As well as I can be," said Minas.

"Good," the king said again. "Good." His feet shifted as if he might rise. Minas held his breath, half in fear, half in prayer—for this was his father surely, though sadly befuddled.

The shadow behind him made no move, but some signal passed. The singer's song, which had muted but not ceased, rose to a buzzing drone. The king stilled once more. His eyes lifted and went blank. The voice that came out of him was his royal voice, deep and strangely flat. "Call the war-council. I'll speak to them tonight."

"Father," said Minas. "It's too early in the year, surely, for us to—there's no time for the clans to gather—we can't—"

It was like speaking to a stone. Minas broke off. He made reverence as if his father were still there to be aware of it. He all but fled then, out into the blessed light.

11

"*Wahai! Wahai!*"

The king's own warband whirled, stamped, shouted, a war-cry like the baying of hounds. They were all naked, their bodies painted in dizzying patterns. Their long hair was bleached white with lime and stiffened into bulls' horns and great arching stallion-crests. They were wonderful and terrible to see.

Minas stood on the edge of the council circle. One arm rested about Dias' shoulders. The rest of the prince-heir's companions lounged about in attitudes of elaborate boredom.

They would dance in their turn, for the prince's honor and their own pride. Their hair was loose, their body-paint simple: red ocher on the brow, yellow on the breast, and the orbs of sun and moon painted on their cheeks. The sun, sinking into the west, limned their faces in gold.

They would dance until the dark, all the warriors of the Wind. Then the council would gather round the great fire, the king's fire, and the year's war would begin.

Westward, thought Minas, looking into the sun's bright eye. Always westward. Maybe they had fled something once, some monstrous horror, some fire on the steppe, famine, merciless war. Not even the grandfathers remembered. Now they themselves were fire and famine. Fools fled them. Wise men bowed and offered them tribute—then well might die regardless, at the king's whim.

The king had not come out of his tent to see the dancing. His warleaders feasted on a fat ox, tossing bones and bits of roasted flesh at the dancers. The dancers darted and spun, evading the barrage. One, too slow or too unwary, caught a thighbone between the eyes and dropped like a stone.

The others danced over and around him. The drums were beating, pounding the pulsebeat. Their feet stamped. They beat the earth into submission.

Minas' companions whirled into the dance. He spun in the midst of them, spinning swifter, leaping higher, shouting louder than any. It was pure mindless bodily pleasure. He lost himself in it.

⇒ ⇐

The council began at full dark. The king still had not come out. Minas was dizzy with drink and dancing, but not so dazed that he could fail to see who was and was not sitting in the council circle. The wardance had moved to another and lesser fire. It would wind through the whole camp before it ended, drawing in new dancers, shedding old ones, till all the tribe was sealed to the king's war.

Minas had danced enough for a while. He squatted on the circle's edge and got his breath back. The sweat dried on his body. He was shivering, but he hardly felt the night air's chill.

Dias dropped down beside him. As usual, he had thought of practical things: he had Minas' bearskin mantle and a wolfskin for himself. Minas wrapped himself in the mantle, breathing its wild musky scent.

The war-council was growing restless. There was kumiss enough, and some had drunk deep of it, but that only made them surly. These lords and commanders were not accustomed to waiting on any man, even a king.

Minas was breathing comfortably again. His heart had stopped hammering. He rose, holding the mantle about him, and walked into the firelight.

Eyes flashed to him. For a moment some seemed to see the one they waited for: quick flares of anger or expectation, even more quickly dulled as they recognized the son and not the father. He smiled brilliantly at them all and took the place to which he was entitled, just outside the canopy that should have sheltered the king.

They ignored him, and his brother behind him. Whatever the princes might be entitled to, they were still little more than boys. This was a council of elders and seasoned warleaders.

Minas' bones were uneasy. His father should have come out for the dancing. As strange and haughty as he had grown, he had never been known to keep his council waiting so very long or in such great ill-humor.

The dancing was far away now. The fire burned steadily. The king's women moved among the council with platters of roast meats, bread fresh from the baking, and skins of kumiss and honey mead. A strangled squeal marked the daring of one man greatly gone in kumiss, laying hand on the woman who bent to fill his drinking horn.

Minas half-rose. He did not know precisely what he would do, whether he would speak to them all or run in search of his father. Still someone must do something, or this council would shatter into squabbling factions.

Just as he began to straighten, the fire flared. In the sudden light, the king came out of his tent. He loomed tall and terrible, like a bull in full rut: great head uplifted, broad horns spearing the stars.

He was wearing the bull's-head crown of the People, and the cloak of the spotted bull's hide. His face was shadowed beneath the sweep of the horns.

Silence fell as he came. Even the dancers, at the camp's far edge, chose just then to pause. Nothing stirred. No one seemed to breathe.

He paced through the circle to the royal canopy. Just in front of it, he turned. The fire blazed on the gold he wore on his arms and about his neck.

When he spoke, his voice was deep, echoing in the silence. "The gods have spoken," he said. "When the moon wanes to dark, we ride, we and all the tribes who look to us as king. Westward, into the setting sun. Westward, to the lands of gold and copper, soft men and willing women, to the lands the gods have given us."

"The gods have given us the world," said the warleader of the North-wind clan.

The others growled assent. It was a chilling sound, soft and deadly. It put Minas in mind of a council of wolves.

"Chariots," said the king. "We shall build chariots—tens, hundreds of them—and train horses, and train warriors. We shall be a storm in the tall grass, a wind across the steppe. All lesser men shall fall before us."

The growl deepened. It no longer sounded like the voices of men, but seemed to come from the earth underfoot.

Minas' hackles rose. The council should have been lively, men speaking in swift alternation, boasting, arguing, planning the war as they had at the beginning of every season since anyone could remember. But they sat still, and their eyes glittered. They said nothing. The king's shadow stretched long across them.

There were no shamans among them. Minas had not looked before, nor thought to look. But the bone rattles were silent, the horn-crowned heads nowhere to be seen. Priests of the gods there were none, no workers of magic, no servants of the Powers. Only the king and his warleaders and the elders of the People.

Minas escaped. He fled, if he would admit the truth. He felt no shadow on him—but would he know if it had already corrupted him?

⇒ ⇐

He hardly saw where he was going. His feet took him where they would. He did not hear Dias behind him, but he was too craven to go back and look for his brother. If it was Dias' mother who had done this, then Dias was in great danger. But Minas was no priest or shaman. He had no power but what was in his hands: to wield a weapon, or to make one.

There was one who had power in truth, whom some were calling a god. He found himself there, in front of his grandfather's tent, on the far side of the chariotmakers' circle.

It was a small tent for so great a man. Two of his daughters kept it for him. His wives were dead long ago, nor had he taken others. Some whispered that he had cut away his manhood as a sacrifice to the gods.

He was man enough, Minas knew. He simply did not care. His spirit burned too bright, with too narrow a flame. All of it was given to his work. He thought of little else.

He was awake as Minas had thought he might be. His tent was full of lamps, dazzling bright. They were one of his few indulgences. His tent was all but bare, his belongings few. If it was not meant for the making of chariots, he did not wish to own it. Every gift that he was given, he gave away. Except the horses. Those he kept—but they were among the herds. Here he had little and would have been content with less.

He sat cross-legged on a single worn hide. He was naked, as if he had been asleep. But his eyes were fiercely awake. Something gleamed in his hand.

Gold, it seemed to be, but its color was odd—too flat somehow. Too shallow. It was shaped into a small blade such as a man might use for cutting his hair.

"A knife of gold?" Minas asked, squatting in front of his grandfather.

Metos tossed it at him. He caught it by the blade; gasped and recoiled. Blood welled from the cuts in his fingers. "*Ai!* It bit me. What spell is on it?"

"That," said Metos, "I should like to know."

Minas lifted the thing gingerly, by the haft this time. That was carved of bone. Minas did not recognize the clan-marks that were on it. "Where did you find this?"

"A trader brought it," Metos said. "He said it came from beyond the river of souls."

"The river that flows round the feet of the setting sun? But there's nothing past that. Except maybe the gods' country."

"No," said Metos. "He said not. He said there's more to the world. Tribes as numerous as ants in a hill. Great wealth. Vast camps—cities, he called them: camps that never move, where men live year after year."

"I've heard of cities," Minas said. "The tribes we overrun, they babble of them. But how can men live so? They'd hunt the land bare inside of a year."

"They keep cattle," Metos said, "and teach the earth to grow fruit at their command. You've seen that, child. You saw the tribe that we over-ran, that had fields growing beside a camp where they lived most of the year. They said they'd learned it from a western shaman."

"We slew every man of them," Minas said. "My father took the chief's wives. They wept a great deal. They all sickened and died before the winter was out."

"They were soft," Metos said. "That is the way of cities. But this . . ." His finger brushed the blade of the little knife that Minas still held in his hand. "This is as sharp as the jaws of death. Whoever wrought this was no soft man."

"What is it?" Minas asked.

"He called it bronze." Metos frowned at it, then lightly, barely touching, ran it down his arm. It left a swath of shaven skin behind it. "He swore he knew nothing of its secret."

"You believed him?"

"He died swearing it." Metos spoke calmly, as a god might, or a king. "He was a thief. He had stolen the knife from a prince. He tried to sell it to me—fool, to tell me how he got it."

"Blades of bronze," Minas said, "would be as deadly as chariots."

"And the king wants a hundred chariots," said Metos. "We've all but exhausted the wood that our allies brought us from the north. There's none to be had here, nor within many days' ride. But westward, across the river, there are forests, the trader said. Great stands of trees. We must have those trees, if we're to have chariots."

Minas stared at him. "It was *you* who moved the king to speak?"

"No," said Metos. "There's gold in the west. The king loves gold. The king's wife loves it even more. But I need those forests. And you—what do you need? Why do you want to stay here?"

"I don't," said Minas. "I want to see the cities of amber and gold, if they are real. And see swords of bronze. But—"

"But?"

Minas ran his tongue over his lips. "There's an ill thing behind the king's face. What it is, why it came, what it wants—I don't know. But it makes my skin shiver. Why does it want to take the war westward? What does it need there?"

"Blood and souls," Metos said. "Tender young virgins. Newborn infants. What does any dark thing hunger after?"

"What," said Minas, "if it wants us? What then? There were no shamans in the council tonight. Already it's stronger than they. The warleaders had no word to say. It's mastered them. It will devour us next. All of us—we who are here, our allies, our kin, our vassals across the plains. Then it will use us to devour the western cities."

Metos did not tell him that he was rambling, or that he was starting at shadows. He said, "I don't doubt that it will try. Did you ask a shaman why he wasn't there?"

Minas opened his mouth, then shut it again. Carefully he said, "My bones knew."

"Your bones were aquiver with horror of the thing in your father. Go," said Metos. "Ask the shamans."

"Will they speak to me?"

"To the king's son, the heir, the prince beloved of the sun?"

Minas flushed. "Now you're laughing at me."

"I am not," Metos said. "Ask them."

That, too clearly, was all Minas would get from that most maddening of men. And maybe, he thought, Metos was a god after all. Gods were beyond the comprehension of mortals. Even mortals who were princes.

12

No warrior willingly sought out the shamans, least of all in the dark before dawn. Minas thought, dimly and very distantly, of sleep. Morning's light would serve him better, surely, for calling on the spirit-speakers of the tribe.

And yet when he left his grandfather's tent, he turned not toward the young men's place but toward the camp's outer reaches. The shamans kept their own circle of tents, their own fires, even their own herds for rite and sacrifice. All young of the herds that were born black or misshapen or on days of ill omen, went to the shamans. So too the men-children marked with strangeness either within or without.

Minas was as unlike them as any man could be. And rightly, for the king must be perfect in all his limbs, unmaimed, unmarred, and beautiful before the gods.

Yet that was nothing to be proud of in this dim cold hour. The stars burned too fiercely overhead, as if they would defy the sun that came to conquer them. Minas was still bare under his mantle, still marked with paint that had blurred and run on his body. He was no very prepossessing figure.

The shamans would be the last to care for any such thing. Minas thrust down the cold grues. He came in good faith, at the command of a living god. He had nothing to fear.

Nothing indeed, though the skin quivered between his shoulderblades, and his manly parts did their best to crawl into his belly. He trod more slowly, the closer he came to those dark and silent tents clustered apart from the rest. His nostrils twitched at the scents that wafted from them. Smoke and tanned hides and unwashed flesh were familiar enough, but there were other things beneath, subtler and darker. Odors of death; of decay. Strange spices, musk, ash, and something for which at first he had no name. Heated bronze, he thought with a start of recognition, though he had never known that precise scent before.

The tents were shut tight. The fires were banked to embers. There was no sound, not even the whisper of wind.

Minas had to drive himself forward. Only pride kept him from turning tail and running back to his own tent and his own belongings and his brother's swift mockery. Each step he took felt like a profanation of holy ground. He trespassed where his like had no right to go. The night itself pressed against him, urging him to retreat.

The sun was coming. The horizon to the east was paling slowly. It gave him strength to advance against the press of shadows.

There was no one in the tents. Except for their ghostly guardians, they were empty. Not even an apprentice lingered to tend the herds.

Minas searched in all the tents. There was no one. Nor did he find any sign of flight, nor any belongings in disorder, nor trail of confusion. For all that he could discover, the shamans had vanished into air.

Surely they were out on the steppe, performing one of their rites— striving perhaps to restore the king to his rightful self. They could not all be gone away. Shamans were the lungs and liver of the tribe, as warriors were its heart and limbs. Without them, no tribe was truly strong.

He hunted them. By then he had little will in the matter; he only knew that he must see them. It was like a geas laid on him.

He went as a hunter goes. He cleansed the paint from his body with ashes and bull's fat and green herbs. He slipped into the young men's tent, where they were all snoring raucously, and gathered his clothing and weapons, and slipped out again under the swiftly lightening sky.

He tracked the shamans by the bending of grass in the wind, and the slant of shadows, and the long rays of the sun climbing over the horizon. He was not truly in the world, nor had been since he saw his father's shadow looming in the firelight.

What he did now, he did for the tribe. He told himself so, over and over, as he caught and bridled a horse and rode out into the grass. It was spring on the steppe, and the sky had been clear when he left the camp, but as he rode, mist closed in about him. The light of morning muted and went grey. The song of birds, the chirring of insects, sank into silence. He was all alone, he and the mouse-colored gelding, in a world without form or substance.

Voices whispered in the mist. At first he thought he imagined them, but they grew slowly louder. They spoke no language he knew: the language of the spirits, he supposed. He thought he heard the faint beat of drums, hardly louder than the hammering of blood in his ears, and a far skirling of pipes.

He neither saw nor heard the thing of horror that sent his gelding mad. He who had ridden before he could walk, who had grown to manhood on the back of a horse, tumbled ignominiously to the ground.

The sound of hoofbeats faded swiftly. He lay in the trampled grass, winded and half-stunned.

It dawned on him, slowly, that he had suffered nothing worse than injury to his pride. He still had his bow and quiver and his long knife, though his hunting spears were gone with his coward of a horse.

He thrust himself to his feet. The idiot gelding was long gone. He had no great desire to go after it. The path ahead was as deeply fogged as ever, but his bones knew the way.

He walked, though it rankled in him, a prince of the Windriders, to be forced to go afoot. He pressed on through the mist, amid the crowding voices. They had stopped laughing at him, at least.

As much care as he had thought he was taking, he had let his guard slip. He nearly fell out of the mist into a circle of dazzling daylight, just barely catching himself in the concealment of the fog.

It was, after all, a grey and clouded light, but it was the light of day on what seemed to be the living earth. It was a hollow in the steppe, a deep green bowl. Stones rimmed it like worn and rotted teeth. Minas had caught himself against one. It was cold under his hand.

Beasts gathered in the hollow. The stag with his horned crown—though in spring he should barely have been in velvet. The bear, the wolf, the wild boar, the lion of the steppe. Black ram and black he-goat. But no bull. The lord of the tall grass was not here, nor had any part in this council.

This was what the king's war-council should have been. The beasts spoke with the voices of men, back and forth in swift alternation. Their language was the language of the People, though Minas could still hear, if faintly, the crowding of spirits all about them.

They were agreed that there would be war. War was the lifeblood of the People. But how it would be waged, and by whom—that, they fought bitterly.

"The king is possessed," said the ram. "The thing that lives in him cares nothing for the People. It will drive him till he dies, and all his people with him."

"It is stronger than we are," the he-goat said. "We have no power to drive it out."

"And so it drove us out instead." The wolf lolled on the ground, grinning as his kind were wont to do. "It won't let us back in. We hardly inspire it to fear, but it does find us tedious. Is tedium a weapon, do you think?"

The boar grunted. "You were always too light-minded. We're going to fold our hands, then, and let that thing rule the People?"

"Do we have a choice?" the wolf inquired.

"It might not be so ill," said the goat. "It's a spirit of war. If the People are warned, and if they fight wisely, they'll suffer no more than if a mortal man led them."

"That thing won't allow that," the ram said. "It will feed on the blood of conquered peoples, but when it tires of that, it will feed on us—on the People."

"The woman was a fool," grunted the boar, "as all women are. If she had taken thought for what she summoned—for what the price would be—"

"Men have no forethought," the wolf said. "Women have too much. Of course she knew what she was doing. She was using a man for her own purposes, and paying her master in the blood of men. *She* will profit from it. I'll wager she won exemption for herself and her women, and bound the demon with great oaths to protect her when it comes to devour the People."

"And her son?"

The wolf shrugged. "The son, too, I suppose. If she can part him from his brother, and dispose of the brother."

The stag stirred. He had been silent, grazing while the others spoke, but his head was lifted, his dark eyes intent. "That one," he said. "The prince. We can use him."

"For what?" demanded the boar. "He'll be dead before the season's out."

"No," the stag said. "You forget what else he is. Whose lineage bred him. He has a god's blood in him."

"Metos is no more a god than I am," the boar said.

"No?" The wolf rolled, laughing. "But men believe he is. And belief makes gods. He's taught his grandson much of what he knows. This is more than a pretty prince. He has the arts of both war and peace, of both breaking and making."

"Little good it will do him among the dead," the he-goat sighed. "And when he comes back, the demon will be waiting, to drive him again from life into life."

"Its mistress hates him most cordially," said the wolf, "and his mother even more. And with cause. We're of little enough account, but those two—they are dangerous."

"We should cultivate danger," the lion rumbled. "Danger protects us. Safety will swallow us all."

"We should go begging to a woman and a callow boy?" The boar tore at the earth with his tusks. "We are the lords of the worlds. *He* is not even lord of this one."

"He can be," the stag said, "of all the lands under the sun. But she who rules his father will give us only the dark and the mists of forgetfulness."

"And who knows?" grinned the wolf. "With us, the boy and his mother might almost be strong enough to face the witch and win."

→ ←

Minas reeled to his knees. His head was spinning. He had been listening to beasts speak in the tongues of men—speak of him. But there were no beasts in that hollow. They were men, and not masked as dancers, either; when he peered through a blur of mist and light, he saw them in the ordinary garb of the People, albeit hung about with amulets and talismans and sacred signs.

He had fallen for a little while into the world of the spirits, but now he was back in the world he knew. He clung to the earth, to grass and stone. The sky was clear overhead. The mist was gone.

They had only to look up, to see him. But they seemed intent on one another. First one, then another swayed to his feet. They began to dance, there in the hollow. The shaking of bone rattles set their rhythm. A thin drone of chanting ran beneath it.

It was eerie, that dance, but it roused no awe in him. They were dancing against the dark—for dread of what they foresaw, and for courage to do what they must. The powers of earth took no notice. The powers of air had no care for them.

It was more than strange to see the terrible shamans, the speakers to spirits, the masters of the worlds beyond the world, and to know that they were only men. Frightened men, set against a power that was stronger than they.

One of them dropped, convulsed. The dance circled him, centered on him. He thrashed, keening in a strange high voice. His fists and heels smote the ground. His body snapped into an arc like a bow.

For a long and terrible moment he hung suspended. All at once, with a sigh, he dropped to the earth again.

He lay in the midst of the dance, breathing shallowly. Minas knew him—rather well, if he could be said to know any shaman. It was a young man, a yearmate; but when the boys were taken away to become men, Phaiston of the crooked foot disappeared among the shamans.

He was nameless now as they all were. Shamans guarded their true names zealously, for in names were power. Insofar as anyone called him anything, he was the Wolf.

He howled where he lay. Then swiftly he spun onto his belly. His head lifted. His face was Phaiston's familiar long-nosed face, and yet it was the wolf of the council: white teeth, yellow eyes, pink tongue unrolling in a lupine grin. "Ah," he said. "Skulker in the grasses. Come out and let us worship you."

Minas' hackles were up, but still he had no fear. He rose under all those staring eyes, and walked down among the shamans. They drew back before him, circling about him. He quelled the urge to turn and turn, to keep every one in sight. He kept his eyes on the wolf.

The wolf, who had been Phaiston, grinned delightedly at him. "Bold is good," he said. "Are you bold enough to make yourself a god?"

"Why should I dare to do that?" Minas demanded.

"Because you have no choice," the wolf said.

"Tell me," said Minas.

"Oh, no," said the wolf. "You'll learn as the gods see fit for you to learn."

"They sent me here," Minas said. "They meant for you to teach me."

The wolf laughed, rolling, kicking, hooting with mirth. "Oh, clever! Oh, wicked! You'll make a marvelous god."

"Teach me," said Minas, though his heart beat hard. "Teach me what I must know."

Rather distantly he heard rumbling: the growls of the shamans. They muttered against him, uninitiate, warrior and prince, trespassing in the realms of magic. But the wolf had leaped up in a dance of glee. He spun round Minas, whooping and yipping.

Minas waited him out. He whirled to a halt, panting, grinning. "Very likely," he said with great good cheer, "we'll all die regardless—and you in agony, for what you'll be presuming to do. Then maybe the gods will be less than amused, too, and torment you in the other-realm. But if against all hope you win the battle—the prize is godhood, the world's worship."

"And the People?" Minas asked. "Will they be safe?"

"You care?" grinned the wolf.

Minas fixed him with a level stare. He wriggled under it, but his wickedness was barely dampened.

"It won't be easy," he said, "or simple. You'll be called when you least expect it, and asked to do things that you never thought to do. You'll humble yourself even to death before you can be lifted up. And it could all be for nothing. You could be broken in body and spirit, and bound in slavery to your most bitter enemy."

"Will the People be safe?" Minas repeated.

"Only if you win," said the wolf. "Maybe not even then."

"Then I had best win whatever battle this is," Minas said. "Now teach me what I must know."

"In time," said the wolf. "You will go now, and be a prince. When we're ready, we'll summon you. Don't look for us. Don't wait. It will only sap your spirit."

Minas did not take kindly to such a dismissal from a man no older than he was. But this was no simple man. This was the wolf-shaman, the wicked one, the teacher and guide. Even Minas who was the sun's child could grant the power of this creature that lolled in front of him, grinning with purest insolence.

"Be sure you summon me," Minas said.

The wolf only laughed.

13

The People of the Wind broke camp and began the long drive to the westward. It was still the first moon of spring, the skies still treacherous, blustery with wind and a threat of snow, but the king was not to be moved. They would ride. They would gather the tribes of their allies, seek out new tribes, and conquer them. They would seize and master the setting sun as they had mastered the morning.

They traveled as they had since the grandfathers' time, in the way of war. Scouts rode a day and more ahead, searching out the lands that the rest would pass through. Then rode the warriors, well-armed men mounted on swift horses. The women and children, the old and the baggage, all laden in the wagons drawn to slow oxen, and the herds in their multitudes, made a great throng behind. The farther they traveled, the greater their numbers became, as more of the tribes and clans came to the muster. They were a mighty horde, a storm sweeping across the plains.

The king led them all in his gold-sheathed chariot, splendid in his panoply. His face, no one could see. The high headdress hid it. He might have been the gilded image of a man, set in the chariot for men to worship.

The rest of the chariots rolled ahead of him, behind the mounted warriors. They would not waste themselves in the vanguard. They were for worthy battles and great conquests, not for marching across lands emptied of people.

"Word goes before us," Dias said. He was charioteer today, while Minas rode in the warrior's place.

The air for once was warm: very warm for spring. Dias was naked but for the belts and baldrics of his weapons. He laughed as the horses danced and skittered. They were fresh in spite of the heat, and eager to stretch out and run. It galled them to keep to this sedate pace, no faster than a woman could walk.

Minas balanced easily as the chariot rocked and swayed. There was some hope of a battle in a day or two: scouts told of tribes gathering, weapons readied.

A battle would be welcome. He had been at odds with himself since he spoke to the shamans. They had not summoned him, nor had he expected it. The king had spoken instead, and begun the long march into the west.

He needed a battle. He needed simplicity: a clear enemy, a plain fight. Something to kill before it killed him, and no mystery in it.

He somersaulted out of the chariot. Dias' squawk made him laugh. He danced to his feet.

It was a goodly way back to the remounts, but he was in a mood to run. The wind in his hair, the sweat streaming down his sides, was blessedly clean. People called out to him. He flashed a grin at them, or the wave of a hand.

On the march the women observed less seclusion than in camp. Many rode in wagons, shut away from men's eyes, but the poor and the bold walked in the open. They were veiled, of course, but that was their advantage. They could slide eyes at a man who ran past, and giggle behind their hands, and offer pungent commentary on his fine young body.

He flushed as he ran, and not only with heat and exertion. They remarked on that, too, as fair as his skin was.

It seemed an age before he was past them and in among the herds. Tonight, he thought, in the darkness past the fires . . .

But not this morning. He found one of the horses he favored—not the coward who had betrayed him before the shamans—and swung onto its back.

He gained a following as he rode again toward the van, others of the young men looking for amusement amid the tedium of the march. They gathered weapons, provisions. It was, suddenly, an expedition.

He had only thought to ride apart for a little while. But with a pack of rowdy followers, and the women laughing, Minas let the wind blow him as it would. Westward, as they all went. Away from the People. Out on the sea of grass, hunting tribes that were not the People.

⇒ ⇐

They rode slantwise from the track of the march, crossing the scouts' trails. They found the marks of many hooves converging toward a single point, but they moved aside from that. They were not hunting the mass of tribes arrayed against the People, not as few as they were, light-armed, without chariots. They were raiding, harrying stragglers, bringing fear where and as they could.

Dias had not come with them. Minas' right side felt oddly naked. But there were others to guard his back, and they were all strong fighters. They would do.

One trail drew him more strongly than the others. There were maybe a score of riders, which would match his own company well enough, and they were riding as if they strove for stealth. They were spying on the People, maybe, and if the hoofprints that came and went were as he thought, they were bringing word to the gathered tribes of what they had seen.

Minas hoped that they were well and truly frightened. The People were the scourge of the world. Tribes of sense or foresight knew it. They surrendered if they were prudent, or fled if they were truly wise. Only the fools and the brave dared to fight.

They had been fighting more often since he was small. Metos said that the world was growing too narrow; that there was not room for every tribe. Nor was the sea of grass endless, as many of the People believed. It had limits, and they were reaching the westward edge of it.

Then they would have conquered it all, from the wall of the world to the river of souls. And perhaps beyond, if Metos' trader had spoken the truth.

Minas turned his mind from these high matters to one rather more pressing. The track he followed was fresh. The sun was sinking; a scouting party might think to camp, if it did not know itself pursued.

He called his men together. "We'll let them camp," he said, "and eat and drink. When they're well on their way to sleep, we'll take them."

"Alive?" asked Kletas. He was bloody-minded but cold in battle: an alarming enemy, but a strong ally.

"Leave one or two for questioning," Minas answered him. "Aias, Borias, if there are guards, dispose of them. Zenon, see to their horses."

They were all quick to obedience. The camp was close, secreted in a fold of earth near a bit of river. Wiser or warier men would have camped on high ground so that no enemy could fall upon them, but these must reckon themselves safe.

They were lolling about their hollow. One or two were even splashing in the little river. They were well-fleshed for so early in the year, soft and fair-skinned young men in richly woven fabrics, ornamented with gold and the gleam of colored stones.

The People were rich. They had conquered tribes as wealthy as any man could imagine, and won booty so vast that it seemed as common as the grass underfoot. But these easygoing raiders were wealthy even by the reckoning of the People.

He who came up from the river with an armful of cloth and gold was perhaps a prince. His hair was very long and plaited in many plaits, and his beard hung to his broad breast, wound with threads of gold and copper. He was a big man but light on his feet, and he was dark as these westerners increasingly often were: a black-haired man, but very white of skin. Maybe a woman would reckon him good to look at.

Minas marked this handsome man for himself, even before he saw what the man carried. He had a long knife, as long as his forearm, in an elaborately tooled and chased scabbard. When he laid his belongings by the fire that one of the others had built, he kept the long knife by him.

The camp settled to eat the young deer that roasted on a spit over the fire, and to drink from skins that emptied as the day waned and the light drained out of the sky. The prince took first share of the meat and first swallow of the drink—whatever it was; kumiss most likely. When he had had his fill, the others were just beginning.

He drew out a stone then and a bit of soft leather, and drew the long knife. It gleamed in the firelight, bright as gold.

Minas' breath caught. The blade was bronze. It put to shame the sliver of a thing that Metos had shown him. It was more beautiful than gold. Its master honed it as he watched avidly, drawing the stone down the edge in long loving strokes.

He took a long time about it. It was a precious thing, and clearly he cherished it.

Minas wanted it. His belly was sick with yearning. It was all he could do not to leap screaming out of his hiding place.

But he waited, because he had learned to be wise. He watched the foreign prince hone his sword till it gleamed. And when he had done that, he drew a shorter knife that was also of bronze, and honed that, too.

One might have thought that he knew there was a battle coming. Or maybe there was a woman waiting for him in the gathering of his tribes, and he made even his weapons beautiful for her.

The darkness fell. The camp settled slowly. Minas was aware of all of it, but his spirit was caught in the bronze. He would have it, both knife and sword.

A small niggling voice observed that such a prize would by right go to the king. If he kept it, he would commit an act of defiance that might not be forgiven.

It did not matter. He would have these things. He would not surrender them to the thing that walked in the king's body.

⇨ ⇦

It seemed the enemy would roister the night away. But at long last, as the stars wheeled toward the middle night, it was time. A soft rumbling in the earth, retreating eastward, gave the signal. Zenon had driven off the horses.

Close upon this, the call of a nightbird sounded thrice. The guards were down. Minas' lips stretched back from his teeth.

He surged to his feet, slipped quickly back to the place where his horse drowsed hipshot, swung astride. The stallion roused with a snort and half-reared. Minas laughed. With a high fierce cry, he sent his horse leaping on the camp.

They had taken the foreigners utterly by surprise. But these were warriors, however soft they had seemed—and their captain was armed with bronze. They were fierce in defense.

Minas' blade was a princely thing, copper honed to the best edge he could give it. The keen bronze hewed it in two. He was mad, he knew as he did it: he grappled with the western prince, body to body, snatching at his belt. The prince twisted. Minas lunged. The bronze knife sprang into his hand.

It pierced the man's breast as if it had been fine curded cheese. He felt it pierce the heart, and the heart leap, protesting.

The prince fell. The knife caught in his breastbone. Minas wrenched at it. It tore free. He whipped about. The man who stooped over him fell with blood spurting from his throat.

Minas swept back and around, caught the hilt of the sword from the dead prince's hand, and whirled into the thick of the fight.

With bronze in his hand, he was like a god. Blades of copper, blades of flint, notched and shattered. Bronze mastered them all.

For all Minas' fine intentions, they left no one alive in that camp. The bronze had thirsted; he had slaked it. It was sated with blood.

He wiped the blades with the well-woven cloth of the prince's coat, and honed them with the stone that had been in the prince's bag. He sheathed them in the prince's fine tooled scabbards and slipped them through his own belt. He rose up then and began to sing. His voice rang like bronze; it clashed like blades. It proclaimed to the stars that he was victorious.

14

They took rich booty from that camp, even as small as it had been. The enemy had been laden with gold, fine fabrics, beautifully wrought leather. The horses were fat and sleek, handsome stallions with long gleaming manes.

And these had been raiders, outriders. The tribes themselves must be glorious in their wealth.

Minas brought his men and his prizes to the king as was proper. Even, in the end, the most precious of all. He was a fool, maybe, but a loyal fool. The king was the king, whatever walked in his flesh.

The king was in his golden chariot, gleaming amid the throng of the People. Young men and boys whooped to see Minas come back with his raiders, trailing gold and bright weavings. Dias circled his chariot round to Minas' side. His grin was swift and brilliant and a little rueful. His slowness had cost him a splendid fight.

Minas led his men to his father. He could see no one he knew in that tall masked figure, but it was still the king. He willed himself to remember that. "My lord," he said, "we bring you spoils of battle."

The king's shadowed eyes passed over the gold, the weavings, the fine trappings for men and horses. The horses scarce won a glance. And the blades, the beautiful bronze blades—Minas' breath came shallow and quick.

The king passed them by as if they had been of no account. He laid his hand on nothing, made no move to claim any of it.

It struck the People somewhat sooner than it struck Minas, what the king seemed to have done. They roared in approval. Kingly generosity, to leave his warriors all their spoils—even gold.

They did not know what the sword and the knife were. Did the king? There was no telling. Nor was Minas going to test it. He took them back quietly, leaving the rest where it lay, and let anyone take it who pleased to.

⇒ ⇐

That night's camp was a war-camp. They were within a day's ride of the enemy's gathering. The scouts had come in with word: the enemy was aware of them. But none of those great warriors would come here, for the People had camped in a circle of barrows, tombs of old kings. They feared no spirits of outland chieftains; their magic was stronger, their spirits unshakable.

Tonight, while the spirits fluttered and chittered helplessly, they made the war-magic, the dancing and singing, the painting of bodies, shaving of faces. The king's men shaped their hair into high crests. Those who could, tumbled with willing women—and sometimes a husband or father caught them, and there was blood to consecrate the warriors' riding to the battle.

No one caught Minas. He had his pick of the young women on any night—they were all eager to lie with the king's son. But tonight, after his raid, not a shadow but was full of soft words and burning eyes. Hands reached out of tents to brush him as he walked by.

One or two did more than that. Most wicked of all was the one who caught him by the belt and stopped him short, then caught him by quite another and far less harmless handhold. He stood rooted.

This was Red Keraunos' tent. The hands must belong to one of his myriad daughters. Minas grinned to himself. They were all as fiery as their hair, and wonderfully wicked.

He slid hands up beneath the coarse fabric of the cloak that she wore.

Bare flesh heated at his touch. She wore nothing under the concealing cloak, not even a loincloth.

Her belly was soft, her secret hair thick and moist. She rocked against his hand. The other moved upward to cup a full soft breast. Her nipple was large and hard.

She drew him into the dimness of the tent. Whispers surrounded him, but this was a sheltered corner. They were alone in it.

She took him into herself with eagerness that left him gasping. He had bruises from the fight; cuts, small wounds. They ached or stung. Then he forgot them.

She ate him alive. She drained him dry. She took all his power to herself, and restored it a hundredfold through the medium of her body.

This was as sacred a magic as any of the exiled shamans could have worked. Minas left her on legs that buckled at the knees, but his spirit was strong—wonderfully so. He laughed and danced, staggering a little, grinning at the stars.

It was some long while before he realized that he did not know which of the daughters it was. He had never seen her face.

⇒ ⇐

He went where he had been going when Keraunos' daughter distracted him. Metos' forge was lit and roaring. His apprentices were mending weapons for men who had left it to the last moment, and seeing to the chariots, making certain that they were ready for battle.

Metos had been in the midst of them: he was stripped for the forge, but the sweat had dried on his body. He sat with his daughter inside of his tent, with the flap lifted to catch the light of his campfire.

Aera smiled at her son. Metos frowned as he always did.

Minas carefully kept his face still. He knelt in front of his mother and his grandfather, and laid the sword and the dagger at their feet.

Metos leaned forward. He took up the knife, balancing it between his hands, and breathed out slowly. "The king's wife knows nothing of bronze," he said.

"And we are fortunate for that." Aera bent over the sword. She did not touch it, but she peered along the length of its blade. "This makes war a terrible thing."

Minas shivered lightly. He felt anew the ease of blade cleaving flesh and slipping past bone.

"War is already terrible," Metos said. "We have chariots."

"Chariots and bronze." Aera sighed. "The gods will grow greedy, with so much blood to feed on."

Women never understood war—even Aera, who understood everything else. "We will feed the gods," Minas said.

"You'll feed the witch who rules the king," she said. She clasped her arms about herself as if with a sudden chill. "He's growing stranger. He never shows his face to the sun now. He goes masked to his wives' beds."

"Yours?" Minas could not keep a growl out of his voice.

"And if he did," she said austerely, "that would be no affair of yours."

Minas looked down. He never could resent her, even when she brought him down from prince and victor to jealous child.

"I think," said Aera in his chastened silence, "that you may do well to prepare yourself. This battle you go to, it will—decide things. Both on the field and in the camp."

Minas' heart clenched. "Mother! Are you safe? Is it Etena? Is—"

"I can look after myself," she said. "See that you do the same."

"Do you know what he'll do?" Minas asked. "Does anyone?"

"Anyone but Etena? Her women," Aera said. "But they never speak. She'll not trust a man, not that one, nor any woman not soul-sworn to her."

Not her son, certainly, Minas thought. And not Aera who had always been her dearest enemy.

"Watch him," said Aera. "Guard yourself. Be wary, and keep trusted men at your back. And remember the morning song in your heart. The gods will hear it, and may protect you."

Minas bent his head. Indeed the world had not ended because that song was silenced—though he had begun to wonder if that end was but deferred.

There was a cold knot in his belly, but a fire in his heart. He bowed to his grandfather and his mother, gathered up his beautiful new weapons, and went in search of what sleep he could find.

⇒ ⇐

He sang the morning song from the eastward edge of the camp, shaping the words without sound, filling his spirit with music. He was dressed in his battle finery, his cheeks and chin stinging with the razor's closeness, his hair plaited and wound tight about his head. He had his sword and dagger of bronze, and his bearskin cloak. He danced, because he had not been forbidden that, and welcomed the sun into the camp of the People.

He began the dance alone, but when he was done, they were all there, the young men who rode with him to battle, and his brother, and the chariots waiting beyond their circle.

It was time. The fighting men were massing on the open plain. The rest of the chariots circled the edges. The king was not late this morning, nor had he ever been for battle. He was mounted in his golden chariot. One of Minas' brothers was his charioteer—Arios who had just come to manhood in the autumn. The boy had a white, wild look to him, as if his soul was given utterly to terror.

It was Arios' first battle, and a great charge was laid on him, to drive the king's chariot while the king plunged into the thick of battle. Minas knew. He remembered.

Now he was a man, and he rode in the warrior's place. Dias was calm beside him, keeping the horses quiet, smiling faintly as he always did before a fight. Minas rested briefly in that calm, before the drums began to beat and the horns to bray. Slowly at first, then with greater speed, the army of the People advanced over the plain.

15

The enemy were waiting on the far side of a long hill, massed on the bank of a little river. Maybe they hoped that that trickle of water would stop or slow the chariots. But it took more than that to do such a thing.

They were as rich as Minas had suspected from the sight of their out-riders. They gleamed with gold. Their horses were splendid. And all along their line, under the banners of princes, he saw the fierce glitter of bronze.

His heart chilled at that. Of all the princes and fighting men of the People, only he had bronze. The rest carried copper or flint or fire-hardened bone.

He raised his voice for as many to hear as could: "My people! Beware of the golden blades. Capture them if you can. But never challenge them. They break flint—they cleave copper. They carve flesh and bone. Beware of them!"

"Gold?" someone asked nearby. "But gold is soft. It can't—"

"Not gold," Minas called back. "Bronze!"

They did not understand. He could only pray the gods that they re-membered, and eluded those terrible blades.

Then there was no time to fret. The mounted warriors had swarmed past the chariots, whooping and shouting and singing their battle-songs. The chariot-teams fretted, fighting strong hands on the lines. But the charioteers held them back. They would have their time, after the riders had swept through the ranks of the enemy. Those in the older, smaller chariots would leave them to fight afoot. Minas' warriors in their splendid new battle-cars would plunge onward, archers and spearmen sweeping through the ranks of the enemy.

Minas was calm now, as Dias was. His heart beat steady. His breath came deep and slow. His hand rested on the hilt of the bronze sword, cherishing the heft and the feel of it. He did not draw it. This was arrow-fight, spear-fight. Later would be time for bronze.

He watched, dispassionate, as the riders hurtled across the stream. Water sprayed. Through the veil of it, he saw how the enemy held their ground; how their weapons glittered.

They met with a ringing clash. The chariot rocked with the force of it. The team jibbed, half-rearing. Dias held them easily, gentling them, crooning to them in the language every horseman knew.

Minas kept his balance lightly, hardly heeding either team or charioteer. The People had fallen on the enemy like a fire on the steppe—as they always did. And as always, the enemy fell before them.

But not as many, not as easily as they ever had before. These had bronze, and bronze was terrible.

The People had chariots. Minas looked to the king, at whose command they must move. He stood in his shining car, erect, stiff and still. The horns of his bull's-head crown swayed in the wind that blew forever across the plain. He had not strung his bow. He seemed blind and deaf to the world about him.

The moment was coming quickly, when the chariots would best advance. But the king did nothing.

The line of chariots had begun to bend and curve, as others of the charioteers saw what Minas had seen. It was time, and swiftly coming past time. Still the king delayed, as he had done in the war-council.

Now as then, Minas lost his strength to bear it. This time the king did not stop him. He flung up his gleaming blade and loosed a great war-cry. Dias, soul of his soul as he had ever been, slipped rein. The team plunged forward. The whole line surged with it, all but the king.

Minas could not watch him and ride to battle. Later, he thought. Now he must fight. The chariot rocked and swayed. The stream scarcely slowed it. He barely felt the water that dashed against his body, though it was snow-cold. He nocked arrow to string and loosed. It fell with the rest of the archers' deadly rain.

The enemy's line was still strong—still holding. Bronze held it. Too many young men of the People lay dead or wounded. Horses thrashed and screamed. Blood dyed the trampled grass.

The chariots struck the line with the sound of hammer striking flesh, crushing bone. Bronze was bright, and it was terrible, but chariots were stronger than swords.

The charioteers at least heeded Minas' warning. They aimed for those of the enemy who carried no bronze, veering wide of the golden blades. They overran the long line. They bowled over the horses, crushed the men who rolled and tumbled underfoot.

"Capture the blades!" Minas roared. "Take the bronze!"

They heard him. Minas' heart swelled with love for them, amid the madness that came on him in the heat of battle. They left the mounted men to killing the lesser folk, and turned on the princes. They wielded the power of their chariots, the weight, the mass, the grinding of the wheels over defenseless flesh.

The princes fought back. Oh, gods, how they fought. They were brave in their extremity. But they were no match for the men of the People.

Minas fought as they all did, driving deeper and deeper into the swarm of the enemy. He let slip his awareness of all but the fall of arrows, the clash of blades, the eyes gleaming, the faces stark and wild, men laughing, shouting, singing, howling.

Minas bared his teeth at them. First his bow and then his beautiful blade plucked the lives from them, and sent the bright blood springing.

Some of them were clever. They went not for the men in the chariots, but for the horses — if they could not sink bronze or copper in the strong arched necks, they sprang to slash at the traces, to cut reins and tangle harness.

Dias gentled the horses through that roil of combat. Hands that reached for his reins fell away. Men who dreamed of springing onto the horses' backs met hooves and slashing teeth, or the darting bronze of Minas' sword.

But one man had his gods' blessing. He came from below, from amid a heap of the dead, and he had a dagger in his hand. He slashed at the belly of the left-hand stallion.

The horse screamed in mortal agony. The man echoed him, tumbling beneath the flailing hooves. The chariot lurched over his body.

The stallion struggled onward, brave heart that he was, with entrails trailing, glistening in the harsh sunlight. His yokemate jibbed, snorting at the smell of his brother's blood.

The battle was thick about them. Minas beat back a new onslaught, even as he felt the chariot lurch to a halt. The stallion went down as if he sank through water, slow, ah so slow.

Dias sprang onto the back of the right-hand stallion, slashing at the traces, as a moment or an age ago, too many of the enemy had tried to do. The other's body dropped, life draining from it even as it fell.

Minas vaulted out of the chariot. On foot, but armed with bronze, he set his back to the chariot and greeted his enemies with his widest, whitest grin.

Gold flamed beyond them. The king came on like fire in dry grass: golden chariot, golden ornaments, wide sweep of horns. His blade was copper, but it was as swift as a serpent's strike. It clove heads from shoulders, plunged into living hearts. It drove back the crush of bodies about Minas.

It dawned on Minas, too slowly, that the king had no charioteer. The reins were wound about his middle. His hand caught Minas, pulling him up with more than mortal strength, into the royal chariot.

There were no eyes to meet inside the bull's mask. The king drove on, fought on, while Minas crouched behind him, gasping for breath. His body stung with a myriad small cuts, but he had no greater wound. His bow was gone. He still had his sword, and his dagger in its sheath.

He straightened. The chariot lurched over a stone or a fallen body. He unwound the reins from the king's waist, slipped past that tall heavy body, settled into the charioteer's place.

The horses knew his hand; he had trained them in their youth. They were light to the traces, willing, and utterly fearless.

The king's sword had broken, but his war-axe wrought terrible slaughter. He clove his way through the enemy. Minas drove the team in a long sweeping arc, as swiftly as the press of battle would allow; for they all threw themselves at the golden car and the king who rode in it.

His father never spoke, never sang, made no sound. His war-axe sang for him. Minas went where his heart bade him go, with no guidance from the king. He was the will, his father the weapon. He herded the enemy, drawing the warriors of the People behind him, driving these western tribesmen back and back toward their guarded camp.

Bronze had great power, but chariots were greater. They rolled over the westerners' tents, flattened them as if a storm had struck out of the turbulent heaven.

The enemy were broken. The battle was lost when Minas took the reins of the king's horses. The rest was conquest, raw and simple. The People were born and bred to it.

They slew the men, took captive the women and the girlchildren, dashed the menchildren against the rocks lest they grow to fight against the People. They made a sacrifice of the enemy's kings—for there were five of them, a full hand of tribes gathered against the People—and offered their heads and hands to the gods. Bronze blades clove them from the bodies, and bronze gleamed before the gods' faces.

What the gods thought, no one presumed to say. The priests and shamans were banished. The king was silent. He performed the sacrifices without a word. His warriors raised the chants, nor did he prevent them. They worshipped the heavens and the earth and the realms below. They bowed before the sun and invoked the moon. They offered the blood of these westerners to the ancestors who, in their greatness before the gods, no longer suffered rebirth, but were made gods themselves.

Minas led the chants. He knew what that could bring upon him, but he did not care. He was covered in wounds, none of which he remembered, and some of which were deep enough to be troublesome. His head was light from loss of blood.

Sometimes he slipped from world to world as he had when he hunted the shamans. Dim shapes crowded thick about the blood of kings: shades of the dead who had not yet come back to the world of the living. They murmured to one another in soft cold voices. Most of them had been living flesh only this morning: warriors of the west who had fallen before the People. They were not all convinced yet that they were dead. They tried to leap on the living, to smite them with ghostly fists, to seize weapons and hew them down.

No one saw them but Minas. He lifted the cup of a king's skull, brimming with the blood of life. The king's shade hovered, glaring with dim eyes, cursing him in a voice no louder than the whisper of wind. He bowed, for that had been a brave king, facing his death steadily, already so torn with wounds that he was nigh dead of them.

The shadow-king started a little. His eyes met Minas'. Minas shivered, though without fear. He was suddenly, fiercely aware of the fire of life in him, the heart that beat beneath his breastbone, the sting of wounds in his arms and breast and side. All that was gone from this spirit. Only memory was left; and even that would fade and die, until he entered again into the body of a living man.

The shade pressed against Minas. It stretched out long shadowy fingers. It reached for his eyes, for the door of his mouth. It strained toward the life that was in him.

"Brother!"

Minas gasped, started. Blood spilled from the skull-cup. Dias braced him with a sturdy shoulder. "Brother," he said in Minas' ear, "you're out on your feet. Come, I'll finish it. You go to the healers' tent."

Minas shook his head, which made him stagger. Dias slipped the cup from his fingers. Others were there, born out of air: familiar faces now blurred and shadowy, as if they too were more dead than living. But their hands were strong, too strong for Minas. They carried him away from the hill of sacrifice.

16

"It's time we taught him what he needs to know," the wolf said.

"Perhaps past time," said the boar. "And if it is too late—"

"Not yet," grinned the wolf.

Minas' mind was perfectly clear. He knew that he was lying in the healers' tent with an unconscionable number of people fretting over him.

And yet he was also crouched on the high steppe, with the wind driving clouds overhead, obscuring dim stars. The shamans stood in a circle about him. Their eyes were brighter than the stars, but no less chill.

"His sight is growing keener," the wolf said, "but his understanding is still a child's."

"He fancies himself a man," the bear growled.

"All men are children," said the wolf. "But this one we can teach."

Minas rose slowly. He felt strange. He came up on four legs—strong legs, with hard round hooves. His head shook. Mane rippled on his long arched neck.

He was a beast as they all were, a red-gold stallion. His body felt as strange-familiar as did his presence in this place. As if he had done such a thing in dreams, or in a life before this.

"Yes," the wolf said, grinning. "You do remember. Good. So much the less to learn, if your memory serves you."

"I am not a shaman," Minas said. He said it calmly, but with deep conviction.

"What, because there's nothing twisted about you?" The wolf laughed. Its teeth gleamed in the starlight. "Don't fret, king's son. You're not condemned to our poor existence. Ruling in the world of the spirits, walking through the gates of the otherworld. Dancing amid the lightings."

"Hiding on the steppe in fear of my father." Minas snorted and stamped. "Tell me what he is. Why you've let him drive you out."

The shamans shifted, growling. But the wolf never stopped grinning. "Let that be your first lesson," he said.

The stars came down out of the sky and whirled about them both. They walked on ways that Minas remembered in dreams. They swam the stream of stars, and trod the moon's road.

A wall of darkness loomed before them. The wolf had circled round before Minas, barring his way. He pressed against Minas' forelegs. His body was trembling, though he tried to seem as insouciant as ever. "Your first lesson," he said. "You can pass that. He—it—doesn't know what you are. But you need to wear a man's face."

Not only the face, Minas thought. Of all the beasts that trod the steppe, only a man had hands. Strong hands, quick fingers.

He stood on a man's legs, with a man's hands, reaching for the wall, opening it as if it had been the wall of a tent. It strained against him. He set his teeth and dug in his feet and pulled. It yielded reluctantly.

He looked out across the camp of the People, standing above it as if on a high hilltop. Though it was starlit night where the shamans were, it was morning here. The sun was just risen, and with no help from him, either.

They had moved the camp from its old place among the barrows, to what had been the camp of the western tribes. Captives huddled under guard still in a circle of alien tents. Heaps of booty lay beyond it, gleaming in the early light—so much, so extravagant, that it seemed as common as grass.

The wolf pressed against Minas' leg. He was trembling still, and whimpers escaped him, as if he could not help himself.

Minas looked for the thing that frightened him so. With these eyes there seemed to be nothing, except that they stood in starlight and before them was clear morning.

The wolf's nose pointed toward the camp's center, where the king's tent always was. The king had taken that of one of the conquered kings, as was his custom. It was as rich as the rest, and wider than any he had had before, full of wondrous things. Minas found that he could see through the felted wool of its sides, and look on whatever he pleased—a skill that made him eye the shaman sidelong.

But he had not been shown this simply to reveal a secret that shamans never told. He saw the king's women in their places, and the young children with them. He saw captive women huddled together under the sleepless eye of an older wife.

He saw the king in a chamber as large as most great warriors' tents, lying on his back, naked as he was born. His hands were at his sides. His eyes were open. He might have been dead, but that the broad breast rose and fell very slowly.

Those wide pale eyes were empty. No spirit looked out of them. It was a shell that lay there.

Etena the king's wife sat beside him with her women on either side of her. Her hands were folded in her lap. Her face was serene. She made no sound, but the women sang in a soft slow drone like the humming of bees in a field of flowers. It was a song to numb the mind, to dull the spirit, to build a wall between the body and the soul.

As they sang, they tended a brazier in which burned sweet herbs. The smoke was full of sleep, of heedlessness, of forgetting.

Minas saw nothing there that he had not already known.

"Wait," whispered the wolf. "Watch."

The song had no end to it. The smoke was gaggingly sweet. Minas was close to succumbing himself, when something made him stir. His hackles rose. The fog of song and smoke lifted a little, enough to see that not all the smoke curled from the brazier. Some of it drifted above the king's body.

It had no shape. It had no eyes. But it had hands, and a mouth. It hungered. It crept in through the king's eyes, through his mouth. It filled his body until it was no longer a shell.

The king sat up. His face was pale. His eyes were alive, but there was still no soul behind them. Only hunger.

Etena's hunger. That was her will, her spirit in him. She had made this. It was born of her, a barren seed, lifeless and yet craving life.

Those eyes fixed on Minas. He had known no fear before then. He knew none at that moment either, but his heart, wherever it was, had drawn in tight and small.

He was raw spirit here, a breath of air, invisible. Yet this thing of shadow saw him. It yearned after him. It wanted—life. Breath. But more than that, the warmth of the living soul.

He could almost pity it. What it most wanted, it could never have, because its coming destroyed the very thing it hungered for. It could never be warm, never content. It could only want, and wanting, devour.

He retreated as an unarmed man backs away from a charging bull. He could not fight it, not as he was, but neither would he fall before it. He drew the shades of night about him, clean night and starlight and the sky above the shamans' circle.

He had returned without memory of passage from his father's tent. No dark thing obscured the stars. The shamans' eyes gleamed on him. He could not read their expressions. Even the wolf's face was blank, expressionless, the alien mask of an animal. "You want me to fight," Minas demanded of them, "against that? But there's nothing to strike against!"

"There is everything," the wolf said. "It eats life. You're full of it, flesh and blood and bone. It's focused now on the king, but if it sees how delectable a morsel you are, it will come hunting you."

Minas rounded on him. "You did that. *You* made sure it would see me!"

"It saw a shadow," the wolf said, "in a stallion's shape. It thinks you're one of us. It will hunt you, but it will find us. We're your diversion, prince. We're going to keep you safe until you can vanquish it."

"That's folly," Minas said.

"Would you rather we let it go direct to you?"

Minas bit his tongue. The small sharp pain, the taste of blood, steadied him somewhat. "It may do that regardless."

"Prince," said the wolf, and its grin had come back, white and mocking, "do trust us to know what we were set in this world to do. We'll defend you. Your part is to live beside it, hide the truth from it, and when the time comes, be the cause of its destruction."

"And how am I to do that?"

"In time," the wolf said, "you will know."

Minas considered any or all of the responses that came to him, but none seemed quite to be sufficient. He settled on silence.

The wolf laughed and danced about him. "Wise, O wise prince! Now go, back to your body. Rejoice in the heat of the blood. Cherish the life that's in you, and the soul that sustains it."

"No."

The word fell in sudden silence. The wolf stared, for once reft of speech.

"First," said Minas, "you will tell me what has become of my father's soul."

None of them answered, not even the wolf. Minas crouched down in front of him, eye to slanted yellow eye. That this was not the waking world, he thought he was sure of. But the wolf was very real, his scent sharp, wild. His breath reeked of old kills. It was, like the stars and the darkness, a thing of living earth.

"I do not think," Minas said, "I will not believe, that my father is destroyed. The witch is too hungry. She has his body and his will, and the power he holds; but she hasn't fed on his spirit. Has she? Where is his soul? What has she done with it?"

"We don't know," the wolf said. He spoke without reluctance, but without pleasure either. "She eats souls. That's what Blackroot witches do. If she hasn't eaten his—"

"She has," said the boar with a clashing of tusks. "Foolish boy. Grieve for you father, that's a good son, but don't deceive yourself with vain hope. Your father is gone."

"Yes, he's gone," Minas said, "but gone where?"

"Gone beyond our recall or yours," the stag said. It sounded almost gentle, and almost sad. "Don't waste what time there is in hunting for him. The creature who devoured him will devour the whole of the People if she can."

"My father is the king," Minas said. "He *is* the People. His soul is our soul. If it is lost, how can we keep our own?"

"If you lose yourself in looking for him," said the boar, "there truly is no hope for the People."

Minas set his lips together. When he did battle, he preferred to do it with enemies.

"Don't do anything foolish," said the wolf, who saw through him as if he had been made of water.

"I'll do nothing but what I must," Minas said. "That much I can promise you."

"Well enough," said the wolf, though the others liked it little. "Now will you go? Your body is waiting."

"Now I will go," said Minas.

Minas lay long in his dream between life and death. After the first day, when the roil of battle was ended, Aera had taken him into her father's tent. No one made a move to stop her, even his brother Dias. That prince hung about like a worried hound, till Aera was ready to fling him bodily out of her way; but her heart was too soft.

"He shouldn't be like this," Dias said on the third day, and far from the first time, either. "His wounds were all scratches. No one hit him on the head. He wasn't struck down. He just—dropped."

"His soul is wandering," said Metos. He had come in behind them, with a sharp scent on him of the forge. He was seeking out the secret of the bronze, and hot odorous labor it was. But it made him happy.

Aera regarded him quietly, but Dias' eyes were wide. "Someone's stolen his soul?"

"Not likely," Metos said. He rummaged in a bag, found what he had been looking for, turned to go out again. But Dias stood in his way.

"Tell me how to get him back again," said Etena's son.

Metos frowned. "Get him back? What do you want to do that for?"

"*Look* at him!" Dias cried.

"He'll wake when he's ready," said Metos, stepping round the obstacle. Dias snatched at him, but he was too quick, though he moved without haste.

Dias crumpled in a heap like the child he had been. But his eyes that lifted to Aera were not a child's eyes. They were wide and dark, and could seem both soft and innocent, but there was strength behind them. Many reckoned him the lesser of the brothers, the quiet one, the follower, but Aera was his foster-mother. She knew better.

"Dias," she said. "He will wake."

"But when?"

"When he's done whatever task has taken him away."

Dias did not understand. She could hardly have expected him to. He was a man of the sun and the green earth. He had nothing of his mother in him.

She comforted him with words that mattered little as she said them, calmed him and soothed him and yes, maybe laid a spell on him, a memory of her voice crooning him to sleep when he lay at her breast. He chose to allow it; he was not a fool, but he trusted her. He went back to Minas' side where he had been since the prince fell, and schooled himself visibly to patience.

Aera sighed. If she had let herself listen to her heart, she would have been pacing and fretting over the still form laid in Metos' sleeping furs. He might have been dead, but that he breathed. He would not eat the gruel she fed him, nor take water. He lay utterly still, save that, once in a great while, his eyelids twitched as if he dreamed.

She had not Metos' surety that this was no ill thing. Her son was not given to fainting fits. Nor had her husband been, upon a time — before Etena came to take his soul away.

Minas had been the king's charioteer, everyone said, just before he fell. If the thing that possessed the king had reached for him through the weakness of his wounds —

She knotted her hands into fists and made herself breathe quietly. Her son seemed asleep, if deeply so. If any ill thing lurked in him, she could not sense it.

She laid her hand on his brow. It was cool, no fever in it. She smoothed the bright hair back from it. His face remained as still as ever.

He was beautiful in motion, with his quick grace and his startling strength. At rest he had the long-limbed awkwardness of a yearling colt. His face was long, its lines almost severe: long arched nose, long mouth stilled into sternness. The brows were level, and darker than his hair, more red than gold. His beard was sparse with youth. He kept it shaven in a fashion of the young men, a glint of fair stubble on the lean cheeks.

She had tended his wounds a little while ago, such as they were. They were none of them enough to fell a strong young man. She took his hand in hers and held it. It was limp. She ran her fingers along the calluses. Every warrior had those, but his were different: he wielded more than rein and weapon. He was a maker, too, a forger of metal, a builder of chariots.

So many arts and skills, and all so quiet now, without word or reason. She came terribly close to hunting her father down and demanding that he tell her what he knew. But if Metos did not want to speak, he would not.

She pressed Minas' hand to her cheek. It stirred, twitching, curving to match her cheek. He gasped for breath; coughed. He sat bolt upright, staring as if he had never seen her before — or never thought to see her again.

She had never wept, even as a child, but she wept now. Minas was breathing deep and hard, like a man who had been drowning in deep water. His hand wrenched away from hers. Dias had it, clutching at his brother, shaking him, babbling nonsense.

Minas shook him in his turn, until he fell silent. "Tell me how long," he said, addressing it not to Dias but to Aera.

She had had time to calm herself, to master her face and voice. "A hand of days," she said.

Minas blanched a little. "But it was only—" He broke off. His head shook; he breathed deep again, as if to steady himself. "It could have been longer," he said to himself.

"Why? Where were you?"

Minas looked long at Dias. His eyes were different, Aera thought. They were the same clear green that they had always been, the same shape, in the same face. But something had happened to them. They were both deeper and brighter—as if they saw farther and understood more than they ever had before. There was a new sadness in them, but a new strength, too.

Dias shook him till he gasped. "Stop that! Stop staring like that! Answer me."

"I was . . ." Minas blinked, and shuddered deep inside himself. "I was learning. I was being taught—what to do. What—what our father is. What's become of him."

"Who taught you?"

The words had escaped Aera before she thought. Minas turned to her. "Shamans," he said. "Priests. She drove them out. They wait—outside. They watch. The wolf could follow me in. The others couldn't, or wouldn't. They're afraid of what rules here."

No need to ask who *she* was. "Why did she drive them out?"

Again the words seemed to speak themselves. And again Minas answered willingly. "They can call on the gods of air and heaven," Minas said. "The eater of souls wants no rival here."

"If we kill her—"

"She won't allow that." Minas lay back as if the strength had run out of him.

"We have to," Dias said—Dias who was the son of Etena's body. "She's a canker in the People's heart. She's swallowed the king."

It made Aera both sad and proud to hear him. This was none of Etena's. And yet that smooth oval face, darker than the wont of the People; the dark brown curling hair, the dark eyes—those were Etena's. He was the evening to Minas' red-gold morning.

Minas spoke from where he lay in the tumbled furs. "You will not kill your mother. The gods would curse you for that."

"But the People would be saved."

"No." Minas covered his eyes with his hands, as if in some way, in the dark, he could see more clearly. "Swear to me by the blood we share: you'll do nothing without my knowing of it."

Dias set his lips together. "Whatever I do, you will know."

Minas accepted that. Aera did not. But she said nothing. It was cowardice, she knew as she did it. And maybe it was the best thing, to let be what would be. To let the men settle it as they would, and for once be a woman as they thought of women, blind and weak and foolish.

III

SEA OF GRASS

18

FEAR HUNG LIKE a cloud over the tall grass. Emry's caravan of traders both true and false found the tribes either little minded to trade, that season, or given to wild extravagance. There was no telling which it would be until they entered a camp—if they were not driven off by packs of howling raiders, or shot at from concealment.

"The world has gone mad," said Conn without perceptible dismay. He was at home here, and the madder it was, the happier he seemed to be. His grief had turned to a kind of dark joy. He who had been so gentle in Long Ford was a fierce fighter here, with skill that Rhian would never have looked for outside the warrior bands of Lir.

She was hardly the same person she had been, either. The people of the plains looked on her as a freak of nature, a woman riding like a man, deferred to by the men who rode with her. Word ran ahead of her, so that after the first tribe or two, those they met knew the grey mare and her rider, and reckoned each of them a goddess.

They had ridden from spring into summer, crossing the broad sea of grass, while the moon waxed and waned, and the stars wheeled overhead. There were no more tribes to meet, except tribes in flight. They were fleeing the scourge of the steppe, seeking refuge to the west. But they would find war there, too, for those who held the lands would defend them. There was nowhere for any of them to go.

Only Emry's caravan was bold enough to journey toward the chariots and not away. One tribe tried to stop them. Its king was young and his brothers were numerous and headstrong, and they had declared themselves protectors of the goddess on the grey mare.

"You can't go on," the king said as the caravan formed its by now familiar line, the donkeys less heavy laden than they had been, but still weighted down with treasures for trade. As Rhian went to mount the mare, she came face to face with a wall of tall yellow-haired men. They were all smiling, as amiable as men could be, but they would not move to let her pass.

"Stay with us," the king said. "Be our luck. Protect us from the scourge that comes upon us."

"I mean to do just that," she said, making some effort at least to keep the exasperation out of her voice. "If you will let me pass—"

"Oh, no," said the king. "If you go on, you'll die. Even you, goddess with the wonderful eyes. The thing that comes on us, it is a fire in the dry grass, a storm of wind across the world. Not even a goddess can stand against it."

She lifted her chin. Her temper sparked. "Do you say that I am weak?"

He flushed and stammered. But he was stubborn, and he was certain that he was chosen to protect her. "Please, goddess," he said. "Don't make us bind you."

"*Bind* me?" She was not afraid at all. She was purely angry. "Do you dare? Let me pass!"

They would not. She dug in her heels and braced. They closed in, stretching to lay hands on her—on one whom they reckoned a goddess.

A whirlwind swept across them, flinging them flat. The mare came near to bowling Rhian over. Rhian caught mane blindly. The force of the mare's speed flung her onto the broad back. She saw a blur of faces, dark men, her own men, fierce with outrage; and foremost of them all, Emry who did not know he was her brother.

They would have trampled the king and his brothers underfoot, and no matter whether they sparked a war among these people; but Rhian's cry, piercingly shrill, froze them in midstride. "No! Let them be. They're not the enemy."

They begged to differ, but the mare spurned them all with her heels. They could stay and fight and be overwhelmed, or they could scramble together their caravan and follow.

The king and his riders watched them go from the safety of the camp's edge. The mare had cowed them perfectly, as she would reckon only proper.

Rhian had begun to know the exhilaration of power. From potter's child to living goddess—that was a splendid leap. She almost forgot the terror of what she went to, rivers of blood and the world's end, in the wild joy of this ride under the endless sky.

⇒ ⇐

On a day of high summer, in breathless heat, they came at last to the war's heart. The land was empty of the living. They had passed a burned camp, and then another; then a hill of skulls surmounted by the head of a spotted bull.

Emry had been sending scouts ahead for days now. Today it was Dal and the silent Nemes. They came back much earlier than anyone had expected, while the caravan paused by a little river to water the horses and donkeys. Dal's face was white. Nemes was even more silent than he usually was.

"Half a day ahead," Dal said, unwontedly brief. "Hundreds of them. Hundreds of hundreds."

"Is there a battle?" Emry asked.

His voice had a hint of roughness in it. He was afraid, too, Rhian thought. They all were. The tribes' fear had infected them.

And they were riding straight into the bull's horns.

Dal answered Emry's question steadily enough. "There was a battle farther on, but days ago. They've camped—who knows how long? They look well settled. There's water. The hunting's good—they've killed or captured all the tribes that would have taken the game."

"Maybe they're finally content," one of the traders said. "They must be rich beyond believing."

Conn laughed. He sat his brown gelding by the riverbank, some little distance away, but his ears were keen. "Those demons are never content. Do you know what they say? They'll ride to the world's end, and conquer everything before them."

"But not us," said Emry. His face was as grim as Rhian had ever seen it. "We'll stop them."

A growl of assent ran through the caravan. They might be afraid, but they were not cowards—not a one of them.

⇒ ⇐

They camped there, even as early as it was, rather than come on the enemy as the sun was setting.

"Remember," Emry told the circle of them all, all but the guards he had set. "They're not the enemy now. They're our hope of rich trade. We're traders—merchants, not warriors."

"Do we have anything they're likely to want?" Dal asked. It was unlike him to be defiant, but he was still pale with the shock of the truth at last: the might and numbers of the force they faced, and the terror—even at a distance—of its chariots.

"Traders always have something," Hoel the caravan-master said.

"Even for people who can take by force whatever they please?"

"Ah," said Hoel, "but that's the game. They take easily, but to trade— that's not so easy. And we carry things that are not common on the steppe. Fine things, things they maybe have never seen."

"Yes," said Conn from the edges where he always was. "They're loaded down with wealth, but they're wild things still. The fine cloth that they weave in the cities, the works of silver and gold and copper and bronze, the jewels and fripperies that we carry—these will captivate them."

"You know them," Emry said.

Conn shrugged. "I know the rumors that run across the steppe. You've heard them yourself."

"Yes," said Emry. "That they worship the sun. That a pied bull leads them. That a god lives among them, and his magic makes their chariots." He leaned toward Conn, his eyes intent. "Tell me what you haven't told us before. Who are these people? Will they possibly trade a chariot for our treasures from the west?"

"You are no fool," Conn said, "but now you choose to talk like one. The chariots are their greatest weapon. They'll never give it to the likes of us."

"Then we'll have to steal one," said Emry.

"You can try," Conn said, "and die."

"And maybe we won't fail. The Goddess is with us. She'll protect us."

"The gods of the charioteers—"

"She made all that is," said Emry, as certain of his words as if he had been a priestess, "all that they worship: the sun and the moon, the stars, the earth underfoot, the bull and the stallion. All that is is hers."

They were all staring at him, and not only Rhian. She had not thought before, what it must mean to be a man, and a Mother's son, and to be given eyes that saw farther than most. She had been refused the choosing—but it had fallen on her regardless. A man could never be chosen at all.

Out here in the grass, the world was a different place. And yet the Goddess was the same. He spoke the truth, this child of hers.

⇥ ⇤

It was an oddly festive camp, that night. They built a fire without care for concealment, and posted sentries but made no effort to be quiet. They sang songs of the cities and the south, hymns to the Goddess, jests and satires and wicked ditties that made the young men blush and look anywhere but at Rhian or each other. They drank the last of the wine, and danced under the moon.

Rhian danced for them. The moon was in her, and the mare was in season, tormenting the stallions in their would-be decorous line. Someone had a pipe and someone else a small drum, and Emry sang in his deep sweet voice.

The night was warm, the moon was bright. She let go her trousers and danced in her skin, in her free hair and the necklet of shells that Dal had given her, with Bran's bronze bells in her ears. The drum set the rhythm. The men beat it out on the earth's breast. She stamped and whirled, swooped and swayed, now like a bird, now like a gust of wind over the grass. She laughed with the joy of it.

Maybe death would come in the morning. Maybe it would come later, after they had tried and failed to steal a chariot. Tonight it did not matter. There was only the moon and the music, and the heat of her blood.

19

Minas heard the music from across the roll of the steppe. He had been out hunting, he and Dias and a handful of the young men, and they had let night catch them half a day's ride from the camp. They had a fat deer roasting over their fire, a skin or two of kumiss, and one another's company—what more could a man ask for?

This was good country, good hunting, ample water. Small wonder its tribes had gathered to do battle with the People, with so much to defend. They were broken now. Their women served the women of the People. Their men's skulls watched over the lands that they had lost.

"We could stay here," Aias was saying as the kumiss went round. "Did you see how the deer all but walked into our arrows? This is the gods' country."

"What, are you tired of fighting?" Kletas asked him—mildly, for Kletas.

"I could rest a bit," Aias said. He was a big man, very big indeed, but gentle. He fought well and killed many, but he never seemed to take such joy in it as the others did. They might have been merciless toward him if he had not been so large or so strong.

"We'll rest when we're dead," Kletas growled.

Aias shrugged and passed him the kumiss.

Minas' bladder twinged. He wandered off a little distance, not quite to the line of their horses, and relieved himself in the grass.

He heard the music as he paused, turning his face to the cool light of the moon. A little wind played about him, brushing his hair with soft fingers. It carried with it a sound like the skirling of pipes and the beating of a drum.

The shamans, he thought. They were calling him. This was just such a night as they loved.

He dug in his heels. He would not go. He was like Aias: he wanted to rest.

Dias came up beside him, fitting there like a sword in its scabbard. "Someone's camped out there," he said. "They don't care much for keeping hidden, either."

"You hear them, too?"

Dias' brows went up. "What, you think I'm deaf? They're not far away."

"Maybe it's a trap," Minas said. "Renegades of the fallen tribes, or raiders from farther west." And that, he thought, would be preferable to a foregathering of shamans.

Dias was already in motion, passing like a shadow in the moonlight. Minas hardly hesitated before he followed.

It was not far at all, just over a hill and down into a shallow valley with a river running through it: the same river that, farther east, flowed past the camp of the People. Dias dropped flat just below the hill's crest and, with Minas close on his heels, crawled up to the summit.

They lay side by side, transfixed.

Traders, Minas knew, seeing the donkeys tethered in a line, and horses that must belong to the guards. They were darker, broader, sturdier than any people he had seen before. The men's beards were black and thick and curling, their hair in single plaits as thick as a woman's arm. They made him think of black rams, with their curly fleeces and their wide blunt-nosed faces limned in firelight.

But he was no more directly aware of them than of his brother barely breathing beside him. They were all men, and however strange they might be, they were starkly ordinary before the one who danced to the skirling of the pipes.

It was a woman beyond any possible shadow of a doubt. She was as bare as she was born, her smooth skin gleaming in the moonlight. Her hair poured like black water down her back, brushing the rich rounding of her buttocks. Her thighs were round and strong, her waist surprisingly small. Her breasts were both full and high, with broad dark nipples. Her face had a beauty such as he had never seen before: full round cheeks, oval chin, long straight nose. Her eyes were large and dark under level brows.

She was the most beautiful thing he had ever seen. She danced with grace that caught at his throat.

He wanted her as he had never wanted a woman before. It was not as a stallion wants a mare, or a bull the heifer. He wanted all of her: not only that white body, but the mind, the spirit that shone in her. She was laughing as she danced, spinning till her hair whipped those wonderful flanks.

A distant part of him remarked on how utterly immodest she was, dancing naked in front of a company of men. But his eyes on her, the spirit in him, knew how all of them saw her: not with lust but with worship. This was a goddess. This dance was a rite of her cult, and these men her servants.

He had gripped the earth till his fingers were sunk deep in it. His heart beat so hard, his breath came so faint, that he was dizzy. He was like to die with wanting her.

It was a pity he was sane. He did not leap up and charge howling on the traders' camp. Nor did he wait till the dance was ended and the fire had died and the traders fallen asleep, then creep in and steal that glory of a woman. No; he watched until she was done, and saw her drop still laughing beside one of the men.

That was a big man with shoulders like a bull, but something about him was strikingly like her. Her brother, Minas thought. He found it comforting, somehow, to see her in the company of family. That was right; it was proper.

It was likewise proper that this brother tossed a tunic at her, and she grimaced at him, but she put it on. It covered her like a cloud across the moon. She was breathing hard, her breast rising and falling, straining the bonds of the garment. One of the men handed her a cup. He stooped to do it, making of it a bow, a gesture of worship. She saluted him and drank it down.

She had the manners and conduct of a man: free of herself, and proud. It should have been appalling. It was splendid.

"Minas."

Dias' voice came faint, as if from far away.

"Minas!" His brother was shaking him, bringing him back to the world from which the sight of this goddess had taken him. He blinked and gasped, remembering at last how to breathe.

"One would think," Dias said dryly, "that you'd never seen a woman naked before."

"A woman, yes," Minas said. "But a goddess, never."

Dias' brow went up. "She *is* a beauty. What will you wager that her men are coming to trade with the People?"

"No wager," Minas said. "Where else would they be going?"

"They're bold. I wonder what country they come from? I haven't seen their like before."

"Maybe they come from beyond the river of souls." Minas had said it lightly, but once it was said, it had the solidity of truth.

"If she comes from that country, then she is a goddess." Dias' voice was light, too. They understood each other very well. "What do you think they came for? To spy on us?"

"To trade with us," Minas said. "And maybe to see what we are. I would do that, if invaders came near to me. To know what I faced."

"Maybe gods from beyond the river are braver than the tribes we've always overrun."

Minas heard that, but his mind was running down another track. "I think," he said, "that we should visit them come morning. We can welcome them to the lands that the People have won, and conduct them to the camp."

"Them?" Dias' glance was wicked. "Or her?"

"I don't think they'll let her come alone," Minas said dryly.

Dias grinned. "Oh, they'd be fools to do that."

Minas rolled onto his back. It was like tearing the scab off a half-healed wound, to take his eyes from her. But the stars soothed him, and the moon bathed his face.

Was this how it had been for his father and Etena? The thought did not frighten him. He felt nothing of the dark in this woman, this goddess from the sunset country. "At first dawn," he said, "we'll put on our best faces and go, and greet our guests."

20

Rhian did not know if she slept that night. She supposed she did. Her dreams were full of moonlight and a strange, wild joy—as if when she woke, she would wake to something wonderful.

She sat up just as the moon was setting. The sky was grey with the first light of dawn. A breath of wind murmured through the grass. They were coming, it said. The morning would bring them. But when she asked it what it meant, it would not answer.

Her companions were asleep, even the guards out past the horselines. It was as if a spell had fallen over them all. None of them stirred as she walked among them, not even Conn, who seldom slept the night through. Bran was deep in dream, snoring softly.

She knotted her hands behind her to keep from touching his face. The distance between them had widened, the farther they traveled in this country. They never spoke at all now, even to be civil.

In the daylight she was too preoccupied with travel to think of such things. At night she was asleep, or preoccupied with the allure of this young man or that—but never Bran. Now in this hour between the worlds, for a little while she had no choice but to remember. What they had been to one another. What her leaving had done to them.

The moment passed. The moon set. The sky filled with light.

She had rekindled the fire and made the bread and set it to bake before the sun was up. Her companions woke just as the bread was baked, as if the spell had lifted from all of them at once. They yawned, stretched, roused noisily to the new day.

Rhian sat by the fire, demure in tunic and trousers, with her hair plaited tidily and nothing left of the night's wildness. Only Emry would look directly at her. She was amused to see who blushed the hottest. So: not every vaunting youth was as bold as he pretended.

Emry approved her choice of garments, from the slant of his glance, but he did not trust it. She flashed a grin at him, approving such finery as he had to put on. He was a beautiful man, and it pleased her to see him show it. These lords of chariots would find nothing to scorn in the Goddess' servants.

�️ ⬅️

They were preparing the horses, brushing their coats till they gleamed, when a cry from the hillside brought them all to a halt.

"Riders!" Dal called out, leaping down from his sentry-perch, running headlong and heedless of dips and stones.

"Chariots?" Emry called back.

Dal stumbled, caught himself, kept on coming. "Horses. No—*ah!*" He tumbled head over heels, rolling, fetching up with a squawk at Emry's feet. His face was scarlet.

"No chariots," Emry said kindly. He pulled the boy to his feet.

The others had drawn in, his warriors and the traders of the caravan. Many had drawn swords. He shook his head at those. "Sheathe them," he said.

"But—" said Mabon.

"We're traders," said Emry. "We don't fight."

It was not easy for some of them, but he was a strong prince, and they were sensible enough when they had to be. The riders found them still in camp, lingering as it seemed over their breakfast, with horses and donkeys tethered and packs of trade-goods laid casually by the fire-circle.

These were men like the tribesmen that they had met as they rode farther eastward: lean, rangy, fair-skinned, with hair that was often ruddy or gold. But there was a difference in them. They were a little taller, a little rangier. Their faces were carved sharp and clean. They had no beards—though Rhian saw the glint of stubble on lean cheeks. How odd, she thought, that they vaunted so of their manhood, yet made themselves look like boys.

They wore a great deal of gold, bright stones, shells and beads. Their coats were heavily embroidered. Their weapons were bone or flint or copper. Only the man who rode first, on a handsome dun stallion, had a bronze hilt gleaming above a richly tooled scabbard.

He must be their captain. He had the look, such as she had seen before on the sea of grass: a headlong arrogance, a glance that raked the strangers and reckoned them beneath him, but he would suffer them, of his charity. He would not meet Rhian's eyes at all. None of them would, in this country.

The riders halted just past the line of Emry's young men. As if at a signal, they sprang down all at once, matched as in a dance. "We are the People of the Wind," the captain said in the traders' argot. His accent was a little surprising: soft, slow, with a hint of a burr. "You are welcome in our lands."

"We are traders from the west," Hoel said. "We bring you the wealth of our people."

The captain's face did not alter. These were not greedy children, Rhian thought, or else they did not like to seem so. She looked for some sign in them of the terrible warfare that the tales told of. None of them wore a necklace of skulls, nor were they stained with the blood of innocents. They seemed ordinary enough young men. There was nothing overtly deadly about them.

"We are pleased to see traders," the captain said. "Our people are camped yonder. They will be glad of your coming."

"We will be glad to come to them," said Hoel. "Will you stop a while, my lords? We have food, drink. Share it with us."

The captain nodded. "Then we will ride to my people."

"And not a moment too soon," someone muttered behind Rhian, but not in traders' speech. The riders did not appear to understand. They settled to eat the last of the bread, and drink wine that Rhian had not known the caravan carried. Traders, Conn had taught her long ago, never brought out all their goods at once.

The riders had smoked meat and the appalling liquid fire that, Rhian had learned many camps ago, was made from mares' milk. Though none of the westerners was hungry, they all ate a little, to be courteous.

She, too, though women did not eat with men here. She remembered that she was supposed to be a goddess. She broke bread and took up a strip of meat, and caught the skin of kumiss as it went round, and suffered a swallow of it. That was more than the men near her could do. It did not persuade the easterners to acknowledge her existence, though she could feel their awareness of her. It must be torture to them to keep their eyes to themselves.

The conversation did not sparkle. The easterners that she had met till now were mighty talkers and tellers of tales, but either these were men of few words, or some constraint silenced them.

Maybe she was that constraint. She amused herself by getting up and wandering about, and marking how they stiffened when she came near.

Why, she thought, they were afraid of her. She could hardly see why, unless some rumor had run ahead of her.

She paused near the captain. He was a lovely young thing, awkward in his length and leanness, but beautiful in his way. His hair was as bright as new copper. His brows were straight and well-drawn and a shade darker. The stubble on his cheeks was more gold than red. His skin was like milk. The sun seemed not to stain it at all.

He had wonderful hands, lean but strong, with long clever fingers. They were a maker's hands, as much as a warrior's: she knew the like of those marks and scars. A man only won those from long work at a forge. It was a pleasure to watch him break bread and drink wine and be ill at ease in her presence.

She sat on her heels in front of him. "What is your name?" she asked him.

For a moment she thought he would go on ignoring her. But it seemed he had no such strength of will. "Minas," he said, as if it had been startled out of him. "My name is Minas."

"Mine is Rhian," she said. "I horrify you. Why? Don't women have speech where you come from?"

His eyes flashed up. Her breath caught. They were as green as summer leaves. She had never seen eyes like that. They transformed his face. It was handsome enough without them. With them, it was beautiful.

"Women have manners where I come from," he said.

"What are those?" she asked him. "To hide in tents and never speak at all?"

"Goddesses know little of men's ways," he said.

"Men of the tribes know nothing of women." She smiled at him, much too sweetly, but maybe he would not know that. "You are in sore need of teaching."

"You will take it on yourself to do that?"

She laughed. "Oh! You do have wit. Who'd have thought it?"

He seemed more startled than offended, which interested her. Some of his fellows were muttering among themselves. He silenced them with a slash of the hand. "You are very bold," he said.

"I'm a woman," she said. She grinned at all their expressions.

One of them could bear it no longer. His command of traders' speech was not as firm as his captain's, but he could make himself understood. "You, woman! You be quiet. He is king's son."

"She," said Minas before she could speak, "is a goddess."

She was not, at all, but it seemed wiser to hold her tongue. He had cowed his people, if not into submission, at least into silence.

This was a very fortunate thing, to have met first with the king's son of the charioteers. Though maybe there was little of chance about it. "Did your father send you?" she asked him.

"No," he said quickly, but not as one who lies. "We were hunting near here. We saw your camp."

Was he blushing? She began to wonder when he had seen it. Surely not this morning. Had he been hunting under the moon, then?

Yes, his fair cheeks had gone scarlet. She bit back a smile. This was beyond fortunate. It was the Goddess' own gift.

She would use it, and well. But for now she simply said, "We would be honored if you would escort us to your people."

"We had intended to do that," he said.

⇢ ⇠

"That was well played," Emry said to her as they rode out of the camp. He spoke the dialect of Lir, which was altogether unlike the traders' speech.

The tribesmen had ridden ahead of them by a little. Rhian supposed the caravan were not to know of the handful who had fallen behind them. Innocents these people might be in matters of men and women, but they were masters of war.

She did not glance at Emry when he spoke, though she was perfectly aware of him. Her eyes were on the prince, who rode not far in front of her. His back was straight, his tail of coppery hair swinging with his horse's stride. He had a lovely way of sitting on a horse.

"He is good to look at, isn't he?"

"Beautiful," Rhian said.

"And," said Emry, "he's their king's son."

"Is that how kings think?" she asked, still watching Minas.

"Kings," he said, "and goddess' servants."

"She sent him to us," Rhian said.

"I can believe it," said Emry.

"I will use him," she said, "as the Goddess bids me." He was silent. She turned to look at him then. His face wore no expression. "Are you judging me?"

"No," he said. "Not at all. I'm only thinking of the day I first saw you, and of what happened after that. The priestess might have done better than she knew, to refuse your choosing."

"She did better than she ever wanted to do," said Rhian. "I was never meant for Lir. I was meant for this."

"It would seem so," said Emry.

21

Traders did not come to the People as often as they might. They were afraid; and well they might be. The People were terrible in war.

But there were things that the People did not make, or that came from so far away that they were both rare and wonderful. For that, traders were welcome, and they were honored like princes.

They rode in through a gathering crowd of children and dogs, men and even a few bold women. As wide as the camp was and as full of people, by the time Minas had brought them to the king's circle, a feast was already in the making.

Even the king had come out to see what came with such delighted tumult. Minas glimpsed his keepers in the shadow of the tentflap, dark shapes with glinting eyes. He was freer of their spells than he had been in a long while: his face was bare to the sun, and though his skin was pale and his eyes blinked as if blinded, he did not hide himself away.

He greeted the caravan-master with courtesy befitting a king. The guards and the lesser caravaneers he welcomed. The woman—his eyes slid past her as if she had not been there.

They were all doing that, but when her back was turned, they stared and muttered among themselves. She stood just behind the caravan-master, next to the captain of guards. She seemed to be taking great pleasure in the sight of this camp, these people, and certainly their tall and terrible king.

Rather fortunately for everyone's peace, she did not address the king as she had addressed Minas. She held her tongue and let the men speak. Her eyes were outrageously bold, dancing over the gathered faces, scanning the tents, narrowing a little as she caught sight of the shadowed women.

Just when Minas could not have borne it any longer, one of those women slipped out of concealment. His mother's eyes crossed his briefly, seeing everything she needed to see. Then she had turned away from him, touching the stranger's arm, murmuring in her ear. The stranger's smile was swift and dazzling. She let Aera lead her away, offering neither objection nor sign of apprehension.

She was safe now. Minas turned his mind from her with an effort that wrenched in his belly. The king was done with his words of welcome. He laid his arm about the caravan-master's shoulders and led him to the feasting-ground, where captives and veiled women of the People had spread the beginnings of a royal banquet. There were finely tanned skins to lie on, heaps of cushions to lean against, and a servant for each man, to keep his cup filled and to choose the best portions for him.

Minas made sure that he sat beside the captain of the guards. The captain's men were light-hearted creatures, like Minas' companions. The captain was a graver soul. He ate in silence, offering no conversation.

Minas let the silence stretch through the platters of bread and the wheels of cheese and the heaped bowls of fresh curds. When the roasted meats began, from the tiny mouthfuls of lark and quail to the slab of roast ox, Minas said as if casually, "It was maybe not wise to bring a woman here."

The captain's brows rose. "Is she in danger?"

"Not," said Minas, "from my mother."

"Then she's safe," the captain said.

"For a while," Minas said.

"You are kind to be troubled for her." He managed, somehow, not to sound stiff. Was that a hint of mockery in his glance?

"She is beautiful, your sister," Minas said. "She is headstrong, yes? How well can she learn the manners that a woman needs here?"

"My—" The captain shook his head as if to thrust that thought aside. "She does as she pleases."

"And you have no power over her."

"No man does."

"Does a woman?"

The captain's lips twitched beneath the black beard. "How strong is your mother?"

"Very strong," said Minas.

The captain's grin broke free. He looked strikingly like his sister then. "I should like to have seen their meeting," he said.

Minas reflected on Aera face to face with a goddess from beyond the river. It was a rather marvelous vision, and rather alarming.

As he paused to contemplate that, one of his father's servants set before them a choice portion of the ox, steaming-fragrant and dripping with juices. Minas half-bowed to the other. The captain drew his belt-knife to cut off his share.

Minas' teeth clicked together. That knife was bronze. So was every knife in the hand of every one of these foreigners, to the last donkey-driver. They were all armed with bronze.

Beyond the river, he thought as if in a dream. Bronze came from beyond the river. The gods made it—or men as wise as gods.

If they would trade—if that were possible—

There would be no trading today. These things had their rites and proprieties. Today the traders were honored guests. Tomorrow they would bring out their wares. And Minas would learn what was to be learned, of the metal that was so strong in its magic.

⤙ ⤚

Rhian had not thought to vanish among the women of this tribe. But while she stood with the men, hearing the king's greeting, a light hand touched her. She looked up a little, into eyes as green as the prince's, but much, much wiser.

These were not eyes to be deceived by simple sleights or veils of pretense. This woman saw clear and she saw deep.

Not so clear and not so deep, Rhian prayed, as to understand why

Rhian had come here. Certainly she betrayed no anger, nor did she call the warriors of the tribe to seize and destroy the invader. She led Rhian into a dim and musty world.

Sometimes in a bitter winter Dura's house had grown as rank as a fox's den. This was a rankness to match the rankest of it: smoke and sweat and ill-washed skin, wool, leather, horses and cattle and the stench of goats.

The tent was very large, and divided into chambers by curtains of leather. Lamps lit it. Some of them were splendid, made of gold or silver, and others were plain clay. The light they shed was a pale golden twilight full of shadows and whispers.

There were no men here, and no menchildren old enough to ride or carry a weapon. This was a world of women and infants. All the men were out in the sun.

Rhian stopped some little way into the tent. Her feet would not carry her onward.

Her guide went on a step or two, then half-turned. "Come," she said.

It took all of Rhian's strength to go on. There was a horror in her, her dream come alive: the cage, the bars, the bird of flame bound within them.

She could turn on her heel and walk away. But she was well raised; she had learned courtesy. And she was stubborn. She had begun this. She would end it.

They must be passing the entire length of the tent, to take so long to come to the end of it. When she began to think that this was a dream indeed, and she was trapped in it forever, they came to a wall, and that wall opened on blessed light.

This was a court of tents, so well hidden that she would never have imagined that it was there. Walls of leather enclosed it. Its roof was the sky.

There were women here, veils laid aside, weaving baskets of the strong steppe grasses, or chattering among themselves. Children played in the sun.

Rhian's guide put aside her veils. She bore a remarkable resemblance to the prince, though her hair was darker. The face, the eyes were the same, the slender height and the breathless grace.

She regarded Rhian steadily, studying her with care. At length she said, "I am Aera. My son brought you here."

"He looks like you," said Rhian.

"People do say so."

Aera gestured toward a heap of hides laid on the ground. The women who had been seated on them had moved on to tend some of the children. It seemed a matter of chance, but Rhian was on edge here; she trusted nothing. As welcome as the light was, and the sky, she was still trapped, still surrounded by strangers, enemies of her people.

This woman, this mother of a prince, seemed amiable. When they had both sat on the hides, younger women brought food and drink. The food was fresh-baked bread and stewed roots and roast meat. The drink was not kumiss as she had expected, but watered wine. The platter and the cups were of beaten gold, extravagant in their richness.

Rhian would have welcomed more herbs in the stew and less grit in the bread, but it was a good enough meal, and plentiful. She was hungry. She ate well and drank lightly, and belched after, with the courtesy of the tribes.

Aera, who had eaten more slowly and with less appetite, nodded approval. She sat erect, with her feet tucked up and her hands resting on her knees. She carried herself beautifully, as if she had been the Mother of a city.

"You are the king's wife, yes?" Rhian said. "Is your son his heir?"

Aera inclined her head.

"Then I'm being paid great honor," said Rhian, bowing where she sat.

"I am certain you are worthy of it."

Rhian shrugged slightly. "I'm no king's wife, nor his mother, either."

"A god ranks higher than a king."

"You think I'm a god's wife?" Rhian bit back laughter. That would have been a very ill thing to do here, in this woman's domain, surrounded by women who, Rhian had been aware for some little while, were watching her subtly but intently. There were women playing with children in front of the flap into the king's tent, and others weaving baskets or sewing garments or nursing babies in a circle about her. She was perfectly closed in.

"I think," said Aera, "that you belong to the Powers."

"Because I ride like a man? Because I came trading with my kin?"

Aera smiled. "Many say my father is a god. He insists that he is not. But he is not as other men are."

"The women of my people are all much like me," Rhian said.

"Indeed?" said Aera. "Tell me of your people."

Rhian sipped wine from the golden cup, taking her time, ordering her words. The king's wife waited patiently. "I come," Rhian said after a while, "from the west. Our country is across the river. Our people—"

"Across the river?"

That was a new voice, one that had not spoken in that place before, nor had Rhian noticed her among the women. She stood beyond the circle, with two or three others behind her. She must have been lovely once: her bones were handsome and her dark eyes large. But time had not been kind to her. Her face was worn, her hair ashen. She spoke the traders' tongue in a different accent, harsher, deeper in the throat.

She must be very high in rank indeed: her gown was embroidered from throat to hem, and her ornaments were gold. Rhian had not noticed till then that Aera wore no ornaments. Her grace was regal enough, without need of gold to brighten it.

Aera sat as still as ever, but she had tensed. "Etena," she said coolly. "You honor us with your presence."

Etena smiled without warmth. "It seems we are honored indeed. So, is it true? We have a goddess among us?"

When Minas had said much the same, it had been an honest question, with an honest heart behind it. Rhian met those eyes, which should have been so familiar, dark eyes set in a broad-cheeked face, and saw nothing that spoke to her spirit.

"I am a goddess' servant," Rhian said, soft and civil.

"There are no mortal folk beyond the river," Etena said, "or so the wise have taught us. The river flows with the souls of the dead. The gods live on the other side."

"There well may be a river of souls," Rhian said, "but our river is water and fish and a god or two. My people are mortal certainly. We are born, we live and die as mortals do."

"How can that be so?" Etena asked. "Can the wise be in error?"

"The wise speak in riddles," Aera said. "Those are men who ride with her, beyond a doubt, with a western look to them, and a western sound to their speech."

"And they crossed the river to come here." Etena's eyes had narrowed. She stepped into the circle of women, drawing close to Rhian, searching her face.

Rhian bore the scrutiny with all the calm that she could muster. She must not betray weakness. She must be like a stone, standing fast against wind and current.

"Yes," said Etena as if to herself, but unless she spoke the traders' tongue by force of habit, she must mean Rhian to understand her. "I have not seen this race before. You are traders, you say?"

"And children of traders," Rhian said. "We travel the world about. Would you be pleased to be shown the finest of our wares, come morning? We have ornaments of pure gold, cloth as fine as a spider's web, jewels of the earth—"

"You will bring them to me," said Etena, "come morning."

Rhian bent her head. Greed, Conn had taught her long ago, was a frequent weakness of the powerful. Rulers of tribes and cities coveted the rare and the beautiful. Traders lived by that. It could, if they were wise, make them rich.

She wondered what Aera coveted. It did not seem to be gold. Knowledge, maybe. If that was so, she was more dangerous than Etena. Etena could be distracted from learning the truth of the caravan's presence here. Aera might not be so easy to deceive.

Rhian rose. "I thank you for your hospitality," she said. "We will bring our wares in the morning, for you to choose."

"*You* will bring them," Etena said. "No man may look on the faces of the king's wives."

"Even a man or two to fetch and carry?" asked Rhian. "Our men are properly tamed. They'll keep their eyes to themselves."

Etena sniffed. But she said, "That may be permitted."

Rhian glanced at Aera. That lady's face was perfectly blank. "Until the morning," Rhian said to them both.

22

Emry feasted as lightly as he could, that night. That was still heavier than he would have liked. He was an honored guest, though not as honored as he might have been if these people had known his true rank. He was given a royal share of the meat, and his cup was never suffered to be empty.

When at last he could politely excuse himself, the stars touched on midnight. Men of the tribe were still dancing and singing, though wine and kumiss had flattened a fair number of them. The traders were still upright. So, he was pleased to see, were most of his men. He caught an eye here, an eye there. They began to rise one by one, not too obviously, he hoped.

Their tents were pitched, their camp made a little apart from the main camp of the tribe. The horses and donkeys grazed in a herd nearby. Mabon and Bran the smith stood guard over the packs and boxes of the caravan's wares. They were awake and alert; Emry caught a flash of bronze before he came into the light of their fire.

Mabon eased first, recognizing his prince. Bran kept his sword drawn till he saw that Emry was alone. Then he lowered the blade. "Trouble?" Emry asked him.

Bran shrugged, a roll of his heavy shoulders. "A foray or two on the baggage. Nothing we haven't faced before."

"And?" Emry asked, fixing him with a level stare.

He shifted his feet, seemed to remember he still had his sword in his hand, thrust it into its scabbard. "We found the chariots, my lord," he said.

"Ah," said Emry.

"They're kept under guard," Bran said, "in a camp of their own. The men who live in that camp—they're makers, my lord. They build chariots."

"Who was guarding the baggage while you were discovering this?"

"I was, my lord," Mabon said, as Bran drew in on himself.

"When you stand guard," Emry said to this man of the villages, "you stand guard. When you are set free of that, then you go wherever you choose."

Bran was knotted tight. Emry held his breath. An instant before he would have spoken again, the smith flung up his head. "Yes, my lord. I'll not do it again, my lord. But that is what I came for—to see chariots. To see how they are made."

"In the morning," said Emry, "you will go and see, by my orders. For tonight, you are a guard, and a guard you will be until I send a man to take your place."

"Yes, my lord," Bran said. From the sound of it, his teeth were clenched.

That was not an ill thing. The man needed strength of will, just as he needed discipline. "You'll never make a soldier, smith," Emry said, "nor should you. But while you play the caravan guard, you stand under my orders. Remember that. We are not in the Goddess' country now. We are among people who make cups of their enemies' skulls, and dash those enemies' menchildren against the rocks. They may smile at us, lay feasts before us, but if they discover why we came, they'll slaughter us without mercy."

"Yes, my lord," said Bran.

Emry nodded briskly. "To your post, sir."

The man went as he should have done, not happily, but with a firm step. Emry let go his breath slowly.

Mabon caught his eye. "It was my fault, my lord. When he said he wanted to go, I didn't stop him."

"You'll stand double shift with him, for that," said Emry. "There can be no slackening here. Our lives depend on it."

"I know that, my lord," Mabon said. "We all know it."

"We must *be* it," said Emry. "We've lived soft, we princes. We think we can fight, because we practice with weapons, and hunt, and once in a very great while meet a raiding-party off the steppe. There hasn't been a war in our country in living memory. The great wars were all so long ago that all the strongholds we built then have fallen into ruin. None of us knows, truly knows, what war is. These people were born fighting. Their year is rounded in war. Either they're preparing for it, or riding to it, or fighting it, or celebrating the victory. They've never known what peace is."

"My lord," said Mabon, "that's a splendid speech. Will you be giving it to the others, too?"

He was not mocking his prince, but his brow was lifted and he had a quirk to his mouth. Emry growled wordlessly at him and stalked off to his tent.

Once inside, in the light of the little lamp that was shaped like a Mother's body, round and full, Emry stripped off his finery and dropped groaning onto his blankets. Haranguing poor Mabon, lashing the smith with his tongue—he was sore in need of discipline himself.

He watched completely without surprise as one of the shadows took the shape of a goddess' servant. "I suppose," Rhian said, "you thought the tents had raised themselves."

"I thought the tribesmen did it," Emry said.

"Bran and Mabon and I did it," she said. "I stood guard for Bran when he went, he said, to look after the horses—but he went farther than that. You were harsher on him than he deserved."

That was exactly Emry's thought, but he was in no mood to admit it. "What did you do to him for running off? Were you kind to him, either?"

"I never said a word to him," she said.

"Then you were more cruel than I was," Emry said.

"I don't think," she said, "that it's your place to judge me."

"No, it's not," he said. "Have you done chastising me? May I sleep now?"

"Don't you want to hear what I did among the women?"

He glowered at her. "What did you do among the women?"

Her eyes were wicked. "I ate. I drank middling bad wine. I talked to the king's wives. One of them is very dangerous. The other is both dangerous and wise."

He set his lips together and waited her out. She wanted him to beg for every word.

After a while he thought she would win the contest: she would leave without having spoken. But she was not so strong of will. She said, "The prince who brought us here—he's the king's heir. His mother made me her guest. I think that matters, somehow. There is another wife, who seems very strong; I'd say she rules there, except that the prince's mother has power she can't touch. She commanded me to bring the best of our wares to her in the morning, as if she has a right to choose first. She'll let me bring a man or two to carry them."

"Factions," he said. "If the heir and his mother are one faction, and this covetous one is another—did you see the king? The man is ill. How long do you wager he'll live?"

"Quite long, if he's not meddled with," she said. "He's as strong as a bull in body. But his spirit is a pale and feeble thing."

"This is not a feeble tribe," Emry said, "as much as we might wish that it were. Its king may be a mask for the true ruler, but she does indeed rule."

"The greedy one," Rhian said. "I'd wager gold on it, if I had any. The other . . . she wouldn't grasp after power. She's beyond that. The greedy one is like a priestess. I think the other may be closer to a Mother."

Emry shivered slightly. A Mother's power went far beyond the ruling of cities. The king ruled men, but the Mother embodied the Goddess. If there was a Mother here, their purpose might be defeated before it began.

He could not let himself think such things. They must do what they had come to do. They could not fail.

"I'll be your porter," he said. "We need a trader with us. Hoel—"

"Conn," she said.

His teeth clicked together.

"Conn lived in this country. He's a trader from his childhood. He'll know how to talk to this wife of a king. And you," she said, "will say nothing at all. Can you do that?"

He could hardly call her insolent: she was the mare's servant. But he could not keep himself from saying, "You don't trust me."

"I trust you as far as a young man can be trusted," she said. "But do remember that in the tribes, young men are never, ever trusted with other men's wives. If you want to ride out of here with your parts intact, you will be the mute servant, and not the prince of Lir."

The parts in question shriveled alarmingly. How she could have seen, he did not know; he was well covered. She laughed at him, tugged at his plait and said, "I see you understand. In the morning, then. Tell Conn. Come sunrise, see that we're ready to trade with a queen."

She went, he supposed, to her blissful rest, now she had burdened him with tasks enough to keep him up till morning. That was her revenge for what he had done to Bran. He snarled, he kicked the pallet that he would see no more of this night, but he did her bidding. He was an obedient servant.

23

Minas woke with a start. For a long moment he could not remember where he was. Not the young men's tent, no—not the old shabby one, nor the splendid new one that they had taken from a prince of the conquered tribes. There were stars overhead. There was grass under him. Not far away, something large stirred, snorting softly.

He was lying in the grass near the horses. The stars were bitter-bright, but the eastern sky had begun to lighten. The air smelled of morning.

Hooves paused near him. They belonged to a mare of unusual color, dappled like the moon. He remembered the mare well. The goddess from across the river had ridden her. She was a goddess herself, he had been given to understand.

She grazed quietly in the starlight, almost within reach of his hand. Her pale coat glimmered. Her long mane ran like water. She was smaller, more sturdily built than the horses of the People, but she was beautiful in her way—just as her rider was.

She looked as if she had been there since the gods made the world: stretched out along the broad back, arms about the strong arched neck, legs dangling easily down.

She seemed asleep, till she raised her head. Her thick plait slid over her shoulder. Her skin was whiter than the mare's coat, her hair blacker than the lightening sky.

She was bare from crown to toe, not even a cloth about her loins. He had seen women naked. Of course he had. But never like this. She slid from the mare's back and bent over him. Her breasts swayed. The nipples were dark and large.

She smiled. He never knew what she did, but he had been properly and modestly dressed in tunic and leggings, and he was no longer. The night air was cool on his burning skin.

She knelt astride him. He gasped. He was near blind with wanting her. But when he thrust upward, her fingers closed about his rod, holding the whole of him fast.

Her smile widened. "I rule here," she said. "Remember that."

Even if he could have shaped the thought to argue with her, the words would have escaped him altogether. He could only think of her—of her skin, soft as sleep, and her scent, both pungent and sweet.

She brushed his lips with a kiss. It felt like a flicker of flame. She traced the line of his chin, his jaw, his neck and breast, down along his belly to the rampant thing that seemed no part of him at all. Till she circled it in kisses, and lowered herself on it. Then it was all of him there was.

He was ready to burst with the urgency of it, but she held him by some power beyond magic, till he knew that he would die if she did not let him go. She did it all at once, with a rush so fierce, and a convulsion so strong, that it sent him spinning down into the dark.

When he could see again, his whole body quivered in spasms. He gasped for breath. She was sitting astride him still, a solid weight across his middle.

He could see her clearly in the grey light of dawn. Her whole body was suffused with a delicate flush. Her cheeks and breasts were rose-pale, like the sky over her. She smiled down at him, long and lazy and sated.

How she could rise after that, still less mount the mare and ride away, he never knew. He followed the sway of her ample hips above that ample rump until they vanished over the rise of the ground. His spirit yearned to stay with her, but his flesh was like unmolded clay. It lay inert in the grass, while the morning brightened about him, and the last of the stars faded into light.

The morning song came soaring out of him by no will of his at all. It was a creature of its own, a power that for that moment possessed him. He was empty of thought. His whole being was that long pure sound.

� ⇐

Aera heard it from the king's tent. There was nothing human or even earthly in it. It sounded like the sun's own voice, bathing the earth and flooding the sky.

It drew her out of the tent into the swelling light. No one else seemed to have heard it. The captives were up as they would have been since long before dawn, tending fires and drawing water and waiting on those of the People who were up and about after the night's debauch. None of them paused or looked up to see what might have made that astonishing sound.

It faded slowly, till there was nothing to be heard but the morning clamor of the camp. Aera's bones thrummed as if the song had settled there.

She turned slowly. She felt as she had when she carried Minas in her body: brimming full, gravid with light.

As she paused to test the limits of this strange new sensation, her eye caught a stir toward the camp's edge. People were coming: the woman of the traders, who had faced Etena yesterday and lived to tell of it, and two men behind her, big black-bearded men as all of them were. One carried a heavy pack. The other was dressed like a tribesman in embroidered leather, with beads and feathers woven into his greying hair.

They walked toward the king's tent. Children and camp dogs followed. Some of the bolder boys were making a game of darting toward the man with the pack, slapping his pack, then leaping away again. He trudged under the weight of it, seeming dull as any captive, but Aera caught the flash of his glance.

This was no slave, whatever else he was. The children and dogs had to stop short of the king's tent, but Aera could pass within. They entered by the main way, where one of Etena's women was waiting for them. Aera chose another, less obvious entrance. She knew where they would go. Etena had let it be known that the courtyard was hers that morning, and no one was to trespass in it.

She had said nothing of spying from the tent's wall. Aera had found several clever slits, so made that they seemed but seams in the felt, from which one could see and hear everything either within or without, but never be seen oneself.

The traders were led direct to the court, but Etena lingered within. She would keep them waiting till they were prowling like wolves in a cage. That was her way. She spent the time in ordering matters about the king's tent, chastising one of his wives with a willow switch, and seeing to it that the king's mind was well enslaved—he would not rouse again as he had the day before, Aera suspected, if Etena had any say in it.

Aera settled for a long watch. The traders arranged their wares to advantage under a canopy that the porter made of the flesh and bones of his pack. Clever, that. Aera would study it later if she could. Her father would be interested to know of it.

Once the canopy was up and the wares spread, the traders settled decorously to wait. The older man sat cross-legged like a tribesman. The younger one took a guard's post, standing alert but at ease. That was a truer face of him, Aera thought, than the other had been. He was a fighting man. Caravan guard, she supposed, and a wise enough choice in a strange camp.

The woman sat on her heels behind the array of gauds and small treasures. Her chin was up, her shoulders straight. Her hands rested on her thighs. She looked like a carven image. Her gown was very fine, woven of cloth like a sunset: deep blue and twilight purple and swelling shades of rose and gold. She wore a necklace of shells, and in her ears swung bells of bronze.

She was beautiful, Aera observed. Very much so. In motion she was almost too quick to catch, but now that she was stilled, she was breathtaking.

Aera considered a number of things. It need not matter to her what became of a pack of foreigners. But these . . . they came from beyond the river. They carried bronze, even wore it as an ornament, as if it had been a common thing. Their caravan guards and servants were remarkably well fed and well dressed.

Etena was still busy within. The drone of the witch-women's chanting rose and fell. That would go on for long enough.

Aera slipped from her hiding place along the wall of the tent, toward the flap through which the traders had been led. She came out with dignity, proper in her veils. The men, she noticed, glanced at the woman, but Rhian shook her head just visibly. The older man eased a little. The younger one, as befit a guard, did not.

Aera knelt on one knee in front of their wares. She did not touch them, but her eyes noted them. "These are very fine," she said. "But if you would sell them to the one for whom you intend them, you would let that one do it." She tilted her head toward the guard.

Rhian's brow rose. "Will he be safe if he sits where I am sitting?"

"As safe as a male can be in this place," Aera said.

"Which is not very." Rhian shook her head. "Thank you, but I prefer him as he is."

"My sister wife," Aera said, "has a distaste for feminine beauty that is not her own. Male beauty, she likes very well indeed."

"Well enough to destroy it lest anyone else possess it?"

The child had a clear eye, Aera thought. "She's not one to geld the colts if they can serve her entire."

Rhian drew breath to speak, but the young guard spoke before her. "I'll take the risk," he said.

"You are wise," said Aera. "Keep silent and let your elder speak, and smile if you can."

He smiled at that, so sweet that even her jaded heart began to flutter. He was fully as beautiful as Rhian, though the curly beard hid a good part of it. "My mother brought me up properly, lady," he said. "Conn will speak and I will smile, and Rhian will do what is best for her to do."

Rhian suffered that—not happily, but Aera had not taken her for a fool. It was more remarkable that the men understood than that she did.

They shifted as Aera had indicated: young guard in Rhian's place, Rhian where he had been—visible but not obvious, nor taunting Etena with the beauty of her face.

Aera nodded. "You'll do," she said.

⇨ ⇦

When at last Etena came, the sun was nearer the zenith than the horizon. Emry's backside ached with sitting, but he had known better than to get up and pace. This was a test, and they must pass it.

The king's wife swept in as regally as any Mother, trailed by a retinue of women. She dripped with gold: golden chains, golden rings, golden collar. Disks of gold were sewn on her veil, so that in place of a face, he saw nothing but a shimmer. He had to struggle to see her eyes.

Dark eyes, and cold. Rhian had warned him. He still had not expected the depth of that chill. This woman loved no living thing. She loved power—that was her heart and soul.

She reminded him rather too vividly of the priestess who had traveled with him from Lir. The thought did its best to quench his smile, but his training held. He lowered his eyes as a proper young man should do, and let Conn speak the greeting for all of them.

The chill at that was perceptible. "You, woman from beyond the river," Etena said. "Why do you say nothing?"

"In my country," Rhian said in tones of perfect politeness, "men are taught to serve. These men serve me. I give them leave to speak for me."

The dark eyes had begun to glitter. "Men serve you? Men serve a woman?"

"Beyond the river," said Rhian, "women rule. Men submit to their will."

"You cannot be telling the truth," Etena said.

"I can indeed," said Rhian. She prodded Emry with her toe. "You, trader. Choose a gift for the king's wife."

Emry bent his head in what he hoped was adequate submission. He considered the baubles in front of him. Some were very fine. Some were gaudy. He might have liked to see that necklace of golden flowers about— not Rhian's neck, no. She was too bold a beauty. But the other of the king's wives, she of the green eyes and the elegant bearing, would have looked most well in so delicate an ornament.

Etena leaned in close, calling him back to himself. Her breath came light and quick. She lusted after gold as another woman would lust after a man.

He smiled at her and spread his hands over the bright array. "Choose, my lady. Choose freely. Whatever you wish, it is yours."

Etena's eyes were gleaming. "Indeed," she said to Rhian, "your men are submissive. How refreshing." She passed her hand over the scattering of baubles. Her fingers twitched. He thought she might seize them all, but she had more restraint than that.

She took a long time to choose. She liked gaudy, and the gaudier the better. The heavier, the more massive it was, the more pleased she was to fondle it.

When at last she chose, it was the bauble he had expected: a massive collar made of plates of beaten gold, each plate inlaid with sheets of colored stones, green and blue and red. There was no fineness in it, nor any elegance. But it was a great deal of gold.

Her glance bade him lift it. She bent her head in its concealing veils, so that he could lay it about her neck. Her shoulders bowed with the weight of it, but straightened soon enough. She stood tall in her black robes, with that massive golden thing seeming all the gaudier against them.

"I will take this," she said, "as the king's tribute. The rest you may trade as you may."

They had been dismissed. Emry for one was glad to go. He gathered together their wares, playing the servant to the last. But as he moved to fold away the flower necklace, some spirit moved him to take it up instead, and go to the place along the wall where he sensed green eyes on him, and offer it with the flourish that he had not seen fit to give Etena.

He did not think Aera was often startled. She hid it quickly; but there was that moment, that glimpse beneath the veils of her dignity.

Other veil she had none. Her head was bare, her hair glinting with red-golden lights. Her face was lovely, even more so than he had imagined. He would never touch her cheek, he would not be so bold, but he could not keep his eyes from caressing it.

He raised the necklet between them. "This belongs to you," he said.

He saw how she loved the shape and the delicacy of it, but her brows drew together. "I require no gifts," she said, "nor tribute either."

"A gift can be freely given," he said.

"A simple man of the caravan can give away gold?"

"I have my share in the venture," he said. He moved quickly, before she could elude him, to slip the necklet over her head. It settled about her neck and over the sweet swell of her breast. It was as exquisite on her as he had thought it would be.

"I can't take this," she said. But her hand that rose to it made no move to strip it off. She stroked the petals of a golden blossom.

"Beauty deserves beauty," he said. He bowed as if she had been a lady of Lir, and left her to her gift and her wide-eyed silence.

24

Aera watched him walk away. He was as circumspect with his eyes as a woman—and like a woman, he knew well how to use them. But there was nothing female in the breadth of those shoulders or the fluid power of that walk. He trod like a panther, light and easy and subtly dangerous.

If that was a simple caravan guard, then the princes of his people must be lofty indeed.

She took off the necklace. Its linked blossoms were cool in her fingers. They were as delicate as if they had grown in the earth, but they were all made of gold.

This was a far more valuable thing than Etena's garish collar. What had he hoped to gain with it? Her goodwill, she supposed, but he could have had that at rather less cost to his share in the caravan.

What else a man might hope to gain with gold . . .

She had a son hardly younger than he was. She belonged to a king. He had no right whatever to cast his eyes on her, let alone to give her gifts.

She would see that the necklace was returned to the caravan. Later. When there was time. She slipped it into a deep fold of her gown. Its weight rested between her breasts, not far from her heart.

⇨ ⇦

The traders opened their camp to trade not long after the sun rose. By midmorning, half the men of the People must have come to see the treasures from the east.

Minas, still dazed by his dream of the dawn, wandered past without great interest in gold or weavings. Bronze he did not see. Nor did he see her—the goddess who had made his dream so very sweet. There were only men in the traders' camp.

He sought out his grandfather's place, and his work on the chariots. Metos had begun a new battle-car, larger than any before, in which two archers could bend their bows while a third man drove the horses. It needed either lighter wood or stronger horses; as he had made it, it was too heavy for two horses to pull above a struggling trot.

"Three horses," Minas said, "or four."

"How would you hitch them?" Metos inquired.

"Three abreast," Minas said. "Or . . ."

He tugged at his chin, frowning at the trainers in the field beyond his grandfather's camp. They were gentling the young ones at this hour, the stallions of three summers who had been broken to the traces the year before and then turned free to run and grow, but who were now asked to be warriors for the People.

"Suppose," said Minas, "that there were a way to hitch a third horse in front of the two. Or if three, why not four? Two and two, maybe."

"That would demand a great deal of the trainers," Metos said, but not as if it troubled him.

"First we need a hitch that works."

"Then find one," said Metos.

Minas' lips stretched in a grin. There was little mirth in it, but his heart was oddly light. How better to forget his dreams of a woman than to lose himself in his grandfather's dreams of chariots?

"If we had bronze," he said, "for fittings and bindings, those would be stronger. You could make your chariot larger."

"They have bronze in the west," Metos said.

"So they do," said Minas.

"Are there not traders from the west here among the People? Would they not know of bronze?"

"Surely," Minas said, "that would be a great secret among their priests and shamans. Bronze has too much power to be a common thing, or easily known."

"Ask them," Metos said.

Minas gaped at him. He had wandered off already, intent on the turning of the shafts for his great war-car. Minas heard him curse the wood he had to work with—it was poor stuff, little better than leavings.

Yet another reason to press the advance into the west, if truly there were forests such as the tales told of.

Minas wavered. He could—perhaps should—engross himself in the matter of hitches and traces. But there was the bronze. And there was the woman, the goddess who rode the moon-pale mare.

The gods favored him. Hardly had he thought of her before he saw her. She was standing outside the ring of Metos' tents, watching the chariot-drills with utter fascination. He barely noticed the shadow behind her: another of her big bearded men, this one even bigger and more heavily pelted than most.

She was wearing a gown of woven blue and green that did pleasant things to the curves of her body. She had bells in her ears, and they were not gold; they were bronze.

He took this gift the gods had given, though his heart beat so hard he was near to fainting. She even spared him the necessity of finding words to greet her. She greeted him with the white flash of a smile. "My lord! Those are the young horses, yes? They're being taught to run in pairs?"

"Some of them are," Minas said.

"They're all stallions. Don't they fight?"

"They learn not to," said Minas.

"I should like," she said, "to learn how that is done."

"Patience, mostly," he said, "and wise choice of the pairs."

"And driving them? Is that so easy, too?"

The thought of a woman driving a chariot was so novel and so shocking that Minas could only stare at her, speechless.

"I should like to see a chariot," she said, "and touch one. There are so many rumors, you see. So many stories. But the reality of them—why, they're but wood, carved and painted, and bits of leather."

"A bargain, trader woman," he said. "If I show you chariots, will you tell me of bronze?"

Her eyes flickered. For an instant she caught her guardsman's glance. His eyes, Minas realized, were much keener than the heavy face might have led one to expect.

"You don't know bronze?" she asked. She seemed a little surprised.

"It is new to us," Minas said. "But not to you, it seems."

"We've known it since our great-grandmothers' time," she said.

He drew a breath to steady himself. "That is a wonder," he said. "And the bronze itself . . . heaven's own power is in it."

"It is strong metal," she said. "Stronger than copper."

"I will show you the chariots," said Minas again, "if you will tell me what bronze is."

She yearned toward the chariots as he yearned toward the bronze. And what, some distant part of him wondered, did she want with the battle-cars of the People?

What indeed? Yet what harm could it do? She was a woman, however beautiful, however powerful. To build the chariots, to fashion the traces, to train the horses to draw them, had taken long years of Metos' life and the lives of the men who followed him.

She was speaking to her companion again in glances. He was not as eager as she was, nor, Minas suspected, as trusting, either. But she prevailed: the tilt of her chin proclaimed that. "I will tell you what I know," she said, "if you will teach me of chariots."

"Done," he said quickly, before she could regret the bargain.

Not that she seemed to do any such thing. She seemed delighted. She followed eagerly, her guardian hound less so, as he went back into the circle of Metos' tents.

Metos was still cursing the wood he had chosen for his chariot-pole. It was the best he had, but it was neither long enough nor strong enough for what he had in mind.

He did not acknowledge Minas' guests at all. The rest of the chariot-makers regarded them in varying degrees of curiosity, and some with more than that, for Rhian was very beautiful; but none was so bold as to question her presence in Minas' company.

She turned in the circle, eyes as wide as they would go. In her face was the pure delight of a child. "Oh," she said. "Oh, this is marvelous! Tell me what this is. Tell me all of it."

"First tell me of bronze," he said.

Some of the light left her face. "Bronze is mingled metal," she said. "Copper and arsenic, or copper and tin."

"Arsenic? Tin?"

"Grey metal," she said. "Red and grey makes the false gold."

Tin, he thought. Arsenic. He knew nothing of any such metals. Maybe Metos did. If not . . .

If not, he knew where they must go, all the People. Westward. Of course. Westward until they all found what they looked for.

Her voice broke in on him, clear and imperious. "Show me chariots! Show me how they are made."

He kept his bargain. He showed her step by painstaking step. At first he thought she might grow bored, but that did not seem possible. Her mind was quick. Her questions were not as numerous as he might have expected, but they were to the point.

"You are a maker," he said after a while, as they watched hunchbacked Patron bend and shape willow-withies into the body of a car. "You know the works of hands."

"I know a little," she said. "I was raised a potter's child."

It was more than that. But if she did not wish to tell him, he would not force her. He watched her instead, saw how she watched Patron. She knew what to look for: she studied the swift movements of those hands. She never shrank from his deformity. He should have gone to the shamans, but Metos had taken him while he was still a small child, nurtured him and cherished him and taught him greater magic than most shamans could know.

This woman from the sunset country leaned close to him, as easy as if he had been her kin. At first he shrank from her, but when she made no other move, he let his work absorb him again.

"Did you make pots at home?" Minas asked her.

She did not glance at him, but her response was clear enough. "I made pots. Toys, too, for children. A bauble or two. Small things, nothing of consequence. Nothing as great as this."

"And your father allowed it?"

"My father . . ." Her lips had drawn thin. "For all I knew, my father was dead. My aunt was my teacher, and she needed me at the kiln."

"No father," he said. "That is a sad thing."

"No mother is sadder," she said.

"For a woman," he conceded, "I suppose it is."

"Even men need mothers," said Rhian.

Patron did something that she did not quite see. She leaned in even closer, so that her breast brushed the maker's arm. Patron seemed too intent to notice. Minas thrust back a surge of pure mindless rage. How dared she touch any man so?

Any man but himself.

He had only dreamed of her. She need never know of it. If she did, he thought she might laugh. She was not the kind of woman to be in awe of any man's rank or wealth.

She left Patron soon enough, to watch someone else fashion a wheel—which fascinated her for an endless time—and yet another man forge fittings for the chariot and its harness.

Her guardian hound paused there when she went on. The copper was good; one of the conquered tribes had been rich in it. But it was not bronze. It had begun to seem a poor thing, weak and soft.

The man from the west watched the forging in silence. He offered neither criticism nor commentary. He offered no threat, either, that Minas could sense. Warily but without great fear, Minas followed Rhian, who had come round at last to Metos himself. She squatted beside him and said, "If you bind several shorter lengths together with metal, it will be stronger than the single pole."

"But also more likely to break if there is a weak link," Metos said, with no evidence of surprise that she, a foreigner and a woman, should speak so wisely.

"All things can break," she said. "Copper is stronger than wood. Wood bound with copper should be stronger than wood alone."

"And bronze is stronger than copper," said Metos.

"So it is," she said.

"Can you forge it?"

"I've never done it," she said.

Metos grunted. He called the smith who was nearest. "We'll brace this with bands of copper," he said. "As strong but as light as you can make it. If you can lengthen it, too—two horselengths in all, and a little over . . ."

Rhian wandered off again, this time toward the chariots that were finished. There were a handful of them, waiting to be tested, then to be given to warriors who had earned them. She paused not by the first or even the second, but by one that was plainer than the others but more finely made. Metos had wrought it for lightness and speed. It was an elegant thing, as clean in its lines as a bird in flight.

She ran her hands over it, murmuring in delight. She lifted the pole, testing the weight and balance. She stroked the wheels. They were spoked—Metos' great genius, to make them light but strong. She wondered at them, peering to see how they were made.

It was a pleasure to watch her, to see how swift an intelligence she had. She was like no woman he had ever met, even his mother. She focused on things that were not women's matters at all—and stranger yet, she seemed to understand them.

He would have her. It was clear to him then, as clear as anything he had known. He had never wanted a woman so before; never wanted one that was his own. But this one he would take.

25

"The prince wants you," Bran said.

He so rarely spoke to Rhian that at first she could not think what to say. The traders were to share the daymeal in the king's circle again, that had been made clear to them, but there was a lull now, as the sun sank toward the horizon. The caravan's wares were put away—nicely diminished since the morning, and a trove of treasures given in return.

Rhian had come looking for Emry. He had gone to bathe in the river, one of the traders said; but as she went to find him, Bran stood in her path. "You should be careful," he said. "When these lords want a thing, they take it. And women to them are things, like gold and fine horses."

"I want him to want me," she said. "He's a gift from the Goddess herself. He's a maker of chariots—do you understand what that means? He's not just a fighting man."

"That makes him even more dangerous," said Bran. "Don't reckon him innocent because he keeps no secrets from you. He's no child or simple fool."

"Oh, no," she said, "he's not either of those. He's beyond even arrogance. He can't imagine that anyone might be stronger or more clever than he is."

"Nor can you," Bran said. He gripped her arms—the first time he had wittingly touched her since she left Long Ford—and shook her lightly, careful of his strength even then. "Watch yourself! Guard your back. I've been listening—I talked to Conn and the traders. These tribesmen will take whatever they want. And they will force a woman to lie with them."

"No man would dare that," she said.

His fingers tightened almost to pain. "These men will. Believe it, Rhian! They are conquerors. Yes, even that one, with his pretty face and his fine manners."

"Oh, he's dangerous," she said. "But he won't force himself on me. Do you think the Goddess would allow it?"

He barely hesitated. "She might, if it served her purpose."

"I think not," said Rhian. But because he would not let her go, she added, "I'll be careful. Will that satisfy you?"

"No," he said, but his fingers slackened. He let her go. "If he harms you, I'll kill him."

She took his hand and kissed it, quickly, and let it go just as quickly. "You'll have to wait till I'm done with him first."

She doubted she had comforted him, but it was the best she could do.

⇨ ⇦

Emry was still bathing when she came to the little river. He had gone well upstream of the camp, where the water was clean. Conn was with him, but had finished, was out and dressed and plaiting his greying black hair.

Rhian sat a little distance from him, drawing her knees up and clasping them. The water looked cool and pleasant, but she was not in the mood to bathe just then.

"You are the child that Anansi brought back from Lir."

Rhian started. Conn's eyes were steady on her. "How long have you known?" she asked him with careful calm.

He shrugged a little. "Long. Your name, Long Ford . . . who else could you be?"

"You never said a word."

"I couldn't find the word to say."

She hugged her knees tightly and began to rock. "Nor could I," she said. Then: "You're not the father of my body."

"No."

"Did she know you knew?"

"She told me," he said, "not long after she brought you back."

"And she was not the mother of my body."

He shook his head. "Our son died in the birthing. You were a gift— a blessing."

"Or a curse?"

"No," he said. "No, never. Never that."

"You went away when she died. You never came back."

His face was too still. "I was weak. I paid for that. I'll go on paying for it till the Goddess takes me into the earth."

"Why? I'm no blood of yours."

"You were the child of my heart."

"Was I?"

There was such pain in him, such deep anguish, that she knew a moment's remorse. But only a moment. Her mood was strange. She was no more merciful than the gods were, and rather less inclined to take pity on him.

"I know who I am," she said. "The priestess who refused me the temple—she told me. Did you know? Did she tell you everything?"

"Mother's child," he said. "Destroyer. You were not to know. You were never to know. I left because I might not be strong enough—I might betray secrets."

"You were weak." But she was not condemning him. Men were not strong in things that mattered. The Goddess had given them strength of body to console them for their lack of strength in every other respect. "I'm safe here—for Lir and for the people. The temple need have no fear of me, now the mare has claimed me."

"I do hope so," said Conn.

Rhian looked past him. Emry was standing there. His face was completely unreadable. She could have no doubt that he had heard. "Surely you guessed," she said to him.

He shook his head. Was he a little rueful? It was hard to tell. "Men aren't told such secrets," he said.

"We can have no secrets here," said Rhian. "If we're to do what we came to do, we must know who we are, and why we were brought to this place."

"Maybe we were simply brought to die," Conn said, but not as if the thought frightened him.

"I won't believe that," said Rhian. "The Goddess isn't capricious. She meant us for something. To learn the ways of chariots. To take their secrets home with us."

"Yes," Emry said. "Yes, we can do that. There's no need to steal a chariot, which would only make us easier to find and kill. If we learn how they're made, no one need know; the knowledge will go with us, till we come home again."

"We need more than that," Rhian said. "The horses—"

"We'll watch," he said, "and remember. Everything."

"And if they guess what we're doing?" Conn inquired.

"I don't think they'll believe we can do it." Rhian shivered a little even so. "Will you turn coward, then, and run away?"

"No, nor betray you, either," Conn said. "I may be no prince of Lir, and no Mother's child, but I have a little courage."

Her cheeks flushed. He had shamed her, and properly.

She more than half expected Emry to be grinning at her discomfiture, but he had not taken his eyes from her. "You really are," he said as if to himself. "You are. I see . . ."

"Your mother?"

He nodded. "You asked me once about my brothers. Our brothers. Yes, we all look much the same. I'm blind, not to have seen before—even not expecting—"

"Who would expect such a thing? The priestesses lied from the day I was born. But the Goddess brought the truth to light."

"I always thought," mused Conn, "that they might have been great ladies and powerful priestesses, but they were still fools to think they could lie to the gods. Gods are never deceived. Sooner or later they see through the ruse—and then the lightning falls."

"Lightning fell when I was born," Rhian said. "The priestess told me. Maybe the gods will reckon that enough."

Conn snorted softly, but he did not say whatever he was thinking.

"I think," Emry said, "that it were best the others not know. It's a terrible thing the priestesses did, but it's not for men to judge."

"The truth will come out," said Conn. "You know that."

Emry hunched his shoulders as if against a sudden blast of wind. "I pray it may not come out soon. We've enough fear to spare, with what we've seen here. I counted chariots today. There were a hundred and thirty and four, and three more in the making. They're lacking the wherewithal to make more: this land is empty of trees. If they learn of our groves and forests—"

"You think they don't know already?" Conn demanded.

"They think there is no world beyond the river—they reckon us gods, or children of gods, because we come from there."

"That will last," said Conn, "only as long as it takes one of us to prove that he bleeds as red as any mortal man."

"Then you'd best not bleed," Rhian said. "Tomorrow I'll visit the chariotmakers again. They'll never expect a woman to understand what they do. Someone should see how they train the horses. If a reason could be found to set up the traders' market within sight of the training-fields . . ."

"I'll find one," Emry said. "When you go among the chariots, take the smith with you again. With luck they'll simply think he's your watchdog."

Rhian shivered with the same chill that had touched Emry a few moments before. But her heart was light—almost dangerously so. She flashed a grin at them both. "We'll see that they never learn what he is. If the prince knew that he can forge bronze, we'd never be let go."

"We'd be killed," Emry said somberly. "They'd keep him captive—and you, I'm sure, shut up in the prince's tent."

"No," she said with certainty that ran to the bone. "I would die first. I'll be no man's servant, nor his prisoner either. Bran will be safe—and so will you, and all who travel with you. You have my word on it, in the Goddess' name."

"Be sure you take oaths you can keep," Emry said.

"I will keep this one," she said. "We will do what we came to do. We will escape unharmed. We will go back to Lir and do all that we may to defend it from these marauders. Did you see how few they are? They have chariots, but their numbers are much less than we were led to believe. We have hundreds, thousands more than they do, and our women aren't kept out of the fighting, either. We will defeat them."

They were no more reassured than Bran had been. Men, she thought, were much given to fretting. It went with the rest of their frailties. She shrugged, sighed, left them to it. Either they would discover their courage in the end, or she would find it for them.

········· **26** ·········

Emry slept poorly that night. The worst of it was not that he had been blind and a fool, but that she had let him carry on in his ignorance—and he was angry at her. It was unbecoming any man, even a prince in Lir, to indulge in temper against a Mother, or that Mother's heir.

Had they chosen a Mother in Lir yet? Had the Goddess allowed that? Or had the priestesses lied as when Rhian failed the choosing, and chosen one of their own to hold the office?

He could feel the earth of his old certainty crumbling underfoot. Priestesses had lied. His Mother had had a daughter. That daughter was here, on this reckless folly of a venture. They could all die, and she could die with them.

The priestesses would be glad of that—at least until the chariots rolled over them and destroyed them.

He was up in the dawn, dressed in his trader's simplicity, pacing through their camp within the greater camp.

There were men hanging about even so early, wild-looking young things with hair that surely had not gone so white so early, nor been formed by nature into such jagged eruptions and uplifted horns. He had seen such extravagances near the king—the king's men, then?

The skin tightened between his shoulderblades as he walked through the casual line of them. None moved to stop him, but one or two happened to stroll in his wake.

Almost he turned on his heel and went back to his own people. But he had his own crazy courage, or he would never have come to this place. He had meant to wander only a little, maybe to see to the horses. Instead he set his path through the camp of the tribe—the Windriders, they called themselves.

It dawned on him soon enough that he was being guided, perhaps herded. Some turns met obstacles, usually in the form of large, unsmiling young men with hair limed and lacquered into horns.

He was not afraid. If they had meant to kill him, he would have been dead before he left the circle of the traders' tents.

He was conspicuous here: taller and broader than most, and notably darker. Children and dogs ran after him, but at a safe distance. None of them, it seemed, had any desire to challenge the king's men.

They were herding him toward the king's tent. That came as little surprise. But now he began—not to be afraid, no. But to be a little wary. If they had guessed what he was here for . . .

He went so far as to turn back. He had not known there were so many men herding him. They closed in a circle, pale eyes level, hands on hilts of sheathed swords.

He stopped, holding his own hands well away from the hilts of both sword and knife. "Only tell me," he said, "where I'm being taken."

"You are summoned," said one of the nearest, a young man as they all were, with a face that seemed somehow familiar. If the hair had been red-gold and plaited down his back—yes, he would have looked very like Minas the prince.

"I'm summoned to the king?" Emry asked. "Is it permissible to ask why?"

"You will come," the king's son said.

Maybe he did not understand the subtler nuances of the traders' speech.

Emry considered escape, but he was hemmed in. He shrugged slightly and let them herd him toward the king's tent.

They herded him into a dim and whispering world. There was light here, light of lamps, but it was dark after the sun without. It made him think of the temple of the Goddess in Lir. But that was high and holy. This was simply suffocating.

Nor was he in a small room as tents went. This was a grand hall, as bright with lamps as a tent could be, and gleaming with heaps of golden spoils.

Here was the king's lair. Here was the king, sprawled on a heap of furs and hides and bolts of rich fabric.

He was an imposing figure, even at his ease, in no more finery than a kilt of fine white leather. His pale skin was laced with scars. His breast and arms were massive, his legs thick, roped with muscle. He was like a great white bull, huge and powerful.

And yet he was growing old. His hair was thin. Softness encroached on his middle. His face was worn, his eyes clouded.

There were women with him, three of them. They sang a ceaseless, droning song. That, and the air thick with something both pungent and sweet, dizzied Emry till he thought surely he would faint. He tried to breathe shallowly. His ears he could not block, but he could do his best to let the chant run over and not through him.

This was magic, dark and old. Women's magic. The king was deep in its spell.

Emry let it lower him to his knees. The earth was buried under hides and carpets, but he felt its strength beneath. He smiled into the king's dull eyes, and said with the ease of prince to king, "My lord, we are well met. Have you a use for a caravan guard? Or are you simply curious?"

"There is reason to believe," said a voice in the shadows, "that you are more than a guard. That you are a prince of a tribe called Lir."

The voice was a woman's, and familiar. She had bidden Emry trade gold for furs and hides and looted treasures, just the day before.

So, Emry thought. This was how a Mother ruled in the tribes: in secret, through the face and body of a man. This man seemed sunk in torpor. The chant, the smoke, wreathed him about.

"In my country," Emry said, "the Mother of the people speaks directly to her children—and yes, to strangers, too. She needs no man to say her words for her."

"It is different here," said Etena's voice. He could see the shadowy shape of her, and catch a gleam of eyes. "Is it true, then? Are you royal born of your people?"

"I am the king's son of Lir," Emry said—for good or ill.

"Have you no fear of our holding you for ransom?"

"You can do that," he granted her. "But why?"

"Many reasons," she said. "Your country is rich. We have not yet conquered it. And," she said, "women rule it. That is greatly against nature."

"We believe that it's against nature for men to rule."

"You, too?"

He showed her his teeth. It was mostly mirth. "I was properly brought up," he said.

"And yet you are a prince," she said. "There is a king, yes?"

"A king to conduct the wars. A Mother to rule."

"There are wars among the gods?"

"Do you think that we are gods?"

"Are you?"

"Does it profit me to be one?"

"Ah," she said. "You are a trader after all."

"May I not be all of those things—prince and god and trader?"

She moved out of the shadows. The drone of the serving-women's chant faltered. This must be a shocking thing, for a king's wife to show herself to a man, even in the king's presence. Only the king seemed not to notice or to care. His eyelids had fallen shut; he snored softly.

Etena stood behind him as if to use him for a shield. Emry could see nothing amid the veils but her eyes. They had a hunger in them that he knew rather well.

Women liked him. Some loved him. That was a blessing of his blood and breeding, and yes, the beauty that went with it. They had bred for it since the dawn time, or so it was said.

"In my country," he said, "it's a woman's privilege to choose the man whom she will lie with."

He had shocked the singers into silence. Etena's hiss of breath was distinct, but she kept her wits about her. "My husband could geld you for that."

"For what? For speaking the truth?"

"For suggesting a thing that is a great crime among the tribes."

"It's a crime for a woman to fancy a man?"

"She may fancy no man but the one to whom she has been given, or who has taken her by right of conquest."

"She has no say in it? At all?"

"None," said Etena.

"That," said Emry after a pause, "is a difficult thing."

"Do you fancy me?"

He blinked. "Lady, I've seen nothing of you but your eyes."

That was perhaps too blunt an answer, but it was the only one he could give.

She stood behind the wall of her somnolent husband, and stripped off her veils. She had been beautiful once, and probably very greatly so; but such a beauty as hers bloomed early and faded fast. The frost was on her spirit, and bitterness cankered deep.

He pitied her. He prayed she did not see it. Because he was well brought up, and because he never could bear to wound a heart, he said, "I see a beauty very like that of my own people. Are you a westerner, too?"

"I come from Blackroot tribe," she said, "far to the east of here." Her dark eyes narrowed, raking his face. "Do you fancy me?" she asked again.

"If I did," he said, "it would never be proper to admit it."

"If I bade you lie with me, would you?"

He raised his shoulders, spread his hands. "In the way of my people, I would be greatly remiss to refuse. In the way of yours, I would be criminal to accept."

"Spoken like a prince," she said. "Now tell me. How long will your traders linger here?"

"As long as there is trading," Emry said, "we will trade."

"Will you go on past us after?"

"That," said Emry, "is for the caravan-master to say. I am but a guard, lady—that is the truth. Perhaps you should speak with him."

"Is he the king of your people?"

That, Emry could answer without prevarication. "Oh, no, lady. He's lord of his caravan, but no more than that."

He could not tell if she believed him. Her eyes seemed unable to turn away from his face. How long had it been, he wondered, since she saw a man who looked like one of her tribe? The white-skinned king asleep at her feet held no more of her heart, he would wager, than if he had been one of the camp dogs.

But a dog could not be a shield for her, nor give her power to rule this most terrible of conquering tribes. He had begun some while since to see why she had brought him here. It was a sad thing, and dangerous. He did not doubt at all that she would kill him if he failed to answer her as she wished. He had seen eyes like hers in tribesmen raiding across the river, empty of mercy and strangers to compassion. She knew only power, and the lure of a fine young body.

He bowed to her with all courtesy, and smiled, and did what a prince could do: undismissed, he left her presence.

As he had hoped, she did not call out to him, nor send one of her women to fetch him back. He was almost pathetically grateful to escape that place and that presence. The open air, even rich with the effluvia of a large and none too cleanly tribe, was dizzying in its purity. He breathed great lungfuls of it.

The king's wild-haired men were nowhere to be seen. He straightened his back and lifted his chin and began to walk back toward the traders' camp.

He had not gone far before someone fell in beside him. It was a man not nearly as tall as he was, but only a little less broad. He was dark, though not as dark as Emry. Emry knew him in a glance: one of the princes, the one who was Etena's son—Dias, that was his name. But, Emry had heard, mother and son were not friends. This prince was closely allied with the one who had brought the traders into the camp.

Factions, he thought. And he had fallen into the midst of them.

He greeted Dias with a nod. The prince strode beside him, matching his stride. After a little while Dias said, "I should kill you, you know. For looking on my mother's face."

Emry slanted a glance at him. "You were listening," he said.

"I saw you go in," said Dias. "I followed."

"Will you kill me?"

"Not today," Dias said. "She wants you, you know—if you really are a king's heir. She can use you as she uses my father."

"Not where I come from," Emry said, yet his heart was cold. There was no true Mother in Lir, and her daughter was here, bound to the White Mare. This woman whose lust was for power, who ruled this tribe from the shadows, well might stretch out her hand toward the Goddess' country.

"If you were wise," Dias said, "you would leave soon, and give no warning. Pack up in the dark and be far away by morning. Then pray my mother has no power to find you."

"Our Goddess is very strong," Emry said.

"Pray to her, then," said Dias.

He looked ready to turn away, but Emry stopped him with a word. "Why? Why warn us?"

"I am not my mother's friend," Dias said.

"That is a great sadness," said Emry.

"It is what is." Dias saluted him as the horsemen saluted one another. "Look to yourself, westerner. And watch your back."

27

Rhian had not gone to the prince in the night. It was a thing she planned carefully, so that he would want her more when she came to him again. But she had not expected to lie awake in the familiar tent, staring at the shadows raised by the lamp's flicker, and remember the touch of his hands on her body. Such skillful hands for a man so well honed in war, so subtle in their touch—and what had surprised her more than anything, so finely tuned to her pleasure. He was not at all as she had thought a lord of chariots would be.

She had gone to him in order to learn what he knew, and to bind him to her will. She had not expected to want him for himself.

It was a long dull while until morning. Then, in the way of sleepless nights, she fell into a sodden doze. When she dragged herself out of it, the sun was halfway toward the zenith, and the air in the tent was stuffy and hot. She pulled on the first garment that came to hand, made what order she could of her hair, and stumbled out.

It was not until she had relieved herself in the trench outside the traders' camp, and washed and combed and plaited her hair beside the river, that the stares of those she had passed made sense to her. She had put on breeches but no tunic. The day's warmth more than justified it, but this was not her own country.

If she was wise she would go back and cover herself, as Hoel put it— echoing the sentiments of the tribes. But she was cross-grained this morning. She skirted the edges of the tribe's camp, turning toward the place where the chariotmakers were.

Somewhat before she came there, she paused. The charioteers were out in force, galloping in companies across the long level. The shouts and cries of men, the rumble of wheels, struck her with almost painful intensity.

She had dreamed this. This was the face of war. They were laughing now, singing and taunting one another in high glee. No one would die, but in this game of war they prepared for blood and slaughter.

It was splendid. Some of the horses were young and inclined to be confused, and some of the charioteers had a green and awkward look, and that caused its share of mayhem. But even that was wonderful. They were a glory of speed: the swift horses, the tossing manes, the dizzy whirl of the wheels over the flattened grass.

He led one of the sides—of course. His hair was as bright as molten copper in the sunlight. He drove a pair of strong stallions, a dun and a bay. The bay was younger, she thought, and hotter. The dun was a seasoned campaigner: he was steady when the other fretted and tossed his head. He was the teacher, the bay his pupil. Minas was the guide and ruler of them both.

The others rode two to a chariot—charioteer and fighting man, the latter armed with a headless spear or a club that looked like the thighbone of an ox. Those were weapons enough to break bones, but the warriors laughed at them.

They howled with mirth when a charioteer, struck full on the head by a war-club, somersaulted over the rim of the chariot and tangled in trailing reins. His team bolted. His fellow in the chariot scrambled to do who knew what, tripped, and fell backward out of the car.

That was hilarious, but when the horses, maddened with confusion, ran headlong into another chariot, the men nearby were nigh prostrate with laughter. Some had even stopped their chariots and flung themselves down, rolling and kicking.

Rhian could not bear it. She ran onto the field, light and swift as the wind could carry her, and darted in among the horses and chariots. Those that had bolted had freed themselves somehow from the second chariot. The charioteer lay groaning near it. He was alive: good. She went after the horses, but carefully, as horsemen did. She did not run behind them, but angled toward them, watching to see how they were slowing and where they seemed determined to be. She met them there, caught reins, set her weight against them.

The horses were well trained to the touch of a hand. They reared in protest, but they did not strike her. They halted with her still on her feet, and the battered chariot still rolling behind them.

She soothed them with voice and hand. They were lovely, deep bays matched even to the star on the forehead, with long glossy manes and finely carved faces. They blew gently on her hands, and breathed deep of her hair.

A scream of pure rage sent them reeling back. Rhian kept her grip on them, and on herself, too. When she knew they would be still, she turned.

The mare was in a furious temper. Her ears were flat back. Her neck was snaky. Her teeth were bared.

Someone, it seemed, had tried to capture her. There was a broken rope about her neck. That would have tried her patience sorely, but she had kept her true rage for the army of men and horses and chariots that stood between herself and Rhian. Not all of them had the sense to clear the way, or could do it in the press of chariots.

She cleared them with teeth and hooves and the sheer white terror of her presence. Then at last she came to a halt, face to face with Rhian, and snorted explosively. The bays cringed. She snapped her teeth in their faces.

"That," said Rhian, "will be quite enough."

The mare flung up her head in outrage, but Rhian stood steady. The mare backed a single, draggingly reluctant step.

Rhian nodded briskly and let go the stallions' reins. As she had hoped, they stayed where she left them. She caught the hank of mane at the mare's withers and swung astride. The mare was still in a temper, but a sigh escaped her. Safe, her body said. Rhian was safe.

Rhian stroked her neck. "Ah, poor goddess. You were afraid for me."

The mare snorted and shook her mane. Rhian smiled but refrained from commentary.

She looked up to find herself the center of a broad circle. Men and horses alike were staring as if they could not stop. Again, too late, she remembered what she was and was not wearing.

She grinned and saluted them. The mare matched the grin. When she began to walk forward, horses and chariots melted out of her way.

All but one. Minas the prince held his stallions steady, though they jibbed and fought. They knew better than to stand in the way of any mare, let alone one who was a goddess.

But Minas was a prince, and she had him—yes, she had him. His eyes looked everywhere but where his mind was. His voice was steadier than she might have expected. "You are very bold."

"I am a woman from across the river," she said.

"Get in the chariot," he said.

She did not think he knew what he would say before he said it: he looked startled once it was out. But he did not try to unsay it.

She hesitated no longer than it took to vault from the mare's back to the chariot. He started; the horses half-reared. The chariot rocked. She caught at the sides.

It moved a little like a boat on rough water, and a very little like a well-gaited horse. It was strange to stand behind a pair of horses, to feel their motion, but to be separated from them by a thin space of air, a shaft, and a few bits of leather and bone and forged copper.

She was beginning to find her balance. She slid her hand around till she touched one of the reins. It was a living thing. Even the slight weight of her hand made the stallion turn his head.

His big dark eye regarded her. He knew her; all stallions did. He cast a wary glance at the mare, who had come up beside the chariot. But she was quiet, biding her time.

A shift of the chariot swayed Rhian against the prince. She felt him stiffen. She did not move away when the chariot shifted again, not at once. Not until she heard his breath quicken. Then she let herself be parted from him again, nearer the chariot's side.

Minas slackened rein and clicked his tongue. The stallions leaped as if shot from a bow—across the edge of the field, and then veering away, out on the open plain. Tumult rose up behind them. The charioteers were roaring aloud, cheering them on.

⇒ ⇐

The chariot was a noisy thing, with the rattle of its wheels and the creaking of its frame. And yet one could grow accustomed to the sound. Then one could hear the wind singing in one's ears, the heart in one's breast and the breath in one's lungs, and the silence of the charioteer.

It was a very large silence. Minas' spirit seemed wholly taken up in the task of driving a poorly matched team over roughening ground. Rhian settled as well as she could in her part of the chariot, which happened to be beside and somewhat behind him. It gave her a fine view of his shoulders, which were as bare as her own, and his long straight back, and the plait of bright hair following the line of it. She allowed her eye to linger over his buttocks, which were very well shaped; for he was wearing nothing at all, as any sane man would on a day so breathlessly hot.

He did not press the horses once the swell of the land had taken them out of sight of the tribe. They slowed to a trot and then to a walk. Their coats were darkened with sweat. Rhian saw the foam between their hindlegs.

The wind was blowing light but steady. It chortled to see them together, danced and teased, plucking her hair out of its loosening plait and brushing tendrils of it against his back. He shivered at the touch, but did not turn or glance at her.

"Don't tell me," she said, "that you've never seen a woman's breasts before."

Sun and heat had brought color enough to his cheeks, but at that he went bright scarlet. "Women are modest here," he said. His voice was somewhat thick.

"What is this 'modest'?" she asked. "Is it shame? Is it fear?"

"It is honor," he said with a touch of heat.

"Ah," she said. "Honor. And yet men walk about naked, and no one seems to mind. Is it only women who have honor?"

"It is only men who have honor. Women have none."

"But if modesty is honor, and only women have modesty, then—"

He brought the chariot to a halt and wound the reins about the post that was set in the rim for just that purpose. She watched with interest as the horses stood rooted, nor moved forward at all; they did not even try to graze.

It was with some effort that she focused on him again. He had turned without thinking, she thought, and been shocked anew by the sight of her.

This time she did not let him turn away again. She caught his face in her hands and held him fast. If he had simply wrenched his head aside, he could have broken away, but he did not do that. "You are a spirit of mischief," he said.

She laughed. "I've been told that before. But really, tell me—how can a woman have modesty but no honor?"

"Modesty clothes her for the honor of her kinsmen and the protection of her family. Without it she has nothing but shame."

"So," she said. "You think me shameful."

"No," he said. "No." But his eyes would not look below her chin.

She let go his face to catch his hands and press them to her breasts. "This is my pride," she said. "This is my glory. I am the Goddess' creation. Man is my flawed image. He exists to serve; to make and rear children; to ornament my house."

Minas' hands had curved to fit her breasts. He was breathing fast and shallow. His rod was defiantly erect.

She half expected him to fall on her like a bull in rut, but he did no such thing. He was as properly restrained as a man of her people.

"You are beautiful and more than beautiful," she said. "You are a wonder among your people."

He was beyond speech, she thought, until he said, "I am no woman's servant."

"A Goddess? Can you serve her?"

He shook his head, but he did not answer directly. Instead he said, "I've destroyed any reputation you might hope to have, by carrying you off like this."

"Did you? Or did you bestow your honor on me, as a tribesman does on a woman he conquers?"

"I didn't—" His teeth clicked together. "Are you allowing me to claim you?"

"No," she said. "But your kin may be allowed to think so."

"And your kin? What will they say?"

"Nothing," she said. "Not a word. My choices are mine to make."

"And if I choose to keep you captive? What will you do then?"

"You won't do that," she said.

She had pricked his pride: she saw how his face tightened. But he was wiser than to rail at her for what was only the truth. "It would protect you," he said as if to himself, "to let them think . . ."

"Surely it couldn't harm your reputation to have conquered a goddess."

She was still holding his hands over her breasts. When she let them go, they stayed. She arched into them.

He gasped, but he seemed unable to move. He could speak, a little. "It—would never harm—oh, gods!"

"Do I please you?" she asked, slipping arms about his middle, catching his rampant rod between them. He spasmed at that, but did not let go his seed.

"Am I beautiful?" she asked him. "Am I splendid? Do you want me desperately?"

"*Yes!*" It was a cry almost of pain.

"You are splendid," she said. "I want you very much."

"Why?"

That made her draw back a bit, the better to see his face. "A man of your age and tribe and beauty has any need to ask me that?"

"I know why I want you," he said with some difficulty, but clearer as he went on. "Why do you want me? What can I give you?"

"Yourself," she said. That was the truth, if not the whole of it. She sealed it with her lips on his, a kiss long enough and deep enough to drown them both.

28

This was no dream. Minas lay with her on the steppe, with the sky a vault of pure and cloudless blue overhead, and the chariot beside them. He had no memory of loosing the horses, but they were free of the chariot, hobbled with a bit of rein, grazing at a respectful distance from the strange pale mare.

The woman rode him as if he had been a stallion, her body arched, her breasts twin moons above him. His hands clasped her hips, feeling the strength and the fullness of them, the broad bones well made for carrying children.

She was magnificent. Beside her, every woman he had ever had was a pale and sapless thing. When she came to the summit, she loosed a cry of triumph. Then, and only then, she let him climb the heights to join her. His cry was fainter by far, breathless, and fading fast.

She held him inside her until it pleased her to let him go. Then she dropped beside him, breathing hard, wet as if she had been swimming in the river. The clean musky scent of her was intoxicating.

He could not speak at all. He could only stare at her, and fight off sleep that was like unconsciousness. He did not want to sleep. He wanted to stay awake, to know when she left, if she left. For the moment she seemed inclined to linger, lying on her back with her arms spread wide, and her beauty all bare to the sky.

He was jealous of the sky. He the reasonable man, the maker of chariots, the prince of men. He envied any eye that could rest on her, even if it were the sun.

This, he knew in his belly, was why men kept their women veiled and shut in tents. Not for honor. Not for protection. Because they could not bear for any other man to see what was theirs.

He could never bind this one in veils. If he tried, if by some miracle of the gods he could keep her bound at all, she would die. And, he thought, she would take as many men with her as she could—and him foremost.

There was a legend from far away and long ago, of a goddess who walked in the form of a beast. She was larger than a lion, striped like the shadows of grasses on tawny earth. She was called the tigress. She hunted men and killed them, and devoured their bones.

And yet, the legend said, she was tender where she loved. To her children she was the gentlest of mothers, just as she was fiercest in defense of them.

This was a tigress, with her tawny skin and her white teeth. She stretched in the grass, luxurious as a great cat. "You," she said in a voice like a purr, "have no art at all. But there is something . . ."

He sat up as if she had struck him. Sleep at least had fled, but with it had gone his deep contentment. "No art? I'm not a good lover? By the gods, woman—"

"Child," she said, cutting cleanly across his words, "for a tribesman, you're a marvel. But it's clear no one ever taught you how to please a woman. That, you've fumbled through on your own; and truly I do love you for it."

He glowered at her. He was sulking, he knew it, just as he knew that she was laughing at him for it. Women had told him how well he pleased them. He had been proud of that. And now this foreigner mocked his vaunted skill.

Her hand was cool against his burning cheek. Her smile was maddening, but tender, too. "Poor boy," she said. "I shouldn't have told you the truth."

"No," he said. "Better the truth than a lie. But that—it hurts!"

She kissed him softly. "Of course it hurts. You have your pride. But do believe me when I say that for all your lack of art, you have somewhat about you that makes the greatest art an empty thing."

"Words," he said. "Such fine words."

"Every one of them is true."

He looked long at her. He saw her, maybe, for the first time. Her beauty. Her strength. Her utter foreignness. "We do not come from the same world," he said.

"May we not meet between?"

"Should we?"

She did not answer that. Could not, maybe.

He rose to catch the horses, to harness them again to the chariot. She helped him—surprisingly skilled, for someone who could not have seen a chariot before she came to the People. She had a good eye; she learned quickly.

He thought—yes, hoped—that she would mount her mare and ride away, but when the chariot was ready, she said, "Show me how to drive the horses."

That took gall. But if he had learned anything of her, it was that she knew nothing of either fear or shame. He could have refused her outright, and by both law and tradition he should have done just that. But his mood was strange, his spirit contrary. He sprang into the chariot and held out his hand.

She grinned her wild grin and let him swing her up in front of him. The horses were fresh and eager. She was warm and alive between his arms. He turned his spirit away from the stirring that roused, and focused himself on the feel of the reins, the stallions' mood and their willingness to leap into flight.

She rested her hands over his. Her touch on the reins was light, barely to be felt. The horses made no objection. He let them walk forward, though they begged to spring into a gallop. They were obedient, even the young bay, who had only gone in harness since the last new moon.

When he was sure of them, he slipped his hands free and left her with the reins. Her breath quickened a little, but she was calm, intent on what she was doing. He could feel the sway of the chariot in her body, the ease with which she followed it.

She had been watching him. She knew the exact click of the tongue that moved the team into a trot. Her hands were not as deft as his; the horses jibbed a little, caught shorter than they liked. But she softened rein, and they settled to a steady gait.

She had begun frowning, deeply intent, but as she settled into the way of it, the smile bloomed.

He had a little warning: a slight tensing of her body, a minute shift of feet. Maybe she had not meant to urge the horses on quite so hard, or quite so suddenly. They leaped forward with force that strained the traces. Minas nearly tumbled out of the chariot. A lurch and sudden sway flung him forward.

She braced against him. He caught the chariot's rim. Her face had gone white. Good, he thought through the whipping of wind. Let her know a little fear.

The dun could run the sun into the horizon and race the moon on its round, but the bay was young and not yet come to his full strength. He tired soon enough.

Rhian brought him down with more care than Minas might have expected. She had no more skill in it than she had granted him as a lover, but she had a certain gift, to be sure. If she had been a man, he would have been swift to number her among the charioteers. But he could not make himself regret that she was a woman.

The horses had run far over the steppe. In the way of horses they had found an upper branch of the river that flowed past the camp. It ran swift and clean, though somewhat low in this season, and the grass on its banks was green.

The moon-colored mare was there already, grazing placidly. She barely acknowledged the stallions' arrival, even when they were turned loose to roll in the grass.

Minas drank long and thirstily from the river, and filled his waterskin from it. When he looked again, a pair of fish hung flopping from a string that, moments before, had laced up Rhian's breeches.

She stood knee-deep in the shallows. As he watched, she swooped and came up with a third fish, larger than either of the others, and giving her a fair fight, too. But she won, strung the fish with its fellows and flashed her white grin at Minas.

"You'll eat them raw?" he asked her.

"Hardly!" she said.

He was in a contrary mood, or he would not have done what he did. He went swimming in the river, swam long and hard, till all the heat and sweat of the day was washed away, and with it the scent and the memory of her. When he came out at last, blue and shivering, she had a fire burning in a circle of stones, and the fish roasting on a flat stone.

Between the sinking sun and the fire, he warmed quickly. The fish was sweet and smoky, as he liked it best. The water had washed away his ill temper. He even smiled at her, and thanked her graciously for sharing the fruits of her hunt.

He stiffened when she left the far side of the fire and her own share of the fish to kneel behind him. Deftly and patiently she worked the tangles from his drying hair. She made no move to tempt him into lying with her again, but her touch, so light and skilled, warmed him to the bone.

Such a thing as this, only a lover or a battle-brother might do. A wife did it for her husband, if she were greatly favored.

He told her as much. She paused in plaiting his newly tamed hair. He felt the swift brush of her lips on his shoulder, and the sharp nip of teeth. He yelped and rounded on her.

She laughed at him. "In my country," she said, "a woman does it for a man she favors. She'll plait her token into his hair, and so claim him; and the other women will let him be."

Struck with sudden apprehension, he pulled his braid over his shoulder. There was indeed something woven in it: a small golden bell.

That was not gold. It was bronze. She had claimed him with bronze.

If it had been gold, he would have torn it out and flung it in her face. But bronze had too much power. It meant too much.

Bindings, he had heard a shaman say once, were twofold. If he was bound to her, then so was she bound to him. Bronze made sure of it.

He had nothing with which to seal it. He had left the camp naked, with no baggage but an empty waterskin. The chariot he would never give her, nor the horses, nor their harness.

Suppose, he thought, that his gift were the driving of the chariot. It was such a gift as few men in the world could give, and no woman had ever had. Women did not ride in chariots, still less play charioteer.

He had broken laws of men and gods. He had cared nothing for it when he did it, and he could not make himself care now. Not in front of her. What did men's laws matter, if she was a goddess?

"You are beautiful," he said, "like a fine bay mare. You are odder than any woman I ever met. No one warned me—no one told me that there could be such a creature in the world."

"I'm ordinary enough in my country," she said.

"Ah," said Minas, "but that is the gods' country. We mortals are different."

She looked as if she might offer objection, but thought better of it. She finished plaiting his hair instead. He allowed it. When it was done, when his plait hung down his back where it belonged, he could hear the faint high chiming of the bronze bell. Binding him. Binding her. Marking in memory this strangest of days.

29

By noon the tale had flown through the camp: how the traders' woman had invaded the chariots' battle, and Minas the prince had carried her away. People were already making songs of it.

It was a scandal among the elders, both men and women. The young folk thought it wonderful. "She rode out as bare as a newborn baby," Aera heard one of the king's wives say to another. "The sight of her struck all the men dumb."

"Surely," said one of the others with a wicked cackle. "All their wits had gone straight to their rods."

Aera bit her lip till it bled. What she felt was not shock, nor yet amusement. It was envy. That one had seen a man she fancied, and taken him. She would never understand what it was for a woman to bow to a man's will.

Why, thought Aera, that was bitterness. She had reckoned herself content—not with what had become of the king, oh no, but with the life the gods had given her. She was mother to the heir. She had power in the king's tent. Her father was the maker of chariots, whom men called a god.

She would have given it all to be riding naked in a chariot, swept away by a bold young charioteer. Nor was it her son's face she saw, but quite another altogether. A strong dark face, a fine curly beard, and shoulders as broad as an aurochs' horns.

She had not been wise this morning. She had known when he came in, and had slipped through shadows in his wake. She heard what Etena said to him, and what he said in return. Then she sent Dias to warn him, but Dias had not reckoned the warning well taken. Better, she realized belatedly, if she had gone herself. These westerners bowed to the rule of women. To her who was a woman, the westerner would have listened.

Too late, she thought as she passed through the king's tent. What was done was done.

Was it?

She stopped short. Her errand vanished, forgotten. She was under a spell, she thought: a western magic. She could not even make herself care.

She went out as she was allowed to do, as a senior wife of the king. She veiled herself in fabric that had been taken from a tribe somewhat to the east of this place, that was not as fine as the weavings the westerners had brought, but it concealed her as was proper. Her gown covered her from her throat to her toes. The sleeves fell to her fingertips, a mark of wealth and standing. There was gold about the sleeves and hem. Gold rings hung from her ears. Gold bound her veil and her girdle. Many would have reckoned her blessed among women.

She felt, walking from shadow to shadow of the camp, as if she were wrapped in chains. The veil suffocated her. The gown was unbearably hot. The boots felt tight enough to crush her feet.

She bore them because she must. She had her rank and position to consider, and the honor of her kin. No matter that this errand might do far more harm to them than if she had stripped naked and danced through the camp. It might not; and she preserved her modesty.

The traders were trading in a great crowd of men and a few bold veiled women. Aera did not see the one she sought, though there were big black-bearded men enough, and one or two almost as good to look at as the captain of guards. Who might, if Etena's spies told the truth, be a king's son of the western tribes.

She had no need to ask who Etena's spies were. She recognized one of the women by the gliding grace of her walk. No doubt some of the king's men strutting about were Etena's, too. Maybe all of them were. Her power had grown great, this season.

Aera moved quietly along the edges of the crowd. The traders were taking in a great deal of gold in exchange for their jewels and weavings and ornaments. Sometimes they traded gold for something that a tribes-man offered: a heap of tanned hides, a finely made bridle, an embroidered coat.

Those who traded, she noticed, had a different look than those who stood on guard. The traders were smaller men, slighter, with darker skin and sharper features. The guardsmen were big men, as big as warriors of the People, and their faces were blunt but very comely. They carried themselves differently, too. They had an air about them, she thought, of inborn arrogance. These were not servants or conquered tribesmen. These were men accustomed to rule.

They had an easy manner with the men of the People. Before the women they were as deferential as if each of them had been an elder of the tribe. It was enough like the respect that was proper among the People that it gave no offense—in fact it pleased the women considerably, though their men were wary.

Aera had brought nothing to trade, except the warning she meant for the captain of guards. Maybe he had gone hunting. There was no one she dared ask. She left the traders' circle with a sensation that was not exactly relief.

She should go back to the king's tent where she belonged. But her spirit was still at odds with itself. She sought her father instead.

He would not be in his tent at this time of day. It would be empty and pleasant, and she could escape for yet a while the duties that grew more onerous, the more powerful Etena became. The time would come, she thought, when she was expected to haul water and gather dung for the cookfires—tasks for a captive, not for the mother of the king's heir.

She came at her father's tent roundabout, circling away from the field of chariots and skirting the makers' circle. And there where she would never have expected to find him was the man she had been looking for. He stood with another man like him, a very big man, massive and silent, watching the makers at their work.

Metos never had seen the virtue in hiding what he did. "If they can understand it," he liked to say, "then the gods bless them."

The western captain seemed more entertained than edified. The other had a heavy, not particularly intelligent face. He seemed asleep on his feet. And yet, Aera thought, a man could conceal great wit and subtlety behind such a mask.

The captain caught sight of her. His eyes brightened in a way that made her heart flutter. His smile seemed honestly delighted.

She resisted the urge to lift her hand to her breast. She was wearing the necklace he had given her—that she meant to return, oh yes, but not yet. He could not see it under her veils, and yet it seemed he was aware of it. Why else would he regard her with such warmth, and sweep such a splendid salute? "Lady!" he called. "Lady! Well met!"

That was beyond improper. It would have won him a spear in the gut if he had been anywhere but here. Metos had never cared for such things, and his makers were of his mind: all the world was the work, and nothing else was of any importance.

Emry the captain went on, oblivious to the infraction he had committed. "A fine day, lady, and a fine spectacle here — such a thing as I've never seen in the world before. Some of it I understand, but the rest . . ."

"That is men's work," she said with a hint of severity. "I know little of it."

He raised a brow. If he was aware that he had been chastised, he did not acknowledge it. "What is women's work?" he asked.

"That would be of no interest to a man," she said.

His smile had faded as they spoke, but at that, the corner of his mouth twitched. He was very difficult to despise, even with his dreadful manners. "Probably it would not be," he said equably, "as feeble of wit as I demonstrably am, and as far beneath your eminence as the earth beneath the moon's feet."

If he had been one of her children, she would have boxed his ear for that. But he was not her child, not even remotely, nor did she look at him as she looked at her sons, both the one she had borne in her womb and the one she had suckled at her breast. Even her king in his youth had not made her heart beat as hard as this young man did.

She settled for a hiss and a toss of the head that set the golden ornaments of her veil to jingling. "Impudent," she said.

He ducked his head as if in submission, but his eyes were laughing at her under the black brows. He knew all too well what he was doing to her.

If he had been a woman, she would have called him shameless. Men did not do such things here. They took what they wanted. They never asked.

Her mouth twisted. "What a day you have had," she said, "lusted after by two royal wives. Is it a game you play? Do you take trophies, or is the conquest enough?"

"Lady," he said, and all the laughter was gone from his face, "if a woman wants me, I must at least, in courtesy, acknowledge the wanting. But I'm given the right to refuse — again, in courtesy."

"You are refusing me," she said.

"Oh, no, lady," he said before she could say what else was in her heart. "Never in the world. If you but ask, I'll gladly give myself to you."

"Would you give yourself to any royal wife who asks?"

"Not at all," he said with all the fervor of his youth. "That one—" He shivered. "She wants me snoring at her feet, enslaved to her will. After I've pleasured her in every way she imagines I know."

"What do I want of you?"

Was he blushing, however faintly? "You may want whatever you please to want," he said, "and I will be pleased to give it."

"If I tell you never again to look on me, or speak to me, or think of me—will you do it?"

"Do you want that?"

She opened her mouth to say yes, she did, she who was the king's wife. But her tongue said, "What I want matters nothing. I belong to the king. Any man who touches me must die."

"Even the king?"

"Oh!" It was a gasp. "Oh, you are incorrigible!"

He bit his lip. "You make me dizzy," he said. "Then I say whatever comes into my head."

"I am old enough to be your mother."

"Yes." He did not seem to understand that there should be anything wrong with it. "And I've never seen your face."

"Oh, no," she said. "I'm not my sister wife. I'll not fall to that temptation."

"She falls to every temptation," he said. "For power; for desire. For whatever strikes her fancy."

"If she were that feeble," Aera said sharply, "she would never have come as far as she has. She is dangerous, child. Believe it. Guard against it."

"I do believe it," he said, though never strongly enough to set her heart at rest. "Great ambition, stunted spirit—I see her clearly enough, lady, though you reckon me an innocent."

"Then you see that you should go," she said. "Go tonight. Take your caravan and whatever you can carry that will not slow you, and escape while you can."

"It's too late for that," he said gently. "We're already under guard."

"Tonight," she said, "the guards can be called off. That much power I do have."

"How long will you keep it, once she learns what you did? No, lady," he said. "We will go, but not tonight, and not in any way that compromises you."

"You do not understand," she said. She clenched her fists to keep from hitting him. "If you don't leave, she'll keep you here. She'll enslave you. She will never let you go."

"Why?"

"Because," she said, "what she wants, she keeps. She wants you."

"She wants what she thinks I am: king's son of a far country. She doesn't understand that a woman can rule the world without the shield of a man."

"If she does understand it, then the world is even less safe than before."

"Maybe," he said, "but there are women who have ruled since the dawn time, Mothers and priestesses of cities old beyond your farthest beginnings. Goddesses, you would call them. She's nothing to them."

"Does she need to be?" Aera demanded. "She has the People. She has this." Her hand swept over the makers' circle, the chariots that even half-formed had a deadly beauty.

She saw how he shivered. So: he was not blind in his boldness. "If she goes too far," he said slowly, "if she loses the king—what then? What will she do?"

"That is nothing that should matter to you," Aera said. "You will be long gone. Pray your gods then that you never see any of us again."

"I don't pray for what the gods won't grant." He was as somber as she had yet seen him; indeed he was grim.

"We may not come to your country in your lifetime," she said.

"You will." He spoke with perfect certainty.

"Have you come to spy on us, then?"

He slid a glance at her. She saw no fear in it. "We were curious. And we had treasures to trade."

"All the more reason to fear Etena," Aera said.

"She has a great love of things that glitter," he said. "I thank you for the warning. The Goddess will bless you for it."

"My gods may not," Aera said a little wearily, "but that's no matter. Look to yourself, and guard your caravan as you may. Trust nothing and no one. No, not even me! For this little time I may tell you the truth, but in the end I belong to the People. Remember that."

"I will not forget it," said Emry.

30

"We should do as she says," Bran said.

He waited till they were away from the chariotmakers to say it, till they had gone back to the traders' camp and sat to the day's meal. Hoel the caravan-master sat with them, and one or two of Emry's warriors from Lir. They had all heard the story, how two of the king's wives had singled out Emry that day.

"We should go," Bran said, cutting through the laughter and light-hearted mockery: the women, it was well known, always cast their eyes on Emry. But Bran was not a man who laughed at trifles. "There is real danger here. No one wishes us well. Even she who warned us—what did she want of us? She'll send her son and his warband, I'll wager, and order them to seize us."

"Not that one," Emry said. He did not know how he knew, but he knew it in his bones. "She meant exactly what she said. The other one— yes, she's as treacherous as a river in flood." He narrowed his eyes, searching Bran's face. It was never easy to read, and no more now than ever. "Are you ready to go? Have you seen all you need to see?"

"Yes," Bran said.

"We can make chariots?"

"No," said Bran.

Emry sat back on his heels. "Then you're not ready at all."

"I am," said Bran. "I've seen enough to know that if there were a dozen of me, and we apprenticed to the chief of the makers for a year, we would have just begun to understand the art and its secrets. What he does to make the wheels, how he cures and shapes the wood and wicker, the length and balance of the pole, the harness, how it's made, and as much as anything, how the horses are trained—we were fools to think we could steal all of that. Even if we steal a chariot and team, we'll only have the one. To make others, enough of them to fight against these warriors trained to the art and skill from childhood—they'll be upon us before we're well begun. We can't do it. It can't be done."

It was the longest speech Emry had ever heard from that man of few words. It struck them all dumb, and struck the laughter out of them, too.

A new voice spoke in the silence. It was light, easy, unafraid. "All very true, and as wise as a man can be. But you're not thinking as you should think. We can do it. It can be done—if we steal not only a chariot, not only the horses, but a maker and a charioteer. We can't invent it, but we can learn. We can be taught."

"And how," Bran demanded, "do you propose to do that?"

Only a man who had known Rhian from childhood would speak so, with no awe of what she was. She did not bridle at it, either; it was familiar, and maybe the more welcome for that. "Do you remember old Anni's potions? There was one, it was very simple. The herb grows in this country. I'll find it, brew it. I'll give it to the one I have in mind. When he's deep asleep, we'll take him. We'll be far away before he wakes."

"And how long will it be," Emry asked mildly, "before the whole tribe comes seeking its prince?"

"Long," she said, "if it thinks him gone on a hunt."

"You really would do it," Emry said. He did not know whether he was impressed or appalled.

Rhian squatted by him, accepted a bit of meat rolled in warm bread, grinned and bit into it, Of course she would do it, her expression said. She had meant it all along.

Women, thought Emry, were wonderful, terrible creatures. And this one was his sister. She was very like their mother, but like their father, too: keen-eyed, clear-headed, and quietly implacable in whatever she set herself to do.

"I thought," Emry said, "that you were besotted with him."

"I am," she said. "That doesn't mean I can't think. I had thought we could steal the old man, the first of the makers, but he would never leave his circle. The young one comes and goes. He's even been known to go out alone, sometimes for a day or two or three. By the time he's missed, we'll be far away."

"That could work," Conn said from the other side of the fire.

"Maybe," said Hoel. "But it would need more speed than our donkeys can muster. What will you do? Leave us behind for the tribe to devour?"

Rhian shook her head. "No. Of course not. You will go on eastward, as if to trade in the sunrise countries. Most of the guards will go with you. As few of us as possible will run westward with our quarry."

"That won't stop them from killing us when they fail to find you with us," Hoel said.

"It will if, once you've made it clear that you're heading east, you turn north or south and do everything in your power to conceal your tracks. Surely you can vanish into the steppe. Or didn't you think this would happen when you insisted on coming with us? We never pretended that it would be either easy or safe."

"We can vanish," Hoel said a little grudgingly. "We knew there was danger when we began. But if you abduct the king's heir, you'll bring down all the wrath of the tribe. Might it not be wiser to steal one of the makers from the circle?"

"The makers, like their master, never leave. Only the prince comes and goes."

That was true enough to give Hoel pause. But Bran said, "If we wait long enough for you to concoct your potion, it may be too late."

"If we leave tonight," Rhian said, "we've done all this for nothing. We've learned too little to be of use."

"Then how long?" Bran demanded. "How quickly can you do what you need to do?"

"Three days," she said, "or four. Hoel, can you be finished with your trading a day or two before that? If we all seem to leave, and a day or two later the prince goes hunting, it will be less suspicious."

"Well enough," Hoel said, "if we're allowed to leave. From what the prince's mother said, we may not be."

"There will be a way," Rhian said.

The Goddess would find one, she meant. It was hardly Emry's place to argue with that. He set his lips together and held his peace. So did the rest of them, good men of the Goddess country all. Rhian smiled at them, well content with herself and her power.

⇨ ⇦

Rhian had gone ahead of Minas, riding the white mare back to the People. Minas lingered till the sun was nearly set. The horses ate their fill of the grass by the river. They were glad enough to see the harness again, and to be yoked to the chariot. As alluring as grass might be, the lure of the herd was strong; and they were far from their kin and kind.

The sun was full in his eyes as he rode back. He drove by feel, trusting the horses' sure feet on the trackless steppe. All he could see, all his eyes knew, was light.

He did not know precisely when he rode out of the world. Grass still rolled away under the chariot's wheels. But the sky was all light, and there was a wolf trotting beside and somewhat behind him. It was a very insouciant wolf, with a wicked yellow eye and an insolent loll of tongue.

The horses seemed unaware of him. They continued their steady pace; even the young one was quiet. It seemed he had learned obedience.

"Good evening, cousin wolf," Minas said after a while. It might not be wise, but he was not in a wise mood, just then.

The wolf grinned its white fanged grin. "Good evening, cousin fool," he said. "Is that a mare's scent you reek of?"

"Is that any concern of yours?"

The wolf yipped with laughter, rolling and tumbling in the summer-ripened grass. "Is it? *Is* it? Cousin, do you know what mare that is?"

"I know she is a goddess," Minas said.

"Then maybe you're only half a fool," said the wolf. "Guard your back, cousin. Trust no one, not even yourself. Your road stretches far, and darkness covers much of it. You will go down to the river of souls. If you cross it, if you walk in the lands that are beyond it, you will never see this country again."

Minas' back was cold, but then the sun had nearly set, and he was naked. "All men cross that river," he said. "All men die."

"Not all men die apart from the People, sundered from them, traitor to them."

That truly was a shudder in his bones. Still he kept his voice light, his face untroubled. "Certainly I shall not do that."

"Will you?" The wolf snapped at a fly. "Ah well. Maybe your sight is clearer than mine. What am I but a shaman, after all? And you are king's heir of the People."

Minas refrained from bridling at that mockery. "I am warned," he said, "and you have my thanks for it."

"Thank me if you live to a ripe and untroubled old age," the wolf said.

"I do intend to," said Minas.

The wolf grinned and spun and leaped into the darkening air. It swallowed him as if in mist. Or it was the mist that took Minas, lifting him out of the spirits' world, back again into the world of the living. The sun dipped beneath the horizon. And there below him, though he had reckoned himself still some distance away, he saw the campfires of the People.

He had come home. And so he always would. He would never betray them; never turn against them. He would die before he did such a thing.

31

It seemed the Goddess would indeed provide. The caravan was still alive and still intact come morning, nor had any threat come upon them in the night. When they laid out their wares to trade, there was already a crowd waiting.

Emry began to wonder if they could give Rhian her three days. The trinkets and small baubles were nearly gone. The richer things were much depleted. They had already begun to trade things that had been traded for their wares, in a circle of exchange that Emry the prince found rather amusing. He had never given much thought to traders' ways until he found himself guarding this caravan.

Hoel did not seem concerned. This was a quite ordinary way of doing things, his manner said. Emry decided not to fret over it. His task was to guard the traders. That art he knew, and well.

Toward midday one of the king's men approached Hoel. He looked a great deal like the heir, who must be his brother: tall and narrow, with hair that might have been ruddy had it not been whitened with lime. His brows were copper, and his lashes, and the freckles on his cheeks.

He was not there to trade looted gold for outland treasure. Emry sharpened his ears. "The king's wife summons the woman from the west," he heard the boy say.

"For her I cannot answer," Hoel said.

The tall boy bridled. But he must have been instructed: he bit his lip and said, "May we know where we may find the woman?"

"She goes where she pleases," Hoel said.

That was more than the boy could bear. Emry intervened before the thunder in his face could erupt into lightning. "I'll help you find her," he said. "Come, follow me."

The boy looked perfectly startled, but by the time Emry had set Mabon on guard in his place and set off toward the camp's edge, the king's son had recovered. He followed a little stiffly, as if for some reason it affronted him to be in Emry's company.

Emry shrugged. He never had concerned himself with the moods of children.

Rhian was where Emry had hoped to find her: in among the horses, brushing the grey mare's coat with a twist of grass and picking burrs out of her tail. She looked like a servant with her ancient breeches and her imperfectly disciplined hair. She was also, in the reckoning of these people, half naked, which had its usual effect. The king's son did not know where to look.

Emry's lips twitched. "O chosen one," he said, "this man would speak with you."

Rhian raised a brow, but greeted the king's man courteously enough.

"You are summoned," the boy said to his feet, "to the king's wife."

Both brows went up. "Take me there, then," she said, mild enough that Emry eyed her suspiciously. When she suffered the king's son to lead her, Emry followed. Neither of them tried to stop him.

⇨ ⇦

The king's wife waited as she had before, but the king was nowhere to be seen. She was alone but for the boy who had been her messenger. The drone of chanting came from a little distance, overlaid with the murmur of the king's women. Emry's nose wrinkled. The air was full of sweet pungent smoke. It made him dizzy.

Rhian had drawn stares all the way from the traders' camp, but the king's wife barely acknowledged her. The dark eyes were fixed on Emry. Were they surprised? Glad? Avid?

Even so, it was to Rhian that she spoke. "You are welcome in my lord's tent."

Rhian bent her head, and then her knees, till she sat on her heels. "I am honored to be so welcome," she said.

"You speak for the traders, yes?" Etena asked her.

"No," she said.

Etena's breath drew in with a hiss. "I shall throttle that boy," she said as if to herself.

"Lady," Emry said—rude, if he had been in a Mother's house in his own country, but here a man could venture great liberties. She listened, as he had hoped, and did not cut him off for his presumption. "Lady, he only did as he was told. The caravan-master speaks for the traders. Shall I fetch him?"

The king's wife paused a moment, frowning. Then she said, "No. Not yet." She glanced at Rhian. "He will do as you bid him, yes?"

"I can ask," said Rhian. "He can choose to obey—or not."

Etena did not seem pleased by that, at all. "Have you people no leaders?" she demanded sharply. "No kings? No one who speaks and you obey?"

"Certainly," Rhian said. "We have the Mother. She speaks for the Goddess."

"Is there no Mother in your caravan?"

Emry's jaw clenched. Rhian betrayed no apprehension. "There is the caravan-master," she said.

"And you? What are you?"

"I am the White Mare's servant," Rhian said. "I go where she carries me."

Etena swept up her hand as if to cast aside Rhian's words. "You— guard. Fetch the caravan-master."

"And while he goes," said Rhian, "will you tell me what you wanted of me?"

Etena had the look of one on a raw edge of temper. She was not accustomed to uncertainty, Emry could see. "I wished to offer a trade. But if you have no power over the traders, you can be of no use to me."

Emry had begun his retreat, but something in her glance made him pause. Her eyes were on him again, fixed in a way that tightened the skin between his shoulderblades.

"I have power over the traders," Rhian said. "Tell me."

"I wish to trade," Etena said. "Give me the captain of your guard."

Rhian's eyes went wide—but no wider surely than Emry's own. "And for what would you trade him?"

"I will trade," said Etena, "for one of our own. I can give you the king's son."

"The king has many sons," Rhian said with more presence of mind than Emry would have had.

"You know which I mean."

Rhian made no attempt to deny it. "How do you propose to do it?"

"That shall be my secret," Etena said, "but be assured that I will do it."

"And then? We leave, with the king's heir loaded among the baggage— and the whole tribe comes after us with chariots?"

Etena's eyes barely flickered. "I will see to it that the tribe does not follow you."

"For how long?"

"For as long as is needed."

Rhian tilted her head as if she could seriously consider such a thing. "Very well," she said. "I'll speak with the caravan-master."

Etena accepted that. More: she let them go, even Emry, and made no move to stop them.

It was all Emry could do to keep his tongue between his teeth, and almost more than he could do to walk from the tent and not bolt onto the steppe. Rhian's pace was leisurely—wise, but it came close to driving him mad.

He was trained as prince and warrior. That saved him. It kept him on his feet, silent, striding in Rhian's wake through this camp that, if the king's wife had her way, would be his prison.

⇒ ⇐

"This is the Goddess' gift," Rhian said.

They were gathered in Emry's tent: Rhian, Emry, Bran and Conn, Hoel the caravan-master and a handful of Emry's young men. Those last had not been invited, but they had seen Emry's face as he followed Rhian into the camp. Nothing short of brute force would have kept them away.

Mabon and Dal busied themselves in rolling up and binding the sides of the tent to let in the light and air. It was maybe not wise, for then everyone could see their conference, but it prevented listening at tent-walls, and above all it gave Emry space to breathe.

He needed a great deal of it. He was glad to sit, to take the wine that someone handed him, to drink so deep and so fast that his senses reeled.

The hand had been Rhian's. She sat at his feet, arm across his knees, and said, "You look ghastly."

He was incapable of coherent speech. She rose, swaying dizzily in his wine-blurred sight, and vanished. After an instant he felt her hands on his shoulders, working into knots that had tightened to pain, and easing them out one by one.

While she did that, Hoel said, "This is the truth? The woman asked to buy one of us?"

"They do that among the tribes," Conn said. "They trade things of value for battle-captives. Usually it's women. Usually," he said, "they kill the men."

"Supposing she wants him dead," said Dal, "why doesn't she just kill him?"

"He's a king's heir," Mabon said. "The gods may take revenge on her for killing him—and it will be worse for him if he's sold away as a captive. She'll keep his body alive, but kill his pride."

"And mine?" Emry had found words at last. "What about mine?"

"Obviously we won't be trading you," Mabon said.

"Why not?"

They all gaped at Rhian.

"Did we ever promise that he would stay?" She regarded them all as women often did, with patience sorely taxed by the dullness of male wit. "Here is our chance. We can take the one we want, thank the Goddess profoundly for her gift, and escape without any of the danger we feared. And you, prince of Lir: you may linger a while, take pleasure with this woman, learn more of the tribe. Then when we've had time to return to Lir, you can escape. The Goddess will protect you. This is all her doing; she'll never let you be harmed."

"We can't do that," Mabon said before Emry could open his mouth. "We can't leave our prince with these savages."

"Not so savage," she said. "Think what he can learn—what knowledge he can bring back to us."

"You don't know, do you?" Mabon demanded. "You don't know what it means that a king's wife wants a man to serve her."

"She wants him for her bed," Rhian said. "That's obvious."

"King's wives don't take men for their beds," Mabon said. "Not men entire. They geld them, lady, and keep them to look at."

"No," said Rhian. "Not that one. Not with those eyes. She wants a man, not a gelding."

"A man of his age," Conn said, "like a stallion gelded late, would be enough for her purpose. It's how it's done, lady. It's the only way she'll be allowed to keep him, and not be killed herself for betraying her husband."

"I don't believe that," Rhian said stubbornly. "She has power enough, and strength of will enough, to do as she pleases. She may pretend that she's done the necessary, but she won't. She'll want the full power that he has, and the danger that goes with it."

"We can't risk it," said Mabon, who seemed to have decided that if Emry would not speak, then he must. "We can't lose our prince. He's too valuable to us and to Lir."

"I may be of more value here."

Emry had some of his wits back. His voice was his own again. He could think, after a fashion.

He went on steadily, with almost his usual firmness. "I think Rhian sees the truth. The king's wife wants all of me. If I let her have me, and watch and listen and do my best to seem harmless, I'll serve Lir better than if I simply ride away. Who knows? I might even be able to turn the chariots aside, keep them from crossing the river. I may be able to prevent the war altogether."

Mabon was not listening. "We had a plan," he said. "If we follow it—"

"We'll be pursued sooner rather than later." Emry cut off his protests. "No, cousin. Think! This lets you go all the way to Lir under the queen's protection. By the time I come back, you'll be making chariots and training horses. The war will be well begun."

"If you come back," said Mabon. "They'll kill you, cousin. This is your death you're chasing after."

"I hope not," Emry said. "But it does seem that the Goddess asks this of me. Should I refuse her?"

"She will guard you," Rhian said.

He looked at her, remembering who and what she was. Mother's daughter. White Mare's servant. He might be mad to trust her, whom the priestesses had called the doom of Lir. And yet she was of his blood. The same womb had borne them. He could not believe that she would condemn him to death or worse.

"This is why I came here," he said. "To win us this. It's a fair trade, yes? Prince for prince."

"It is fair," Hoel conceded, "though we're not given to trading human souls. If we offer treasure, particularly gold—"

"She does love gold," said Rhian, "but if we offer her that, she may wonder why we want her husband's heir so badly. She may begin to reflect on what he knows, and what he can teach us. We can't give her time to do that. Much as she loves gold, it can't keep her besotted. It can't talk sweetness to her in the nights. Nor can it convince her to turn the war away from our country."

"I will do it," Emry said in a tone that silenced them all. "Hoel, go. Play the trader. Gain us as much as you can. Win from her a surety that you will not be pursued. Let her be concerned with capturing and securing the prisoner."

"I think," Hoel said, "that you should come with me. Best she see what she lusts after, even as she haggles with me for it."

Emry's privates tried to crawl up into his belly at thought of entering that dim and smoky place again. But if he would do this, he would live there for Goddess knew how long. He stiffened his spine and firmed his spirit. "Go on, then. Let's get it over."

For a moment he feared that Hoel would bid them wait, but the caravan-master nodded. "Yes. This one we end quickly."

That, Emry thought, was a mercy. There would be little enough of it hereafter.

32

Etena of the Windriders bought Emry prince of Lir in return for the living person of Minas the prince and for a quantity of gold that would, she assured Hoel, convince her people that it was a fair exchange. She was getting, as far as he would let her know, a captain of guards from his caravan—and a young and handsome one, too.

They made the bargain in the secrecy of the king's tent, well guarded against spying eyes. It would be complete when the caravan left and Emry stayed behind. As to how Minas would be delivered to them, the king's wife said, "You will receive it all together on the day after tomorrow, in the morning. See that you are ready by then to leave us. Need I bid you keep silent as to the particulars of this trade?"

"I think not," Hoel said dryly.

"Good, then it is done," said Etena. "Go. We shall not speak again."

But as Emry moved to escape in Hoel's wake, she stopped him. "Guardsman," she said.

He turned to face her. He kept his eyes on his feet, although she was veiled.

She rose from her heap of cushions. She was a small woman, round and full-breasted—what he might in Lir have reckoned a delightful morsel, a plump partridge. But this was no toothsome bird. She was as dangerous as a starving she-wolf.

She had to stand on tiptoe to span the breadth of his shoulders with her hands, and to run her fingers through the curls of his beard. He willed himself to stand still and not shy away. This he must endure. This the Goddess had laid on him.

Etena lowered her hand and stood looking up at him. He had seen men look at horses so, with pride and possession. "You are even more beautiful than I remembered," she said.

He did not know what to say to that.

It seemed he need say nothing. "Go," she said. "Until your caravan leaves, you belong to them. Let us both remember that."

He bent his head and let himself be dismissed.

⇒ ⇐

When Rhian found him, he was standing by the riverbank, upstream and out of sight of the camp. He had been swimming in the water. His clothes were in a heap beside him, and his hair was a wet tail down his back. He had shut his face tight, and his heart, too.

"Is it that unbearable?" she asked him.

He sank down on his heels, hands fisted on his thighs. "I can learn to bear it," he said.

"If you truly can't," said Rhian, "we'll do as we planned before."

"No." He rolled the tension out of his shoulders, and drew a long shuddering breath. "Then she'll come hunting me as well as her own prince. What's done is done. I consented to it. I'll not go back on my word."

"She won't geld you," Rhian said.

"No," he said. "She won't." He believed it, too. Her touch, her eyes—she wanted all of him.

Rhian dropped to the grass beside him. "This is the Goddess' will, or I would never have urged it on you."

"Nor would I ever have accepted it." He turned to face her. "Sister, believe me when I say, I do this of my free will. It only horrified me for a while. Now I know I can do it. What's so difficult about it, after all? I please a woman who wants me to please her. I live with a tribe that treats its own well enough. Everything I see and hear, I'll take back with me, the better to wage the war when it comes to us."

"You're a brave man," she said.

He heard no mockery in her voice. "I'm no braver than I have to be."

"That's brave enough."

She had been eyeing the water. He watched without surprise as she stripped off her breeches and dived smoothly from the bank. She swam as well as she did everything else: with easy grace, as if there were no effort in it.

It was astonishing, he thought, that she had lived her life in a village as small as Long Ford, and no one had ever wondered to find such a swan amid the common geese. If the priestesses truly had feared what she would become, then they had been fools to let her live.

Now he the prince, the heir, the one born with blessings on his head, was sold a slave to the conquering tribe, and she was going to the city that had been forbidden her. "Strange are the ways of the Goddess," he said to the air.

⇒ ⇐

Minas heard the man's deep voice speaking in a language he did not understand. He had gone hunting that morning, because the young men's tent needed meat—and never mind that he had both yearned and dreaded to see the western woman again. He was fleeing her as much as hunting down a fat doe for his fellows. He had come back, he thought, by a way known to few, and there the gods had set them, the woman in the water, the man on the bank, both as naked as they were born.

He shocked himself with the force of his jealousy. Even knowing that that was her brother—that they should see each other so, and be so at ease . . . he ground his teeth at the thought of it.

He hid in the grass and watched them. The man lolled at his ease. The woman rose out of the river like the goddess she was. Water streamed down her body. She lay beside her brother, close but not touching. They spoke together in their own language, idly, as if they had no worry in the world.

Minas wondered if they were speaking of him. As soon as he thought it, he felt a fool. Of course they were not. Why should they? He doubted that he mattered excessively to either of them.

He was in a black mood and no mistake. Dias had taxed him with it this morning, when he stalked out with his bow and spear, and would accept no companion, not even the brother he loved most. He had growled wordlessly and left Dias still upbraiding the morning air.

The traders would be leaving soon. Traders never stayed long; they always moved on. She would go with them. If he saw her again, it would be in another age of the world.

And that he could not bear. Twice now she had lain with him, and when he tried to think of other women, he saw only her face. When he tried to remember the others he had lain with, his memory called up her body. She had swept all the rest away.

He would not let her leave. He could not. And yet, how was he to do that? She did as she pleased. Prince he might be, but she was a goddess. She would laugh at anything he did to bind her.

As he lay in the grass and watched, her brother sat up. She began to comb and plait his hair as she had done for Minas—was it only yesterday? Jealousy gusted anew, so fierce that he was like to die of it. This was her brother. She was his sister. There was nothing between them that spoke of man and woman. They were as easy with one another as Minas was with Dias. Yet he burned to be the one who sat so, with her light fingers in his hair, and her breath gusting soft on his back.

It took her a long while to make order of that thick black tangle— much longer than it had taken her with Minas. She was patient. The man was less so, but she cuffed him when he fidgeted. He submitted as any sensible brother should do, growling a little, but half-heartedly. Minas could imagine what she was telling him: that beauty has its price, and it was his duty to pay it.

When her brother was as tidy as he could be, he returned the favor. She fidgeted even worse than he had. He laughed at her for it.

Minas ground his fists into the earth. He would go to her tonight, as she had gone twice to him. He would bid her stay when the others went. He would beg her if he must. He would give her all that he had, trade her his every treasure, if she would stay with the People. With him.

He slipped away before she saw him. It was as hard a thing as he had ever done, but he had a little sense left. If she knew that he had been desperate enough to spy on her from the grass, she would drive a bitter bargain. Worse: she would refuse to hear him at all, but mock him for a pitiful besotted thing, and leave him to die for want of her.

⇒ ⇐

The young men were glad to dine on venison that evening. Minas, who had hunted and brought it back, had no stomach for his own kill. They had kumiss, and that he could swallow; and Aias had procured a skin of wine, Minas did not know where, nor care.

His friends and yearmates were not the only ones round that fire that night. Some of the king's men had wandered over; most were his blood kin, sons of his father. They had brought wine, a better vintage than Aias'. It was good wine, sweet and strong, and no one was overscrupulous in watering it.

It was a grand feast. In the morning, Minas thought, he would go to the woman, stride up to her and claim her. How could she refuse him? He was the king's heir of the People.

He told his brothers of this, at length, in figures of noble oratory. It dawned on him somewhere in the middle that he might do better to tell Dias. Dias he loved; Dias he trusted. He did not trust any of these young men with their wild white hair. But Dias was not there. He had not seen Dias since the morning. These were his brothers, too. They were his great good friends. They gave him wine. They gave him kumiss. They listened gladly when he told them of the woman whom he must, he utterly must have.

It was good wine. Very, very good wine. He swam in the river of it. He danced round the fire, light as air, swift as a flame. All the faces now were narrow ruddy-browed faces. They were all his brothers, his blood. The rest had whirled away with the sparks from the fire.

"A raid," they were singing. "Let us ride on a raid!"

He paused. He was far gone in wine, but a minute part of him found wits to ask, "What, tonight?"

"Why not tonight?" they said. "Are we not strong? Are we not wonderful? Can we not see in the dark?"

"I have eyes like a hunting cat," he declared.

"So," they said. "Lead us! Let us raid—westward. Let us find a tribe that still has its gold and its women. Let us take it and conquer it and bring back the spoils. And then," they said, "you can lay all of them at her feet. She'll love you then. She'll fall headlong into your arms."

"*She*," he said distinctly, "will fall into *my* arms. Not yours! Not anybody's. Mine."

"Yours," they agreed willingly. "She is yours. You'll win her with the prizes of battle."

"All mine," he said. "Mine."

They all had arms about one another in a long chain of laughing, staggering men. Horses, he thought. Chariots. They needed horses and chariots. "We raid in chariots," he reminded them.

"In chariots!" they echoed joyfully.

It was a grand confusion, finding horses and chariots in the dark, harnessing them, gathering weapons, preparing for a raid that was altogether glorious and altogether mad. Adis declared that he had found an unconquered tribe within a day's chariot-ride. It was small but it was rich, and it thought itself safely hidden in the vastness of the steppe. "Its priests and shamans are strong," he said, "but I found them, I, because the gods love me."

"And us!" his brothers sang.

They mounted the chariots two by two. Minas rode as warrior—of course. Adis was his charioteer. The horses were fresh and wild in the night. They leaped at the touch of the lash.

The wind was stronger than wine. It whipped Minas' face and sent his hair streaming out behind him. Something bumped against his foot. A wineskin—wonderful! He hooked it with his toe and flipped it into his hands—laughing as the chariot rocked and swayed—and drank till the world reeled.

It reeled straight down into the dark. There were stars in the heart of it, and the murmur of wind, and a sound like a wolf's laughter.

33

Rhian, hidden in shadows, saw how the king's men—his own brothers—plied Minas with wine and laid their mistress' spell on him. This served her purpose amply, and yet she did not have to like the taste of it. It hurt to see him staggering, giggling, his lovely keen face gone slack and stupid.

When they took chariots and rode on their lie of a raid, she found the mare beside her. She had barely time to swing astride before the mare was in motion.

The king's men rode far enough out to escape any scouts or spies, but not so far that it would take any of them overlong to creep back toward the camp. There they stopped, circling round Minas' chariot. Minas sprawled in it, snoring loud enough for Rhian to hear. His brothers rolled him out onto the ground.

She could not see what they did, but the snoring stopped abruptly. They stripped him, bound him, wrapped him in something dark and voluminous. Then they flung the limp bundle of him over the back of a horse. One of the brothers rode with it, leading it. The rest circled and circled, trampling all traces of what they had done there, and rode away westward. They had not been lying about the raid, then; or they would not wish their fellows of the tribe to think that they had.

It was terribly clever. Rhian pondered any number of things, wise and not so wise and frankly insane. But the mare had her own purpose, and that was to follow the man who had taken Minas.

He was not riding direct to the camp, though it was nearly dawn. He had angled off somewhat to the north. Rhian rode as close as she dared. He had no apparent suspicion of her presence: he rode in leisurely fashion, asking little of his horse. Sometimes he drank from a skin of wine—not, she would have wagered, the skin that Minas had had in the chariot. That was drugged, she was sure.

The sky had lightened in the east when he stopped. They were farther out from the tribe's camp than they should have been, and not angling closer. The place he chose had nothing to distinguish it from a myriad other hollows in the endless roll of the steppe. It was convenient, that was all. He slid from his horse's back and turned toward the horse on which Minas was flung like a sack of trade-goods.

He nigh jumped out of his skin. Rhian smiled at him in the pale light, sitting on the back of her pale mare. "Good morning, king's son," she said. "I see you have my baggage."

The boy was too astonished to go for his sword. Rhian's smile widened at that. "Go on with your raid," she said. "I'll take this as we all agreed."

"But she never said—" The boy bit his lip. Rhian could see how glad he was, how eager to ride with the others, and how sulky he had been to be relegated to this duty. And what, she thought, might it have been? Might he have been bidden to deliver a dead man to the traders?

She sweetened her smile even further and said, "Surely you didn't think you'd be denied a raid? Here, give me the rein—and be quick. If you ride fast, you'll catch them."

That might or might not have been true, but clearly he wanted it to be. He all but flung the rein at her, scrambled onto his horse, and kicked it into a run.

Rhian drew a long breath. The shape on the horse's back never moved. It was too securely wrapped for her to hear if it breathed.

She had to trust that their poison had not killed him, and that they had bound him living in his wrappings. Time was short. The caravan would be ready by sunrise. She had to have him secure in the baggage then, one bundle among many, neither more nor less valuable than anything else the caravan carried.

And yet if she rode back now, she would be seen; the tribesmen would know that this baggage mattered. And if they asked to see what was in it—to trade for it. . . .

The horse on which he was bound was of no particular distinction: bay without markings, thicker and heavier than the chariot-teams, a beast of burden rather than a prince's prize. It looked, in fact, a great deal like the caravan-guards' horses.

Rhian undid the bindings and eased the dead weight to the ground. She arranged it as best she could, and hoped it was face up and alive. "Guard him," she said to the mare.

The mare was grazing with perfect aplomb. She did not acknowledge Rhian, but neither did she fling up her tail and bolt. Rhian mounted the bay and turned him toward the camp. She could only pray that when they came this way, the mare would still be here, and her charge with her, and that he was still alive.

⇔ ⇐

The caravan was all but ready to go. Most of the gold had come. They were waiting for the rest of it, not obviously, but she knew the look. And there was Emry, the only guard not in armor. More of the king's white-haired boys stood about him. They were guarding him, though like the caravaneers, they were not proclaiming the fact to the world.

Rhian had left the bay horse among the herds and walked to the remains of the traders' camp. The tents were down and packed, the line of horses and donkeys falling into place. She slipped in between Hoel and Conn and said, "He's on the steppe. The mare's guarding him."

Neither of them permitted his expression to change, but Conn's eyes sharpened. "Treachery?"

"It seemed so," she said. She smiled at a tribesman who was eyeing her sidelong, and reduced him to blushing confusion.

"Then we can go," Hoel said. His signal was subtle: a glance, a lift of the chin. It brought his people together. In a bare few moments, the caravan was fully formed, gathered and moving away from the camp.

A fair number of tribesmen had come to see them go. Rhian mounted one of the guards' remounts, falling in with the guards. They all, even she, did not look back to where Emry was standing. Their hearts were with him, but if their eyes followed suit, one of them would break. They could not do that. Not for themselves. Not for Lir. And certainly not for Emry the prince.

⇔ ⇐

Emry knew why they had turned their backs on him with such seeming cruelty. He did his best to believe that it did not hurt. Why should it? It was done to preserve his life.

They rode away safe. He, with whom they had bought this, stood alone in a tribe of strangers. His weapons, his armor, were in the caravan. He was a slave now. He owned nothing, not even his body.

His keepers closed in. They made it clear enough where he was to go. He put on his most harmless expression and let them herd him. That, to his surprise, was not into the king's tent.

He knew real fear then. He had caught what Rhian said to Hoel and Conn. If they had intended to deliver a dead man—might they intend to keep a corpse in his place?

If he was to die, then that was the Goddess' will. He would not shame her by weeping and begging for mercy.

They took him to a tent, after all, not far from the king's. It was filthy and cluttered and had obviously never seen the hand of a woman. From the look and smell of it, it belonged to the men who herded him.

Their leader pointed to a corner. "You sleep there," he said. "You eat what we leave. You fetch our wood, draw our water. You serve us, and you live. You refuse . . ." He stabbed with his hand, straight to the heart.

"I understand," Emry said. He did not, not entirely, but he understood enough. He could play the servant. That was what the king's wife wanted, it seemed; strange that she should pay so high for a slave for her husband's sons, but who knew what was in her heart? Certainly not Emry.

He did not wait for the king's sons to leave. He set to work silently, making order of that midden of a tent.

The king's sons lingered for a while, watching, but he was doing nothing of compelling interest. They wandered off one by one. Soon enough he was alone. He went on cleaning and scouring, because it kept him busy; and busy, he had less leisure to think.

When he was done, he would wager that these young men had never seen their tent so orderly. His corner had a pallet in it, and a coverlet of tanned cowhide that was not too frayed. His belongings, such as he had kept, were secure in his pack, rolled and flattened into a bolster for his bed. It was rough comfort, but it would do.

Even as he pondered a bath in the river, one of the king's sons came in search of relief for his hunger. Emry watched him consider striking a blow when he found that Emry had done nothing about the daymeal. Something held him back: royal orders, perhaps? He snapped instead, "Find me something to eat. Be quick about it!"

Emry bent his head as if to one who was entitled to respect. "If my lord will bring somewhat to cook, then I will cook it. Or will bread be enough?"

"Meat," said the boy. "I want meat."

"Bring me meat," said Emry, "and you shall have your dinner."

The boy looked ready to strike Emry in spite of the king's wife. Emry braced himself for it. But one of the others was calling in the language of the tribe. The boy aimed a half-hearted cuff at Emry's head, which Emry eluded easily.

Such reprieves would not be frequent, Emry thought. He set to work making bread, for which at least he had the wherewithal. Meat he would not have unless he hunted for it, and he had no weapon. Nor was he at all certain that he would be allowed to wander away from the camp.

"Don't fret over Samias," someone said behind him. "He's all snarl and no teeth."

Emry looked over his shoulder. This one of the king's sons wore his own hair in its own curly dark-brown semblance, and his face was broader and blunter than the others'—more like Emry's own. "Dias," Emry said. "You are the prince Dias."

Dias nodded. "And you are the westerner whom my mother traded for gold. Were you expecting a life of ease in her company?"

"Truth?" Emry asked. "I was expecting to have my throat slit as soon as my kinsmen rode out of sight."

Dias laughed, as much startled as amused, and squatted beside Emry. "So why did you do it?"

This was an amiable man, and a pleasant man, and a very dangerous one. He was Etena's son, and the prince Minas' best-loved brother. Emry answered him with a shrug and a lift of a flour-smeared hand. "I was curious. Maybe I was bored. It's not the adventure I'd thought, standing guard on a caravan. Mostly one rides. One rides a great deal. Then one stands about and looks fierce while the traders trade. And there's precious little fighting."

"You think we'll let you fight with us?"

"I'm good at it," Emry said.

"You think so?"

"I know so."

Dias looked him up and down. "Yes, you look strong. But can we trust you?"

"Probably not," Emry said, "if you ride against my people. But otherwise . . . I gave my word. I belong to your mother. I'll fight as well for her as if she were my own."

"Is that what you think she wanted you for?"

"She wanted me for my pretty face. But she'll be needing to get some use of me. These boys need a keeper, and badly, but there's more I can do. I'm sure she knows it."

"Do you have no pride?"

Dias did not ask it in shock or disgust, but as if he truly wanted to know. Emry considered the different sides of the question. Pride to a tribesman, pride to a man of the Goddess' country, pride to a prince from Lir. His answer came a little slow, but he meant what he said. "I have pride enough and to spare. I'll not creep and moan and lament my condition. No one here will see me as less than a keeper of his word."

"You are . . . different," Dias said.

"I'm a westerner," said Emry.

The bread was made. He buried it in the ashes of the fire to bake, and sat on his heels to wait for it.

He thought Dias might leave, but he lingered. "I warned you before," he said after a while, "and this I suppose was your response: the caravan left, but you took the bargain my mother offered. You know she'll be the death of you."

"I hope not," said Emry.

"She breaks men's spirits," Dias said. "And that may be worse."

"The Goddess protects me," Emry said.

"Truly," said Dias, "I hope that she does."

So did Emry, but he would not say such a thing to this man. Well-disposed he might be, but he was not a friend. Emry could have no friends here, only enemies of his enemies. And if Dias knew what had become of the brother whom he loved . . .

It would all come in its time. That was truth, and Emry could be sure of it.

34

The caravan rode away from the camp under a strange, sultry, heavy sky. The heat was oppressive, the air thick, cloying in the throat. Far off as the day lengthened, Rhian heard a mutter of thunder and saw the flicker of lightning.

They went as quickly as Hoel judged prudent, which seemed draggingly slow. A handful of boys and young men of the tribe had followed them. The caravan could not seem too hasty, nor could they turn at once toward the place where Rhian had left the mare and the prince. Both of whom, she prayed, were still there, and still alive.

Near noon at last, they saw the pale shape of the mare grazing on a hilltop. A dark bundle lay near her. By then they were alone in the sea of grass, no pursuit, no companions, not even a vulture circling overhead. Rhian flung herself from the grey stallion's back, running headlong up the hill.

The bundle was stirring. She ripped off its bindings and pulled the wrappings from his sweating face. He was scarlet with the heat, gasping, thrashing blindly, but there was no awareness in his eyes. They were blurred with the drug his brothers had tricked him into drinking.

Conn dropped beside her, and Mabon beyond him. "Do you have the potion you brewed for him?" Conn demanded.

"Yes," she said, "but—"

"Give him enough to put him under," said Conn. "We can't afford a delay—we're still too close to the tribe. If hunters come out here, or raiders—"

"Raiders," she said. It had been growing in her since the dawn, a thought so wild, so mad, that she had not allowed herself to finish thinking it. But here under the lowering sky, with the heat weighing on her like a hand, she knew what was laid on them to do. "Conn, take him, get him on a horse, guard him and keep him safe. Mabon, call the rest of the company. Bid them string their bows and sharpen their spears. We're going hunting."

"But you can't—" Conn began.

"There are a dozen chariots out there," Rhian said, "and a dozen teams, and a following of remounts. Trained horses, Conn. War-chariots. Driven by drunken boys who will never expect a raid on their raid. If we come on them with the dark, we can take them all."

"You are completely mad," Conn said.

"I suppose I am," she said. "But this is a gift, just as the prince was. How can we fail to take it?"

"These are men in chariots," Conn said. "We have horses, well enough, but if they ride against us—"

"We'll take them in camp," she said. "It takes time to harness chariots, far more time than we'll give them. We'll be fighting men on foot, slowed with wine, and at most a man or two on horseback."

"And if they're ready for us?"

"If they're ready and waiting," she said, "we'll know it was folly, and we'll escape before they see us."

"It will never be as easy as that," Mabon said. But if Conn had hoped to find an ally, Mabon swiftly proved him mistaken. "If they really are camped for the night, and if we catch them soon enough, we'll take them. And if we stampede the horses—"

"We need those horses," Dal said, "to pull the chariots. Let some of us draw them off while the rest fall on the camp. They're all stallions, yes? And we have the mare."

"Yes," said Rhian. "Yes! The mare can call them to her. Without horses they'll be helpless."

"I suppose you know where to find them," Conn said, "and can come on them before dark."

"The mare knows," Rhian said. Her eyes took in all of Emry's young men. "Well, sirs? Are you with me?"

They were, to a man. And so, unwillingly but unflinchingly, was Conn. "At least one of us should have a little sense," he muttered.

It was not easy to entrust Minas to Hoel and the caravan, but Rhian was driven by more than her own will. The mare waited, pawing impatiently, while Rhian dosed the prince with her tincture of herbs in strong wine. When he was deep asleep, breathing steadily and strongly, Rhian tore herself away from him. "Keep him alive," she commanded Hoel. "Keep him safe."

The caravan-master was keeping his thoughts very carefully to himself. "I will guard him," he said. "We'll come to you by morning."

The mare smote the ground with both front feet and squealed. Rhian knew better than to linger in the face of that.

⇀ ↽

The mare knew where she was going. The pace she set was not quite killingly fast. Rhian crouched over her neck and clutched mane and let herself be carried. The others were swept in her wake.

The sky was like a vast colorless hand, pressing down on her skull. The sun seemed to hang motionless in it. There was no wind but that of their speed.

They paused twice to rest the horses, to let them graze a little, to drink from streams that crossed their path. How they found those on the steppe in the summer, when even rivers ran dry, only the mare knew. This was her venture. They were but her servants.

The charioteers must have made camp early. Their chariots rested in a circle, the horses in a herd under little guard. They were well into the last of their wine.

It was still some time until sunset, but the sun was hidden in a bank of cloud edged with lightnings. It had built along the horizon while they rode. It heaped on itself, climbing the flat pallor of the sky.

In that greenish dusk, the riders paused and began to dismount. Rhian stopped them. "No. We go now."

They exchanged glances. She knew what they were thinking. No time to reconnoiter, no time to be certain that the men in the camp were all there were; that there were no scouts hidden in ambush.

This was the mare's battle. Mabon bowed his head to it. Rhian left him there, borne away on the mare's back, angling toward the horses. Those must have wandered off from their masters, for surely even drunken boys would not have set the herd out of sight of the camp. Only one man stood guard, and he was asleep with his head on a half-empty skin of either wine or kumiss.

The horses were grazing, but uneasily, snatching mouthfuls of grass, watching the mare as she came toward them. She sidled coyly, turning her rump to waft her scent in their faces, borne on the thin wind that had begun to blow.

Nostrils fluttered. One of the stallions squealed softly. Another rumbled deep in his throat. With a flick of the tail that was pure laughter, the mare lured them out onto the open steppe.

Behind them, under and about the sound of hooves, Rhian heard the clamor of battle. She had never heard it before, but there was no mistaking it. Metal on metal. Shouts, cries. Screams of pain.

Completely without thought, she flung herself from the mare's back. She landed rolling, somersaulted to her feet, and ran headlong back the way she had come. She had no sword or spear, no blade but the knife she used for cutting meat, but she had a bow and a full quiver. She strung the bow as she ran.

Battle was a milling, scrambling, untidy thing. Surprised and unhorsed the tribesmen might be, giddy with wine or dazed with sleep, but they fought as they had been bred and trained to fight. The men from Lir had been wise, had divided them from each other, each choosing his own target, but Rhian saw a thing that made her heart sink. The men of Lir struck to stun or wound. The men of the tribe struck to kill.

She nocked arrow to string. She was on a rise of ground, which was well; she had a great advantage. Her mind was clear. The world seemed to slow. She had ample time to think, to choose her target.

Too much time, maybe. One of them killed Conn. She saw the blow, saw it begin, saw it fall. The copper sword hacked his head half off his shoulders. The tribesman who wielded it was familiar—they all were. He laughed as he wrenched the blade out of the still-twitching body and whirled on Mabon.

She aimed for the heart. The wind was treacherous, gusting, whirling bits of dust and dried grasses, tangling the men's hair in their faces. It whipped a streamer of hair across her eyes just as she loosed.

The arrow flew straight and true. Just as with a deer in the wood. Just so. It pierced the boy's narrow breast with force enough to whirl him half about. His expression was incredulous.

Rhian had no time to waste in reflecting that she had taken a life— that she had killed. She nocked again. Another wild-haired boy, another bloody blade—spear this time. She could not see whom he had killed. It did not matter. She shot him in the throat, not intending that, but the wind had a mind of its own.

They had all seen her now. They called to one another, drawing together, beating off the men of Lir with ease that was almost contemptuous. They laughed at wounds. Only death won their respect.

She had given them death. Two of them stayed behind to hold off her kinsmen. The rest dropped flat in the grass and slithered up the hill toward her. They were as fast as snakes, and their eyes were fully as cold. She saw in them the death she had given, returned in full measure.

Thunder rumbled. Lightning cracked. The wind rose to a gale. There was no shooting of arrows in that. Rhian drew her bronze dagger. She had no thought of running.

These tribesmen must not escape. They must die, or she must. Otherwise they would bring down the whole of their tribe on the caravan, and then on Lir.

With a sound like a wolf's howl, Mabon cut down one of the men who blocked his way, and fell on the rearmost of those who stalked Rhian.

As if that had roused the rest, they surged in his wake. Their blood was up at last. They had remembered what they were trained for. They were defending the mare's servant, the Mother's daughter of Lir.

Dal was dead with a spear in his heart, and Gwion who had been Emry's cousin. And Conn—Conn was dead on the steppe that had become his home. The others were wounded in varying degrees. Rodry might not live out the night.

But all the men of the steppe had fallen, every one. Their horses, their chariots were safe. All the harness, the weapons, half a dozen skins of kumiss, had fallen to the victors. Rhian must think of that, must see it as a victory, even though the man she had long thought of as her father had died for her whim.

They gathered all their plunder together in the teeth of the wind. Lightning danced from cloud to cloud. Sometimes they saw it strike—not always afar off. There was no rain. The air was grittily dry. Rhian's skin prickled. When she reached to scrape her hair out of her face, it snapped at her fingers, clinging to them, tangling worse than before.

"We can't linger here!" Hoel bellowed in her ear, fighting to be heard above the wind. "But we can't go on, either. This is the wind of the gods below, the wind of fire. If it kindles the grass . . ."

The grass was dry. The women of the tribe had been using twists of it for tinder. If fire began on the steppe, with this wind to drive it, it would burn with a terrible swift flame.

"We'll hitch up the chariots," Rhian shouted back at Hoel. "We'll take the dead with us—all of them—and take every vestige of the camp, and leave the rest to the wind. We'll get the wind at our backs—see, it's blowing westward. We'll take shelter past yonder ridge. Doesn't it dip down into a valley?"

"No closed places," Hoel said. "No traps. If the grass catches fire, we'll burn like rats in a kiln."

"But the ridge will block the wind," Rhian said, "and maybe the fire too, if it comes."

"It will come," Hoel said. But he did not try to stop her.

She had only memory to go by, and two dozen fretting, anxious horses to bind with the tangle of lines and fastenings that made up their harness; and night was falling fast. But Bran's eye was quick and his memory good, and he had studied the chariots more carefully than she had. He instructed the others, such as were not too badly hurt to walk. They managed, if not well, then at least adequately. The lightning was nearly constant, granting flashes of vision. It was enough, just.

Rhian took the reins of the first team, a pair of long-legged blacks.

There were not enough men, wounded or hale, to drive all the chariots, but their teams would follow the mare, she hoped, and the lead of their own herdmates, as did the remounts and the guards' own horses.

She could barely see the team behind her. The mare was a white glimmer ahead. She followed the mare from flash to flash of lightning, through the by now incessant growl of thunder, with the wind buffeting her back. She did not pretend even to herself that she was driving the chariot. None of them was. The mare led, and the stallions followed. She wound the reins about the pole and clutched the sides and let herself be carried wherever the Goddess willed.

35

Rodry died in the chariot that carried him to such refuge as there was. They did indeed find shelter below the ridge, up against a sudden steep slope. The wind swooped and howled above them, but the air below was still. There was no water here, nothing to drink but what they had brought with them from the charioteers' camp.

They buried the dead under the loom of the cliff, in the sand and scree that was at least easier to dig through than the matted grass of the steppe. They laid the charioteers together, with respect, for they had died in honorable battle, and their own they laid side by side and a little apart. Then they built a cairn over them all, no very great or high one, but enough to keep wild beasts from digging up the bones.

There were no words to say over them that could be heard above the wind, but they all prayed silently, gathered in a circle. No one wept, not even Rhian. That would come later, when there was time.

They snatched what sleep they could, with men taking turns on guard, hour by grueling hour. It seemed a long time until dawn. The wind never slackened. The lightning did not cease its lashing of the steppe.

Somewhere in that endless night, Rhian began to smell smoke. She might be dreaming it. Lightning had its own sharp reek, and the air was full of it.

Bran was on guard just then, sitting on the edge of their makeshift camp, beyond the circle of chariots that enclosed both men and horses. He had his back to one of the chariots, his face toward the shrieking dark.

She crouched beside him in the flicker of the lightning, and bent toward his ear. "There's smoke in the wind."

He nodded. "The grass is burning behind us."

"That will destroy whatever traces we left behind," she observed.

He nodded again. He did not say what he must be thinking, as she was. That the caravan was still up there, moving slowly, at donkey-speed.

And that Minas was with it, the prize they had won at the cost of Emry's body and perhaps his life, and the lives of Conn and Dal, Gwion and Rodry.

"At dawn," she said, "I'll take the mare. I'll find them."

"You can't risk that," he said. "Send someone else."

"No," said Rhian. "No one else can ride the mare. You go on. Make for the river. If we don't catch you before then, we'll find you in World's End."

"We can't leave you behind," he said. "The steppe will burn. If you go back—"

"We need the prince of chariots," she said. "But if we lose him, at least we have the chariots themselves, and the horses. It's a better outcome than we ever hoped for."

"Not if we lose you."

She laid her hand on his cheek. It was rough with grit, his beard caked with it. "Dear friend. You know what welcome I can expect in Lir. Maybe it's best if I not come back. And if I do—I'll bring their master chariot-maker, their tamer of horses, their charioteer. That's worth my life, yes?"

"No."

"I am going, Bran," she said. "As soon as it's light, I'll take the mare and one of the stallions and go back for him. I'll bring the caravan if I can—but that I can't promise."

"Just come back," he said. His voice was thick. "Just come back alive."

It was not wise, maybe, but she slid arms about him and laid her head against his broad familiar breast. He did not thrust her away. There was no passion in it, only the comfort of body to body and spirit to spirit in this night like the wrath of all the gods below.

⇨ ⇦

She left in the first grudging glimmer of dawn. The wind had abated somewhat, but was still blowing strong. The lightning had moved off to the westward. There was a flicker of ruddy light in the sky to the east, but it was not the light of the sun. The steppe was burning.

She caught the acrid tang of it as she ascended the slope of the ridge. The mare clambered stoically upward, but Emry's grey stallion shook his head and snorted.

As she rode onward, the line of fire lengthened. It had begun somewhat to the north, and was running south and west. From the angle of it, she reckoned that the camp of the Windriders was on the other side—a wall of fire to bar any pursuit.

Indeed the Goddess was protecting her own. Rhian could only pray that that protection would extend to her as she went back for the caravan.

It was not easy in this featureless country, to know where she had been or where she should go. Yet again she had to trust the mare. She recognized the charioteers' camp, at least, as she rode past it. It was a trampled circle in the grass, dark stains of blood, gouges of hooves and chariot-wheels. A blind tracker could tell what had happened there.

The fire would scour it. The wind whipped her face. The smoke was stronger. She coughed. There was a brown haze over the world, dimming what morning light there was.

The caravan must be somewhere close by the broken camp. She had to trust the mare. She was a tracker of sorts, but not in this country, nor in this wind, or in this veil of smoke.

She was beyond exhaustion. She clung to the mare's back and to the stallion's lead. She saw without understanding, how much closer the fire was than it had been a little while ago. The wind was driving it. It was coming, she thought without emotion, faster than a horse could gallop.

She was the bird of flame. Fire was her element. She flew free in it. If she escaped the cage of her body—what matter? Nothing would ever bind her again.

She all but fell into the caravan. It had taken such refuge as it could in a fold of the earth, by a wide shallow pool. The donkeys were covered in mud. Their masters had wet down the leather of their tents and taken shelter beneath. There was no grass in a broad circle about them—they had stripped the earth bare.

Wise men. They greeted her as if she had been an apparition of the dead. "Mount," she said, "and ride. Ride for all you're worth. The fire comes."

Hoel shook his head. "No, lady. We can't outrun it. We'll pray that it runs past us."

She opened her mouth to protest, but shut it again with the words unspoken. What he had said was manifestly true. There was no way a company of men on foot, with donkeys, was going to outrun a wildfire. They were as safe in this place as it was possible for them to be.

"I'll take the prisoner," she said at length. "He has to come to Lir. If he stays here—if the tribe comes upon you before you can escape westward—"

If Hoel thought her a fool, he did not say so. Two of his men slung the limp burden of the prince over the grey stallion's back and bound him securely. They covered him with a dampened cloak, and gave Rhian another. "Goddess keep you," Hoel said for them all.

"And you," she said. "May she hold you in the hollow of her hand. Look for us in Lir, caravan-master."

He bowed to her, even to the ground, and all his men with him. Long before they rose, the mare had turned away, and the stallion in her wake.

⇒ ⇐

They raced the wind and the storm of fire. They paused only to drink from the little rivers. Smoke engulfed them. Rhian, taking Hoel's lesson, tore her shirt asunder and wetted it in each stream they passed, and bound the halves of it to the bridles of the horses, to protect their noses and shield them from the smoke.

Rhian could feel the fire's heat searing her back, crisping the tiny hairs. Flames reared up in a wall behind her. Their roaring filled the world.

She was going to die. Even she, the bird of flame, had no power against this. And yet, because she was Rhian, she could not surrender. She must fly. The mare bore her. The stallion, brave heart, forged on in her wake. Westward on the wind's back. Westward to the river of souls; to death, or to·Lir.

36

Minas lived in a black dream, a darkness shot with fire. Sometimes he hovered just beyond the circle of shamans. They spoke to one another, but in the languages of beasts, which he could not understand. And sometimes he sat with the wolf, kicking his heels against the wall of the world, that dropped away to infinity beneath him. The wolf never said anything intelligible, either. It merely laughed at him, with its red tongue lolling and its plumed tail waving in mockery.

This world was a dizzy, rolling thing. It had the pitch and sway of a horse's gait, but oddly skewed, as if—

As if he lay face down on a horse's back, and the horse moved at a steady canter. When he tried to move, he found he could not. He was bound. The darkness about him had a distinct scent of horses, and a less distinct one of damp wool, and a powerful tang of smoke. There was a roaring in his ears. His head ached with pounding insistency, his mouth tasted of a solid month's debauch.

He remembered firelight; feasting. He remembered wine. He remembered—chariots? A raid. Had he dreamed that?

This seemed a nightmare, but it was as real as the raw chafing of horse-hair ropes on his wrists and ankles. He was a captive. He was also about to be catastrophically ill.

Struggling only made it worse. In desperation, he raised his voice and howled. The effort nigh split his skull—but it brought the horse to an abrupt halt.

He heard running feet. A hand plucked the coverings from about his face. His stomach let go all at once and completely.

The bindings slipped free. Someone lowered him to the ground, turning him on his back, laving his face with blessed coolness.

He blinked till his eyes cleared as much as they were going to. There was still a thick haze over the world, and a gagging reek of smoke, but the face above him was one he knew—oh, gods, well indeed.

"I should like to pamper you," Rhian said, "and let you rest, but there is no time. The grass is burning. If I untie you, will you give me your word, sworn on your name, that you won't try to escape?"

His spirit was still half lost in a fog, but he could think, after a fashion. When he tried to speak, he erupted in a coughing fit.

She set a waterskin to his lips. He drank in small sips, as a wise man did, though his thirst was terrible. When he had had enough to soothe his throat, though never enough for his thirst, she took the skin away. "Will you swear?" she asked him. "And mean it?"

"What will you do if I won't?" he asked her. His voice was a rough whisper.

"I'll tie you on the horse again," she answered, "and get you out of here before we both burn."

"I will ride," he said. "I swear—to you, on your name as a goddess' servant. Until we escape the fire. Then—"

"Then if I have to bind you again, I will." She set her shoulder to his, lifting him with surprising strength. His legs were totteringly weak. His head was throbbing. But he had been riding since before he could walk. Once he was up, he stayed there. She wrapped his face in a wetted cloth, as if he had been a woman in a veil. But no woman had ever ridden stark naked but for a flapping tatter of cloak.

The fire's roar had risen to fill the world. Even the mare was more than eager to escape it. Once her rider was safe on her back, she leaped into flight. Sparks swirled about her. Minas, swept in her wake, thought he saw wings, as if she were a great gleaming bird: a bird of fire.

⇨ ⇦

The wind saved them. It had been blowing strongly westward, but as they fled, it shifted into the south. Above the roar of fire, Minas heard the rumble of thunder. He almost thought he caught a scent that was not smoke, an achingly clean scent, the scent of rain.

Whatever the truth of that, the wind's shifting shifted the fire, driving it toward the north. When he glanced back, he could see the terrible splendor of it, the burning wall mounting up to heaven.

The horses dropped from a gallop to a canter. The stallion on which Minas rode was laboring. The mare seemed tireless; but was she not a goddess? Her pale coat was darkened with sweat, with soot and smoke.

The woman on her back looked like a spirit from the realms below, with her soot-blackened skin and her matted hair.

From a canter they slowed to a walk. They were going due west, and steadily away from the wall of fire—away too from the People, and from the lands that Minas knew, where he had hunted or raided. They were riding, he thought, toward the river of souls. Toward her country—the country where bronze was as common as flint, and women ruled like kings and gods.

He was mortal and he was ill, and his head was full of aches and fog. He did not understand. He could only ride. The grey stallion followed the mare, close as a foal to its mother. He shut his eyes and lowered his head to the coarse mane and left himself be carried. It would end when it ended. Until then, he would simply endure.

⇨ ⇦

He was dimly amazed when at last they stopped. He was even more amazed to discover that he was shivering. He was cold; he was wet. It was raining. The thunder had given birth at last.

It was a fireless camp, but Minas had seen enough of fire to last him a while. Rhian raised a tent, a small one, and drew out bread and cheese from the pack that had ridden behind Minas on the stallion's back. Minas was too sick for hunger, but he choked down what he could, sipping water laced lightly with kumiss.

Rhian washed the soot and ash from her body and her hair, standing naked in the downpour, laughing as it lashed her skin. When she was clean, she crawled into the tent, still smiling. He could feel the heat that radiated from her. She was like a fire herself.

He, poor shivering filthy thing, could only huddle in his corner and stare. When she reached out a hand, he stiffened. But there was nowhere to go.

She cleansed him with a cloth wetted with rain, taking her time about it, going gently where there were bruises and raw skin. Her touch was light. It warmed him. After a while he gave up his resistance, sighed and submitted. It was only wisdom, he told himself. He was too sick to go far, and he had given his word. He would stay until the morning. Then he would go back to the People.

She lay beside him, her warmth against the chill of his mortal flesh. He half hoped, half feared that she would do more; but she only held him. Her breast was a soft swell beneath his cheek. Her arms raised a wall against the chill and the rain. "Sleep," she murmured. "Sleep."

⇨ ⇦

The morning was bright and cool and scoured clean. The wind had borne away the stench of smoke. The fire was still burning: as Minas stumbled out of the tent, he saw the black pall of smoke on the horizon, and the daylight-dimmed flicker of flame. It would burn long, he thought, and burn far.

The People were on the other side of it. He could only pray that they had had warning; that they had escaped.

"That is the wrath of the Goddess," Rhian said, coming out beside him. "Is she not mighty?"

He glanced at her, then quickly away. Her only garment was her hair. It covered her most insufficiently.

He was no better dressed than she. He turned to dive back in, to find something, anything to cover himself, but she barred his way. "Come here," she said. "Warm your bones in the sun."

He could not make himself thrust past her. He spun away instead, and flung himself to the grass. It was wet. He was almost glad of the chill.

She brought him bread and a handful of dried meat. His stomach was less unsteady than it had been the night before. He was almost hungry. But he clenched his fists and set them on his thighs. "Tell me what this is. Tell me why I am here. There was a raid—I didn't dream that. How did I come to be with you?"

She drew a long breath as if to steady herself; and coughed. The smoke was in her lungs. She did not appear to take any notice. "There was a raid on the raid. Your brothers—your brothers are dead."

He surged to his feet, but his knees could not hold him. He sank back down again. "All of them?"

"All." She knelt in front of him. "One of them had taken you—bound you, drugged you. He was going to kill you. I stopped him."

Minas was not surprised. Not angry, either. He felt nothing at all. "Etena?"

She nodded.

"And you knew?"

"I . . ." She had never had such difficulty meeting his eyes before. "We bought you. She sold you to us."

She was speaking words in the traders' tongue. He had thought he knew it, and well. But the words made no sense. "You . . . bought me?"

"Traded you. You, and gold. In return she took the captain of the guard."

"Your prince from the west? You sold her your prince?"

"It was his will," said Rhian.

Minas' head ached worse even than it had when he first woke on the grey's back. "I think I must dreaming. Or mad."

"This is the waking world," she said. "Your father's wife wanted to be rid of you. She could have killed you—but this, she seemed to think, was better."

"But why—"

"So that you would suffer. So that you would be a slave."

He looked about, and laughed. "You tell me this here? Now? You're alone. You don't even have a scrap of cloth to cover yourself. Are you the one who is mad?"

"I am the one who cannot lie to you, even to save myself. You can't escape. The mare won't let you. And if she would, where would you go? There is a wall of fire between you and your tribe. That wall will stay as long as you try to go back."

"Fire dies," Minas said. "It burns everything there is to burn. Then it goes out."

"How much is there to burn? How wide a sea of grass?"

"It can't—"

"If the Goddess wills, it can. You belong to me. Believe it. Accept it."

"I'll kill you," he said, a snarl in his throat.

"If you were going to, you would have done it before now." She regarded him with calm blue eyes. "I think it best if I bind you again. To be safe. And to spare you temptation."

"Why? So that you can use me as a man uses a woman?"

Did she flinch? He could not be certain. "We will use you," she said. "That much is true."

He fought her. But she was stronger than she had any right to be, and he was still weak from hunger and the drug. Even then he might have eluded her, but in his struggle he fetched up against the forelegs of the mare. Her head loomed over him. Her breath blew lightly in his face. She opened her mouth and gently, very gently, took his wrist in her teeth.

Those jaws could crush bone. He did consider it—but a cripple could not be king over the People. He lay stiff and still while Rhian bound his wrists and ankles together and heaved him onto the grey's back. She said no word. She broke camp swiftly, packing everything tightly, slinging it behind Minas. The grey lurched forward, with the mare just ahead of him.

It was deliberate, he thought, that she held the horses to a trot. Face down and bound, he felt every stride in the roots of his teeth.

This was torture, clever and cruel. After an endless time she paused to let the horses drink and graze. She pulled his head up and thrust the neck of a waterskin into his mouth. He had to drink or drown. She gave him enough to take the edge off his thirst. She did not feed him or let him off the horse. He would not beg, though his belly was rubbed raw and his shoulders were all but pulled from their sockets and his bladder was ready to burst.

It was that last which broke him. He endured well past noon, but came a time when he must either wet himself or ask for mercy.

She said no more than she had since the ride began. She unbound him from the horse. He fell feet-first, which was better than headfirst, to be sure. She did not unbind his ankles. He managed to kneel, and to relieve himself with a sigh that was almost a groan.

She watched him without expression. He had no blushes left in him. He met her stare with one just as flat.

"A bargain," she said. "I will let you ride like a man, but with your hands tied, if you swear to make no effort to escape. If you prove your good faith, I may even unbind your hands."

He hunched his shoulders. "I give my word," he said.

She unbound his ankles, and then his wrists—but only to bring his hands round to his front and bind them again. His shoulders cried in agony. He set his teeth against it.

It was rather less miserable to ride sitting up. Minas fixed his eyes on her back as she rode in front of him. So straight, it was, with the heavy black braid brushing the mare's loin. So wide and straight in the shoulders, so full in the hips—so perfectly a woman.

He hated her. It was a perfect hate, honed and flawless. It was purer and somehow cleaner than the hate he bore Etena, or the brothers who had conspired with her to do this to him. Etena lived, unless the fire had taken her. His brothers had died—the gods' justice, and yet he owed vengeance to those who had killed them.

His hate for Rhian was remarkably close to love. It was a pure thing, a simple thing. She dared to own him. She dared to bind him with cords and oaths, to compel him who was born to suffer no woman's compulsion.

And to think that he had wanted her once, yearned for her so badly that he had dreamed of keeping her with the People. Was this her Goddess' revenge for that, or his own gods' mockery?

37

"What use will you make of me?"

Rhian looked up from building a fire in the evening's camp. Minas sat under the mare's guard, his bound hands clasping his knees. The evening was cool; his skin was pebbled with chill, even with one of the cloaks thrown over his shoulders. And yet, she thought, his anger was warming him enough to keep his teeth from chattering.

She answered his question with a question. "What use do you think I'll make?"

His lip curled. "The same use I would make of a woman I had captured."

"That would be pleasant," she granted him.

"But that's not all of it, is there?" he demanded. "Even as a bedmate, I'm hardly worth an exchange of prince for prince."

"I have many brothers," Rhian said, "and most are princes. What makes you think we can't spare one?"

He hunched and glowered. He looked like a half-fledged bird. She wanted to comfort him, but she was the last person, just then, that he would look to for such a thing.

"Etena I understand," he said. "She'll reckon herself well rid of me. But you, I don't understand at all."

"I'm simpler than you think," she said. "Consider what you have that we do not. What you know, that we can use."

He was fuddled and furious, but he was far from dull-witted. "Chariots," he said.

"Yes," she said.

"You should kill me now," he said, "and have done with it."

"We won a dozen chariots," said Rhian, "and the horses to pull them. They'll teach us much. But you will teach it faster."

"I will teach you nothing."

"What if I offer you a trade?"

He glared under his brows. "What can you possibly offer that would cause me to betray my people?"

"Bronze," she said.

He snapped erect.

"Bronze for chariots," she said. "Secret for secret."

"I am not a merchant!" he snapped.

"No," she said. "You are not. You are my slave, whom I bought with my brother's life."

He shrank into himself. Something about his expression frightened her—not for her safety but for his.

When she was small, one of the village boys had captured a she-wolf in the wood. He had kept her in a kennel, and plied her with such dainties as a wolf might love to eat, and done his best to tame her. She had spurned him. She had curled into a knot of ragged fur and shut out the world. In a few days she was dead.

Minas looked as the wolf had. As if captivity were beyond unbearable. As if, unless he were free, he would die.

She knelt beside him. His hair was matted and filthy, its copper darkened to ruddy brown. The bell that she had braided into it, plaiting it tight, was still there. It chimed softly as she touched it.

A shudder racked him.

"We will give you the secret of the bronze," she said. "All of it, in the forges of Lir. Only teach us to build chariots, and to tame horses to draw them."

"So that you can fight against my People," he said.

"So that we can fight against the tribe led by Etena and the king who is under her spell. Etena, who sold you to us, because killing you would have been too merciful."

"Etena doesn't know," he murmured. "She doesn't see. Bronze—she doesn't understand."

"We will give you bronze," she said.

"Indeed? And then let me go?"

"After you have taught us to build chariots," she said, "and train horses, we'll reward you. Have you thought, prince of the Windriders, that you might find allies against your enemy? That you might be able to oppose her, even defeat her?"

"What, with an army of westerners? Against my own People?"

"Your own People will destroy you if you go back now. Your enemy will see to it."

"Not everyone follows her," he said.

"No one can follow you, if you are dead."

He scowled. She breathed out slowly. He was not ready to hear what she had said, not truly. But the death was gone from his eyes. He was secure in the world again. He wanted to live.

She left him to his thoughts, with the mare to guard him. When the evening's bread was baked and the wild goose that she had shot on the day's ride was cooked, he ate his share of both.

He was still scowling. He was very young, she thought. And however bloody his hands might be, however many wars he had fought and tribes he had conquered, he was a sheltered creature. Intrigue was alien to him.

No doubt his father had been the same, and so Etena had snared him. Minas had been kept safe. Aera's doing, she was sure, and Aera's fault, too, for not teaching him to be subtle. He had had no defenses, in the end. Etena's plotting had trapped him with effortless ease.

In Lir he would learn how princes ruled in cities. If he had the will. If he set himself to the task.

She had been simple, too, thinking only that if she stole him, he would do what she wanted of him. She had taken no thought for what it would mean—to him, to his tribe, to Lir.

But the Goddess had known. This was the Goddess' doing, all of this.

The wall of fire, the charred ruin of the steppe, would hold back the tribe until her people were ready. Then they would come, that was inevitable. And when they did—what might Lir not do, with the son of their king within the city, and the tribe divided against its rulers?

Rhian was simple enough, too, when all was considered. Such thoughts made her head ache. She would leave them to the Goddess, and to Mothers and priestesses. It only mattered, for now, that she bring this man safe to Lir.

IV

A PRINCE IN LIR

IN THE END Minas was no better than Etena. Her lust was for gold and a man's body. His was for bronze—and a woman's body.

It hurt his head to think as Rhian wanted him to think. To see the world as she saw it; to understand how he could use this terrible thing to break Etena's power.

The eastern wall of the world was fire. It burned for day upon day, but the wind blew steady from the west and south, driving it away from them. Squalls of rain lashed them, wetting down the summer-seared grass.

On the third day Rhian let him ride unbound. That night, when she was fast asleep, he slipped away from the bit of fire toward the shadow that was the stallion.

A shape of moonlight rose in front of him, set shoulder against him and threw him down. For the second time he lay on the ground and looked up into the mare's calm dark eye, and knew that if he resisted her, he would die.

Time was when he would have sought that. But the dream of bronze had weakened him. He retreated in as good order as he could, went back to the blanket by the fire, wrapped himself in it and glared at the stars.

He, lord and warrior of the People, man grown, taker of many skulls, maker of chariots, tamer of horses, king's heir, lay captive to a lone woman and a white mare. He might have been a newborn child for all the power he had to oppose them.

He could gnaw his liver till there was nothing left of it. He could seethe with anger till his belly was an aching knot. But as he lay there, with naught but her blanket to cover him, and no possession but the bronze bell knotted in his hair, he made a choice. He would not accept this. But he would endure it.

He was up before she was in the dawn. When he left his blanket this time, the mare raised her head but did not stop him. He went down to

the stream by which they had camped, with a handful of ash from the
fire mixed with the last of the fat from the goose that she had shot a day
or two before. That, and certain herbs from the streambank, scoured the
dirt and the stink of smoke from his body and his hair. He even shaved
his face with her bronze dagger, which he had slipped from its sheath
beside her while she slept.

He came back to the fire in the first of the sunlight, no happier than
he had been before, but notably cleaner and better kempt. Rhian was up
and tending the fire. She carefully said nothing, but as he approached,
she tossed him a bundle of something.

He shook it out. It was a pair of leather breeches. They were wide in
the hips and snug in the waist and a good foot too short, but they covered
the parts of him that mattered. He decided not to mind that they belonged to a woman. He pulled them on and laced them tight, and squatted to eat the morning's bread and a handful of tubers baked in the coals.
"Good," he said as he licked his fingers.

She raised a brow but refrained from comment.

At least, he thought, he was slave to a woman who knew the uses of
silence. That silence deepened considerably when he returned her dagger
to its sheath and sat to work the tangles out of his drying hair.

She made no move to help him. Nor did she hurry him onto the
stallion's back. She let him finish on his own, while she bathed herself,
then basked naked in the sun. He refused to stare at her. He worked out
the mats and tangles, grimly, and freed the bronze bell. For an instant he
considered flinging it in her face. But when his fingers moved, they plaited
it into his hair again. Its soft chiming had become part of his world. It
reminded him of what this ride was for, and why he suffered it.

It was midmorning before they mounted, but Rhian seemed in no
hurry even then. She sent the mare out at a walk, riding easily. She was
half-naked as she mostly preferred to be. His eyes rested as usual on her
back, on the heavy black plait that divided it, and the swell of her hips in
her ragged breeches.

The core of his anger cast him into a daydream of riding up beside
her, flinging her off the mare's back, and taking her whether she would
or no. But he had never raped a woman even in battle, and he did not
honestly want to begin now. When he took her again, she would be
willing—she would be begging him. And he would refuse her more than
once before he gave in to her pleading.

That was a pleasant dream to indulge in while he rode through the tall
grass. He became aware, somewhere in the middle of it, that a wolf was
running beside him. The stallion seemed not to see it: no lifting of the
head, no startled snort. And yet it was very real to his eyes, very solid,
loping at his heel. "Brother wolf," he said.

"Brother stallion," said the wolf. "You're a long way from the People."

"Are they safe?" Minas demanded. "Did they escape the fire?"

The wolf shrugged with its whole body, ending in a fillip of the tail. "That won't matter to you now, will it? You belong to this woman from the west."

"I am still clanborn and blood kin to the People," Minas said tightly.

"Well then," said the wolf, "they were never in danger. The wall of fire has stayed west of them. They'll not be taking the war farther westward this season, but they'll live to conquer the world."

"Is that the gods' word?"

"You think they talk to me?" said the wolf.

"I think you spy on their councils," Minas said.

"As you spy on ours?"

Minas bared teeth at him. "We all do what we must. Does this visitation mean that I've not been abandoned, now I'm defeated? That my lessons will continue?"

"We can't cross the river," the wolf said. "When you go there, you go out of our sight and our power. There will be no gods to defend you, and no shamans to watch over you. Only the Goddess who rules the west."

"She already rules me," Minas muttered.

The wolf howled with laughter. "O wisdom! Have a care, prince of slaves, or you'll be a shaman yet."

"Gods forbid," said Minas.

⇀ ↽

Minas had lost count of the days when they came upon a circle of chariots and a herd of horses that Minas knew very well indeed. Both were in better state than he would have expected, with thieves who knew so little of either.

The thieves themselves were in comfort, having shot a pair of antelope and set them to roasting over a fire. The horses were tended, tents pitched. The men were mending garments, plaiting one another's hair, playing a game with a set of marked bones. One, seated cross-legged near the fire and intermittently turning the spit, was doing something with a bit of harness.

They greeted Rhian with a great whoop of welcome, leaping up all together, dancing, spinning, singing a wild whirling song. Minas gaped at them. The People were not restrained in welcoming their great ones back to the tribe after a raid, but this put them to shame.

He was swept up in their exuberance, borne off the back of the grey stallion, carried to the fire and set on his feet beside a laughing, blushing Rhian. "Alive!" they sang. "You came back alive!"

"Of course I did," she said. "Both of us."

That quelled them for a long moment, as they stared at him. It was as if they had never seen him before.

Maybe they had not seen a slave in borrowed breeches before. He stared back steadily, till some of them looked down as if abashed, and the rest shrugged and went back to their celebration.

He did not know if it was a victory. He decided not to call it a defeat. There was meat, there was kumiss. There was a tent for the newcomers—only one, but it seemed they all expected him to share it with Rhian.

He had no intention of doing such a thing, but he kept quiet while they ate and sang and told stories. Mostly they spoke in their own language. He slipped into a doze, sitting and then lying curled in a knot by the fire.

He spent the night so. They were up much earlier than he would have expected, after the night they had indulged in. They broke camp, rounded up the horses, harnessed the chariots. They were no more clumsy at that than boys of the People would have been.

One of the wheels had broken—he could see where it had been mended. There was a pin of bronze in it, and bindings of leather stretched tight. It was oddly but cleverly done.

In spite of himself he walked among the chariots. He had meant to stand back, to refuse to give them help they had not asked for, but there was a tangle in a harness here, and a bit fitted upside down there, and an axle-pin that was ready to slip loose. As he finished securing that, he found himself face to face with one of the dark bearded men. This one he thought he recognized: the big bear of a man who had always seemed to be hanging about Metos' circle.

"You'll drive the chariot," the man said, "and teach me as you go."

"To drive it?" Minas asked.

The man shook his head. "To make it. Tell me how it's made. How the harness is made, how it should be fitted to the horses. I changed this one—see, I shortened this here, and made this stronger here. And if the bit were bronze instead of hardened bone—"

"You have a maker's mind," Minas said.

The man nodded. "I'm a smith. I forge copper and gold and bronze."

"You . . . forge bronze?"

"Yes. My name is Bran," the man said. "Yours, we all know."

"And if I won't teach you?"

"She said," said Bran, "that I was to teach you of bronze."

Minas sucked in a breath. "But I thought—"

"That all the smiths were on the other side of the river?"

"I thought you were all fighting men."

"I can fight if I have to. I'd rather be making things."

Minas pondered that while he harnessed a team that had, on a time, belonged to his brother Adis: a handsome pair of duns, full brothers to his own stallions who were still among the People. He was aware of Bran's eyes on him, marking every move he made. The smith had watched the chariotmakers in just the same way.

It was rather remarkable how quickly they broke camp and set off to the westward. Now that they had Rhian with them, they were in haste to return to their own country. The pace they set was the pace the People set on raids, when they would travel as far and fast as they could without exhausting the horses.

These people did not take poorly at all to riding in chariots. They were skilled riders of horses, and they were quick to learn. They loved the wind of speed, the roll and rattle of wheels, the creak and snap of the traces.

"Our forefathers were horsemen of the steppe," Rhian said. She had taken Bran's place in the chariot after a pause to breathe and to water the horses. Bran was riding with Mabon, teaching him, no doubt, what Minas had taught him through the long morning's ride.

Rhian did not ask to be taught anything. She seemed inclined to teach instead. "Long ago," she said, "in the dawn of the world, horses came to us, and horsemen who thought to be our conquerors. Our foremothers took them into the cities, and lay with them and taught them the way of the Goddess. And now we are all one people."

"Is that what you expect to do with us?"

"Do you think we won't?"

"I think," he said, "that your horsemen were not as strong in war as the People, nor as firmly bound to the gods of blood and slaughter."

"You are not a bloody-minded murderer."

"No?"

"No." By accident or design, the chariot's motion swayed them together. He felt the softness of her breast against his arm.

He set his teeth. "We have never been conquered, not ever, not since the gods begot our ancestors on the daughters of men. You may conquer me, because I am weak and I am mortal, but you will never conquer my People."

"We may not, but the Goddess will."

"If she chooses."

"Did she not bring you here?"

"And maybe," he said, "I am the arrow in the heart of your people."

"Maybe you are," she said, with a shift of mood that left him speechless. "And maybe that is the Goddess' will, too."

39

Guardians waited at the river of souls: a company of men and armed women, watching over the sea of grass from a lofty camp, a fortress new-built on the steep bank of the river. Their outriders met the chariots half a day's journey from the river, greeting them with the same wild joy with which the warriors from Lir had greeted Rhian.

Minas did his best not to gape at the sight of women in armor. They made no such effort themselves. Their stares were frank, their fascination unmarred by either fear or shyness. They grinned at him, bold as young men of the tribes, and said words he did not understand, but he could guess what they meant.

When he saw the high wall looming above the river, at first he thought they had come to the city called Lir. It was some little time before he understood that it was not even a village; it was a distant outpost, half a day's journey downriver from the last of their cities, with half a hundred warriors in it, and as many of them were women as men. They lived inside those walls, not in tents but in round houses built of precious wood and willow-withies and reed thatch. All their weapons were bronze, and the trappings of their horses.

These people were rich beyond the dreams of kings. What had seemed great wealth and easy excess on the steppe was proved here to be a notable measure of restraint. His captors had been concealing the true extent of what they were, and what they had.

When the rest of the People saw what was here, even in this outpost of the realm, they would want it with all their wild hearts. Minas did his best to keep his eyes to himself, to keep his hands from twitching toward so much bronze, so much silver and gold, so much pure unheeding extravagance.

The feast of welcome was, they professed, a poor thing, a rough makeshift for a camp of war. The bread was finer than any he had eaten. There was cream and honey, an abundance of fruits, fish from the river, meat, cheese, flesh of birds, eggs prepared in half a dozen ways, cakes both sweet and savory, wine of more sorts and flavors than he had known existed. There was so much of it, and all so strange, that he barely touched it.

Nor was he set where a slave would have been among the People: bound with the rest of the captives, fed what leavings there were after the People were done. He had been given rich garments to wear, ornaments of gold, and a place at the feast between Rhian and the commander of the garrison, who was a woman. If he had come to them as a prince of his people, he could hardly have been accorded more honor than they gave him as a slave.

The women were open in their admiration. They all, it seemed, found occasion to wander past him, and excuse to touch him, especially his hair. They said a word when they did it, a word that, he thought, meant "Copper." They touched his cheeks, too, wondering at the lack of beard in a man of his age; one, bold beyond belief, proved to her full satisfaction that he was not a eunuch. He regarded her in shock. She laughed and kissed him on the mouth and danced away.

It was all he could do not to break and run with his jewels clutched in his hands. He was too proud for that. Too proud to complain to the woman who had bought him, either, though she sat next to him and said nothing while the women of her people made a plaything of him.

The end was merciful. A young person who appeared to be a servant — male, somewhat to his relief — conducted him to one of the round houses. It was mostly one large room, but there were smaller rooms divided by walls of wicker.

One of these, the servant indicated, was his. There was a pallet in it, raised on a wooden frame, and a box that proved to be full of fine weavings, and a cluster of clay lamps; and a jar with water in it, and a cup of fine pottery, and in a niche in the wooden wall, a small carved image. It was incontestably, overwhelmingly female, with great round breasts and great round belly and deeply carved sex; but it had no face.

This must be the Goddess who ruled beyond the river. Had they set her on guard over him? He felt no more confined than he had before he found her in her niche. It seemed she was like the mortals who served her: light-handed, easygoing, but in her heart implacable.

He bowed to her only half in mockery. Almost he did not undress in front of her, but she had no eyes. He stripped out of the beautiful borrowed garments and the collar and armlets of heavy gold, and lay on the pallet.

Rhian's bronze bell chimed softly in his ear. He closed his fingers about it. He was surprised, and more than a little, to be alone here. Even if Rhian would not come seeking him, he would have thought one or more of the other women would have done it. From all he knew of these people, there was nothing shocking in a woman's coming to a man's bed.

He did not like to admit that he was disappointed. These dark full-breasted women were delectable. Part of him wanted to hate them, because they were so like Etena who had sold him and Rhian who had bought him. But they were beautiful, and however little beard he might have to offer the razor, he was a man. He had not lain with a woman in close on two moons' turning — since the second time he lay with Rhian, outside the camp of the People.

He lay on his belly. It was chill in the room, the first breath of autumn along the vale of the river, but he was a warrior of the People. Cold was nothing to him. Maybe it would cool the heat in his loins.

He had never slept in walls before. They had none of the motion about them that tent-walls had. They stood stiff and still even in the flicker of lamplight. Sounds came through them muffled or not at all. He was both more and less aware of the people about him, all crowded within the walls of the fort, but separated from one another by the walls of their houses. He felt utterly alone and yet crowded beyond endurance.

He was not under guard. When he escaped the room, he found the outer room full of sleepers, men and women mingled without regard for either modesty or propriety. He slipped through them with a hunter's skill, out into the dark and the starlight.

The wind blew soft across the sea of grass. The moon was riding high. Minas sat on the wall and gazed eastward. He had passed a guard on the way up, an armored woman who greeted him with a perfect lack of either surprise or alarm.

If he rode out tonight, he wondered, would anyone stop him?

Something stirred out in the moonlight. It might have been a wolf. It might have been a man with a crooked foot, limping through the tall grass, white face lifted to the moon and the loom of the wall.

Minas thought he might be dreaming. And yet Phaiston seemed very real, both as wolf and as man. He had always been quick on his feet, even the crippled one. He paused at the foot of the wall and stood staring up. His eyes had a faint gleam in them, as if they had kept the wolf's semblance while the rest of him walked as a man.

"Brother wolf," Minas called down softly.

"Brother stallion," Phaiston called up. "That's a tall fence you're shut in."

Minas had come up with the help of a ladder. The guard had gone round the curve of the wall. She did not come running back when he drew the ladder up and, balancing it precariously, brought it to the place where Phaiston still stood. Minas was a little surprised that he had not melted into the moonlight.

He climbed up not too clumsily. There was no mistaking the reality of him now: he was dressed in a filthy wolfskin with the snarl of its head for a hood, hung about with bones and beads and scraps of fur and feathers, and surrounded by a sharp animal reek.

"You walked a long way," Minas observed.

"Mostly I ran four-footed." The shaman turned slowly about. His nose wrinkled. He spat. "Pah! This place stinks of women's magic."

"That surprises you?"

"It's strong." Phaiston sneezed. "You're dead, you know."

Minas raised his brows. "I am?" He drew a breath, held it, let it go. He pinched his arm hard. "The dead breathe? They feel pain?"

"You're dead to the People. Nothing came living through the storm of fire. The steppe is ash. Everything burned. Your raiders, your horses, your chariots—all gone. The king lost a dozen sons and one. Great was the mourning, nine days of ashen grief. Etena led the chorus of women in the long dirge."

"Etena? Not Aera?"

"Aera has shut herself away in her father's tent. No one can come to her or speak to her. Her grief is absolute."

This was not real, no. Minas felt nothing but a kind of dim amazement. "Dias?"

"He's king's heir now," said Phaiston.

"He would hate that," Minas said. "Oh, he would loathe it."

"What, he should have thrown himself on the pyre of your remembrance?"

"Gods forbid," said Minas. "He never wanted to be king. King's brother, king's right hand—that was the height of his happiness. All the privilege, none of the dull duty. Do you know how much he hates sitting in judgment?"

"He's judge of the tribe now," Phaiston said. "Who else is there? The rest of your brothers who live are children. Your naked goddess killed the three eldest, shot them with her bow. Her men killed the rest who had passed the rite of manhood."

Minas' shoulders tightened. "Rhian killed three of my brothers?"

"An arrow in the heart, an arrow in the throat, an arrow in the eye. Quick as that, and cold-hearted as any man."

Minas sank down against the rim of the wall. He could feel those arrows in his own body. And yet he mustered a flare of anger. "How do you know any of this? How can you? You've been on the steppe as long as I have. Longer. What do you know of what passes in the tribe?"

Phaiston rattled his bone necklaces and grinned as a wolf grins. "What, king's son? No gratitude? Here I came half across the world to bring you news and offer wisdom, and you call me a liar. It's lucky for you I'm a shaman and not a warrior, or I'd slit your throat for that."

"You could try," Minas said sweetly.

"Ah, and what's the use in killing a dead man?" Phaiston prowled along the wall. "Trusting people, aren't they? Anybody could get up here."

"Maybe," Minas said. And after a pause: "Is it true what you said? You can't cross the river?"

"Did I say that?"

"In a dream," said Minas.

"Dream-sendings can't cross that wide a river."

"But you—in your body—you can?"

Phaiston tilted his head and peered at Minas through narrowed eyes. "Why would I want to do that?"

"Curiosity? The gods' will?"

"Or maybe for love of you, O prince of the dead." Phaiston leaned over the inner edge of the wall, staring down at the fort. He had not once looked at the river, Minas realized. "No. No, I can't do it. I'm not that brave. The river of souls will flow on without me."

"Why? Are you afraid?"

"Yes!"

"And you a great lord of wolves."

"If I cross that river," Phaiston said, "I'll have no magic left. Even here I feel the Goddess' power sapping my strength. If I'm no more than mortal man, what use will I be to you?"

"Much," said Minas. "As you knew. Or why would you come so far?"

"To see the river of souls," Phaiston said.

"And now you shall cross it."

"Do you think you can force me?"

"I think," said Minas, "that I can raise my voice and summon a garrison of women, and persuade them to take you captive. Is your magic strong enough to stand against that?"

"The garrison are women?" Phaiston said faintly.

"Women in armor, with swords of bronze."

"Gods," Phaiston said.

Minas smiled at him with the love of a wolf for its tender prey. "And goddesses," he said.

But Phaiston was a wolf, too, more surely and truly than he. "Threaten all you like, but I stay in the world of the living. May the gods help you, prince, and the spirits of your ancestors, because no one else will."

40

Phaiston went down the wall as he had come up it, shrinking to four legs and rough grey fur as he touched the grass again. He paused to look up. Minas stared flatly down, feeling more truly alone than he ever had in this world.

The wolf tucked its tail and flattened its ears and turned, running off eastward under the moon.

⇒ ⇐

Rhian found Minas at first light, dozing fitfully on the wall. She ventured no judgment as to where and how she had found him. She only said, "You're wanted. Come."

He rose stiffly, working knots out of his back and shoulders. His expression was anything but amiable, but he followed when she turned toward the ladder. She led him down from the wall and through the fort, which was already wide awake, to an open space near the wall, where all the chariots were drawn up side by side.

Bran and a handful of men and women were there, stripped for work. They had begun to take apart one of the chariots, piece by piece, peg by peg, noting how each part was made and where it went and how.

Minas stopped short. "What in the gods' name are they doing?"

"Learning," Rhian said.

"Gods," said Minas. But he did not try to stop them. He watched instead, arms folded, saying nothing.

Caleva the garrison commander came to stand beside Rhian, watching Minas watch Bran and the others. "I think you should go to Lir as soon as may be," she said.

Rhian glanced at her. "You don't think it's better to keep him here till he's more nearly tamed?"

"As long as he can see the grass, he'll be as wild as a wolf." Caleva rubbed a scar that ran the length of her arm, absently, eyes on the red-headed prince. "The sooner he's in Lir, building chariots, the safer we'll all be."

"Him, too?"

"He's less likely to run," said Caleva, "if he's farther from the steppe."

"One would hope so," Rhian said.

Minas had left off watching and gone to show Bran how to separate a wheel from its axle. One of the women took the wheel and inspected it, feeling out the joining of the spokes to the rim.

"Do you see how that's made?" said Caleva. "He must have been a god who conceived such a thing."

"The people of his tribe do believe so," Rhian said.

"And we are mortal," Caleva sighed.

"We have his grandson here with us, who was his pupil. He's a great gift of the Goddess."

"And that gift were best delivered to Lir," Caleva said, "and to the king."

"And the Mother?" Rhian asked steadily, though her heart had begun to beat hard.

"The Mother is dead," Caleva said.

"No one's been set in her place?"

"The priestesses rule in council," said Caleva. "Some are declaring that the age of the Mothers is over; that this is the time of kings and councils. Others say the priestesses are afraid—they tried to choose a Mother from among themselves, but every woman they chose was given some sign that she was not meant for such an office. One, it's said, went as far as to sit in the Mother's place, and was blasted for it, struck dead where she sat."

Rhian heard her as if she spoke from very far away. It was strange to be told these things, and to remember how she would have heard them if she had been in Long Ford. Now when Caleva spoke of the Mother, she spoke of the woman who had given Rhian life; whose heir Rhian should have been, but the priestesses had forbidden it.

Rhian was going to Lir. She could hardly avoid it. Minas was her captive. She was not about to hand him over to any troop of guards, though they were chosen of the king.

"We had better go tomorrow," she said with sudden decision. "Can we be ready then?"

"It can be done," said Caleva.

"Good," said Rhian. "Will you help us see to it?"

"With pleasure," Caleva said. She rose, creaking a little, for she was not a young woman. She stood looking down at Rhian. Her expression was more approving than not. "You did a great thing, bringing this tribesman here. But have a care. He's not a tame thing. Nor may he ever be."

"We'll keep him under guard," Rhian said.

"Guard yourself," said Caleva.

Rhian frowned at her. "Are you afraid for me?"

"I think that one can break hearts as well as take heads. Be wary of him."

Rhian considered a number of things that she might have said. She elected to say none of them. She nodded and pushed herself to her feet. Caleva was already on her way, Rhian supposed, to prepare for her guests' departure.

They were all in the midst of the chariot's scattered bits now. She heard Bran say, "That would be stronger if it were metal rather than wood."

"Is metal so common," Minas asked, "that you can stud a chariot with it?"

"How common is wood on the steppe?" Bran inquired.

Minas grinned. He looked like a wolf indeed just then, though his manner was easy and his humor light. "Less common by far, I would wager, than it is across the river. Is it true what they say? That you have whole great forests in your country?"

"We have forests," Bran said, "and mines for our metal, or traders who bring it to us from our allies far away."

"Rich," Minas murmured. "So rich. Your Goddess has blessed you."

"She has," Bran said. "Now look here, what does that do?"

Rhian did not listen to Minas' explanation. Caleva's words had affected her oddly. She saw Minas as clearly as she ever had, surely. Yet when she heard him speak, she heard things she had not heard before.

Not tame. Indeed. And in no way willing to accept either his captivity or his death to the tribe. He would be dreaming of revenge; and in that dream, he was lord of a country richer than his people might ever have imagined.

Still she was not afraid. All men were weak at heart, and it was through the heart that she would rule him.

41

Minas stared at the hollow shells that floated on the river. Boats, those were boats. All the chariots were laden in them, and heaps of baggage, and guards in armor. But not the horses. Those were on the other side, with more armored guards to watch over them. They must have swum the river in the dawn. Surely they had not crossed over in boats. No horse would endure such a thing.

Minas did not intend to, either. "And why," he asked as reasonably as he could after numerous repetitions, "can I not ride with the horses? I was born on horseback. I was never born to swim like a duck on the water!"

"You go with the chariots," Rhian said implacably. The garrison commander, who had been hearing Minas' arguments, had turned away to see to something with the boats.

He had hoped to find more softening in Rhian, but she was like an image carved in stone. She beckoned to a pair of burly guards. As if to worsen the insult, one of them was a woman.

Minas glared at them all, but especially at Rhian. "Call off your dogs! I'll go."

The woman in particular seemed to regret his surrender. Both guards hovered close while he scrambled into the boat that waited, drawn up on the bank.

It was no worse, he told himself, than a chariot drawn by restless horses. He sat where the boatmen directed, in the middle, atop a bale that carried a strong scent of new wool. There was no chariot in this boat, only baggage and trade-goods, and half a dozen guards, and Rhian.

She was seated in the bow, leaning against the high curve of the prow. "Isn't this marvelous? Comfortable, too. Won't your feet be glad not to be standing in a chariot day after day?"

Minas' feet wanted earth under them. But he held his tongue.

There was, he had to admit, a certain pleasure in lying in the shade of a canopy that the boatmen raised as the sun ascended and grew warmer. The boat rocked gently. The oars dipped and swayed. The oarsmen rowed to the strong slow beat of a drum.

In all his life he had not imagined such a thing: not only riding on a river but riding upriver against the current. Once he had put his dread of the water aside, the maker in him roused and grew curious. He looked to see how the boat was made, how the oars were shaped, how the men wielded them against the ever-running water.

He slid to the side, leaning over it, peering down. The river slipped past, dark water shot with a gleam of sunlight. He saw nothing in it but once the silver flash of a fish. No dead souls. No spirits from the realms below.

There was power here. It was strong, and deep and old. But it had nothing to do with men or the souls of men. It was as purely itself as the wind of heaven.

Maybe he simply lacked the eyes to see. He trailed his hand in the water. It was cold and strangely smooth, and it parted before his fingers, streaming over them.

He laved his face. In one of the other boats, the rowers had begun to sing. It was a slow song in a strange mode, weaving the voices of men and women. There were no such songs among the People. Women did not sing with men. It was highly improper.

Impropriety was a different thing here, if indeed these people knew it at all. He had passed from world into world, as sure and as complete as if he had entered the land of the dead.

Toward evening the river curved away from the sea of grass. There had been trees enough on the farther bank, but now they grew thicker. Rhian gave him the words to name them: a copse, a wood, the outriders of a forest. And in among the trees, amid fields of green or ripe gold, he saw a place like the garrison's fort, but much, much larger. It filled the inward curve of the river's bend and stood high over the wooded lands beyond. It was a fortress, Rhian said, and a traders' town. Its name was World's End.

With trees, Minas had gone from copse to forest, so that he better understood how they grew together. With dwelling places of these people, he began with a forest, as it were: with a stronghold too large to encompass with his mind. Even in the gathering of tribes he had never seen so many people, so closely crowded together, as he saw here.

They moored the boats on the western bank in the shadow of the crag, where wooden piers jutted out into the river. All the chariots were covered and guarded, not obviously, Minas noted, but as if they were no more than traders' cargo. The crowds of people on the shore barely took notice of them; there were other boats, other guards, and a tumult of coming and going.

Somewhat to his startlement he realized that he was not unusual here. There were other rangy fair-haired men, even some whose hair was red, though none that he saw had his true bright copper. They wore tribesmen's garb, some in fashions that he knew, from tribes that his had conquered in this season or the season before.

He, who was dressed like a westerner, attracted barely a glance. Such of those who did notice him were usually women, and they looked him over boldly, with an expression that he could hardly mistake.

He sidled as close to Rhian as his pride would allow, stepping from pier to trampled earth.

A long sigh escaped him. It was living earth. These were mortal people all about him, and a strong mortal scent to them, too, in the heat of the day. The sky overhead was the same sky he had left behind on the steppe, as blue and remote as ever, though he was hemmed in human bodies.

He walked in a circle of men, the dozen who had come as traders to the People. There was a sort of comfort in them, a familiarity that, just then, was welcome.

They brought him up a steep and narrow track under the frown of a high wall and a massive wooden gate. He shuddered as he passed under it. His heart felt small and cold, his spirit crushed down by the weight of these walls.

The others waited for him within, in an open space under a patch of sky. This outer wall was just that. There was a second, smaller wall inside, and that, he could see, held up a roof.

This commander, like the last, was a woman. Her name was Britta. She was not young; her hair was shot with grey, and her face was seamed with lines of care and laughter. Still she looked strong, and her dark eyes were clear.

She had received them in the center of the second tower, which like the space within the first wall was open to the sky. There were lamps lit round the edges, and a table laid with a feast that put that in the garrison to shame. It was, he was beginning to understand, a simple meal as these things went here; she apologized for it, as if he could find fault with such richness as would have befit a festival among the tribe.

Minas found that he was hungry. He could eat, and sleep, too; there was a pallet spread in this court under the stars, as if they had known how little he liked to sleep in walls.

He slept alone. Rhian was within—and likely with company, too; he had caught one or two of the garrison making eyes at her.

He had no cause for jealousy. She was as heedless of either modesty or propriety as the mare whose servant she was. No man could own her, though one might dream of it.

He lay in the starlight on the far side of the river of souls, and his dreams both waking and sleeping were full of her. There was a spell on him, a curse of desire. He doubted she even knew she had laid it on him. Nor, he thought, would she care.

He had crossed the river into another world. It was not the world of the dead; and yet, if he was dead to the People, was it so very different?

42

Past World's End the river turned away from the sea of grass and into the heart of the Goddess' country. Minas had learned the different words for gatherings of trees. Now Rhian taught him how gatherings of people could be divided: village, town, city; garrison, fort, stronghold. World's End was a fort. Villages clustered on either side of the river, no larger sometimes than camps of a tribe. They were almost never walled. Towns might embrace the river, or might sprawl along the bank or straggle away inland. Raw and half-built walls rose about many of them. And where there were hilltops, there were fortresses, large or small, rising out of ruins of old stone.

Cities were always walled, as warriors of this country wore armor to protect their vitals. The heart of each city was not a stronghold of warriors but a temple: a structure of wood or stone in which the women worshipped their Goddess.

Men did not worship in temples. The great mysteries were forbidden them. They were a lesser creation, beloved but weak. They could fight battles, ride horses, even call themselves kings — and, Minas discovered to his astonishment, rear children, too, while their women went about the real business of ruling the world.

He was learning to speak the language, a little. He might not have stooped to it, but he had a little wisdom. People talked among themselves; maybe they told secrets. And maybe it was simpler, sometimes, to understand what they said before they remembered to say it in the traders' speech.

⇒ ⇐

At the gate of autumn was a festival. They stopped for that, for three days, in a city between World's End and Lir.

There for the first time Minas saw the Mother of a city. She was the living image of one of their carven goddesses: vast breasts, vast belly, great round thighs. She suckled a child as she sat on the threshold of the temple, receiving guests and hearing petitioners and judging altercations as if she had been a king.

Minas, as one of those guests, found himself meeting eyes as deep as the river on which he had come to this place. She was not old, he realized; she had seemed as enduring as mountains, but she was still young enough to bear and nurse a daughter. Her hair was black and thick, rippling down her back to her ample hips. Her skin had the color and smoothness of cream. She was splendid.

She smiled with warmth that made him blush from the loins upward. "You are welcome in Larchwood," she said.

He bowed as if to a warleader of the People, but he found no words to say. A person—a man, for a wonder—was waiting to take them to their lodgings. They had a whole house here, ample for all of them, and servants to look after them. There was even a place for the horses, a house built for their comfort. Cut grass was brought in to them, and handfuls of barley, and bits of fruit and sweetness to please their taste. They were looked after like honored guests.

The autumn festival was bound to the harvest: to the gathering of fruit and grain, the pressing of wine, and the laying away of provisions for the winter. Minas had seen the laborers in the fields, men and women and children side by side and toiling in the sun. Great heaps and sheaves attested to the length of their labor; vats of grapes from the vines on the hillsides, and baskets of fruit from the orchards and grain from the threshing-floors.

So much labor, for so many, put Minas well in mind of the simplicity of the tribes: meat and milk from the herds, meat and hides from the hunt, fish from the rivers and wild fruits and grain where the women might find them. But the winters were lean, with poor grazing for the herds and poor hunting on the steppe; and there were no granaries and storehouses. Such could not be moved from camp to camp.

He had begun to see, as the river bore him through this strange country, what use a warrior people could make of these sleek comfortable farmers and dwellers in cities. Their fighters were few, and many of those were women.

They had so much to defend, and so much of it built on the earth or growing in it. They could never sweep together the whole of their country and carry it away to another camp or another realm of the world. Their cities bound them like chains to the earth on which they were born. Their fortresses were still rising on the hilltops, their walls half-built, their garrisons raw recruits or grey-haired veterans whose scars were few and whose bellies were soft with good living.

Swift warriors in chariots could conquer them, take their wealth from them, keep them like herds to till the land and feed the People. They built fortresses for protection, and stole a prince of the People to make chariots for them, but their wealth was their weakness. All the gathered tribes and clans of the People would roar over them as the fire had roared over the steppe.

He could call that gathering. He could send the spear of war to every tribe that was kin or conquered, and summon them all to take this soft rich country. Horsemen in thousands, chariots in hundreds—the muster would be like none the world had ever seen.

Rhian's voice brought him back to the waking world. He was in a wooden box of a room, one with a window that opened on the horses' house. A servant waited to help him dress in garments that the Mother had sent: rich garments, soft garments, wonderfully woven, and ornaments of gold and copper and bronze, set with amber and precious shell. He walked naked to the window and looked out to see where Rhian was.

She was outside the horses' house. The mare was with her. Minas had never seen the mare gleam so, like a cloud over the moon. Her mane and tail were as white as a fall of moonlight. There were flowers woven into her mane, bronze and purple and gold.

Rhian seemed none too pleased. Her voice had an edge as she addressed the child who stood beside the mare. "And whose command was it to deck this horse like a beast for sacrifice?"

Minas was pleased that he understood her, for she was speaking the tongue of the west. The child was more difficult, but he thought he caught the meat of it: "Lady, this is harvest festival, and this is the White Mare. We celebrate her, not sacrifice her."

"Will there be any duties in that celebration?" Rhian inquired.

The child shrugged. "If you wish, lady, she could ornament the third-day rite and the sacrifice—but not as the victim! It's tradition, lady, that if the mare is in a city during a great festival, she graces it with her presence, and her servant stands beside the priestesses in the rites."

"In the temple?" Rhian's voice sounded odd, as if she was not quite able to trust it.

"Yes, lady. But I forgot, you are a chosen one, yes? Not bred or raised to it. You should talk to the Mother. She knows the things that the mare's servant should know."

"Do you know them, too?" demanded Rhian.

"I know a little," the child said. "I looked after the Old Mare once when she came to Larchwood. Her servant was very gracious. She taught me some of the things that she knew."

Minas wondered if Rhian would notice that she had been rebuked. It seemed that she did not; or maybe she chose to ignore it. "Teach me, then, till the Mother has time for me."

"Sir," said the servant behind Minas. "Will you dress?"

Minas had been rebuked, too. He considered ignoring it, but he could hardly go out as he was. He let the man dress him as if he had been a wooden image, and hang him about with ornaments, and plait his hair; but he refused the garland that looked a great deal like the one in the mare's mane.

He looked rather fine, he thought, though he had no weapon to mark him a man and a warrior. Slaves did not carry weapons, nor, that he had observed, did most of the men in the west. At most they had a knife for cutting meat.

Certainly he was not dressed like a slave. He was not confined, either, except by the walls of this city. He walked freely out of the house and into the maze of streets, more of them and more tangled than in even the great gathering of all the tribes.

They were all dark-haired people here. Tribesmen did not come so far up the river. Minas was somewhat taller and much fairer than anyone he passed. Children, and a few people who had not been children in some while, trailed after him in fascination, or darted in to stroke his hair. They made a game of it, daring one another, giggling and running away when he spun to see who had touched him.

He caught himself wishing for his guards. Even one would do. But that was cowardly, and none of these invasions was hostile. They were curious, that was all.

The city was hung with banners, a richness of woven fabric that would have been worth a whole tribe's store of gold. There were flowers everywhere, and people singing, and where there were open spaces, there were people in them, dancing to the music of pipe and drum. Nearly always, there was food near the dancing, tables spread and women or more often men inviting passersby to eat, drink, share the bounty of the harvest.

He ate their fine white bread and their roasted meats and their extravagances of fruit and grain and sweetness. He watched their bold half-naked women dance with their maiden-eyed men. He heard the songs they sang, some of which he understood, most of which he did not.

He had been wandering aimlessly, but he was aware that the circles of the city were growing smaller. In time he came to the center, to an open space that startled him with green: grass, a ring of trees, a structure of wood on a foundation of stone. Here, he could suppose, was the temple.

He had expected a crowd of dancers and a greater feast than he had yet seen, but there was no one about, not outside the temple. Within he heard singing, voices of women and none of men, high and eerie.

He ascended a tier of steps to the temple. Its gate was open. Scented smoke wafted out. They were burning sweet herbs such as must be pleasing to their goddess.

He peered within. It was dim almost to darkness, but there were candles lit. He saw the women in a circle, white naked backs and haunches, white breasts, broad hips bound with a garment of knotted crimson cords. It hid nothing of their sex, but rather enhanced it.

Here was pure raw woman, power such as he had never imagined. They were singing spells to bind the world.

Defiance bade him enter their temple, hear their song within the curve of those age-darkened walls. But he found his feet would not obey him. As proud as he was, royal born, descended of gods, here he was only a man.

He was no lord of creation here. He was an upstart, a child, his gods but children of the one great Goddess. All his dreams and sureties, the conquest he foresaw, the rule that he would hold, dwindled to folly. He would never rule here, nor would any man. There was no such power in him.

He recoiled with a gasp, stumbling backward into the sunlight. Its warmth bathed his face. Its strength weakened the women's spell.

For spell it was, no more if no less. He was stronger than it willed him to be. He was of another creation, a lord of sun and sky, begotten of the free air and the open grass.

"I will conquer you," he said to them from the sanctuary of the sun. "I will rule you. By the gods of heaven I swear it."

43

Rhian had done very little thinking since she rode away from the tribe. She plotted and schemed. She acted accordingly. She . . . killed. But she pondered none of it. Even on the river, when she could have faced all the things that she had been and done, and contemplated what was in front of her, she had chosen to lose herself in the running of the water and the turning of the sky. All too often, too, she had watched Minas when he was not aware of it, till she knew his every line. She had not sought him out in the nights; it was a strangeness in her, a desire to sleep alone, to be alone. She did not want a man at all, even that one, except to look at.

In Larchwood during the three days of festival, she could no longer avoid the inevitable. The mare and her servant had duties. Those were not many and not excessively onerous, but they were real; they were inescapable. They reminded her of everything she had been evading.

Even while she was awake she saw the faces of the men she had killed. Waking and sleeping she saw the faces of the men who had died in her battle: Dal who had been a pleasing lover, Conn who had been for a while her father, Gwion and Rodry the noblemen of Lir. They haunted her in dreams, dying over and over again. Even when they let her be, she faced another ghost, and another bitter guilt: Emry as she had last seen him, standing alone in the midst of the tribe. Was he dead, then? Had they killed him in retaliation for their prince's loss?

She had to hope and pray that they had not; that her vision was simply memory. He would come back, alive and whole. She had prayed the Goddess for that, and dared to hope that she had been heard.

She stood with priestesses in the rites of the festival. It was more than strange to know that the mare gave her this right, and yet to feel like an impostor; then to remember what she would have been if the priestesses in Lir had not forbidden. That would have been she in the Mother's place, center of all the rites, strongest and clearest voice of the Goddess in these lands that had been hers since the dawn time.

There was still no Mother in Lir. Nor would there be, unless Rhian took that place.

She saw that, there in the temple of Larchwood, in the circle of priestesses. It was clear in the sacred fire. It was truth.

She sat with the Mother on the third night of the festival. They were all gorged with feasting, weary with revelry. In the city, the sounds of celebration had faded somewhat. People were falling asleep where they danced or ate. Come morning they would wake to a duller world.

"You will be glad to go," said the Mother.

"Not for your sake," Rhian said, "or for your city's."

The Mother smiled. "No, of course not. But Lir is waiting."

"The king sent us a message," Rhian said. "Not to lay any compulsion on us, but the sooner we bring our cargo there, the better for us all."

"The king is wise," the Mother said.

"So I'm told." Rhian turned her wine-cup in her fingers. It was nearly full, but she had no desire to drink.

She let her eyes wander over the Mother's hall, half of which was under roof, and half under the stars. A great number of people were there, but there was no one near enough or alert enough to hear what they said to one another.

After a while she said, "It may be best if I leave Mabon to deliver the cargo, and go . . . wherever the mare's servant should go. Back to World's End, maybe. I'd be welcome there."

"And not in Lir?"

Rhian met the Mother's quiet dark stare. "I was born there. I was sent from it on the day I was born. There were those who would have preferred that I die that day, and never have lived to discover what I am."

"If the Goddess had meant you to die, you would have died."

"So one would think," Rhian said. "But will Lir be glad to see me? I think not."

"What is Lir? Is it walls? A city? Or a gathering of people, not all of whom might be of the same mind?"

"Are you saying," said Rhian, "that I should not care what the priestesses think, or what their prophecies have told them?"

"What is done is done," the Mother said. "What is still to do—that is laid on you, as the Goddess wills. Will you run away from the place where she has been leading you since the day of your birth?"

"Maybe I was never meant to go there at all. I was never to know who I was."

"Yet she made certain that you did."

"Does that come when one is made a Mother?" Rhian asked. "Does the knowledge of everything come then?"

The Mother laughed, and for a moment Rhian saw the girl she must have been—and not so long ago, either. "Oh, I know very little! But when signs are as clear as this, I can see them well enough."

"I don't know what I see," Rhian muttered, "and the wind won't speak to me."

"Have you sought it out?" the Mother asked.

"It always came to me," said Rhian.

She sounded petulant even to herself. But the Mother's expression did not change. "If you call on it, it may choose to answer. What have you to lose by trying?"

A Mother's wisdom, thought Rhian, could be wonderfully exasperating. She left the food she had barely touched and the wine in which she had had no interest, and sought the open air.

The wind was chained here, trammeled in walls. But down by the river it was free to play as it would. It was a small wind tonight, a playful wind, dancing on the water, brushing her cheeks with soft quick fingers.

Truth, she thought. She had been shutting it away, as she shut away remembrance. It had been tugging at her, calling to her, for long and long, all the way from the sea of grass.

It was not as easy to open her ears to it as it had been when she was a simple potter's child in Long Ford. Too many thoughts crowded in on her; too much knowledge, too much awareness. She had become a power in the world.

The wind cared nothing for powers among human children. It was in a light mood tonight, too light to heed any will of hers. It teased and tormented her. It told her secrets that were perfectly useless: how a shepherd had gone to the pasture with his sheep and found two black ewe-lambs born long out of season; how the grandfather fish from the eddy downstream had come into a fisherman's net, but had broken free again. Nothing that could profit her; nothing even interesting.

She perched on the end of a pier, knees drawn up, clasping them tightly. The wind was cool, not winter-cold yet, but hinting at it. It was the dark of the moon tonight, and the sky was thick with stars. They shimmered on the water.

She felt his tread on the pier long before he crouched beside her. "The Mother said you would be here," Minas said.

"Did she send you to me?" Rhian asked without taking her eyes from the river.

"She said that I should find you," he said. The burr of the tribes was strong in his voice tonight, as if the longer he stayed in the Goddess' country, the more he strove to remember what he had been.

"Did she tell you why?"

"Only that you might wish to see me."

And be reminded, she thought, of why she should go to Lir, and with whom she should do it.

"We're leaving tomorrow," she said. "Riding—you and I and two of the king's guards. The chariots will follow in the boats, and the rest of the company."

She heard his long sigh. His relief must have been enormous; he hated the boats. And yet he asked, "Is it wise to do that?"

"Wiser than to linger," she said. "I think we should come there quickly. The king's summons was urgent. He needs us now, not half a month from now."

"We could," he said, "take one of the chariots, and two teams of re-mounts, and be there even faster."

She slid a glance at him. He was keeping his eagerness well reined in, but his expression was livelier than she had seen it in a long while.

She hated to dull it again. Indeed, why should she? Need they make any great secret of this thing that they brought to the king? It had seemed best when they first agreed, she and Mabon and Bran, to bring the chariots on the river and not to risk them by land. Yet one chariot, with such a charioteer, surely would come safe to Lir.

"Good, then," she said. "We'll do that. The guards can follow on horses."

His smile was swift, and swiftly suppressed, and yet it warmed her. "Will there be fighting?" he asked a little too brightly.

She was not sorry to dash that hope. "Here, in the heart of the Goddess' country? Not likely."

"Then why did we come slowly, in boats, and not quickly, in chariots?"

"To keep the chariots safe," she said, "and unbroken, till they come to the king."

"They would have been safe," he said. "They're strong enough for battle." He peered at her in the bright starlight. "That's what you fear, isn't it? That they'll terrify your people. They're new—different. They promise things that your country hoped never to see."

"We've known war," she said, "since the dawn time. There have been battles, invasions. What we are now, we are because horsemen came from the steppe, rode over our people, and made themselves kings at the side of our Mothers. Those old forts on the hills—those went up when great hordes swept across the river and did their best to crush us. Many of them won, or thought they did. But here we are. And yet . . ." She sighed. "It's been a long time since anyone challenged us. We're not as strong now as we were then. And you—your people—are very strong indeed."

"I belong to you now," he said, soft and bitter. "I am your slave. They who rule the steppe, they are no longer my people."

"Not even in your heart?"

He did not answer that. She rose and held out her hand. For a long moment she thought he would not take it, but in the end he did. She drew him up. "We should sleep," she said.

She did not mean that they should sleep together. She wondered if he was disappointed when she left him at the door of their lodging and went alone to her bed. She hoped that he was.

As it happened, she did not sleep at once, nor indeed till very late. There were preparations to make. She had to choose the two armed men who would ride with them. Mabon could not go: he had to see that the chariots traveled safely on the river. But when she went looking for him to ask for two of his men, she found him in the common-room of the lodging with Bran, lingering over wine.

They welcomed her with wine-warmed gladness. Neither of them was awash in it, but they were much at ease. Mabon filled a cup and held it out.

She took it but did not drink. "There's little time for wine," she said. "I'm taking one of the chariots, and the charioteer, to Lir. Mabon, will you lend us two of your guards? They should be ready to ride at dawn, and ride fast."

Mabon raised his brows. "Trouble?" he asked.

"No," she said. "But my heart bids me go."

"Ah," said Mabon. "The Goddess. Or is it the mare? Is she eager to see her kin again?"

Bran spoke before she could find an answer. "I'll go. I'll ride."

"You're not a guard," she said. "You belong with the rest of the chariots."

"And not with you," he said. His tone was flat.

She stared at him. He had seemed over the months of their journey to come to acceptance of the world as it was. She had even thought him happy, surrounded by chariots, learning what Minas and the chariots themselves had to teach.

The wine had loosened his tongue. He met her stare with defiance that made her think, painfully, of the boy he had been. He still was, in his heart. And he still wanted her—a wanting that was close to anguish.

She loved him. He was her yearmate, her friend, her heart's brother. But her desire for him was lost somewhere between Long Ford and the camp of the Windriders. She had taken Dal as much to spite him as for the boy's beauty and his ready smile. But when Dal died, she had wanted no one else of her own people. She only came close to wanting the man who, by now, hated her perfectly: the man she had bought in return for the king's heir of Lir.

All this filled her heart as she met Bran's stare. "You will stay," she told him as gently as she could, "and guard the chariots, and continue to learn all you can of them. When you come to Lir, there will be a forge for you, and apprentices, and whatever else is necessary. Tell me what you need, and we will have it."

"I need . . ." His voice caught. "Be careful what you promise. I'll hold you to it."

"I'll see that you get it," she said.

He had mastered himself, wine and all. "I'll get word to you before dawn. May I have your leave to go?"

Rhian had never in her life given Bran leave to do anything. Mothers did that, and elders, and priestesses. Rhian was only Rhian.

She was the mare's servant. Bran bade her remember it. "You have my leave," she said stiffly.

44

Minas was up in chilly starlight, choosing the chariot-teams and the chariot, and harnessing Adis' duns that were most apt to his hand. By the time the others came out yawning and stumbling, he was ready to go.

He carefully said nothing to any of them of the ease with which he had done all this. There had been no guards on the boats, and the herds had only the mare to watch over them. Everyone else was asleep in a haze of wine.

Conquerors had only to know when the festivals were, and attack in the wake of them. Thieves could have made off with all the chariots and every one of the horses, and no one been the wiser.

There seemed to be no thieves here. When anyone wanted a thing, he asked for it. Most often he was given it, either in trade or as a gift.

But Minas could not ask for his freedom. That, they would never grant. He was too valuable.

He had thought, there in the dark with its faint threat of frost, of taking the chariot and riding out—east, not west. He had gone so far as to gather the reins and rouse the team.

But he did not bid them take him home. He had his honor. And, he admitted, he was curious. He wanted to see this city everyone spoke of as if it were the gods' own dwelling place, and meet this king whose son had so captivated Etena that she traded gold and a prince for him.

He had come this far. He would see it through to the end. Therefore he was ready before the others had even come out, and waiting when they came. He had half expected them to insist on a baggage train, soft creatures that they were, but apart from the remounts, who carried small burdens, they traveled as light as tribesmen on a raid.

There were only the four of them: Minas and Rhian in the chariot, and two black-bearded young men on horses.

As the first light swelled in the sky, Minas took up the reins. The dun stallions snorted. They were eager to go.

But he held them in. The Mother herself walked toward them down the long sloping way from her house, with a pair of young women for escort. She moved lightly for so massive a woman, with grace that must have been remarkable in her youth.

All of the guards who had come from World's End were there. To a man and a woman, they bowed before the Mother. Only Minas kept his head erect, and Rhian, who was distracted: the mare, relegated to the remounts, had chosen that moment to put one of the stallions in his place.

Even a Mother had to wait on a goddess. When the flurry of squealing and kicking had died down, with no bloodshed but with the stallion much subdued, Rhian turned as if to speak to Minas, caught sight of the Mother and started. "Lady! I didn't see you. Please, if you'll pardon me—"

"The mare's servant serves the mare," said the Mother. "The rest of us are of lesser account."

Rhian looked as if she might have contested that, but the Mother gave her no time.

"I came simply to bid you farewell," the Mother said, "and to give you blessing upon your journey."

"You honor us," Rhian said, "and your blessing is most welcome."

"Even to you?"

The Mother was not speaking to her but to Minas. He still had a prince's instincts: he had spoken before he thought, stumbling in the western tongue, but managing to find the words. "Even to me," he said, "blessing is always welcome."

He had startled them all, and Rhian not least. Only the Mother seemed unsurprised. She smiled at him and raised her hands. "Then may the Goddess bless you and watch over you, and bring you safe to your journey's end."

They all bowed to that—Minas, too, as a prince might before the gods.

He was a most imperfect slave. But these were most indulgent masters. He brought the team round in the flame of the morning, saluted the Mother as if she had been a king of the People, and swept his little company out of the city.

⇀ ↼

It was a glorious morning, bright and clear, with a light wind blowing, just enough to cool the heat of the sun. The horses were fresh but obedient. The road was broad and clear, as if it had been meant for a chariot. It ran along the river, so that there was always water to drink and bathe in. Often there were trees, but never so thick as to shut out the sun.

They skirted the villages that owed service to the cities like hunting-clans to the greater tribes. Even so, they could hardly escape notice. Nothing like them had been seen in this part of the world before.

People were not afraid. That astonished Minas. On the steppe, everyone knew the rumor of the terrible chariots and their even more terrible riders. Here, that rumor had never come. What the lords and priestesses knew, it seemed, was not open knowledge. Their people lived in innocence.

To them the painted box on wheels, drawn by horses, was a marvel. They followed it in open delight, chattering with questions. They wanted to know who and what the charioteer was, how the chariot was made, how the horses had been taught to pull it. They plucked at the harness, peered at the fittings. Sometimes, if they were bold, they begged to drive the chariot.

"Gods," Minas said on the second day, after they had escaped from a particularly persistent mob of villagers. "Your country has nothing to fear from the People. You'll overwhelm them with curiosity."

Rhian was riding the mare just then, leaving Minas alone in the chariot. She grinned at him with an utter lack of sympathy. "The women were all remarking on your skill as a charioteer."

"They would know?"

"They know a good hand on the rein, whether the man be sitting on a horse or standing behind it."

That was not the part of him she was speaking of, and she made sure he knew it. He was glad of the sun and wind that had turned his fair cheeks to ruddy bronze. They hid the blush.

He would never grow accustomed to women with eyes as bold as men's, and tongues that if anything were bolder. He almost began to regret how quickly he had learned to make sense of their language.

When they traveled by night, it was less difficult. The roads were nearer empty then. Under stars and a sliver of moon, they sped through the darkened villages. Those were closer together, the farther they went, till it seemed there was hardly open space between them.

Late the second night, they stopped to rest, camping in a grove of trees. Past the trees the land rose in a long swell. The stars were very close; they seemed to sit atop the hill, resting as the riders rested, waiting for the morning.

Minas slept as a wise warrior did, with one ear alert. That ear heard Rhian rise, just before the sun came up, and creep softly away from the others.

He woke at once and completely. She was climbing the hill, alone, without even the mare to bear her company. Something about her, some turn of the head, some tensing of the back, brought him up and in her wake.

She might reckon herself quiet, but he was silence itself. He could pass like a shadow in the starlight. The horses barely raised their heads at his presence.

She ascended the summit of the hill and sat there. Minas, making himself part of a shadow of trees, looked to see what she was gazing at with such intensity.

It was a village, he saw, on a long level of the river. There was nothing remarkable about it. It was smaller than some. The hill on which she was sitting held the ruins of a fort, but none had been built in its place, nor did the village boast a wall. It was a cluster of huts and houses, no high roof of a temple. Sheep grazed between the hill's summit and the village. Minas did not see the shepherd. Either there was none, or he had hidden himself in a fold of the land.

"Long Ford?" Minas asked.

She started like a deer. It was fair revenge, he thought, for her laughter of the morning before.

She settled quickly: like the mare she served, she was not at heart a skittish creature. She kept her temper, too, which surprised him somewhat. "Yes," she said. "Long Ford."

"Will we ride through it?"

"The road passes by it."

"We could," he said delicately, "go round this hill, and keep it between ourselves and the village. If we would avoid the curious, and the women who so admire my hands on the reins."

"It would delay us," she said as if to herself. "If they knew I was here— my aunt—the friends I had—"

"It would be rude simply to ride through without stopping. And the errand is too urgent to let us linger."

"You don't think I'm a coward?" she asked him.

"No," he said, and that was the truth.

"It would be cruel, too. Wouldn't it? To let them see me, but not pause to speak, or explain. Because explanations would take so long, and a proper welcome even longer. And we have to come to Lir."

"That is so," he said.

"Then we will go round the hill," she said, "and leave the river."

She did not sound relieved to have made the choice, nor content with it, either. But it was wise; it seemed she saw that.

He did not greatly like to deepen her wisdom, but the sun was close to rising, and they were clearly visible from the village, if anyone had looked up. "Come away," he said, "before we're seen."

She looked as if he had struck her, but she let herself be led down from the hill.

45

When Rhian had killed three men with arrows from her bow, she had known less pain of spirit than she knew in choosing to pass by the village that had raised her. It was an older pain, she thought. She had evaded it longer, and given it more time to fester.

She wanted, that morning, to run back into Dura's arms; to hide herself in the small cluttered house, in her old bed between the hearth and the potter's wheel, and not emerge again until all this strangeness was gone.

That was foolish, and she knew it even as she thought it. The strangeness had become her world.

She had never been born in Long Ford, or bred there. The place of her birth had cast her out. Now she traveled toward it as if to invade it.

The two guards, circumspect men both, said nothing of her taking the long way round that particular hill. Once they were past it, at full speed of chariot and remounts, they were a bare day's journey from Lir.

When she was a simple village child, that had seemed a great distance. Now that she had crossed the sea of grass, and known that her many days' journey there was but a portion of a vast whole, this day seemed as short as the blink of an eye. She had lived out her life in the shadow of Lir, and never known what she was to it. For that, she had needed to travel beyond the shadow, into the cold glare of the truth.

Maybe that was why she had been sent to Long Ford, and not farther away. Not simply because the priestess from Long Ford had happened to be in the temple that day, with a child that had died, and breasts that had ached with untasted milk. If she was not to be sent to the lands of the dead, which were both farther away than anyone could imagine, and nearer than the next breath or the next heartbeat, then she would be kept within the sight and the power of the priestesses in Lir.

The mare had taken her to the sea of grass, to free her. But now Rhian came back. She rode in a chariot on ways that she had never traveled before, westward through the close-gathered towns to the city of the Goddess.

It lay like a jewel in a broad ring of open land: fields and groves and orchards now stripped by the harvest. The leaves of the trees had turned, so that the city was ringed in scarlet and gold. The river shimmered with it. Boats rode the water, fleets of them, traders' boats and fishermen's boats and pleasure-boats of princes.

The city itself was walled in golden stone. It had five gates, one for each quarter of the wind, and one for the Goddess who ruled them all. Her presence was everywhere about it. Her image was carved in the stones, and stood at the turns of the road, and hung from the branches of the trees. Even the wind was hers, the breath of her spirit in her oldest and most beloved city.

The road was broad and clean. Stones were laid on it to ease travelers' passage. The chariot's wheels rumbled over them, deafening those who rode in it.

They had a following of people afoot and on horseback, women and men and children, in a chorus of barking dogs and a tumult of questions. The horses, trained in war and accustomed to a close press of bodies, still had not had to pull their chariot along a paved road before. They were fractious, and more so the closer to the city they came.

Rhian gripped the sides of the chariot as one of the dun stallions bucked hard enough to rock the car. Minas kept the horse in hand. His face was quiet, intent. He seemed in no difficulty. Yet there was a tightness in his jaw, a deepening of the frown with which he contemplated the horses.

"Stop the chariot," she said abruptly.

He glanced at her. After a moment he shrugged, as if he had considered asking why but decided against it. He gentled the horses down, taking his time about it, letting them settle little by little.

When they were still, Rhian turned to the crowd that had stopped with them. "Please," she said. "Of your courtesy. Draw back, move softly. Be a guard of honor. For the horses' sake, I ask it of you."

"Are you the mare's new servant?" demanded one of the women on horseback, a proud gold-bedecked creature on a splendid black mare.

For answer, the white mare herself came between Rhian and the rider,

flattening ears at the black mare, sending her in swift retreat. The others
bowed, even the children for once somewhat subdued, and opened a ring
about the chariot.

Rhian smiled at them all. "I thank you," she said, "and my charioteer
thanks you from the bottom of his heart. Will you escort us, then? Will
you conduct us into Lir?"

They were pleased to do that, and in reasonable order, too, now they
understood that it mattered to the horses. That was the courtesy of the
Goddess' country, and the fine manners of Lir.

The way opened before them after that, although it had been thronged
with travelers. They made a path for the chariot, a road of honor. The
horses, as if aware of that, arched their necks and danced a little.

Minas' jaw was still set, but his frown had eased. He was merely intent
on what he was doing. She wondered if his heart was beating as hard as
hers, as they drew closer to the high gate. There were guards above it in
bright armor, and people in it, watching their advance.

"The king?" Rhian asked the nearer of Mabon's guards.

The man, whose name was Huon, was farsighted; he could see faces
where she saw only a blur of dark and pale. After a moment he shook
his head. "It's guards, mostly, and people from the city. No one of
rank."

"He would wait inside," Minas said, "if he is a king like our kings.
They never come out. It would be beneath them. They send their sons,
maybe, or their warband, for escort. But not themselves."

"That is how it is," Huon agreed. He tilted his head toward the great
circle of their escort. "Did you think these came on us by accident?"

Rhian had not been thinking. Whatever the mother of her body had
been, she was a potter's child. She knew little of kings and Mothers, ranks
and courtesies.

"You'll have to guide me," she said, "through the city's ways. I come
from a simple village. Cities are all strange to me."

"And this is Lir." Huon nodded. "Yes, I'll guide you, if that's your
wish. Follow me now. Remember who you are, and what you are and
why you came here. You are higher than kings, but your grace permits
you to bow to the will of kings."

Minas startled her with a sudden smile. It was crooked, but it understood more, just then, than she did. "Will your proud people accept such
a thing, if they see it in a slave?"

"Are you not a king's heir?" Huon asked.

Minas stood straighter. His shoulders went back, his chin came up.

He was as beautiful as his horses. The rush of heat startled her. She
had felt so little for so long, that to feel it now, almost under the gate of
Lir, left her breathless and barely able to see, let alone think.

She must be as clear-headed as she had ever been, to face this city. Its gate opened like a mouth, gaping to swallow her.

She fought free of that vision. She had ridden through gates of cities before, though not a city as great as this. She had seen crowds of people, been stared at, remarked on, followed. That was the lot of the mare's servant, the woman who had brought the chariots into the Goddess' country.

Lir was a city. Yes. A great and beautiful city. Some of its houses were of stone. Most were of wood carved and painted with wonderful artistry. There were green places, avenues of trees, flowers cascading over walls and down staircases. The brilliance of the colors, the crowding together of trees and houses, the throngs of people in bright clothing, in gold and shell and amber, dizzied her; dazzled her.

Huon led them down the long wide way. It was straight, not twisted and tangled as streets were in towns and villages; nor, because the city was so great, did it curve round the circuit of the walls. It led to a circle, a gathering of great houses. One was of stone, one of wood, one of both.

King's house, Mother's house, temple. That much Rhian knew from the teachings of her childhood. King's house of stone, for men and war. Mother's house of wood, for women and peace. And temple wall of both, for the alliance between them.

The temple was silent. Its doors were shut. The Mother's house was shut and barred. Only the king's house was open to their coming.

Huon led them to the open gate. Armored men stood there. They had spears in hand, held lightly, either to ward or to show the way.

Huon dismounted in front of them. Rhian chose to take that as a sign to the rest. She stepped down from the chariot, tugging at Minas till he secured the reins and followed her. On foot, leading the horses, they entered the king's house.

It was the largest house she had ever been in, and the highest. Yet at heart it was like any other house in this country: a great room with a hearth, and a cluster of lesser rooms behind, where the kitchens and the storerooms were, the guardrooms, the servants' quarters, the armories.

There were two stories to it, and a stair that ascended to the second, where the king and his family and his guests would sleep. The whole of Long Ford could have lived there, with all their kin, and taken up but a portion of it.

They left the horses in the outer court, which in a lesser house would have been an entry no larger than the stretch of a woman's arms; but here it was as large as a whole house in a village.

The hall was wide and airy. Its roof was held up on pillars that had been great trees, and the center of the roof was open, letting in the light and air, and letting out the smoke of the fire.

The king sat by the hearth, flanked by half a dozen young men whose faces made Rhian catch her breath. Emry seven times over, from beardless youth to man of solid years: for each was an image of the other, and the king no less than the rest.

These were his father and his brothers. Her father; her brothers. She had the answer to the question she had asked Emry, so long ago and so far away. Yes, they were all like him, and yes, they were all beautiful.

They stared at her as if she were a spirit come back from the dead. With a soft clatter of hooves on stone paving, the mare came up behind her and rested her head lightly on Rhian's shoulder. They eased at that, all at once, and the youngest said, "Oh! It's the mare's servant." And somewhat belatedly: "Lady, we welcome you to Lir."

His elders frowned at him, but indulgently. He flushed. He was very young; his voice was barely broken. It cracked as he said, "I'm sorry, lady. My father should have said that."

"It was a fine welcome," Rhian said, "whoever gave it. I'm honored to be in your city."

"We are honored with your presence." The king's voice was like Emry's, dark and sweet. He rose; he was a tall man, and broad, towering over all but the eldest of his sons. "And this is the prince from the sea of grass?"

"This is Minas, king's heir of the People of the Wind," said Rhian.

Minas was silent, standing very straight, eyes fixed on something only he could see. She had insisted that he put on the clothes he had worn to the festival in Larchwood; that he look like a prince and not a slave. He had obeyed her without a word, but without any particular delight, either.

He did look well, and to her eyes, properly royal. How he might seem to the king of Lir, she could not tell. The king studied Minas at his leisure, in silence.

His sons followed suit, with the same careful lack of expression, except for the youngest; his eyes were not friendly as he looked Minas up and down. Minas came back from wherever his spirit had been, and met those eyes, and said levelly, "Yes, I was reckoned worth your brother's life."

"One life means little beside the lives of all the Goddess' people," said the king. If he grieved, he held it at bay. "Gerent, you will look after our guests. See that they're housed and bathed and fed, and treated with every possible honor."

The boy looked as if he had been slapped. Still, as spoiled as he might be, he was properly brought up. He bent his head in obedience.

"My lord," Rhian said before Gerent could take them away, "will you see the chariot first?"

"Are you not tired?" the king asked. "Hungry?"

"That will wait," she said.

The king deferred to her. That was startling. But she was a goddess' servant, and he belonged to his people. Her rank was above his.

The chariot was waiting where they had left it, with their two guards standing by it. A small crowd had gathered, mostly men and boys, but a few women standing in the midst of them. None was dressed as a priestess.

They gave way before the king. He nodded to one or two of the men, and bowed somewhat more deeply to the women. He walked a circle around the chariot and its restive horses, examining it as closely as he had examined Minas, and with the same lack of expression.

When he was done, he said to his sons who had followed him, "See to the horses. Bring the chariot into the stables. And Gerent, do as I bade you before."

"Huon," Rhian said equably, "show the king's men how to tend the harness. Rory, help with the chariot."

No one dared contradict her. It was an odd feeling, not exactly pleasant, but not too greatly unpleasant, either. With the horses taken care of and the chariot as safe as it could be, she allowed Gerent to do his father's bidding.

······· **46** ·······

Minas' captivity was as easy here as it had been on the way to Lir. There were no chains. He was dressed and tended and fed like a prince. His bed was soft, the room airy, and part of its wall opened and fastened back, so that he could look out on a stretch of green toward a house such as he had seen before, in which these people kept their horses.

There was no feast of welcome that night, at least not for him. He bathed alone but for a pair of silent menservants. He ate alone, and it seemed he was expected to sleep alone. He was more weary than he had reckoned, weary to the bone. He lay on the too-high, too-soft bed and fell into sleep as into deep water.

⇨ ⇦

The sun woke him, casting a beam across his face. It was high enough to have risen above the wall of the house, and bright enough to dazzle him. He sat up blinking, struggling for memory. He was not in a tent. Nor was he on the steppe. The air was strange, heavy with the scents of water and green things.

It came to him all at once, as he staggered to the window and leaned on its frame. He was in the king's house of Lir. His room was two men's height and more above the ground. Horses grazed below in a green paddock between the house and the stable. He recognized Adis' duns and the grey mare who was a goddess.

There were clothes laid out, clean and new. They fit as if made for him. They were plainer than the festival garb of Larchwood, but more finely woven, and sturdy: made for use. There were no ornaments and no weapons. That much of captivity, it seemed, he must suffer.

He ventured out of the sunlit room into airy dimness. He stood on a gallery above the great open space with its banked fire. A few servants were in it, but none acknowledged him.

He inched his way along the wall. He was a warrior of the plains. He was not meant to perch on ledges. It was a great relief to come to the stair, though that was its own horror. He edged down it, sliding a foot along each step.

The tiling of the floor was not blessed earth, not quite, but near enough. He restrained himself from clinging to it like a child to its mother.

Even before servants he would not show himself weak. He walked steadily away from the stair. A man approached him with a basket. In it were bread, fruit, cheese. "To eat when you work," the servant said with a dip of the head, offering respect with the gift.

Minas took it half-blindly. "Work?" he asked.

"Come," the servant said, smiling as if to a child. "Come and see."

Clutching the basket, Minas followed the servant out of the king's house and into the sunlight. There were people out and about, a good number of them, men and women both. They busied themselves with tasks, some of which he recognized, some not. One gathering out beyond the stable—that was familiar.

They were gathered round the chariot. They had not, at least, taken it apart. A pair of sturdy legs protruded from beneath it; a woman's voice echoed from the box. He understood enough to know that she was commenting on the fastening of the axle to the body of the chariot.

The others listened with deference that warned him: when she emerged, wriggling out from beneath the chariot, she reminded him rather fiercely of Rhian. It was little to do with her looks—she was no beauty; she was sturdy, rather, and foursquare, with a broad pleasant face and callused hands. But something about her, the way she carried herself, the clarity of her eyes as she raised them to him, spoke of the mare's servant.

It was authority, he thought. Among the People, men had it; particularly men who were clan chieftains and princes.

She looked him over as women did in this country, frankly, letting him know what she thought of him. It seemed she approved. Mostly they did, though he had heard a few remark that he was somewhat thin and very pale, and they did not like it that he did not grow his beard. Such of it as he had, which was little beside the men here.

But this woman seemed content with him as he was. She said in the traders' speech, "You'll be teaching me to build these. The rest of these here will do your bidding. Tell them of the wood, the leather, the metal, how the wheels are made—one by one, in order, as it must be."

"Is that a command?" Minas asked her.

Her smile had the same implacable sweetness as Rhian's. "You are not given a choice, no. But we do ask. In courtesy."

"You are very courteous people here," Minas said.

"Teach," she said. Courteously.

That was his work: to teach. These outlanders knew nothing, but guessed much. They knew the potter's wheel and the wheel of the oxcart, if not the chariot-wheel. They knew the carving of wood, the curing of leather. And they knew bronze, which he did not.

Metos would covet their wealth of wood and hides and metal, and their great numbers of willing craftsmen. When Minas began, there were half a dozen. Before the sun touched the zenith, there must have been half a hundred. He could not be sure: as many seemed to leave as to arrive, and those who came later brought things that he had indicated a need for earlier. Some had set to work splitting and cutting logs of wood. Others had begun to cut and sew harness.

However soft these people might be, they had no fear of hard work. They listened and they learned, and they remembered well.

He forgot to eat that day, and only remembered to drink when a bold-eyed girlchild brought him a cup brimming with cool water. When the light began to fade, his pupils left him—they were not like Metos' apprentices yet; they did not have the strength to work through the night.

He let them go. He lingered till dark, alone and it seemed forgotten. There was feasting in the king's house, lamps lit, a fire burning, savory scents wafting out into the chill of evening. He welcomed the bite of hunger and the fiercer bite of loneliness. Those well befit a slave; and that, after all, he was.

He dozed, maybe, sitting beside the chariot with his back to the wheel. When he roused, the king sat beside him, wrapped in a mantle, and a second lay warm over his own shoulders.

He blinked at the lord of Lir, still half in a dream. He had been on the steppe, or perhaps in the shamans' country, and yet he was also here beside the river of souls, under the power of the western goddess. The king's face seemed part of the dream, so like Rhian, and so like the man with whom she had bought Minas.

Out of that dream or waking vision, Minas said, "He is your son, isn't he? The one who stayed behind."

"He is my heir," said the king. His voice was quiet.

Minas nodded slowly. "Yes. Yes, the gods would reckon that a fair exchange."

"They would," said the king, still in that soft expressionless tone.

"But you," said Minas, "know a deep and abiding anger."

"Do you not?" the king asked.

"To the bottom of my heart," Minas said. "But what is done is done. I gave my word, and I will keep it."

"I have made no promises, secured no alliances. The mare's servant does not speak for me."

Minas sat still in the darkness. "And yet you use me."

"Why not? Doesn't your king use every weapon set in his hand?"

"And many that are not," Minas said, "but which he can take."

There was a pause. The night wind played about the space between the walls. At length the king said, "I will not ask you to assure me that my son is safe. That is with the Goddess. But will he be treated well?"

"He was bought and not captured," Minas said. "And she who bought him is intrigued by him. If he's clever and circumspect, he'll keep her intrigued, perhaps for a long time."

"We do learn here, how to fascinate women," the king said. He sounded almost smug.

"If your son learned it well," Minas said, "he'll be as safe as a man can be in this world."

The king seemed, if not satisfied, then willing to let it go. He rose. "Come," he said. "Take the daymeal with me."

"As a guest?"

"You are our guest," the king said.

An odd sort of guesting, Minas thought: bought and paid for, and no choice in it. But it was preferable, surely, to the lot of a slave.

47

Rhian was offered a bed in the king's house, but some spirit in her sent her to the stable instead, to the mare's stall. It was bedded deep with sweet straw, and there was water, and a servant brought food for her to eat. In the morning she was offered a bath and fresh clothing, all that befit a guest. But all night long she had the mare's warm familiar presence.

She had slept in cities. World's End and Larchwood had been pleasant enough, and Britta and the Mother had welcomed her with honest warmth.

In this city she had been born. Here were her blood kin. Yet she felt no warmth. Men had greeted her, but her father, her brothers had not known her. She had seen no women who were not either artisans or servants. There was nothing here that spoke of honest welcome.

She went out in the morning after a restless night. The mare did not see fit to follow. There was grass here, and leisure. She meant to pursue both.

Therefore Rhian was alone, walking out of the king's house, past guards who bowed but made no move to stop her. The city was awake. Bread was baking, potters' wheels turning. She saw a weaver at the loom and a goldsmith at the forge. Children tumbled and played in the street.

The temple was as silent as it had been the day before. She hesitated in front of it. Her heart was beating hard enough to deafen her. She would faint, she thought rather distantly.

This was the greatest of all temples, sacred to the Lady of the Birds. It was wider than the king's house, and higher. No one knew how many priestesses were in it. Many: that much was certain. They were all brought here, schooled here, then chosen for temples in every city; but the best of all stayed in Lir.

Not one of them had come out to see the chariot or its charioteer, or to look on the mare's servant. The gates were shut. Rhian would have thought them dead, as the Mother was, save that she heard, dim and muffled by walls, the soft high sweetness of women's voices. They were chanting the morning hymn.

After a long moment, she turned away from the locked gate. The Mother's house stood dark and silent. It was truly empty, truly deserted.

Its door gave to the touch of her hand. She recoiled, startled. She had not meant to go in, not till she did it.

The court was dusty and unswept. Banks of flowers along the wall had overgrown their ornamented pots and begun to die. The trees that guarded the inner gate had let fall their leaves.

It would have been beautiful when the Mother was living in it, a place of warm golden stone and rich greenery, full of the singing of birds. Their nests clung to branches of the trees and to curves of carving along the roofbeams. But they were all empty now. Nothing stirred in this place but the wind swirling a handful of wan leaves about her feet.

The wind had nothing to say, or nothing it was willing to let her hear. She walked through the linked chain of round houses that surrounded the great house like a necklace about the neck of a Mother. All of them were empty. She could see where the potters had been, the weavers, the cooks and bakers, the woodworkers, the minders of children. All gone now, vanished into the city, she supposed, or sent back to their towns and villages.

The center of them all was a hall like the king's, but wider, higher, airier. Its walls were carved and painted so that it seemed a forest of trees and flowers, full of beasts and birds. The hearth was dark and cold. The carved chair beside it, the Mother's chair, had been a nest for mice: its cushion was sprung, the soft goosefeathers scattered on the floor.

Rhian felt nothing as she stood there, except a kind of distant sadness. She was not meant to sit in this chair. Her place was on the mare's back. Home was the wind and the sky and the freedom of the earth. This city, these people, were not kin in the spirit, whatever their blood made them.

"I am more kin to the wild horsemen than to these my own people," she said. She spoke softly, but her voice echoed in the hall.

She turned away from it. Now, she thought, she would go where she should have gone at first.

⇒ ⇐

This gate was shut and barred. Rhian went over it. If there were powers on it, she never felt them.

She came down a hill of grass divided into stone paths. They looked like the spokes of a chariot-wheel, leading to the temple at the hub — strangely bitter to see it so, like the image of the thing that would destroy it. Houses lay in circles about it, many houses, and rich. But the temple was small in the midst of them, and low, and very, very old.

She saw priestesses here and there within the walls. They were dressed for the most part as she was dressed, in trousers with or without tunic. Few wore the robes she had thought all priestesses must wear, and none proclaimed her beauty in the skirt of scarlet cords in which they celebrated their great rites. And none was masked.

They were women like any others — like Rhian as she began to move along the path. She attracted no notice. If they had been guarding against her, they had failed.

She approached the temple slowly. Its gate was open — here, there seemed to be no need to protect it. It was not as large as the temple in Larchwood. It was dark and low and redolent of age.

Here was power. Here was the Goddess' oldest place of worship. Here women had come since the dawn of time. Here Mothers had ruled the rite, here they had died. And here they had been born, in a dark and ancient room lit only by lamps, so thick with holiness that surely it had suffocated no few of them.

Rhian had been born in that room. She stood in the outer room of the temple, before the most ancient of all images of the Goddess, lit by the fire that, she had been taught, had been kindled in the first morning of the world. She felt the spirits all about her, old priestesses, old Mothers, her ancestors and her kin.

Home, this was not; no more than the Mother's house was. But it was hers in ways that she could hardly begin to understand. Her blood, her bone, were bound up in this place.

"So," said a clear and bitter voice behind her. "You come at last where you should never have been."

She did not turn to face the priestess who had refused the Goddess' choosing. "I come where the Goddess leads me," she said.

"You were not led here."

"Would you know?"

She heard the soft tread of feet on the earth of the floor. Her shoulders tightened. If the priestess meant to kill her, it would happen now. She would not stop it. There was a wildness in her, a kind of madness.

But she was still alive when the squat sturdy figure halted beside her. The priestess carried no weapon, unless she reckoned that her eyes would suffice.

Rhian had never been hated. Long Ford had been stifling to her spirit, but it had been a gentle place. Even on the steppe, among the lords of slaughter, she had been made welcome.

This was hatred, pure and unalloyed. She met it with calm she had to fight for. "Has it ever struck you," she asked, "that by opposing the Goddess' will, you may be bringing on the thing you fear? That because you cast me out, you made the rest inevitable?"

"No," said the priestess. "Not ever."

"This is no place for lies," Rhian said.

The priestess' breath hissed. "How dare you?"

"You know how I dare," said Rhian. "Look about you. Think! Because of you, there is no Mother in Lir. The temple is shut and barred. Only the king is left to rule. When the tribes come, this city will fall, not because its walls were weak or its defenses feeble, but because there is no one to lead its people."

"The king rules well," the priestess said. "We maintain the Goddess' rites as we have always done."

"But there is no one in the Mother's house," Rhian said. "There is no heart in Lir."

"This is the heart of Lir," the priestess declared. She struck the earth with her foot. "Here, in this place. This is the center."

"You are as blind as you ever were," Rhian said. "You were born blind. But when you die, your eyes will open. You will see."

"Are you threatening me?"

"I am telling the truth," said Rhian.

"You should not have come here," the priestess said.

That was a threat. Rhian turned on her. She recoiled slightly. Rhian had no time to indulge in satisfaction. "Listen," she said. "You listen to me. Hate me all you like. Loathe me till your heart turns black with it. But you will defend this city. You will help the king. You will do whatever is needed to protect the charge that has been given you."

"That is not yours to ordain," said the priestess.

Rhian began to understand hate. It was a great deal like rage, and a great deal like frustration. "You will do it," she said. "For Lir's sake, you will."

"Not for you. Not ever for you."

"Blind," Rhian muttered.

"Perhaps I can see."

Rhian turned to face a woman she did not know. It was a woman of no age in particular, as this first priestess was, but Rhian thought she might be older. Her eyes were clouded with the veil that sometimes fell with age, and yet they saw farther than most eyes that Rhian had known. It was her spirit: it saw clearer, the darker the light of mortal day became.

"Lady," Rhian said in deep respect.

The second priestess inclined her head. "Lady," she responded. "I will not say you are welcome here, but I greet you in the Goddess' name."

"I care little for courtesies," said Rhian. "But I will not see this country fall for a simple lack of good sense."

This second priestess was not lost in hate or fear: she laughed at that, and said, "There is a little sense among us, though you might not believe it."

"Open the temple, then," Rhian said. "Summon the king and his counselors. Bring me in front of them, and I will tell you everything I learned on the sea of grass."

That sobered the priestess. "Have you spoken with the king?"

"No," said Rhian.

"Ah," the priestess said. Then: "I can summon the priestesses. But the king—I doubt he would come at our command."

"Ah," said Rhian in much the same tone as the priestess had, with much the same understanding. "Very well. We meet in the Mother's house, tomorrow morning. I will see that the king is there. Will you do the same for the ladies of the temple?"

"I will try," the priestess said.

⇒ ⇐

"I do not go at their bidding," the king said.

She had found him in a field outside the city, shooting at targets with a bow of remarkable length and heft. It was a bow only a strong man might bend, a man who took great pride in his strength. It made her think, somehow, of the warriors of the steppe.

His greeting was courteous, even warm. But when she told him of her errand, his deep blue eyes went cold. The men about him had drawn back as if in anticipation of trouble, but he did not shout or strike. "They do not rule me," he said.

"They are the Goddess' servants," said Rhian.

He was trying, she could see, to remain calm; to remember that she was an outsider, and very likely an innocent. Which she was, but not to the point of idiocy. He said, "I am not their servant."

"Tell me, then," she said. "What they did."

His companions glanced at one another. Innocence, she thought, had its advantages. As did the mare, who had appeared, quite casually, just behind her.

The king was master of his temper. He answered levelly, brief but clear enough. "They attempted to make a Mother of one who was never blessed with the right to that office."

"It seems they failed," she observed.

"She died," he said. "In her sleep. Before she could be consecrated."

"Was she helped into the Goddess' arms?"

"Not by me," he said, "or by anyone under my orders."

"There is still no Mother in Lir," said Rhian, "so it seems that your will and the Goddess' were the same. Why are you still at war with the priestesses?"

"Because once they failed with their false Mother, they formed a council. That council attempted to impose its will on me."

"You are a man," she said. "They are women and priestesses."

"Surely," said the king. "They bade me abandon my plans for the defense of this country, call back the caravan, and above all, permit no chariots to cross the river, and no charioteers, either. If I had done as they bade, you would still be on the steppe, and there would be no prince of chariots teaching our people the secrets of his craft."

"What would they have had you do?" Rhian inquired.

"Nothing," he said. "Build walls. Train soldiers. Both of which I was doing already. And pray—that, they urged me to do in all zeal and piety."

"Every breath we draw is a prayer," Rhian said. Dura her aunt had loved that saying, and found frequent occasion to recall it.

"Indeed," said the king. "I will not be ruled by these priestesses."

"Will you come for me, then?" Rhian asked. "In the Goddess' name?"

She held her breath. He took his time in replying. He was a proud man, she could see, and well aware of his rank and position. And yet he was also a man of sense, or so she had always heard. "For you I will come," he said. "But only for you, and for the Goddess you serve."

"That will do," Rhian said, "and I thank you."

He bowed to her, lower maybe than he strictly needed, but there seemed to be no mockery in it. "The mare chose well," he said. "That comforts me."

"We all need comfort in these days," she said.

48

Rhian wanted a man that night—the first night in a long while that she had hungered for the warmth of another body in her bed, and the comfort of arms about her. There were no few men both young and not so young who indicated that they would have been pleased to answer her summons. But when night had fallen, when the daymeal was eaten and the wine had gone round, the bed she went to was none of theirs.

It was empty. Starlight shone through the open shutters. The room was clean and rather bare, scented with herbs that a servant must have scattered on the coverlets. She undressed, folded her clothes tidily, and shook her hair out of its plait. The chest at the bed's foot yielded a comb carved out of white bone, and a knot of colored cords. She sat cross-legged on the bed and began, with more patience than she usually had, to make order of her heavy black mane.

She heard his tread long before he reached the room. He walked lighter than men here, almost soundless, but the wooden floor of the gallery had a faint echo to it. She was almost done with her combing, and all but ready to begin plaiting. She knew that lamplight flattered her. He would find nothing to object to, when he came in upon her.

She had her smile ready when his hand parted the curtain—unmistakable, those long white fingers. His expression was as startled as she could have asked for. His cheeks flushed scarlet.

She widened her smile. His face locked shut. He was angry, she thought. Still. Like the king, he was proud; and he did not like to be bested by anyone, even a woman.

She watched him consider turning on his heel and stalking away. But he was as predictable as any other stallion. Pride kept him where he was, glaring at her.

When he was angry, his eyes were clear green. She smiled into them. "I don't want you," he said.

She looked down at the part of him that said the exact opposite, then back up into an even fiercer blush than before. "Come here," she said. She had no expectation that he would refuse. Particularly when she sat up a little straighter, and let him see how beautiful her breasts were.

He groaned as if in pain, but he came at her summons. She took his hands when he was close enough, and drew him stiffly down. He dropped to his knees with what must have been bruising force.

"Never lie to a goddess' servant," she said.

"I don't *want* to want you!" he burst out.

"Now that is truth," she said. She slid forward till her breasts were almost touching his breast. "But I want you. You've ruined me for black-haired men."

"Good," he said nastily.

"And I?" she asked. "Have I spoiled your taste for fair-haired women?"

"You've spoiled my taste for women at all."

"So angry," she said. "So young."

She brushed his lips with hers, light as a breath of wind. And again, just a little less light.

He moved so swiftly she had no time to react, gripped her hard, kissed her till she gasped for breath. He drove her back and down, with the full weight of him on her, and there he held her.

She regarded him without fear. That made him even angrier. She thought he might strike her. In a way he did: driving his hard rod into her, as if he would impale her.

She locked her legs about his middle. When he moved to pull back, she gripped him fast. He was deep inside her, his anger so strong, so hot, that it burned her to the very center.

She saw the horror as it struck him what he had done, or tried to do. It killed his anger. It would have killed his ardor, too, but that flame was hers to tend. In his moment of defenselessness she dipped and rolled till he lay on his back. She rode him like a fine red stallion.

She took her time about it. It had been too long since she lay with him—far too long. He, wise creature, surrendered at last, and gave himself up to her. Then there was no anger, and no horror, and no despair, either. Only the heat of the blood, and their hearts matching beat to beat. She tasted the salt sweetness of him, drew in his scent of musk and man and horses, and reveled in the ruddy splendor of his hair. It was as thick as a horse's tail, but softer by far, and bright as copper in the lamplight, shot with streaks of bronze and gold.

Men's release was always swift, not like a woman's that could go on and on. She held him just short of it, till he begged her to let him go. Then at last she did, driving him deeper even than before, and holding him while he spasmed, till his eyes rolled up in his head. He gasped like a man who was dying.

But he was very much alive. She slid down, still holding him in her, till they lay face to face, her arms about him, her thighs about his hips. His eyes now were the deep green of leaves in the summer, soft and sated. "Witch," he breathed. "Daughter of witches."

"We have been called that," she said lightly. She ran fingers down the line of his cheek, from smooth skin to prick of coppery stubble, past his chin to his shoulder, till her palm came to rest over the still-rapid beating of his heart. "Beautiful man," she said. "Did you think you could take me by force?"

"I tried," he said. "I wanted to. Gods, I wanted to!"

"Long ago," she said, "in the time of the dawn, a young man of the horsemen took a woman of the Goddess' people against her will. He did not imagine that he had committed a sin. It was only what men did. But it was a great crime against our people. He paid for it with his life."

"So," he said. "Do I die?"

"We still need you," she said. "And we promised to teach you of bronze."

"But then," he said, "I'll be put to death."

"No," said Rhian.

"But—"

"Dear fool," she said. "If you had truly meant to force me, you would not be lying in my arms. You would be gelded or dead."

He sucked in his breath. For so great a taker of heads, he was remarkably easy to appall. He could not have heard such things from a woman before: certainly not a woman who was lying in his bed.

"You couldn't have forced me," she said. "It's not in you. I took you because I wanted you, and because in your heart you wanted me."

"I'll never forgive you for what you did," he said.

"Never is a long time," she said.

He twisted away from her. She let him go. He went only as far as the wall; he huddled there in such a knot of confusion that she came near to pitying him.

"Come," she said. "Can't we declare truce?"

"Truce?" His face twisted. "What do you care for truce? You're the captor, I'm the captive. You can bind me to your will, and I will serve you as you command. But never ask me to give you more."

"If it were only your body I wanted," she said, "there are a hundred men in Lir who would be delighted to serve my pleasure. I want you, prince. Not only your rod in me or your hands on me. Your heart, too."

"You won't have it," he said through gritted teeth.

"I will win it," she said.

"I will die first."

"Maybe," she said. "Shall we wager on it?"

"No."

"It doesn't matter," she said. "I will have it in the end. And I will have you."

"I will fight you."

"Men always fight," she said. "It's how they are made. Women always win, because they are made to win. Here we understand that. On the sea of grass, people forget. They're too far from the Goddess—from the knowledge of what she is."

"That knowledge will die," he said. "Our gods will kill it."

"The Goddess can't die," said Rhian. "She is above any gods of men."

She had silenced him. She stretched on her side, wriggling till she was comfortable. She blocked his escape from the bed.

He had a strong fire of anger, and a worse one of confusion. But under her eyes, little by little, his body surrendered. It was tired; he had worked it hard. She watched him loose it into sleep.

It was true, she thought, what she had said to him. When she looked at the men of her own people now, they seemed too broad, too dark, too thickly furred with hair. She wanted slender and pale and smooth-skinned almost as a child. But no child would be so tall or so strong. And where a man was most a man—that was not a child's, not at all.

Carefully she moved in toward him. He did not thrust her away in his sleep. She slipped arms about him and laid her cheek against his breast. His heart beat slow and steady. The breath sighed like wind in his lungs.

He was like the steppe from which he came: slow drumbeat of horses' hooves, whisper of the wind through the grass. This city barely sufficed to hold him. He was as wild as the hawk of heaven.

And yet he was hers. No matter that he refused to accept it. He fought it, but he could not escape it. She was wilder than he. He was a child of the tall grass. She was a child of the Goddess.

Was this what the priestesses feared? They had locked the world in walls and bars. They had made the Goddess into a creature of secrets and of hidden rites. They had taken her away from the common run of women, and weakened her teachings.

Maybe it was best if Lir fell, after all. Maybe the temple should be broken, and its secret places opened to the sky. Maybe then the Goddess would show herself clear to her children, and no power of man or man's weapon would stand against her.

These were terrible thoughts. Yet Rhian could not stop thinking them. Lir was troubled; its spirit was dark. The Mother was dead, the priestesses at odds with the king. The Goddess' harmony was not in it, or anywhere near it.

Even as troubled as the tribe had been, its king ruled by a sorceress, his wives and sons divided, it had been singleminded in its purpose. It would invade, it would conquer. It would pursue the horizon, westward and ever westward, until it came to the edge of the world. Lir had no such singleness of mind. It was all scattered in confusion.

49

Rhian had sent some of the king's servants, by his leave, to prepare the Mother's house for the morning's council. When she came there at first light, she found the hall swept, the shutters opened to let in the light, and chairs set in a ring for those who would come. There was wine waiting, and new-baked bread, and sweet cakes.

There was no fire in the hearth. That would not be kindled, for there was no Mother to kindle it. But there was light enough, and warmth as the day brightened.

Rhian marked the place where she would sit, a chair no higher than any other, facing the door and the hearth and the Mother's empty chair. As she investigated the table laden with food and drink, Minas prowled the hall, restless as a young wolf.

She had not commanded him to come here. When she rose early, he was up just before her. He watched her bathe and dress, did the same himself, and followed where she went.

There was some comfort in his presence, and some use also. It were best he hear what she had to say, and better if he understood it. The priestesses and the king's men should know him; he was the center of everything they did to defend this country.

He seemed slight to be worth so much, and terribly young. This house meant nothing to him; he was curious, but he was not in awe. The painted walls fascinated him, and the pillars carved like trees, and the floor with its many-colored tiles.

He was on his hands and knees, peering at the tiles, when the priestesses came. There were six of them. Their leader, who walked first, was she of the clouded eyes. The bitter one followed. The rest were of lesser note, though none was young.

He crouched, wary as any other wild thing. They regarded this creature kneeling on the Mother's floor, with his bright hair and his startled green eyes, as if he had been an invader from the world of the spirits. One even made a gesture of warding. Minas grinned at her, which startled her out of all useful sense.

The king arrived then, which was a mercy, maybe. And maybe not. The warmth of sun in the hall became suddenly chill. The priestesses drew away from those half-dozen men in their warlike finery.

They faced one another like adversaries in a fight. Rhian stepped between them, glaring impartially at both. "You will sit," she said, "and eat and drink, and swallow your anger. This is no time or place for it."

They were so appalled by her impudence, and so shocked that she would dare it, that they had obeyed before any of them found words to protest. They ate; they drank the heavily watered wine. They warmed slowly in the sun.

She sat and watched them. Minas came to sit at her feet. He was playing the slave, and not too badly, either, if he kept his eyes down. Those were as defiant as the rest of him was submissive.

When both sides of the battle were quiet, Rhian said, "You will settle your differences now. You will not leave until you have done so. This city will be ruled in amity, or it will fall. That is the Goddess' word."

"Oh, it is," said the priestess with the clouded eyes. She sounded amused. "So, child. You hear her, too."

"If you hear her," Rhian asked, "why have you not spoken for her?"

"And I her Voice," said the priestess wryly. "I can speak, but I may not be heard. The Mother's death deafened us all."

"Now you will hear," Rhian said. "And you will listen well."

"We will not listen to you," said the bitter priestess.

"I do wonder," the king said, his deep voice startling after the voices of the women, "that you take this thing on yourself. The mare's servant has never been a ruler. She comes and she goes. She passes like wind among the people of the Goddess."

"In that wind," said Rhian, "is the Goddess' voice. I speak for her now, since no one listens to her Voice in the temple."

"You speak for nothing," the bitter priestess said. "You are the destroyer of Lir."

The men glanced at one another. They did not know, Rhian saw. The father of her body, the two who must be her eldest brothers, saw only a village child who had been chosen for this strangest of priesthoods, the service of the mare.

The priestesses knew, all of them, who she was. She could not allow them that advantage. She said, "I am the Mother's daughter, the child whom you would have destroyed. But the Goddess forbade that. She willed this. You will accept it."

She looked as she spoke, not at the priestesses, but into her father's eyes. Eyes as deep a blue as the sky at twilight, like Emry's, like her own. Whatever face the Mother had worn, her children had inherited their father's.

She watched him understand. She saw the astonishment; the shock. The memory, as he recalled her birth. "They said you had died," he said. "She said it. Did she know?"

"She did not," the Goddess' Voice said.

He drew in his breath with a hiss, a sharp sound of anger. "Even then," he said, "you defied your Goddess."

"You speak without understanding," said the bitter priestess. "You do not see what we saw, and still see. The fall of Lir, O king. The end of the world. Because of this child. Because of her."

"Because of her?" he demanded. "Or because of what you did to her in your cowardice? What you did to Lir—this is the Mother who should have been. This—"

"No," Rhian said. "I am not to be Mother. I belong to the mare."

"You must be Mother," he said. "We must have a lady in Lir. Otherwise there is no heart, no spirit here. There is no one to rule us."

"The Goddess rules you," Rhian said. "I will speak for her, and you will listen, but I will not sit in yonder chair, nor claim the title or the office."

"That matters little," he said, "once it is known that—"

"It will not be known," she said. "The truth of what I am, that stays within these walls."

"That is wise," the Goddess' Voice said. She did not even sound surprised.

"I do think it is," said the king slowly, as wisdom overcame anger. "We will all swear that no word leaves this place."

"That, we were sworn to on the day she was born," the Voice said.

"Perhaps that was ill sworn," said Rhian, "but it's done. It's too late by far to tell the truth. The people will be troubled enough without the burden of that."

The king inclined his head. He was trying, she thought, not to stare at her.

No matter now. "There will be a truce," she said. "The king will see to the preparations for war—in full freedom, bound to no one's will but that of the Goddess. You," she said to the priestesses, "see to the welfare of the people. Keep their bodies fed and their spirits strong. The king will defend the cities. You will see that there are cities to defend."

She met each of their stares. It was like taming horses. The stronger will won. And Rhian would not give way. She had nothing to lose here. They had everything.

That was the duty and the purpose of the mare's servant, the child in Larchwood had told her: to be free of all the lands under the Goddess' sway. To speak when no one else could safely speak. To command when command was needed, but when the need was past, to ride away.

A Mother was bound to her city. The mare's servant was bound to nothing but the mare.

Rhian rose. "You will settle matters now, as king and priestesses should. How you settle them, I care little. Only that you do it."

When she left, Minas followed. She had half expected him to linger. But he was making it clear: he was her dog. Not theirs.

"Go to the chariots," she bade him once they were out of the hall. "I need no guard now, and your pupils are waiting."

He kept his eyes on his feet; he bowed somewhat too low, and did her bidding.

⇀ ↽

Much later in the day, after the sun passed noon, the king found her where she well should be: in the stable, tending the mare. He had put aside the gold and finery of the council. He was dressed in plain leather and well-woven cloth, with sword in baldric and dagger at his side.

"Ride with me," he said, "if you will."

She raised a brow, but the mare was ready, and she too. She had had enough of walls.

His horse was waiting, a tall and sturdy red mare. Two of his sons waited with her, mounted on horses of like quality: the eldest but for Emry, one must have been, and the other was the youngest.

They kept their eyes to themselves as their father mounted and as they rode through the city. The people smiled at their coming, bowed and waved and called out greetings. There was no fear in them, and no crippling awe, but love and great respect.

Some of that was for the mare, and therefore for her rider. Rhian had yet to become accustomed to it. She followed the king's example as best she could: smiled, bowed, waved in return. It was a little easier the longer she did it.

It seemed an endless while before they passed the outer wall of the city. The fields were blessedly open before them, stripped of their harvest, lying bare under heaven.

The king, it seemed, had a place in mind. The mare was content to follow his mare. Rhian let the sun fill her, dimmed though it was by a rising veil of cloud. The wind sang in her ears. It was full of secrets.

They passed flocks of sheep in autumn pasture, and goats perching precariously on hillsides above the road. They crossed a narrow band of beechwood, pale gold and sighing in the wind. The clouds by then had thickened, obscuring the sun. Rhian's nostrils flared, catching a scent of rain.

Past the wood they left the road and followed a narrower track that wound up the side of a hill. The wind freshened as they ascended. At the summit it whipped their faces, cutting through even leather and well-woven linen and wool. Rhian shivered, but she was not truly cold. It was exhilarating—glorious.

From here they could see the whole of the country that they had ridden through to come here, the valley of the river and the patches of woodland and the circles of villages and towns. The chief jewel of them all, the city of Lir, lay within its golden walls, a patchwork of green and gold and brown.

This must be how the Goddess saw it, small enough to enfold in her hands. "Do you often come up here?" she asked him.

"Whenever I can," he answered. "From the high places, even the greatest of troubles can seem small."

"When I was younger," she said, "and my spirit needed comfort, I always went up on the hilltop above Long Ford, and listened to the wind."

"The wind knows all that goes on in this world," the king said, "though it may be difficult, sometimes, to make it care for what we care for."

Their eyes met. His were warm. She found herself smiling. "It loves gossip," she said, "and secrets."

"Some of which are even useful." He swung down from the red mare's back and held up his hands. Rhian let him catch her as she slid from the white mare's back. His hands were warm and strong, his body a bulwark against the buffet of the wind. Today it neither whispered nor laughed; it sang shrill and keen.

He shifted his hands to her shoulders, and looked her in the face. "When did you learn what you are?"

"Before I crossed the river eastward," she said, "it was made known to me. I should have died there on the sea of grass, and never come back. Certainly there were those who hoped for it."

"Priestesses," said the king. His voice was a growl. "They took your life from you, your right, your office. They deprived your mother of your living presence. And I—I never knew I had a daughter. I may make alliance with them because our country has sore need of it, but for this I will never forgive them."

"They were afraid," Rhian said. "They did as best they could, as blind as they were with fear."

"It was not enough," he said, fierce enough that he reminded her vividly of his son whom she had left on the steppe. "It will never be enough."

"Please understand," she said as gently as she could. "They foresaw ruin on every path, as long as I was permitted to live. Yet they did it. They left me alive. They took away my blood and my kin and the name I would have had, and made me a stranger. Maybe I would have been better dead. Or maybe all of this serves the Goddess, and we mortals are too feeble to comprehend her purposes."

"She brought you back," he said: simple as men were, driving direct to what mattered to him. "If I could stand before the world and name you your mother's child, I would do it. I know why I must not, but it's great pain to be so wise."

"May the mare's servant be ally and friend to the king in Lir?" she asked him.

"It is permitted," he said.

"Then let it be so," she said.

He hesitated. She saw how he moved, then stopped, as if afraid of her, or himself. Her fear was maybe stronger than his, but she had not had his years of being king to make her cautious. She pulled him to her and held him. Her own blood. Her own bone.

After a stretching moment he returned the embrace. He was a solid presence, broad and strong. A bulwark, she had thought before. A strong wall against the terrors of the world.

And maybe it would break, as the priestesses had said of the walls of Lir. But for now it was here, and it was strong, and she—she realized as the rain came, lashing her face, that she was happy. It was a strange, sharp-edged, utterly mortal happiness, but it was none the less real for that.

50

The steppe burned from horizon to horizon. It was the wrath of the gods, people said—Emry's understanding of their speech was feeble still, but he could see the fear in them, the roll of eyes toward heaven, the hands lifted as if to thrust aside a blow. The wind blew from the east or the south, which kept the fire from the camp, but the air was thick with ash and smoke.

The whole of the west was walled away from them. Emry prayed to the Goddess that the caravan had escaped before the fire overwhelmed the world. It was her doing, he hoped with all his heart, to protect her children from pursuit, and to conceal what had been done between the traders and the king's wife Etena.

How well it had succeeded, he discovered on the third day of the fire. People were beginning to pack up their tents and flee, but the king showed no sign of leaving this camp.

That morning the sun barely had power to pierce the pall of smoke. The air cut at the throat with each breath. More of the tents were coming down than before, herds being gathered, oxen hitched to wagons, women and children emerging from seclusion, laden down with baggage.

The king's sons who had been using Emry as a servant were up far earlier than usual, muttering to one another, hanging about as if they could not find anything useful to do. When Emry tried to wait on them, they snarled at him. One, who until then had been almost friendly, cuffed him and kicked him and spat at him in the tribesmen's language.

Emry was too startled to strike back. He kept his head down instead and escaped under cover of a scuffle between two others of the princes.

There was little enough difference between the scant light of the tent and the brown dimness of the outer air. He had thought to seek out the river on pretext of fetching water, but a dark figure was standing near the king's tent: a woman where women were not accustomed to be. She carried no burden, had no child in her arms. She simply stood there, wrapped in veil and mantle though the morning was breathless with heat.

He knew her by the eyes in the veil: green as summer leaves, lifting to meet his. Something in them drew him to her, as unwise as that might be; but he could not stop himself.

"Lady," he said.

"Prince," she said.

"Not that," he said, "lady, nor guardsman either, now."

"You submitted to this."

It was not a question, but he chose to answer it as if it had been. "The others are free," he said, "and alive, I can hope. If the Goddess allows. If they escaped ahead of the fire."

"Why?"

"Your sister wife," he said, "was insistent."

For a breathless moment he feared that she would press him closer to the truth, but she sighed and gave it up. "A dozen of the king's sons," she said, "went raiding westward. None of them has come back. One of them—" She clasped her arms about herself, shivering in the smoky heat. "One of them is the king's heir."

"They may have escaped, too," Emry said, "if your gods were kind."

"Our gods are not kind," said Aera. "When I look in my heart, I see flames. When I pray for their safety, I see bones charred to ash."

Her voice was so quiet, so still, so perfectly calm, that Emry closed his arms about her and held her to his breast. For a long moment she suffered it, thin as a bird in his embrace, trembling with grief she would not set into words.

Then she stiffened. He let her go. Her eyes blazed at him, but not with anger. Not exactly. "Do not ever do such a thing again," she said.

"Not unless you ask," said Emry.

⇒ ⇐

It seemed the king had been resisting all counsel to break camp, because if he did that, he would be turning back eastward; and that, he would not do. But the wind shifted, and the wall of flame advanced inexorably toward them. Even the king's will wavered then.

These children of the steppe could break camp, even such a great one as this, in hardly more time than it took to command it. They divided into bands—clans, Emry suspected; they abandoned the slow heavy wagons and mounted even the women on horses, and fled the fire.

Even as the last of them took the eastward way, the wind shifted yet again. The wall of flame slowed its advance. But they were in motion, and there was open country ahead of them, country that they had conquered.

They were on that road a hand of days. They ate what they had brought with them, taking no time to hunt. Yet when they did stop at last, the hunting would be splendid: there was ample sign of game, beasts fleeing the fire as did the people of the tribe.

Emry traveled with the king's clan: his women, his children, the men of his warband. The maker of chariots came with them, and a full half-hundred battle-cars, each with its charioteer. They were a terrible number, and strong, with all their men and weapons.

The camp they settled in had the look of a place that had been occupied often before. It was a wide grassy bowl atop a hill, with a stream running round the foot of the hill, and a wonder in the bowl's heart: a spring that bubbled up out of the rock.

From the rim of the bowl one could see a great expanse of the steppe, and mark the line of fire along the horizon. It was dying down, maybe, or burning farther away. The whole of the west was barred, like the wall that so many in Lir had hoped would be enough to hold back the chariots.

But no wall would stop them for long. This year, yes; and if the Goddess willed, Rhian had taken her charioteer back to Lir and persuaded him to teach the people what he knew. But next year, or the year after, the chariots would come. Emry was as sure of that as of the winter that would follow this searing blast of summer.

The king's sons did not come back from their raid. When the fire was dead at last, some of the king's warband went to look for them. The wait for their return seemed endless, and the mood in the camp was brittle. Emry became adept at dodging sudden blows. Etena never called for him, never showed herself to him. The son of her body, the prince Dias, who would be king's heir if Minas did not come back, took to spending his days on the western rim of the bowl, standing or sitting like a stone, unmoving for sun or wind, clouds or rain.

He had been as close to his brother as the two halves of a nut's kernel. Born on the same day, nursed at the same breast, though never nurtured in the same womb, they had been all but inseparable.

"Not that they went everywhere together," one of the princes said.

He was in a talkative mood, and the weather that day was vile. He sat just inside the opening of the princes' tent and looked out at Dias on the rim, being buffeted with cold rain. Emry was mending harness for another of the princes, a more exacting task than usual: one of the colts had objected to it with excessive vehemence. It was a ghastly tangle, much torn and broken, but Staris professed himself greatly attached to it.

Emry pieced it together fingerlength by painstaking fingerlength, while Kritas, who was bored, amused himself with chatter.

"They would go off alone or with other people," Kritas said. "Usually it was Minas who did it, mind; Dias would be asleep or off in the privies, and Minas would disappear on him. When Dias was young he'd pitch terrible fits, but when he grew into a man he taught himself to endure it. Minas was always the leader. Dias would follow. Day and night, we'd call them: the sun and the moon. Minas could live without his brother, but Dias—I don't think he'll want to live alone."

"He may have to," drawled another of the princes from the shadows of the tent. "Do you know what I heard? It wasn't a raid they all went out on. They tricked Minas, took him away and killed him, because Etena wanted him dead."

Emry kept his eyes fixed on the rein he was repairing.

"And the gods took their revenge by setting the steppe afire?" Kritas shivered, and perhaps not entirely from the gust of wind that chose that moment to rock the tent. "That's a terrible thing, to dispose of a king's son. And why not dispose of his brother, too? You know that if Dias discovers that Etena had Minas killed, he'll take revenge."

"He won't kill his own mother," Staris said.

"For Minas he might."

"No, not Dias. Dias fears the gods."

"Etena doesn't. And that may be her undoing."

"Or Dias'. She's a witch. If she lays her spell on him as she did on the king, she'll have everything she could ask for, for as long as she wants it."

Emry labored diligently over the harness. He was not easily astonished, but he had been thinking that if he had been given to these of the king's men, then they must be bound to Etena. Evidently that was not so. Equally evidently, they had not been part of the conspiracy that took Minas out of the camp.

Could it be, he wondered, that Etena's most loyal men were gone, lost in the fire? If it was her will that drove the king, and that will was weakened, its support taken away, it might be possible to delay the tribe's advance—perhaps for years.

A war within the tribe, he thought as he stitched the torn and broken rein. If he could foster that, who knew how long it would last, or how much harm it would do?

Truly the Goddess was great, to have set him in this place. He sang a hymn to her in his heart, as he mended harness for an enemy's chariot.

The king's men came back when the moon had begun to wane, when the fire was but a rim of ash along the horizon, and the first breath of winter was blowing over the steppe. Their faces were blank with shock. They brought back word of the wagons in the abandoned camp: that enough of them were whole for a herd of oxen to be sent for them, and men to drive them.

But that was not why their faces were so bleak. They bore a burden wrapped in cloaks, pitifully small: a few bones, a handful of ornaments half-melted by the fire, and a thing that, when Dias saw it, made him howl aloud.

It was a sword of bronze, darkened with fire. Emry recognized the hilt. Minas had carried this sword; had cherished it as a woman cherishes her child.

"The heir," said the man who had led the hunt. "The heir is dead, consumed by fire. And his brothers — all who went with him — dead. Dead and burned. The fire consumed their camp, their chariots, horses, everything. This is all that was left."

Dias' howl rose to a keen. Others echoed it, till the whole camp was one great wail of lamentation. The king's heir, the prince, the lord of warriors, was dead.

Nine days they mourned him and the brothers who, they thought, had died with him. Nine days of fasting and dirges. All the royal clan rent their garments, heaped ashes on their heads. The surviving sons shore off their limed and stiffened hair, and offered it to the shades of the dead.

The king himself came out, whitely naked, shaved bare. Three whole days and nights he lay on his face before the bier on which was laid the few remains of his sons. He took no food or drink. He lay like the dead himself, save that, intermittently, he wept.

When at last he rose, gaunt and ravaged, a handful of his women came out unveiled, their hair cropped short, their gowns torn and smudged with ashes. Emry knew the one who led them. Her beauty was all the keener with her hair in cropped curls and her face stripped of flesh by grief and fasting. Her eyes were all but blind. She saw nothing but the bier and the sword that was laid on it.

The women who followed her, who must be the mothers of the rest, shrieked and wailed. She was silent. She took the sword from the bier and cradled it. The rest she left, nameless remnants all.

The others began a wild dance of grief and anguish, dipping, whirling, flinging themselves to the earth and beating upon it. Aera turned and walked through the tumult, light on bare feet.

She did not return to the king's tent. She crossed the camp instead, still cradling the sword, and vanished into the chariotmakers' circle.

Few seemed to notice. Emry followed her, drawn as he had been in the early days of his captivity. He told himself that he did it to help his people: to feed the dissension between the most powerful of the king's wives.

But in truth he went for her sake. Her beauty, her strength, captivated him. He grieved for her, even knowing that her son might not be dead; and knowing that he could not tell her what he knew. She must mourn, nor would he be at all wise to comfort her.

She sought her father's tent and shut herself within. Emry hung on his heel, wisdom warring with the heart's urging.

The heart won. He lifted the flap, pausing in surprise; for the tent was not the dim closed space he had expected. The rear of it was open in a sort of portico, a canopy that looked out upon the camp's rim and the western horizon.

Aera stood there, still with her son's sword in her arms. "I will not go back to the rite," she said.

"I haven't come to ask that of you," said Emry.

She started and half-spun. "You!"

He lifted his shoulders in a shrug and let her see his hands, that they were empty, and that he was unarmed.

"Where is Dias?" she demanded.

"I haven't seen him, lady," Emry said.

"Then he didn't send you?"

"No, lady," said Emry.

"You should find him," she said, "before he does something desperate."

"Would he let me stop him?"

"He might."

"Or he might kill me; but what matter? I'm a slave. My life is worth nothing."

"Your life is worth a little," she said. "Maybe more than a little if we come to your country. Do your people know what it is to keep a hostage?"

"We've held hostages from the tribes," he said. "What would you hold me for?"

"Whatever we could." Her arms tightened on her son's sword. Emry's heart was in his throat, though she could not have known the truth of his presence in this place. But after a while she loosed her grip; her shoulders drooped. "Who knows how long that would be? The west is walled in fire. By the time it's passable again, winter will have come. Your country is safe from us for now. Later . . . it's as the gods will."

"Lady," said Emry, "I grieve for your loss."

Her glance was clear and hard. "Do you?"

"He had great gifts," Emry said, "in war and in the making of chariots. I saw him sitting in judgment—young as he was, he had skill in that, too. And he was your son."

"Yes," she said. "He was my son. I know he did not lead that raid. I suspect that there was more than wine and kumiss speaking in the brothers who instigated it. None of them had ever been his friend."

"I have heard," Emry said, "that they were encouraged to set him in harm's way. Though I doubt they expected to die in fire."

"Do you think that he died then? Or that he was dead when the fire came?"

"He could have died by the sword," said Emry, "which would be a gentler death than fire."

"She will pay," Aera said quietly. "For the king's soul, for my son's life—there is a price, and I will take it."

She was as straight and strong and keen as a bronze blade. Emry drank in the glory of her. "In my country," he said, "you would be a Mother—a woman who is a king."

"Women are not kings," she said, but without passion. Her mind was not on him. She was rapt in grief, and in anger so deep it had gone stone-cold.

He began to withdraw, but she astonished him: she said, "No. Don't go. Stay."

He was glad to obey her. As soon as he stopped, she seemed to forget him, and yet it also seemed that she needed his presence, or a presence. After a little while he sat on his heels, at his ease, and let himself slide into the guard's stillness: empty of thought and yet keenly alert.

The sun had sunk halfway to the horizon before she turned. Her eyes were full of its light. Yet she saw him clearly. "You belong to my enemy," she said.

"I belong to myself."

"She owns your body."

"She may think she does," Emry said.

"Are you loyal to her?"

"I serve my Goddess," said Emry.

"Do something for me," she said. "Guard my foster-son, the son of her womb. If you have any power to protect his soul, do it."

"You trust me for that?"

"I think," she said, "that you would destroy my tribe without a qualm.

But when you give your word, it is truly given. Will you protect my foster-son?"

"While I can," said Emry, "while my city and my Goddess have no part of it, I will guard him with my life and heart."

"That is enough," Aera said.

⇒ ⇐

That was his dismissal. She was safe here in her father's tent. Emry had but to walk out of it, past a circle of empty chariots and up the slope to the rim of the hilltop.

Dias the prince sat where he had sat since they came to this camp. He wore nothing under his mantle but a smearing of ash. Unlike the rest of them, he had not cut off his hair; it hung in matted locks. His cheeks were rough with unshaven beard.

"Have you come to kill me?" he asked the sky.

"The lady Aera sent me," Emry said.

"She trusts you?"

"I gave her my word."

"See that you keep it," Dias said.

Emry bowed slightly.

Without warning Dias whipped about and seized him by the throat. Emry stood still, his body loose, his eyes level. Dias' fingers tightened just short of pain. "If you had anything—anything—to do with his death, I will break your neck."

"In the Goddess' name," Emry said, hardly more than a whisper against those cruel fingers, "I never in this world wished him dead."

"You're lying."

"If he is dead," Emry said, "it was none of my doing. That is the gods' own truth."

Dias let him go abruptly. "No. No, of course you had nothing to do with it. You are her plaything. He was her enemy."

"She is your mother," Emry said.

Dias laughed, harsh as the cry of a raven. "She is no kin to me. She cast me out when I was born."

"I heard she went mad as some mothers do, and forsook her child. But I think," said Emry, "that she may remember you now. The king is weak. The king's heir is gone. She'll be wanting another man through whom to rule. And you are her blood and bone."

"Are you a shaman? A soothsayer?"

Emry blinked, startled. "Why, no. How can I be? I'm a man."

"You are a—" Dias seemed startled himself, and more so as he began to understand. "In your country, shamans are women?"

"And kings," said Emry.

"How strange." Dias peered at him. "You look a great bull of a man, and yet you crawl at women's feet. Is that why she bought you? For your servility?"

"I think it was for my beauty," Emry said.

Dias' bark of laughter had true mirth in it, however brief, however swiftly it darkened. "Can you seduce her, man of the west? Can you win her to your will?"

"She is a sorceress," Emry said.

"Cannot a sorceress be ensorcelled? She found you fascinating enough to pay gold for you. Gold, westerner, is life and breath to her. She's half yours already. Win all of her, free my father, and I will undo your slavery. You'll be a free man again."

"Can no one here do such a thing?"

"Men of the People do not have women's arts." It seemed Dias was more proud of that than ashamed. "Do it, Goddess' man, and you shall be free."

"And if I fail, I shall be dead," Emry said lightly. "That's a fine bargain, prince."

"Why, don't you value your freedom?"

"My heart is no one's slave," Emry said. "But to see my own land and people again, yes, I would be glad of that. I will take your bargain. Only promise me one thing."

"What is that?" Dias asked when Emry did not go on.

"When you are king," Emry said, "give me one gift, one boon—whatever I ask. Will you do that?"

"If I become king," said Dias, "I will not give you my kingship. Anything else that is in my power, if you do this thing, I will give."

"May the Goddess witness it," Emry said.

"And the gods," said Dias, "above and below."

They made their bargain there on the rim of the high hill, in the long rays of the setting sun. The Goddess witnessed it, and Dias' gods of wind and sky. When it was made, the sun touched the horizon. Dias bowed low to it, and sang a long winding song, a chant that seemed to unfurl from him with no will of his at all. That was the seal of their bargain; that, and the swift fall of night.

52

It was Etena and not Aera who sang the princes to their long rest with the gods below. That, Emry gathered, was a remarkable thing, and a bit of a scandal. That song belonged to the mother of the king's heir. In refusing to sing it, Aera had abdicated from her position. In taking her place, Etena had laid claim to the office—for her son as well as herself.

So ended the nine days' mourning, in darkness and raw cold rain; and so, it seemed, ended Aera's power among her people.

Emry tumbled out of an unexpectedly deep sleep. The first blow woke him. The second half-stunned him. He blinked up at an indistinguishable but unmistakably princely face. "Get up," said the boy. "The king's wife wants you."

So she did, Emry started to say, but he bit his tongue. He scrambled himself up and into some sort of order. His ribs stabbed where the prince had aimed a kick. One was maybe cracked. He took care to breathe shallowly, and to move with care as he dressed and plaited his hair.

The camp was bleak in the grey light. There would be no sun today: the clouds were heavy and low. It had rained in the night, and would rain again later, or even snow. The camp dogs huddled in the lee of tents or tried against the threat of kicks and stones to claim places by the fires. Even the children were subdued, their usual footraces and noisy games of stick-and-ball reduced to a somewhat lifeless mock war in the deserted council-circle.

Emry gathered his wits and his courage, drew a deep breath and let it go, and entered the king's tent. The king was not in the common space; maybe Etena was giving up that pretense. She was there with two of her women. He thought he heard the third keeping up the spell of chants and drugged smoke, somewhere not too far away.

He bowed in front of Etena, and sat on his heels, and waited. She spoke no greeting. He let her look at him, steadying his spirit, so that his skin was like armor, and his face a mask. To her he was a thing, a possession, an image of gold or a fine jewel. He was content to be that, and no more.

"You will do a thing for me," she said to him. "My son is now the king's heir. You are now his servant. You will serve him, guard him, share his every breath. And when I ask it of you, you will tell me what he does, and when, and with whom."

"I am, in short, your spy?"

"You are whatever I bid you be."

Emry bent his head. "As you wish, my lady," he said.

⇒ ⇐

Thanks be to the Goddess, he was too shocked to say more, still less to burst out in hysterical laughter. Now he was doubly charged, and doubly sworn to watch over the prince Dias. And Dias had bidden him weaken Etena's power in the tribe.

Great was the Goddess, and wonderful her ways. If she could use a man to work her will in this world of men and veiled women, why not?

He learned by inquiry that the king's heir kept little enough state. He shared a tent like the one in which Emry had already been a slave, no larger and certainly no cleaner than the other had been when Emry found it. The dwellers in this one were not king's sons, except for Dias. They were yearmates, or close enough; kin through the royal clan, who had been the prince Minas' warband before Minas was taken away. They had all shaved their hair to the skull, and some had slashed their cheeks and breasts and arms with knives.

They looked like a pack of demons in the lamplit clutter of their tent. Dias in their midst was easy to find: he was clean, which surprised Emry, and his hair was combed and plaited, and his skin was unmarred. One would think he did not mourn, until one met his eyes. Then the visible sorrow of the rest shrank to nothing.

He greeted Emry as if he had expected him. "Which of them sent you?" he asked.

"On the face of it," said Emry, "your mother."

A shadow crossed Dias' face. "To kill me?"

"To spy on you," said Emry.

"That may be worse." Dias spoke lightly, as if he did not care. "Come then, there's a place for you. Can you hunt?"

"I can hunt," Emry said, but not with his full attention. The others had stiffened when Dias spoke of the empty place. He could well guess whose it was.

But Dias did not care about that, either. He pointed with his chin at the heap of furs and hides nearest him. "You'll sleep there. Can you sing? Tell stories?"

"A little," Emry said.

He held his breath, but no one asked him to entertain them just then. There was a low growl, hardly to be heard, when he approached Minas' old place. Dias stared his kinsmen down. He had power here, Emry thought; he was more than a shadow of his brother who was gone.

In this tent, it seemed, Emry was not to be their general slave. They let him make order of their chaos, but none of them ordered him about. They made rather a point of ignoring him.

As he went out with the last armload of moldy hides and threadbare furs, Dias trailed after him. The air was raw, and had grown more so as the day advanced. Snow, Emry thought, for a certainty.

He flung his burden in the midden pit which was dug beyond the outer line of tents. When he turned to go back, Dias barred his way. The prince thrust a bow into his hand, and a filled quiver. "We go hunting," he said.

"It will snow by nightfall," said Emry.

Dias flung a bundle at him. It unrolled into a mantle: bearskin, well tanned and almost clean.

"Horses?" Emry asked.

They were waiting, bridled, fleeces strapped to their backs, and bags of provisions laden on them. Emry rolled his eyes at the sky, which lowered forbiddingly.

Dias was in no mood to hear any objection. Emry had his orders, threefold. He mounted the nearer horse, a sturdy and somewhat nondescript bay. Dias was already astride, already in motion toward the rim of the camp.

⇒ ⇐

The first spit of snow caught them on the plain. Dias had found the track of a herd of deer, and was following it as if nothing in the world mattered but that. Emry kept his head down against the bitter wind, and his eyes on the track, with glances upward to be certain of the path. It was a great trust, he thought, for this man to arm a slave and set him in the rear. If Dias wanted to die, this well might be how he meant to do it.

Emry had no intention of obliging him, if that was his purpose. Dias dead was no use to Lir. Dias living might breed enough dissension in the tribe to keep the war at bay for a while at least. Emry very much wanted Dias alive, well, and able to stand against his mother.

So Emry guarded Dias, there on the plain, with the wind whipping his face and clawing at the bearskin wrapped tight about him. There was sign enough of game, and not only the deer Dias was tracking. But of living things they saw nothing. All the beasts were gone to earth, the birds gone to roost, against the coming of the storm.

And yet as they rode onward and the snow began to fall, Emry caught flashes in the corner of his eye. It seemed he saw beasts after all, like shadows in the snow: a stag, a boar, a shambling bear. Dias did not turn to shoot the stag. Bear and boar made no move against the hunters.

They were watching. Emry saw the gleam of eyes. Beasts did not stare at men as these did.

Spirits, he thought. In the snow, in the wind, they trod the edge between worlds. Maybe Dias had opened the door, in his grief that drove him from his people's camp in the threat of snow.

Dias grieved, but he was not altogether mad. They camped before dark in a sheltered hollow, where a shelf of stone made a shallow cave. Dias had brought fire in a little jar, and dry tinder to feed it. There was bread, kumiss, dried meat. The horses' big warm bodies blocked the wind. They were in decent comfort, while the snow fell outside and the wind howled its frustration.

Dias rolled himself in his mantle and lay down between the fire and the horses. Which left Emry the warmth of the inner cave, but also no easy escape. He shrugged and fed the fire a twist of dried grass. His belly was full; he was warm. There was no snow falling on him. His mantle was even beginning to dry.

One of the horses sighed and groaned and lay down. The other stood hipshot, already asleep. Beyond them was the dark. Now and then as the fire flared, Emry saw a swirl of snow.

There were shadows in the storm: bear, boar, stag. Stag was closest, the great swell of his neck, the spread of his antlers dark against the night.

Emry blinked. The horses raised their heads, ears pricked.

A man slid past them. He moved slowly, as horsemen knew how to do, and with care not to startle them. He wore for hood and mantle the hide and horn-crowned head of a stag. The face beneath that regal head-dress was human enough, a long-nosed, sparse-bearded tribesman's face; the plait of hair on the narrow shoulder was faded copper. Only his eyes were truly odd as he came into the light of the fire: one was blue, and one was moss-green.

Dias did not stir as the stranger stepped over him. Emry sat still, alert but unfrightened. "So," he said, soft lest he wake the prince. "This is where you all went. Did you call him to you?"

"We called you," the shaman said. "He had the ears to hear."

"Are you going to bid me guard him, too?"

"Oh, no," said the shaman. "We have a message for you."

That did surprise Emry, for a moment into speechlessness. Then he found words. "From the White Mare's servant?"

"From the one who is above the gods."

That robbed Emry of all speech.

"The prince of chariots lives and is well. The chariots have come to Lir. You are free, if it pleases you."

Emry's heart thudded in his breast. Free. And where fire had covered the White Mare's track, snow covered his. If the storm continued, he could escape at dawn, and be well to the westward and his tracks utterly obscured before anyone came after him.

And yet.

He had given his word many times over. And he could do more to defend Lir here than in the crowd of his brothers and cousins and kin.

He was sick with wanting to be home again; to see his father's face, and walk in the king's house, and hear his own language spoken by his own people. This was exile beyond the nightmare of a miscreant in Lir, abandoned on the steppe among a barbarous tribe.

Still, it was the path the Goddess had chosen for him. He had accepted it. If the shaman told the truth, then that was well indeed. But Emry's word was still given, and he had still his duty to do.

He would stay.

The shaman was watching him steadily, mismatched eyes fixed on his face. This man knew the secret, knew what Emry had come for and where Minas had gone. He was deadly dangerous.

"Swear to me," said Emry, "by whatever gods you serve, that you will tell no one in your tribe of this message which you brought me."

"I was driven out of the tribe," the shaman said, "by the one who is the enemy of us all. In this I serve my gods. If by it I help to destroy her, I will be content."

"And if it destroys your tribe?"

"I have no fear of that."

"You should."

The shaman shook his head. "Dream as you will, man of the west. Leave if it pleases you. There is no more need of you here."

"I think there is great need," Emry said.

"You act alone," said the shaman. "Our gods will do nothing for you."

"I don't know your gods," said Emry. "I only know my Goddess."

"Then pray she may protect you," the shaman said.

53

Dias shot a stag in the snow, and Emry a doe. There was meat enough there to feed the young men's tent, and some of their less fortunate kin, too; and hides and bone and sinew that could be turned to good use.

The sun came out as they rode back to the camp on its hilltop. They could see the smoke of the campfires from out on the plain. As they rode up the steep hill, men and boys on horseback came whooping down. It was a grand welcome, and a royal procession.

Dias seemed disconcerted, but he let them sweep him up and over the rim and into the broad circle of tents. Emry, following like a good servant, saw to it that no one came close enough to be a threat.

The prince's warband, which had been Minas' and now seemed to have elected to belong to Dias, came at the gallop from the far side of the camp, howling like exuberant wolves. They plucked Dias from his first escort, relieved his horse of its burden of the stag, and carried him off to the place where the charioteers trained their horses and had their wild rattling races.

The chariots were put away today, covered and protected against the melting snow. The young men had been playing a game on horseback, a mad trampling melee with a very dead goat as either prize or victim. Some of them went off with the stag; the rest pulled Dias into their game.

Emry was no part of that. He still had the doe, gutted and drained, slung in front of him on the bay gelding's back. Dias was surrounded by men who, Emry had reason to believe, were devotedly loyal. Emry elected to leave him there, and to withdraw a little distance, toward the circle of the makers' tents.

Aera was still living in her father's tent. He found her in front of it, grinding the seeds of the wild grain into the rough flour of these people. Two women were with her, both somewhat younger, and both very like her: slender and tall, ruddy-haired, but the eyes of both were more grey than green.

None of them was veiled in the wintry sunlight. That surprised him. The two he did not know—her sisters?—turned their faces away at his coming, but Aera seemed not to care how proper or improper she was. She looked full into his face. The sun was bright but certainly not blinding, and yet she seemed barely to see through the light in her eyes.

Emry laid the doe in front of her. "For the maker," he said.

She blinked, and seemed to focus. Her brows drew together. "For my father? Not for me?"

"I think," said Emry, "that it might be improper for me to give you a gift."

"It's improper for you to approach me at all," Aera said.

"Even if I meant to approach your father?"

"Did you?"

"Well," he admitted, "no. The gift is still for him. Dias shot a stag for the young men's tent. This is for the maker of chariots. And for his daughters."

"Ah," she said. "All three of us." Her sisters did not believe that any more than she did: they were all dubious alike.

"Lady," said Emry, "you may do with the gift as you will. I wish you well; I wish you good day."

He had startled them, he hoped as he turned and strode away, but it was more likely that the sisters were laughing at him. It was a long while since he had felt like a raw boy, but just now, he was close to it.

He shrugged off his doubts and fears. Dias was still at play in the field. Emry stood in the crowd of watchers and tried to understand the game. It seemed to partake of a great deal of galloping and shouting, and no little bruises and bloodshed. The purpose, as far as he could tell, was to gain possession of the goat's carcass, but then it seemed that one was supposed to go somewhere with it—and the rest of the players did their roaring best to stop it.

It was entertaining, if incomprehensible. He could not tell whether Dias had won, but everyone seemed delighted with the outcome. They hauled off the wounded, returned the horses to the herds, and went in a noisy crowd to find food and drink and the warmth of a campfire.

Emry was cold, his feet were wet, and he was hungry. He was more than glad of food and fire. One of the boys brought him heated kumiss. The stuff was even more vile hot than cold, but it was warm. Warmth was welcome, just then.

They were not treating him like a slave. Nor was anyone looking askance at him for taking a place near the fire, beside Dias, and being given a share of the prince's portion.

"The prince's dog," Aias said. He was one of the warband, a huge man by any reckoning: he towered over Emry, who was not small. For all his size, he was a gentle creature, and he was patient with Emry's attempts to learn his language.

"A prince may have a dog," he said. "That is, a man who lives in his shadow, serves him, protects him, does his bidding. There were many who called Dias the dog of the one who is dead. Now Dias has his own dog. It's a comfortable office, outlander. Whatever he has, you share."

"If he has enemies, they're my enemies?"

"Of course," Aias said. "They'll threaten you as they threaten him. And if he dies, you die with him."

"Dias didn't die with his brother."

Aias grunted. "Clever, aren't you? Dias is a prince. The king will name him heir, come solstice."

"It's different for a prince," Emry said.

"Yes," said Aias. "Here, will you have more kumiss?"

"No more," Emry said. It was a cry for mercy.

Aias laughed at him but let him be. Some of the young men, indefatigable, had begun to dance round the fire. Someone had a drum and someone a pipe, and someone else began to sing. The music was simple but there was a strong rhythm to it, the rhythm of the blood.

Emry would have thought himself too weary and too homesick for any gaiety, but this music set deep in his bones. He rose and slipped in among the line of dancers. They made space for him. Dias was on one side, Aias on the other. Emry fit well between. They linked arms as the music quickened. It still matched the beating of Emry's heart, swifter, swifter, swifter, round in a dizzy whirl until the stars spun away.

⇨ ⇦

Aera saw him dancing with the young men as the icy dark came down. She should have been safe and warm in her father's tent, sitting in companionable silence with her sisters. Instead she was out here in the trampled snow, wrapped in a mantle that her son had given her, watching the outland slave conduct himself like a warrior of the People.

She should hate him for being alive when Minas was dead; for being a slave, but clearly suffering no inconvenience from that condition. She should loathe his broad-cheeked foreign face, his thick body, his pelt of black hair. But she could only think that he was beautiful, like a young bull; and that—oh, gods—she wanted him.

The king had not taken her to his bed in time out of mind. She had told herself that that was a good thing; that she was well rid of his weight on her, his rod thrusting in her, the rank man-smell of him as he took what he wanted. After Minas, he gave her no more children, not even daughters to be set out for the wolves. Now she was old enough not to want that burden, even if she was still able to carry it.

Yet when she looked at this boy who was no older than her son, she felt as if her loins would melt. He was as big as the king—broader, maybe—and he did indeed smell of man. But it was not a rank smell. It was sharply pleasant and somehow clean, as if he rubbed his skin with green herbs. She wanted to bury her face in the hollow of his shoulder, and feel his arms about her, and—

Her wits were all shattered with grief. That was why she did this. It was permitted that she leave her husband for a time of mourning, that she return to her father. But that she should cast eyes on a man to whom she was not given by law and custom, that was a terrible dishonor.

It was very difficult to care, as she stood in the dark and the cold, and neither of them any bleaker than her heart. Her son was dead and burned in fire. Was it so horrible a thing for her to want a little warmth for herself?

He was a warm man. He had been raised to defer to women, and yet he was not weakened by it. Certainly he could ride and dance and hunt as well as the common run of tribesmen. He could sing, too, in a voice like dark honey, while the drum beat slow and the pipe sang sweet beneath.

Her wiser self knew that even to stand here was betrayal of the king her husband. However dead his spirit might be, his body but a shell for Etena's will, he was still her king and her rightful lord.

She cared remarkably little for that, just then. Her son was dead. Her husband was worse than dead. The People were scattered across the steppe, driven back by fire from the path they had been following for years out of count. Was it so terrible or so ill an omen that her heart yearned for a pair of strong arms and a sweet smile?

She turned her back on him and clasped her arms tight about herself, shivering with cold that ran deeper than that of snow underfoot and ice in the air. As troubled as her world had been before the traders came to the People, it had at least been whole. Now it was shattered. She did not know that it would ever be mended again.

54

Winter set in swift and hard. After that first early storm, the sun came back for a little while, but then the storms rolled in, one after another, with blasts of bitter wind and unrelenting snow.

Emry had always dreaded winter; it could be terribly dull, shut in the city day after day, with nothing to do but tell tales, polish weapons, and vie to be chosen by the strongest of the women. Tedium could be a terrible curse, unless one found an occupation to while the time. Emry had learned the whole of the Great Song of Lir one winter, that told the tales of all the Mothers since the dawn time.

And yet, as tedious as winter was, he had always been warm, and his belly had always been full. Even in a lean year, the dwellers in the king's house were well enough fed.

Winter on the steppe was hard. There was kumiss and dried meat laid away, but not a great deal of either. The cattle and goats and sheep grew thin, and their milk dried up; nor were there as many as there should have been, for they had lost a great number in the flight from the fire. If they slaughtered the flocks and herds to eat, they would have no young in the spring, no milk, no cheese. As good as the hunting had been when they came to this camp, as the storms closed in, it grew harder to track and find the game; and the game when they found it had barely enough flesh on its bones to make a mouthful.

Everyone was hungry, to greater or lesser degree, and cold—for tents could not keep out the wind as walls of wood or stone could do. The only warmth in them was that of bodies crowded together. There could be no hearth inside a tent, and these people had no braziers, no ovens or firepots; the best they knew was a stone heated in the campfire and wrapped in a bit of hide and laid in the sleeping-furs. There were stories and songs enough, and weapons tended and harness mended, and the chariotmakers kept on with their craft; but mostly people huddled together and struggled to stay warm.

At the heart of this black season came the feast of the solstice. With the priests and shamans all driven out of the tribe, there was no one to declare the day on which the shortening of nights ended and the first faint glimmer of a longer day began. The king, or Etena speaking through

him, made the decree; and whether or not it was the day itself, the tribe
was glad of its coming, and the three days of festival that went with it.

The king had not been seen in long enough that people had begun to
whisper that he was dead. But he came out of his tent for the festival:
pale, blinking in the wan sunlight, but patently alive. He performed the
sacrifice of the black ram, of the bull and the stallion. He laid their bones
in a cairn that his men built on the steppe, and set their skulls on guard
about it.

When the sacrifice was made and the gods propitiated, they feasted.
They slaughtered oxen and roasted them whole on great fires of dung
and dry grass and precious, hoarded wood. They brought out what they
called summer wine, which was made from honey; it was sweet and
strong, like a taste of summer in the heart of winter.

For those three days they were warm and well fed. The king sat among
them, silent and aloof, but they reckoned that kingly. On the day of the
sacrifice he did as they had all expected: he brought the head and hide of
the spotted bull to Dias who stood among the young men, and bestowed
them on him. So without a word was Dias named king's heir of his
people.

The women did not show their faces through any of this festival. Boys
and men of lesser clans tended the fires and prepared the feast, then served
it to the warriors and the elders, and to the king. To Emry it seemed a
strange unfinished thing, this world without faces or voices of women;
and most of all in a time of festival, when they should have shown themselves in their greatest glory.

The solstice feast was a little like the feast of the dark of the year in
Lir. There were sacrifices there: the king offered a bull, the Mother a
heifer to the Goddess, and fires burned on every hilltop, warming the
chill of the winter night. They did other things to warm it, too; things
that he saw little of here. He heard of it; young men loved to boast. But
he did not think they had as much of it as they pretended.

Tonight the young men put on the heads and hides of beasts—Dias
in his bull's hide foremost—and painted their faces with sacred signs, and
wove a skein of dancers through the camp. They were binding it together,
sealing it with the blessing of their gods.

Emry was pulled into the dance, caught up in it from the young men's
fire, round in a winding track to the king's tent. It spun him off there,
by accident it seemed, but it was no accident that brought him up against
the tentwall, and a woman standing by it. He recognized one of Etena's
three servants, the tall one with the cold grey eyes.

She beckoned. The tent's wall was folded here, and the fold was an
entrance.

It admitted them to a space that startled him. There was light, not a great deal of it but still dazzling after the firelit dark. A tree of lamps illuminated a shimmer of fine fabrics that he well remembered, for they had come from Lir. A bed of furs lay in the midst of them. And there was a pot from which radiated a wondrous warmth. A firepot after all, and in the king's tent—where else would such a rarity have hidden itself?

His guide had slipped into shadow and vanished. He was alone in the light and the warmth.

It was clear what was expected of him, and who expected it. He opened the chest half-hidden in a hill of cushions, found a jar of southern wine and a pair of golden cups. Another jar carried about it a distinct scent of musk: rarity indeed, unguent from the cities beyond the southern horizon, too rich almost to bear.

He considered preparing himself in every way possible, but it might be excessively shocking even to her, to find him naked in the bed she had laid for him. He sat cross-legged on it instead, and basked in the warmth.

She let him wait for a very long time. He drowsed sitting up, as a warrior could. The dizziness of the dance faded. Music wound through his heart, the Great Song of Lir from its beginning.

He had come to the ninth Mother, she who wore three faces, three daughters born at the same birth, when the inner curtain stirred. He ended the verse in the chamber of his skull, and looked into Etena's unveiled face.

She had painted it, though not as they did in the west: this was a white mask with a thin dark curve of brows, and lips painted small, like a scarlet bud. It was like a goddess' face, but a goddess from a country he did not know.

She was wrapped in a mantle of gleaming black fur. She let it fall from shoulders that were still beautiful, and a body that, though softened with years and idleness, had kept its loveliness more readily than her face. He let her see the pleasure he took in looking at her.

She bloomed with it, so much that he was taken aback. Had no one ever let her know that she had beauty? Or had it all been power, and a face that no man who did not own her must see?

"Is it true," she asked him, "that in your country a woman can command anything of a man, and he must obey?"

"True enough," he said.

Her dark eyes glittered. "Stand, then," she said. "Undress yourself."

"Would you not prefer to do it for me?"

She sucked in a breath. He had outraged her—but he watched her reflect on what he asked of her. He saw the glint of curiosity, and the spark of heat that came with it. Her fingers found the fastenings of his coat and worked them loose one by one. Her eyes were narrow; she frowned, focused like a child.

She would kill him in a heartbeat if he displeased her. She would break his spirit if she could, and rule it utterly. Yet he knew a softening of compassion for her, that was almost pity. So much power; so little peace.

She undressed him as if he had been a child's doll. Surely she had seen men naked before—the men of this tribe wore little enough in the summer. But maybe not in front of her, smiling at her, offering himself for her pleasure. Emry had gathered that the woman's pleasure was seldom the man's concern, here.

When all his garments were laid aside, she explored the whole of him with her hands, meticulously. She ran her palms across the width of his shoulders, down his breast, over his arms. She lifted his hands, measuring her own against them: hers were swallowed in his, her fingers soft on the calluses of bow and spear and sword. She spanned his waist, his hips, the strength of his thighs. She shied from the thing that must be most clearly on her mind.

She circled him slowly. He felt her touch on his back, the firm tug on his plait. She stroked him as if he had been an animal. He arched and sighed, purring in his throat. She shied again. Poor creature, never to have known this of all delights there were.

She came round to face him. "Take me now," she said. "For the gods—for the festival. Because the king—"

"You ask me to be your sacred king?" he asked her.

She was perhaps beyond answering.

"When I am done," he said, "do I die?"

She seemed to recover a little at that, enough to speak rapidly, in swift gusts of breath. "Do your duty well and be a king where a king is needed, and you will live to give me your strength again. Fail me, or breathe a word of it outside this place, and there will not be enough of your bones to scatter on the wind."

Emry understood a great deal just then, that had not been clear to him before. She had the king utterly subdued to her will—but one part of him accepted no such compulsion. She had made her king a gelding; but for certain purposes she needed a stallion. Nor could it easily be one of the tribe, not if she would be safe from betrayal.

She must have looked on Emry as a gift of her gods. "So this is why you bought me," he said.

"I prayed to the gods," she said, "and they brought you to me. I asked for a king, or a king's son. You are that, my divinations tell me. And you have sired sons."

His teeth clicked together. Of course she would want him for that. He would wager that her next son, once he was born, would not be given to a rival to nurse. And she would see to it that it was a son, whatever rites or potions she needed in order to ensure it. It would not even matter that it would be a dark child: she was dark herself.

She had planned this with great care, he could see, and considerable patience. He made no effort to hide his admiration. "Lady," he said, "you are remarkable."

"I do what I must," she said, but he could tell that she was pleased.

He moved carefully, slowly, as one approaches a beast of uncertain temper. She did not recoil. Very gently he stroked her as she had stroked him, with the same soft touch. She shivered. He persevered, slowly; where she quivered most strongly, he lingered.

Little by little her tautness melted. Her heart would not stop beating, nor her mind cease scheming, but he could make her body forget all the world but itself.

When her knees gave way, he eased her down, still playing the parts of her like the notes of a pipe. The song he made was subtle and ineffably sweet, traced in touches and in kisses and, when she opened to him of her body's own accord, in the rhythm that was oldest of all but for the beat of the heart.

She caught fire in his arms. Her lips fastened on his. Her arms and legs locked about him. She drove him deep inside her, gasping a little as if in pain, but taking no notice of it.

He was hers now as a moment before she had been his. He gave himself up gladly. She was eating him alive. But one thing he kept that was his own: his will to hold until she had come to the summit. She gasped then in what sounded for all the world like shock. Her body spasmed. Her eyes went empty, as empty as her king's.

Emry's own shock broke his hold on his body. They must have fallen together: when he could see again, they were lying side by side in the heap of furs. Her head was flung back, her eyes wide and staring. Tremors ran still through her body.

Just as he was about to give way to horror, her eyes snapped shut. She drew a sharp breath, then another. She sat up with a stifled cry, but fell back as if all strength had drained from her.

"Out," she said, so soft he barely heard it. Then louder: "Get out."

He rose on wobbling knees and gathered his clothes. The last few articles of those, she flung at him. Her aim was dreadful. "Get out! *Out!*"

No matter how angry she might fancy herself to be, he had no intention of running naked into the cold. He dressed quickly but with care, under her smoldering stare. When he was fit to go out among the people of her tribe, he stooped and kissed her lightly on the brow, and slipped through the slit in the tent-wall.

55

Etena sent no one to drag Emry out and fling him off the rim of the hill. Nor did he wake choking in blood. She had taken what she needed from him, however angry it had made her. Now once more she left him to his own devices.

He could be patient. If he had gone too far, he would have died that night. That she let him live told him much.

Once the festival was over, winter's grip closed tight and hard. Emry took to spending a good part of the days in the makers' circle, when he was not preoccupied with Dias: guarding him, riding or playing at mock battles with him, or listening and trying to understand the words as he sat in judgment as king's heir.

But when Dias was well protected by the crowd of his warband, or sleeping through the cold of another bitter day, Emry slipped away. The makers had brought their tents close together. Their fire was the warmest in the camp. When the forge was going as well, there was no warmer place on that part of the steppe.

He went for the warmth, and to learn what he could learn. Metos was glad of a strong pair of hands; Emry, as he said bluntly, had little gift for making chariots, but muscle enough to make him useful.

But he went also for the one who was there, though she did not show her face outside of her father's tent. He knew she watched him: he felt her eyes on him. She never summoned him as Etena had. Nor would she. She was too much a child of her people.

So too was Emry. But he was in her country. He could try to play the game as her people played it.

One day in the dead of winter, when for a little while there was a thaw, and the sun came out and the air was almost warm, Emry lent his strength to the shaping of a chariot-wheel. That fascinated him most of anything the makers did, and they were glad to teach him the way of it.

When that was done, it was still barely noon. Dias would be in council with the elders for some while yet. It was not a war-council; that could not be held without the king. They were settling other, lesser matters of the tribe, the small and dull but indispensable things that every king and king's heir must concern himself with.

Emry was not excessively sorry to be spared that duty. Today it meant that, for a while, he was free. He could take a horse and ride. He might sleep. Or he could leave the new-made wheel and withdraw, without fanfare but without secrecy, to Metos' tent.

He had seen the two sisters go out not long since, each laden with empty waterskins. Metos was completing the turning of an axle. The tent was quiet, but he had not seen Aera leave it.

She was within, weaving on a loom. The thread was wool from the sheep, dyed green and blue and, here and there, dusky red. She wove a subtle pattern, like the steppe in autumn; she was intent on the task, her hands deft, making swift work of it.

He crouched a little distance from her and watched her. She ignored him—deliberately, he thought. He was content to wait her out. Her hands were slender and strong, the fingers delicate in their touch, pale as ivory. Her profile was carved fine, finer than any in his own country. Her hair, cropped for mourning, curled softly on her forehead. The sight of it struck him with a sudden, piercing tenderness.

He had loved many women, and been loved by many in return. But this was different—stronger, clearer. When he was away from her, he felt her absence. When he was with her, he had come home.

Even with her refusing to acknowledge him, and making it clear that she would not ask him to lie with her. She was not like Etena. She could not break the vows she had sworn to her king.

He pitied Etena. He did not pity Aera at all. She was too strong.

But that strength was brittle, and close to breaking. She would be too proud, he thought, to ask anyone for anything, not for herself.

After quite a long while she said, "You should not be here."

"I think I am needed here," he said.

"You," she said tightly, "of all men living, are the least use to me."

"Am I?"

"Why are you not with Dias? He could die, and you would be here, smirching my honor."

"Dias is with the warband," Emry said, "in front of the elders and the clan-chiefs in council. He's as safe as he's likely to be."

"And I am not?"

"Your body is well defended here," Emry said. "Your spirit . . . who protects that? It's the spirit she destroys."

"Why do you think I came here?" Aera asked him. "I know what I risked in doing it—I'm safer from her under my father's eye, but I lose any power I had under hers."

"You have allies, surely," he said, "and spies."

"Such as you?"

"Surely I'm not alone."

"You are not," she said. "Now tell me, if you are my ally—how it is that you performed the midwinter sacrifice with her, the rite of kings. That now, though she tells no one, it is known that her courses have not come on her since before the sacrifice."

Emry dropped back on his heels. "So. She did as she intended. But what use will a child be to her? It might be a daughter. Even if it is a son, it will be years before she can make him king."

"Power," said Aera. "A king's wife who is with child is sacred. And once she has the child, if it is a son—and you may be sure, outlander, that if one does not come out of her body, one will be brought forth before the People—she can raise him as truly her own. She failed in that before. I will wager that she has no intention of doing so again."

"But," he said, "in the long years before he can be king, what will she do? Dias' hatred is unshakable, and he never comes near her. How will she rule him, if she can't touch him?"

"Does she need to touch him? She has you."

She lifted her eyes. Their clarity struck Emry like a blow. She was angry—not with Etena, and certainly not with Dias. With him. "How could you do it?" she demanded. "How could you let her—"

"She summoned me," he said. "I belong to her. And . . . she's a sad thing, for all her power."

"You did it because you *pitied* her?"

"And because she asked me," he said. "When a woman asks, a man can refuse—never doubt that. But—"

"But you wanted her."

"She wanted me," he said, "and she needed what I had to give."

Aera looked long and hard into his face. Her eyes were like green stones, full of light but snow-cold. "You are no one's friend here," she said, "or ally. You belong to your own country. We are nothing to you but enemies—makers of war, who will destroy your people. Are we not?"

That was true enough to silence him for a moment, but then he said, "You bade me win her heart. Surely you knew her body would come with it."

"Did you truly do it because I bade you?"

"No," he said. "But I did remember it. Are you so angry because you never thought I could do it?"

"I am not—" She bit her lip. "You are too different. I believe again that you come from the gods, from beyond the river of the dead. Surely no human man can be as you are."

"I am utterly mortal," he said. He stretched out his hand and closed it about hers. "See? Warm. I'm as alive as you are."

She snatched her hand free. "She bade you, didn't she? She bade you seduce me."

"She did not."

"Don't lie to me."

"I do not lie," he said. "My people, we abhor the lie. She laid nothing on me that concerned you."

"And Dias? What did she ask that you do to him?"

"Protect him," Emry answered. "Spy on him, too—but she has never asked me to tell her what I see."

"And if she did, would you?"

"I would tell her nothing that any spy of hers could not tell her for himself."

"What, nothing?"

"I may be her slave," Emry said, "but I am not her ally."

"Nor are you mine."

"But maybe," he said, "I am your friend."

"No man can be my friend."

"No man of this tribe, maybe."

"No man in this world. Go. Are you not bound to obey any woman who commands you? I command you to leave, nor ever come back."

"I am not bound to obey any woman who is not my Mother or my mistress, or my commander in battle."

"Commander in—"

"Not," he said reflectively, "that that would be particularly likely, since my father commands all the warriors of Lir, and I am his heir."

"So you are—"

"Oh yes," he said. "I hide it terribly badly, don't I? She wanted me for that. Royal blood, you see, for the things that one needs a king for, or a king's heir."

"For the—" This time she spoke again too quickly for him to intervene. "Do you know all of the things she needs a king for?"

"Those that the king himself is too soul-lost to do, or too perfectly enslaved."

"Or too valuable to waste." She seized his hands in a grip strong enough to bruise, hardly aware perhaps that she did it. "She made you king with the midwinter sacrifice. Do you know what becomes of the king at the coming of spring? When the new year is born, and winter's grip breaks, and the gods put on their crowns of new green? Do you know what happens to him then?"

He saw it in her eyes. It was a memory, too, a very old one, sung in the measure of the Great Song of Lir. "The year-king," he said. "The royal sacrifice. But—"

"She wanted you for that," Aera said. "To give her a son, then to feed her power with your life and soul. Your blood shed in the new moon of spring, in the midst of the great rite, will give her more than she ever took from the king of our People."

"But your king—she's sucked the soul out of him. What will she do, fill him up with mine? Doesn't she fear he might turn rebel?"

She hissed at him. "This is no game!"

"It is not," he agreed. "But it's a long cold while until spring, and who knows what might happen? I'm forewarned. She's preoccupied. She may not even want me for that at all. Can a king's heir be sacrificed? Surely, if the heir of a king from across the river can fulfill the gods' decree, then the son of the king who rules in this tribe—"

"Dias did not take the place of the king in the dark of the year," Aera said.

"But he was given the bull's hide by the hands of the king. He was named heir in front of the tribe. Surely that matters more here than whatever the king's wife did in the night?"

"Him," said Aera, "I can protect. You cannot even protect yourself."

"Can I not?"

"So," she said. "You're a man after all. I'll pray my gods you can stop strutting long enough to feel the axe on your neck."

"Why? So that I can know the pain of my own folly before I die?"

She slapped him, hard. His head rocked with the force of it; it dizzied him. "Gods," she said through set teeth. "Gods, if only I could hate you."

"It would be simpler," he agreed.

She struck him again, laying him flat. He stared up into her white wild face. She stooped and kissed him as hard as she had struck him, and with the same passionate intensity. Just when he must breathe or fall into the dark, she let him go. He might have taken her glare for hatred, or rage, but he did not think it was either.

She bent once more. Her hands cradled his face, her fingers tangling in the curls of his beard. This kiss was soft, and tasted of salt. There were tears on her cheeks. "I should not," she said, "I should never—in this life—"

She was not weeping for him, not in her heart. She thrust herself away from him. "Get out, before we dishonor all our kin."

"There is no dishonor in this," he said. But he rose, because plainly she could not bear that he saw her weep. Such pride; so much pain. And beauty to break the heart.

He kissed the tears from her cheeks, and pressed her hands for a moment to his heart. Then he left her to mourn her sorrows in peace.

56

Aera wept till her throat was raw and her ribs ached. All the grief that she had held tight in her heart, all the pain, the anger, the pure blind rage, burst out of her with no hope of restraint. Not only did she weep for her son. She wept for his father, who was worse than dead; and for his brother, who might be dead by spring. And she wept a little for herself, because she had been so perfectly, utterly a fool.

She had reckoned it enough to raise Etena's son as if he had been her own, and to keep him safe until he was a man. For her own son she had taken too few precautions. She had never thought that Etena would dare to touch him, once the king had named him heir. Folly—for Etena had dared to corrupt a king. Mere princes would be as nothing to her.

Now Minas was dead, and Dias was in danger. Did Etena hope to keep the king alive until the child within her was grown? Or had she chosen another of the sons to be king between? That would not be Dias. Dias would never submit to her magic.

If two royal heirs were sacrificed come spring . . . what power would that give her? Would she hoard it, or would she wield it in ways that Aera was too befuddled to conceive?

The storm of grief had passed. Aera lay in her father's tent beside the half-finished weaving, all empty and wept clean.

Her mind was very clear. She rather thought she understood what Emry had done to her, though she could not be sure why. He truly did not think as men did here.

He was no ally, no. Enemy? Without a doubt. And yet she did believe that she could trust him—until they came to his country. Very likely he hoped to prevent that for as long as possible. This conflict of kings and kings' wives would serve his people very well.

It seemed he had chosen her side of this battle. Because she did not own him, and Etena did? Because she was the weaker, and he had a soft heart for the downtrodden? Or simply because he wanted to lie with her?

Not so simple, that. She wanted to lie with him—oh gods, desperately. If she had been even a fraction less firmly bound by honor and grim good sense, she would have taken him as a man takes a woman, headlong and heedless, instead of casting him out.

She gathered herself together and washed the traces of tears from her face. She returned to the loom and began where she had left off, her hands moving swiftly but with care, so that no thread was awry.

Her sisters came back when she had woven an armlength of new cloth. They were silent women, as odd by now as their father. Aera beside them was a bright and frivolous spirit.

She had not realized before how stifling their silence was. As maddening and sometimes dangerous as the king's tent could be, with its factions of quarrelling wives and concubines, its squalling babies, and its perpetual drone of Etena's spells, still it was a lively place. Maybe she had not been happy there, but she had been more honestly alive than she was here.

Her son was dead. She was not. The westerner had proved it in ways that still heated her loins when she thought of them.

She thought long on what she would do. That night she slept more deeply than she might have expected, and woke certain of her choice.

With no need to protect her son, with Dias as well guarded as he could be, she could afford to be reckless.

She chose her time carefully. In the mornings Etena rose at her leisure, lingered over her toilet, held audience for her allies and spies. Then the king was lightly guarded, only one of her witches with him to sustain the spell. If he was to go out, he would do it at noon or after, when Etena had let him know what she wished of him.

In the morning then, a handful of days after she had decided on it, Aera approached the king's tent by one of the less conspicuous ways. She made no attempt to be furtive, for that would draw suspicion. She had a basket over her arm, laden with bread that she had made, and flesh of the deer that Emry had brought, dried with herbs and berries in the way that she had learned from her mother. It was gift and tribute, and excuse as well, so that she seemed to have an errand in the king's tent.

She entered that world which had once been hers. It was dark and close and seemed unutterably crowded, and yet she saw no living thing. The women were all hidden away, secreted in the inner reaches.

The king was hidden less thoroughly than his women. Who but Etena would dare to touch him? Her spell bound them all, warriors and women alike.

It was time they began to break free.

Aera entered a space of dim light and cloying smoke and the ceaseless, maddening chant. The woman who intoned it had the same empty stare as the king, the same absence of life or soul. She was a vessel, that was all; a voice for Etena's will.

Aera silenced her with a honey-sweet. She sank back in her cushions, her face rapt in bliss, as the drug that Aera had baked in the cake sent her wafting down into sleep.

The king lay hardly more conscious as Aera covered the incense-burners and did what she could to clear the heavy air. She knelt in front of him. He was naked in a nest of foreign weavings and rare furs, his big body slack. His skin was soft and cool. His hair was thinner than she remembered, and greyer.

She laved his face with water that she had brought, steeped with herbs that sent a strong green scent through the smoky sweetness of Etena's spells. Did he rouse a little? She washed his neck and breast, his arms— trying hard not to think of another body, another big bull of a man who was as strong and clearheaded and free as this one had been when first she knew him.

He stirred under her hands. He looked as if he were swimming up out of deep water. She slapped him lightly with the wetted cloth, first one cheek, then the other. He groaned. His head tossed.

He blinked at her. His eyes were deeply clouded, but his brows were knit.

Her heartbeat quickened. There was a glimmer of awareness there. He had a soul still. It was a poor feeble wandering thing, and it did not like to linger in this hulk of a body, but that it was there, still in his possession, she could not mistake.

She had hoped for this, but not dared to expect it. So, she thought: Etena's magics were not as strong as fear made them.

Or this was a trap, and she had fallen headlong into it. She had gambled on that, in coming here.

She heard nothing beyond the room, sensed no spy behind a curtain. Nothing in the king's tent had changed, except the light in his eyes, brightening slowly.

Just as she thought he might have recognized her, the light went out. His eyelids drooped. His body was slack again, his soul lost.

Aera regarded him in something that was not quite grief. Not much longer now, she thought. Even Etena could not keep this broken thing walking, speaking, fighting in battles. Very soon she would need another slave to her will.

But as Aera rose to retreat, the king's hand closed about her wrist. Its strength astonished her. His eyes were still shut, his face still empty of expression. He said, "Minas. Minas my son. Where is he?"

She realized that she was gaping at him. His grip on her wrist tightened. She gasped at the pain.

"*Where?*" he whispered.

"Dead," she said baldly.

He let his breath out in a long hiss. "So that was not a dream. And the other? Dias? I gave him the bull's hide. Was that true, too?"

"Yes."

"She'll kill him. She'll kill them all, in the end: every son of my body. She hates us beyond reason."

"You slaughtered every male in her tribe," Aera said, "and enslaved or killed the women. She has reason enough, when all's said."

"I made her my wife," he said. Then: "Enough. She'll come soon, to put back all my chains. Do a thing for me."

"If I can," said Aera.

"Kill me."

Aera stared at him.

He opened his eyes. They were clouded, but much less than before. His hand groped among the heaped fabrics of his bed, found something, brought it out clenched in his fist. "She made this," he said. "Help me. Help me drink it."

She saw how it was: how he struggled to raise it, but his arm trembled violently, until his grip on the vial slackened. It fell to the coverlets. It was a foreign thing, finely carved out of pale green stone, and tiny to be so deadly.

"Did she give it to you?" Aera asked.

His head shook—tossed. "Stole it. Kept it . . . long. Could never . . ."

"Better to kill her," Aera said, "and set you free."

"If she dies first, her soul enters me," he said. "Kill me first. Then kill her."

Aera took up the vial. It was cold, and heavy for its size. He lay like a dead thing, but his breath was coming in gasps. It was fear—but not of death. Of living as he did now, bound and helpless.

Aera slipped the vial into her garments. "Can you endure until spring? Can you do that, my lord?"

His fists clenched in the coverlets. "My death then will only feed her power."

"Not if we perform the rite," she said.

"Too long," he said. "Too long."

She hardened her heart. "If you die now, you weaken us. If you wait—"

"If *you* wait," he said, "her power will be unshakable. She will take the new heir, and take me, and rule this tribe more completely even than before."

"Is that so ill a thing?" Aera asked.

"Once she no longer has me," he said, "she will break us. She will see that the clans divide, and the kings and chieftains and warleaders go to war with one another, and all our power scatters in the wind. And no one will remember us."

"No," said Aera. "Maybe once she wanted that. But now she tastes power. She will bring the clans together under a new king, unite them and strengthen them and drive them westward. Just as she has always driven you—toward the lands of gold, to wealth unimaginable. She forges us into a weapon for her hand."

"She will destroy us," he whispered. "However she does it, she will conquer us all."

He gave her no warning. He surged with startling strength, lunged at her, bore her down. The vial flew free of her mantle. He caught it with warrior's swiftness. The tremors began as soon as his fingers closed about it; but this time he did not succumb to the weakness. He linked both hands, gasping with the effort, and brought the vial to his mouth.

She scrambled toward him. But he was too quick.

It was a swift poison. It seemed the vial had barely touched his lips before he convulsed. "Kill," he gasped with the last of his breath. "Kill her." And as he died: "Go. Live! Kill—kill—"

His will, that had been broken for so long, was strong in his death. It drove her out as if she had been flung by a hand. She had wits at least to cover her head and face, to move without haste, to slip through the murmuring dimness and out into the cold of the winter morning.

Wisdom would have taken her back to her father's tent, to her loom, her sisters, her wonted tasks. But she could not be wise.

She found Emry, by the gods' grace, alone in the young men's tent. Dias and the rest were preparing for a hunt: she heard them whooping and laughing out by the horses. Emry must have been sent to look for something: he was rummaging in a bundle of oddments, bits of fur and tanned hide, harness-straps, arrowheads, coiled bowstrings. He took up one of those with a grunt of satisfaction and turned, and started like a deer.

Aera was in no mood to be proper, just then. Nor could she be discreet. "The king is dead," she said, quite calmly she thought. "It will be a little while before they find him." She held out her basket, which she had kept with her even in her flight. "Here is bread, dried meat, sweetness. For your hunt. See that Dias is safe. Will you do that?"

"I always do that," he said, but not as if he took much notice of his own words. "Did you say—I thought I knew your language. But did you say—the king—"

"The king is dead," she said.

"Did you kill him?"

Straight to the point, and no foolishness about it, either. She smiled at him, unable to help herself; it was the beginning of hysteria. "No."

"Etena?"

Her hand flicked, warding off the ill luck of the name. "No. I wouldn't, you see. Because I wanted him to wait, to hold on till spring. But he couldn't do that. He had poison. Her spells kept him from drinking it, till he had me there. I think I made him strong enough."

"You would strengthen any man's spirit," he said a little faintly. He rallied himself: his shoulders came back, his chin came up. "You want us to go on this hunt? It might be better if the king's heir is here—when—"

Aera sank down where she stood. Her mind was clear. Her heart was steady. But her knees, all at once, had lost their power to hold her up.

He dropped to one knee in front of her. If he had touched her, she would have broken, but he kept his hands to himself. "Lady," he said, "I think Dias should stay in camp. The more of his men he has about him, the clearer it is that the succession is assured, the safer he'll be. And, lady," he said, "I don't know all the intricacies of power here, but I think it would be less than wise to let her live."

"He said that, too," Aera said, "before he died."

"I'll do it," Emry said. "I'll kill her."

She stared at him. He was not jesting, nor was it bravado. He meant every word.

He had seemed a gentle creature, and soft, with his rich clothes and his meek manners. But he was a warrior after all, and a king's son.

She caught him before he could rise. "No. This is not for you to do."

"Who better than I? A slave, a foreigner, not bound by kin or clan. Any of you who does it becomes subject to the laws of kinslaying. I a slave, killing a king's wife, am simply condemned to death. I'll run, lady—and maybe I'll escape. Or maybe not. Does it matter which?"

"It matters," she said, too low she hoped for him to hear. Aloud she said, "You will do as I bid you. Go, stay close by Dias. Trust no one, not even his yearmates. What must be done with Etena, I will do."

He opened his mouth to protest.

She silenced him with a stroke of the gods' own inspiration. "This is a women's matter. Do you question it?"

He bent his head. "Lady," he said. There was enough of a growl in it to make clear his reckoning of her wisdom, but he was too much a man of his people to disobey her.

When he was gone, she had to stay for a while where she was. She did not think she could walk, just then.

It dawned on her much too late, that she had not settled with Emry whether Dias would go or stay. She had to trust that he would do what was best.

Oh, gods. The king was dead—had sacrificed himself. And she was utterly unprepared for it.

But so was Etena. Etena could not even know it yet; it was still early, though it seemed as if days had passed since she watched the king gasp out his life. Aera had to get up, to move. To be ready when the first shriek pierced the icy air.

Metos. Metos must know. She should have gone to him at the first. Fool that she was, and besotted, to run to the foreigner—but he had proved useful after all. If he did as he was told. If he did not break free of her command and get himself killed.

She raised herself to wobbling knees, and after a long moment, to her feet. She drew a deep breath, and then another, to steady herself. Emry had left the basket behind. She left it where it was, for the young men to find when they came back. Carefully, a little slowly lest she break and fall, she walked back to the makers' circle.

57

Emry knew perfectly well what Aera had done to him, but he could no more defy her than spread wings and fly.

Nor was it only obedience that held his hand. The part of him that was prince and not simple man knew that it served Lir better to keep Etena alive. Lir needed contention among these people. The more bitter the battle for the kingship, the more likely it was that the tribe would crack, even shatter.

He found Dias still among the horses, and several of his men squabbling amiably over taking out chariots. There was snow, but wind and sun had thinned it. It would not be such heavy going, they insisted: just enough to keep the teams from running wild.

Dias seemed disinclined to call a halt to the bickering. He was whiling the time with one of the young stallions, who, it appeared, had been broken to harness but not to ride. The horse was amenable to bit and saddle-fleece, but he sidled and snorted at the man leaning over his back.

Emry moved in to take the bridle and gentle the stallion. Dias swung up and landed lightly. The stallion staggered but held his ground. Emry from below, Dias from above stroked him till he stretched his neck and sighed.

Dias slid down to stand again by the stallion's side. Again he mounted and dismounted, and then a third time. When he had done that, he looked Emry in the face. "Tell me," he said.

Emry had thought himself sufficiently masked, but it seemed he was not. He had had a shock, to be sure; he was still reeling with it.

He considered keeping silent or evading the question. Better not, he thought. "Your father is dead," he said.

Dias frowned. "That is not a thing for jests here."

"Nor in my country," Emry said.

"You said—" Dias leaned toward him. "If you are lying, or mocking, or playing a game of princes, I will have you dragged behind yonder chariot."

"I tell the Goddess' own truth," Emry said, "through the lady Aera. He is dead. He took his life in her presence."

"Gods," said Dias. He had gone white. "Oh, gods." He straightened. "Then why do we hear nothing? The women should all be wailing."

"No one knows but the lady Aera," said Emry, "and we two. He'll be found soon, but—"

"She came to you? She told *you*?"

"She came to your tent," Emry said, "and I was there."

"You belong to Etena. And she told you. What, is she trying to get herself killed?"

"I am no danger to her," Emry said. "She thought that you would be wiser to stay in camp, and not be out hunting when they find him."

"When they— Gods." Dias scraped his hand across his face. "This means that I'm—"

"Yes."

"I'm not ready."

"I think," said Emry, "that few princes are."

"I have to be ready," Dias said. He stiffened his back. "I must be strong enough. I must—be—king."

"I think," Emry said slowly, "that you should take it into your head to visit Metos. This squabble will go on all day, and you weary of it, yes? And we all know the hunting is abominable, unless we ride far; and is that snow I smell on the wind?"

Dias smiled thinly. "You're a clever man," he said. "Now swear to me that you do none of this in your mistress' name."

"By my own name I swear it," Emry said.

Dias nodded, satisfied. He and Emry between them freed the young stallion of his bridle and saddle-fleece, and let him run back to the herd of his fellows.

Dias called easily to some of the warband who were standing about. "Aias, Kletas, Borias! Come."

They were willing. The others glanced at them, but the squabble was erupting into a fight. That was more entertaining than whatever Dias might be up to.

The three who went with him were his most trusted friends, the ones who were closest to him. Emry took note of that. Dias was thinking like a prince, if not quite, yet, like a king.

⇒ ⇐

Metos was waiting in his tent. Being Metos, he worked at something while he waited: carving a casting-mold for a bit made of copper rather than bone.

He looked up at the young men's coming. Emry had seldom seen him look at a human creature; he kept his attention for the works of his hands. But he looked at Dias, and then at each of the others, and at Emry last of all. His eyes were piercingly keen. Emry began to believe what the tribesmen said, that this was a god.

He seemed to be alone. But Emry sensed another presence behind a curtain, the mingling of softness and brilliance that was Aera.

That was well. Aias and Kletas and Borias, innocent of the thing that had brought Dias here, bent their heads in respect to Metos and sat politely until he was ready to speak. Dias prowled the space that, though not wide, was empty enough to indulge his restlessness.

Aera emerged, veiled, from behind the curtain. She brought cups, jars, a basket of bread. There was salt with it, very precious, very rare, so that the young men's brows rose.

The jars were full of honey mead, the summer wine of the tribe. The bread was newly made. Even Dias ate a little bread dipped in salt, and drank a sip of the mead. This was a ritual, a ceremony that bound them all to more than simple hospitality.

Emry shared it. He might not have done that, but Aera brought the basket and a jar and a cup to him, eyes lowered in the propriety of the tribe. So was he too bound, and this council sealed to the silence of those who took part in it.

Once the needs of hospitality were fulfilled, Aera did not retreat behind her curtain. She sat quietly in a corner, out of sight of most of them, but not Emry.

Metos, as the host, spoke first. He had drunk a cup of mead and eaten half a loaf of bread. He belched, as was polite, and said, "If I were a wise king, I would send men now, before the truth comes out, and take the woman captive."

"The woman is a witch," Dias said. "Who will dare take her? She turns men to toads, it's said, and shrivels their members till they piddle like women."

His companions glanced at one another. They could not but know whom he spoke of. Hands flicked, warding the omen.

"I will take her," Emry said. "I'm not afraid of her spells."

"You're her slave," Dias said.

"A woman owns nothing here. Yes? Everything that is hers belongs to her through her husband or her husband's heir. Am I not therefore the property of the king? And is the king not—"

"The king is completely in her power," said Aias.

"I am not," Dias said.

"But you aren't—"

"The old king lies dead in his tent," said Emry. "No one yet has found him. Shall we sit here talking the day away, or shall we seize the woman before she expects any such thing?"

"Since when are you one of us?"

Emry grinned at Aias. "I'm a man and she's a woman and a witch besides, and you need to ask me that?"

It was not exactly true, but a man of this tribe would never have understood the truth. Aias subsided, though he eyed Emry with the remnants of suspicion.

"Go," Dias said abruptly. "All four of you. Take her and bring her here. Try to be quiet about it if you can."

"You'll need these," Metos said. He unrolled a bundle of leather, baring half a dozen bronze blades. Emry recognized them. The traders had carried them, though he had not known they would be traded or sold.

One was his own, his sword with the silver hilt. He had reached for it before he thought, moving swifter than the others, lifting it, sighing as it settled into his hand.

It was the best of the blades, as well it might be: it was made for a prince in Lir. Belatedly he remembered what and where he was. But he could not let the sword go.

The young men did not know enough to tell one blade from another. But Metos and his daughter clearly did. Metos seemed amused. Aera he could not read behind veils and lowered eyelids. Neither moved to prevent him, or to advise Dias that the slave had taken the blade fit for a king.

They were armed, all four of them. Dias would not go. He wanted to, but Metos stopped him. "If they bring her safe here, you'll have her in your power. But if they have to kill her, you won't have that stain on your spirit."

Dias did not like that, but he had to yield to its wisdom. He settled for seizing Emry by the shoulder as he prepared to go, and saying harshly, "If anybody has to kill her, let it be you. But then you'd best run—because I'll be bound by my honor to avenge her."

Emry bowed without mockery. "I understand," he said.

He did not meet Aera's gaze. She had tried to prevent this. But this was fate; however great her wisdom, she could not stand against what must be.

⇒ ⇐

They went as casually as they could, four idle young men passing through the camp, looking to occupy themselves late on a winter morning. Their weapons were hidden in their mantles of fur and hide. They sauntered with deceptive slowness, closing in on the king's tent.

It was unguarded. No sound came from it but the usual murmur of women's voices and the laughter and cries of children. The king's men were elsewhere. They had passed some of them idling about the council fire, playing at the bones. In a well-ruled tribe, Emry thought, the king would have been in council, and his men would have been nearby to defend him.

Emry had taken the lead. None of the others, he would wager, had been inside those walls. They seemed content to follow him.

He was following his heart, and the roiling in his gut. He did not fear

Etena's magic; that was the truth. The Goddess protected him. But he did not trust this quiet, not altogether.

He breathed a prayer to the Goddess as he entered the king's tent, most of it wordless, pure will and pure entreaty. He did not know if she heard. He could only hope.

They found Etena where she often was. Only one of her women was with her. She greeted Emry's arrival with a glance that shook him: it was briefly, unguardedly glad. Even when his companions come in past him and seized her and her servant, she kept her eyes on him. Trying to lay a spell on him, maybe. He felt nothing, not even a breath of wind.

Aias and Kletas bound and gagged her. Borias did the same for her servant. Neither resisted. It was as if they could not conceive of such a thing, and so could not respond to it.

They wrapped the women in cloaks and carried them out. It was eerie, how nothing changed; no one saw them, no one cried a warning.

Emry could not bear it. Every drop of wisdom that he had cried out to him to go with the others. But he had to do it—he had to find the king's body. If it was there. If his death was not a dream or a spell.

It was there. It was already rigid in death. Its face was livid. There was no sign of the maid who had been with the king, nor of the other whom Etena must have sent to fetch him. He was all alone, rigid and still.

It was a terrible thing, this death of a king. Emry's heart yearned to bring him out into the sun, to give him honorable grief, but that would be rankest folly. A slave found with the body of a king would have been put to death in Lir. He doubted that the penalty would be any less here.

He slipped away as softly as he could. Dias' young men were already gone.

He could have escaped then, gathered his belongings and taken a horse and run. But when he turned, it was toward the makers' circle again, and Metos' tent, and the new-minted king.

58

The wailing began before Dias' yearmates returned to Metos' tent. Aera, sitting in tense silence with Dias and her father, started as if she had been struck. If the boys had failed—if they had been hurt, or killed—

The flap lifted. She braced for attack.

But it was Aias with a long limp bundle slung over his shoulder, and Kletas behind him with a second. Borias followed, empty-handed. There was no one behind.

They had Etena and one of her maids. The others, said Aias, had been nowhere to be found.

They laid their burdens on the floor of the tent.

"Go," she said to them, and to Dias, too. "This is for us to do. Your part is out there—where the keening is."

"But—" said Dias.

"They've found your father," Aera said, though none of them could fail to know it. "Be sure to be astonished, and suitably horrified."

"It is a horror," Dias said. He turned to the others. "Come, be quick."

They went out at the run. Their absence felt like the aftermath of a storm, still and unnaturally quiet.

Metos broke the silence with the hiss of bronze from leather sheath. He had drawn the one sword that remained. Swiftly, coldly, without a glance at her, he ran it through the burden that Kletas had carried.

The woman within died without a sound. The other, Aias' captive, began to struggle, as if somehow, in all her wrappings, she understood what Metos had done.

Even knowing what a fool she was, Aera interposed herself between her father and the captive. That it was Etena, she did not doubt at all. "Not this one," she said. "Let the People judge her. Let them know what she did, and how she did it. Then let them decide her sentence."

"You may regret that," Metos said.

"I'm sure I will," she said. "But this is what must be."

He sighed, but he shrugged. "On your head be it," he said.

Wise boys: they had bound Etena tightly and gagged her before they wrapped her in cloaks. She lay in the nest of them, glaring at the two who stood over her.

"It's ended," Aera said to her. "The king is dead. Now there will be justice."

Etena's eyes narrowed. Aera saw no fear there. There was laughter—at herself, at the ease with which she had been captured, who knew? She was perfectly defiant. If Aera cut her throat then and there, she would never beg for mercy. She would embrace her death.

Aera loosed the gag, though she suspected she would be sorry for it. Metos, watching, said nothing. He kept the bronze blade in his hand, stained still with the servant's blood.

Aera held a cup of snowmelt to Etena's lips. She drank gladly enough. When she had had her fill, she turned her head away.

The wailing outside had risen to a crescendo. Aera knew as if she had a shaman's sight, that Dias and his companions had brought the king out into the light, so that the People might see the manner of his death.

Etena was impassive. "Did you do it?" she asked.

"He did it himself," said Aera.

Etena's lip curled. "Oh, surely. That is the gods' truth as you will swear it."

"Would you know truth from black lie?"

Etena smiled thinly. "He won't kill me, you know. You should have let your father do it. My son is a weakling—he'll never have the courage to put to death his own mother."

"There are worse things than death," Aera said.

Etena only smiled.

→ ←

The king lay dead in the council circle, laid on the hide of a spotted bull, under a blue and empty sky. The People circled him in a wild dance of grief. For this, even the women came out, rent their garments, tore their hair that was shorn already for Minas the prince. The men slashed their arms and faces and breasts, shed blood in the king's name.

Emry had thought their grieving extravagant before, when they mourned a prince. Now he saw how they mourned a king.

Dias was king now, no one disputed that, even the flock of his brothers. But until this king was laid to rest, he would not rule with the full force of the name. The elders and clan-chieftains performed much of the office that he would hold; the rest was laid aside.

He had sent out riders, strong young men on the swiftest of the horses, bearing word of the king's death and bidding the scattered tribes and clans to gather. That would be no simple thing in the dead of winter, nor a swift or easy one. He summoned them for the moon of spring, the moon after the next, and they would gather to the westward, near the fire's edge. The hunting would be better there, and grazing for the herds; and all the tribes in that region were broken or dead.

But now, on this bitter-bright day, it was only the royal clan. They raised the king up, sat him as if on a throne, clothed him in royal finery and crowned him with gold. He stared sightlessly over the camp of his people. In truth, Emry thought, he was more strongly present now than he had been since Etena's spell took his soul away.

Emry kept his head down. This was not a time for outlanders. The slaves and captives, who usually were out and about, laboring in their rags, were nowhere to be seen. He, who had kept his distance from them, could hardly seek refuge with them now.

In the end he went where he might not be safe, but he might be of use. He found Metos' tent even more bare and silent than before. Etena and her maid were not to be seen, nor did he see or hear Aera or her sisters. For once even Metos and the makers had left their place. They would be mourning the king, he supposed.

He should have expected that. He considered withdrawing to the young men's tent, which would likewise be deserted, but he seemed to have lost the will to move. He settled in a corner, knees drawn up, cloak wrapped about him, and did his best to find both warmth and peace of mind.

⇨ ⇦

With the coming of night, the tumult of grief muted for a while. Those who could sleep had fallen where they danced; the fires kept them warm, or not. By morning some would be frozen dead. They were an offering to the gods, an escort for the king.

Emry woke in that stillness. He was still alone in Metos' tent. It was black dark. His bladder twinged; he rose stiffly, groaning, shaking with cold. He hobbled out of the tent.

The stars were thick overhead, scattered like hoarfrost across the blackness of the sky. The cold numbed his cheeks and the tip of his nose; he was grateful for the beard that grew so thick. His breath ached when he drew it in.

He relieved himself as quickly and discreetly as he could, a stream so hot it seemed to burn. When he was done, he turned to go back into the tent, which though cold was at least warmer than this. But something stopped him. The stillness. The utter lack of wind. The glitter of starlight on the bare and trampled earth.

At first he took it for the pulse of his own heart. But that was nothing inside of him. It was a drumbeat, swelling slowly, and a skirling of pipes, and a thin eerie singing.

They came from the east and the south and the north. They came with drums and pipes, bone rattles and chiming of bells. They walked upright like men, but their heads and shoulders were those of beasts: bear and boar, bull and stag.

The shamans had come back, and the priests of the People. They circled the camp sunwise, and then against the sun, three times three. They bound it and warded it and sealed it with their magics. And when that was done, they raised tents in a quarter that had been empty.

Emry stood watch until dawn. His skin quivered as the wards went up one by one. The air seemed warmer for their presence.

To his surprise, the tribe acted as if nothing untoward had happened. Almost he thought them oblivious to the powers that had returned, until at midday the rites of mourning paused. The priests came into the circle and danced solemnly round the king. The people ceased their own dancing and wailing, fell back and stood still.

The priests were priests of the Bull, in mantles of bull's hide and horned headdresses. They were naked under the hides, painted with ash and red ocher, and warm in the bite of the cold. They pawed the ground and snorted; they did battle, horn to horn; they played a long moaning song on the horns of bulls.

When the last note died away, the priests linked arms, facing outward, and knelt, a circle of guard about the corpse of the king.

They knelt as still as images carved in stone. As if that had been a signal, the young king's warband advanced together. They led a captive, bound and staggering. She was naked, her aging body pebble-skinned and blue with cold. Her face and her eyes were covered with a hood of tanned leather that fell to her shoulders.

Aias and Kletas flung her before the priests and the dead king. Dias set his foot on her back.

He was dressed, or not dressed, as a priest. The bull's head concealed all of his face but the mouth and chin: firm chin, mouth set thin and stern. The wheel of the sun was painted in ocher on his breast and thighs, and on the palms of his hands as he lifted them.

"Father!" he cried. His voice boomed from the bull's mask. "You have gone to be lord among the dead—and may the gods grant that your soul is yours again, and your spirit whole."

The dead king sat unmoving. The living priests had no more motion in them. Only the wind stirred, plucking at the trailing edges of mantles.

Dias swooped down without warning and heaved Etena to her feet. Her knees buckled. He held her up with one contemptuous hand. "This, Father, is the thing that destroyed you. This stole your soul and gnawed your life away. I would sacrifice it, Father, on the altar of your spirit— but it is never worthy of such a thing. Better it be stoned to death and its carcass flung out for the dogs."

"I did not kill him." Etena's voice was startlingly clear. "If you would punish his murderer, then look to the one who suckled you at her breast."

"You will not speak of her," Dias said in a low growl. And louder: "People of the Wind! Judge this creature. What death shall we give her? What torment shall she suffer?"

"What is worse than death?"

They all looked astonished at Metos. He who never left his circle except in a chariot, who never saw aught but the chariots that he made, was standing just outside the circle. He stood taller than any near him, with his face like a falcon's and his eyes like green stones.

He spoke again. "If we give her death, we give her oblivion—for is it not known that as we did in life, so is it done to us in death? Would you give her up to the peace of forgetfulness? Is that sufficient atonement for what she has done?"

"If we let her live," Dias said, "we leave her free to commit her crimes again. She is a witch, a sorceress. She destroys men's souls."

"They call me a god," said Metos. "Exile her. Cast her out. Take her name from the memories of the People. Curse her soul and her spirit, so that when death takes her at last, she may go into the claws of the gods below, and not into the peace of silence."

He spoke with the voice and authority of a god. Even Dias, king that he was, bowed before it.

They cast her out as she had been brought to the circle, naked, masked, without food or weapon. The king's warband took her in chariots, far out on the plain, too far to return on foot, and there left her.

Emry rode with Dias, clinging behind in the warrior's place. Aias' chariot carried Etena. Emry half expected that they would fling him out with her, for Dias had said no word to him beyond the simple command: "Get in." But once he was there, it seemed he was forgotten. When they turned back to the camp, Emry was still in the chariot.

It was not until the mourning was over, the king laid in a barrow with his chariot and horses, and the head of bull and stallion set on guard above it, that they knew: a handful of the king's sons were missing with weapons and chariots. There was no fire to consume them, no raid to destroy them. Hunters tracked them westward into the devastation of the fire, but they were too swift. They were gone.

Emry, standing on the edge of that plain of ash and blown snow, knew in his heart that she had gone with the king's sons; that she was leading them. She was riding westward into Lir.

He would wager that Metos had expected that—that the maker of chariots knew precisely what he had done in loosing that serpent upon the west.

But Lir was strong, and well accustomed to the power of women. She would not find it so easy to corrupt. Nor would she ever again seduce a king as she had seduced the lord of these people.

The tribe was free of her. It was waking, stretching, rejoicing in its freedom. In a little while it would begin the march toward the great gathering and the kingmaking.

And then, he was sure, the Goddess would see that Dias was much delayed before he could begin his own conquests. Then maybe he would turn north, or south. Maybe the west would be safe.

Maybe the moon would come down and pour its light in molten silver over the earth, and the sun's light turn black, and the stars fall in a shower of ash. Emry was only intermittently a fool. He knew as well as any seer, that this tribe went west. It had gone west since before living memory. It would go until there was no more earth to ride on—and then, he supposed, it would set sail on the sea, or spread wings across the stars.

Emry turned his back on the sunset. He was no longer a slave. What he was, he was not certain yet; but they had not cast him out or killed him. He was, as far as he could tell, the king's companion. Servant, maybe. Protector of his right hand.

And that was strangest of many strange things, that Emry prince of Lir should be trusted guardian to the king of chariots.

59

Dias did not take possession of the king's tent, though he was entitled to it. The king's wives and concubines, Emry gathered, would be returned to their kin or offered as gifts to the new king's friends and allies. Or he might keep them; but Dias showed no inclination toward his father's leavings.

All the old king's wealth, like his women, was Dias' to keep or give away. That at least he considered with care and some little wisdom. He gave great gifts in the gathering of tribes: gold and treasure, women, a share of the flocks and herds. But he kept wealth in plenty. He made a name for generosity, but kept a name for great riches. And that, everyone agreed, was altogether befitting a king.

It was a splendid kingmaking, in a splendid spring after so bitter a winter. There Emry saw in truth the numbers that could be mounted against the west, and his heart went cold. They were as innumerable as the birds of heaven. And all of them, to the last and poorest, mounted their warriors in chariots.

They made Dias king on the day of high spring, as ordained by the priests of all the tribes and clans. It was a glorious day, clear and warm. The seared earth to the west was coming to life, waking to a shy new green. The steppe round the great camp, where fire had not come, was lush with grass.

They raised Dias up on a high mound of earth, the barrow of an old king or god. Its summit was bright gold, carpeted with flowers. Red blood stained it, blood of sacrifice: a hundred bulls, glorious extravagance, offered up to the gods of the air and the gods below. The hides, the thighbones wrapped in fat, sent a rich black smoke to the gods. The lesser meat made a feast for the tribes.

While the last bull's bellow was still fading into the earth, the priests laid on Dias the hide and head of the king of bulls, the white bull, the lord of the steppe. He braced under it as if it were as heavy as stone. Then he straightened, easing to the weight of it. His shoulders broadened. His head rose. He spread his arms. The roar of his people bore him up.

Emry felt that roar in his bones. Hundreds, thousands of voices acclaimed their new king, his youth, his strength, the simple splendor of him after Etena's fading shadow.

It was a beautiful, terrible thing, this tribe and this king. Emry withdrew from it, retreating to such solitude as there was. He would go; now, truly, he would set out for home. The one who had bought him was gone. His purpose was completed. He only stayed—why? Because he was a coward?

Because he was a fool. He had not seen or heard from Aera since the priests came back to the tribe. She was secluded in her father's tent. She had traveled from camp to camp shut in a wagon, who he knew hated to be so confined.

Now that the king was made, the gathering proper would begin: feasting, dancing, marrying and giving in marriage. Men took wives from distant clans, and women—if secretly—inspected the young men. Often they did more than that, if what he heard was to be believed.

He did believe it. It was in the Great Song of Lir, how gatherings had been on the steppe, long ago when his ancestors were wild horsemen such as these.

And it was in the song that when a king died, his wives either went with him into the tomb, or went to his sons, or were free. Emry knew that no wives had been sacrificed in this king's name, nor had his sons taken any of them, even Dias. There would be marriages made, that much he understood; chieftains of the clans, lords of the tribes would take the choicest of the women as gifts.

It repelled him to think of them so. It sickened him to think that *she* might go to some thick-bellied clan-chieftain, to share his bed and bear his sons. Daughters were not welcome among these people.

The thought when it came was almost unthinkable. But he had to think it. He could not bear to see her sent away, given like a gold collar or a fine heifer. Even when he told himself that Dias would not do such a thing to his foster-mother—what after all did Emry know of any of them? They were not his people. They did not think as he thought.

He went to Dias in the morning after the kingmaking, choosing his time with care. The feasting had gone on late, but Dias was a man who liked to rise with the sun. Indeed, this morning Emry heard him before he saw him, a deep sweet voice chanting in the dawn. The young men snarled and muttered and buried their faces in their furs, all but Aias, who grinned at Emry and said, "The sunrise-song. Now I know we have a king again."

Emry saw him coming back from the eastern edge of the camp, looking like any other tribesman, though darker and broader than most. He greeted Emry with a swift smile. Emry returned it almost before he thought. Dias' good humor was difficult to resist. As heavy as the king's mantle had weighed on him the day before, this morning it seemed the burden was light.

"A fair morning to you," he said in greeting.

It was fine indeed, bright and warm and clear. "I heard you singing," Emry said.

"What, did it wake you?"

Emry shook his head. "I gather it wasn't approved of while your father was king."

"While that woman was king in all but name," said Dias, "it was forbidden."

"She's gone," Emry said. "The priests have come back. The sun shines here as it didn't before."

"Ah," said Dias, looking keenly at him. "You feel it. You would be a priest here, you know. Or a shaman. The gods speak to you."

Emry shrugged at that. They had come to the tent in which Dias was living, a very handsome one, though not as handsome as that in which the old king had died. There were no women in it yet, but by gathering's end there would be. Already the lords and chieftains were offering their daughters. Dias would choose among them—it was part of his duty, like judging disputes and leading the armies to war.

The tent's flap was fastened back, letting in light and air. No darkness or dimness or drugged smokes here. All was open, bright and clean.

Dias settled in the shade of the tent, beckoning Emry to sit beside him. A boy, young and shy, brought the perpetual bread and kumiss. It was an honor, Emry knew, to break bread with the king; but Dias did not put on airs. He was as easy as he had ever been, speaking of this and that, undertaking with considerable skill to put Emry at ease.

"Kingship suits you," Emry said as they passed the skin of kumiss back and forth.

"Are you surprised?" Dias asked him.

"Are you?"

"This was never meant for me," Dias said. "I was going to be my brother's warleader, his right hand. That was all I cared for. I never dreamed, even in nightmares, that this would come to me."

"It seems the gods willed it," Emry said.

"And you? Do you still hope to be king, if you can go back to your people?"

Emry considered the wisdom of an honest answer. "If the Goddess wills," he said, "I will be king."

"And my enemy?"

"Or your ally." Emry leaned back in the heap of furs and cushions. "Tell me, king of chariots. What am I now? Your slave? Your servant? Your guest? Your hostage?"

"What do you wish to be?"

Emry hesitated. Now, he thought: say it, or forever keep silent. It was difficult to the point of pain to speak as he must speak, so that this man would understand him. "I would wish," he said at last, "for the gift that you promised me when you were made king."

Dias raised his brows. "Would you now? Yes, you've earned a reward for what you've done for us. If it's in my power to grant, you shall have it."

"It is in your power," Emry said. He could hardly get out the words.

"Then it is yours," said Dias, as an innocent man would. "Only name it."

"The lady Aera," Emry said.

Dias was as taken aback as Emry had thought he would be. He was not angry, not at first. "The lady—my foster-mother? What in the gods' name would you want with—"

"I would like," said Emry, "to have your leave to approach her. To ask her—if she would be—"

"A concubine? She who was chief wife of a king and mother of his heir?"

"She would be whatever she wishes to be. Wife, concubine, mistress of a slave—it doesn't matter."

"You are mad," Dias said.

"Maybe," said Emry. "Maybe I'm simply foreign. I don't know the proprieties here. In my country, I would be unspeakably bold in daring this; but I might also let it be known that if she were to ask, I would be glad to accept."

"Gods," said Dias. He seemed too shocked for anger. "You truly are asking for her. Why? What use do you think you can make of her?"

"She can make of me whatever use she pleases."

"She has—had—a son no younger than you."

"Yes," Emry said. And why that seemed to trouble these people so excessively, he could not understand.

"Tell me why, apart from my given word, I should allow you to do this thing. She is a great lady. You have been a slave. It's dishonor for you even to look at her, let alone make her your wife."

"That may be so," Emry said, "but I should like to ask her. By your leave, my lord, since that is required here."

Dias shook his head in amazement. "You're clever, foreigner: tricking me into giving my word before I understood how truly outrageous you could be. Well then. You may ask her. If she refuses, you're bound by it. Do you understand that?"

"Perfectly," Emry said.

"And if she declines to accept your suit, you'll ask no more of me. The gift is given. It can't be given again."

"That too I understand," said Emry.

"Then it's done," said Dias, "and may the gods help you."

Emry bowed to him, as low as to a Mother.

He would not understand that, but certainly he could understand Emry's smile. He shook his head again, sharply this time. "Go, get out. You're making my head ache."

<hr>

60

Aera had thought that Etena's exile would set her spirit free and undo the confusion that had beset her. But as Dias rode to his kingmaking, and then when he was made king, she found that she was more troubled than ever. Instead of walking in the light as even a respectable wife might do once her husband was dead, she shut herself up as tightly as any maiden. She even traveled in the wagon, with its curtains lowered and both light and air shut out.

It was a living thing she ran from: a pair of deep blue eyes, a set of broad shoulders, a white smile. When she slept she dreamed of him. When she was awake she struggled to keep from spying on him. She wanted him more, the harder she tried to deny him.

She was a woman of full age. Her son had grown to manhood before he died. Her husband was dead. She was subject still to her father and to the young king; but custom permitted her to ask them to choose her a new husband—even to name him, if she was discreet.

She did not want a husband. She wanted a living man in her bed, a warm body and strong arms. She wanted the sweetness of him, the gentle way he had, but with no weakness in it.

She wanted him. And that was folly touching on madness, for a woman of the People to yearn so for an outlander.

On the morning after the kingmaking, she was mending one of her father's tunics, straining her eyes in the dim light of the tent, when she heard that too-familiar voice in the outer room. He was asking for her. Her sister Dania responded with suitable stiffness, reminding him that he was male entire and Aera was a woman of unblemished reputation.

"I come," he said to that, "by the king's leave. Lady, of your courtesy, ask the lady Aera if she will speak with me."

He spoke softly, but the crack of command must have taken Dania aback. When she spoke, it was much more faintly than before. "I will ask. But I cannot promise—"

"Ask," he said sweetly, but still with that ring of royal bronze.

Aera took pity on Dania, or so she told herself. Before Dania could part the curtain, Aera emerged from behind it, abandoning her mending to stand in front of Emry with lowered eyes and folded hands. "You asked for me?" she murmured.

He was not dismayed as a man of the People would have been. Gods, he was smiling—did he know how that made her heart melt?

He knelt in front her, still smiling, and spread his hands. "Lady, I did ask, and the king gave me leave to ask you."

She looked down at him. She understood what he was saying. It did not shock her: and that surprised her a little. She felt . . . what? Surely not a wild white joy.

"You know how impossible it is," she said. "I was chief wife of a king. You are a foreigner and a slave."

"I am a king's son," said Emry, "and a king's heir, and no longer a slave. Your king has set me free."

"You are still a foreigner," she said.

"I see men here taking wives from tribes that are, maybe, as distant kin as I am to you. My father's father's grandfathers in the dawn time were horsemen of the steppe. White Horse People, they were called. Now we are the Goddess' people, and the White Mare's children."

"That sounds very noble," she said. "But what power or wealth do you have here? How will you keep me? Is it my dowry you need, to make you a man of substance?"

"I am the king's guardsman," Emry said.

"Provide me with a tent," she said, "and all that is necessary for its comfort, with servants to tend it and a wagon to carry it and herds to feed it, and I will ask my father to consider you as my husband."

He blanched a little at the price she set on herself, but he was hardly deterred. "If I can give you all those things," he said, "will you accept me?"

She threw down her heart and set her foot on it before he heard how it sang. "Give me what I ask, and I will give you myself."

His smile blinded her with its brilliance. He leaped up, as light on his feet as a much smaller man, and bowed low before her. "When I see you again," he said, "it will be under the wedding canopy."

⇥ ⇤

As Emry was leaving the makers' circle, Metos himself came to meet him. Emry paused. Metos knew, he thought: the green eyes raked him from head to foot. "You are a brash child," Metos said.

"I'll be more than brash," said Emry. "She sets a price on herself—but they tell me that the bride's father offers a dowry to the man who would marry her. Is that so, my lord?"

"It is so," said Metos. His eyes were glinting.

"So," Emry said. "As her dowry, will you offer a tent and servants and a wagon and cattle? Goats, too, I suppose. And sheep."

"She has a dowry," Metos said, "of two wagons and a large tent and threescore spotted cows and a bull to serve them. I will trade one wagon with its oxen, for three maidservants and a score of milch goats and a flock of sheep."

"That," said Emry after a respectful pause, "must be a splendid wagon indeed."

"I made it," Metos said, as if that answered everything. Which to be sure it did.

"Then I will trade it," said Emry.

"There is another thing," Metos said, "which I will demand of any man who takes my daughter."

Emry's glow of self-satisfaction died.

"I am the maker of chariots," said Metos. "If a man would claim my daughter, let him be possessed of a chariot and a team and suitable remounts. I will give my child to none but a charioteer."

"Then I will be one," Emry said, "to be worthy of her."

Metos lifted a brow, but said nothing. Emry bowed to him as he had to Aera, but without quite the insouciance. This price was higher than the other, and notably more difficult.

But he would pay it. What he had seen in her eyes when briefly they raised to his—if she had been a woman of Lir, she would have summoned him to her bed long ago.

Brash, Metos had called him. Well then, he would be as bold as a man could be.

⇥ ⇤

He waited till night had fallen. Dias, as he had hoped, came back to his tent at not too late an hour, and not too drunk with kumiss. He was warm with it, expansive; he grinned when he saw Emry. "Well, westerner? Did she throw you out on your ear?"

There were others with him. Not all of them were men Emry knew. For that he curbed his tongue, and only said, "She offered a bargain, which I took. But her father wants more."

"Does he now?" Dias paused in entering his tent. His hand flicked, dismissing the strangers, but keeping Aias by him.

Emry slipped in behind Aias' broad back. Lamps were lit; Dias' bed was spread, ready for him to fall into it.

Instead he rounded on Emry. "What does Metos want in return for his daughter?"

"That I be a charioteer," Emry said, "with chariot and horses."

Aias snorted. "He should ask for the moon and a basket of stars. You'll get them sooner."

"Not if the king gives me a gift," Emry said.

It was audacious. Deadly, maybe. But he trusted in Dias' equable temper, and the charm of his own smile.

"And why," asked Dias, "should I give you a clan-chieftain's wealth?"

"Because I've served you well since I came here," Emry answered, "and will serve you as I can, for your sake as much as for hers."

"You have gall," Dias said. "We admire that here. I'll give you horses, you've earned those. But a chariot? That's too much, westerner. Too much by far."

"What," said Emry, "if I were able to make one? Would I be allowed to keep it?"

"That would be a marvel," said Dias. "Hasn't Metos himself said that you have no gift for making?"

"I will pray," said Emry, "that the Goddess will give me the gift."

Dias laughed. "Yes, pray! Maybe she'll favor you. If she does, what you make is yours. I'll see that Metos knows it."

"I thank you," said Emry.

"Thank me when your prayers are answered," Dias said. He was still grinning, as if it were a grand jest that Emry would do what he had sworn.

⇒ ⇐

Metos did not laugh. He said flatly, "You'll build a chariot when yonder camp dog stands up and sings."

"Maybe," Emry said with determined lightness. "I do have the king's leave. He hasn't forbidden me to ask for help."

"You may ask," said Metos, "but your own hands, and only yours, will do the making."

"If I ask, may I be answered?"

"You will be answered," Metos said.

"And will I be given what I need?"

"Ask," said Metos, "and it will be given."

Emry let out his breath in a long sigh. Metos saw it: the corner of his mouth twitched. He went back to the wheel that he was shaping. Emry went to discover what he must do to fulfill this task he had taken on himself.

⇒ ⇐

Necessity, the Mother had told Emry long ago, was the best of teachers. He was not gifted with the maker's art, but his will was strong. When yet another wheel-rim warped and snapped, or when the copper he was smelting for the fastenings tried to leap out of the pot, he made himself remember her face. He persevered doggedly, learning the craft little by little.

From the first he suffered under the eyes of every idler in the gathering. They were not circumspect in their reckoning of his talent. There were wagers on how soon he would give it up, and how broken he would be when he did it.

He set his teeth and endured them. They all knew why he was doing it. He was half a laughingstock, half a legend: the western slave who labored to win the maker's daughter.

On the day when he made two wheels that matched, and that rolled smoothly on their axle without wobbling or cracking, his mob of watchers cheered as loudly as if he had won a race. There was still the body of the chariot to build, and the yoketree, and the complexity of the harness, over which he struggled in the nights after the long grueling days in the makers' circle. But the worst of it, the part he had dreaded most, was done.

He never saw the one he did this for, nor tried to visit her. That would come after, for good or ill.

He was aware, sometimes, that Metos watched him. The maker's stare was different from that of his perpetual audience: keener, brighter, colder. He never said anything then to Metos, nor Metos to him. All their conversation was of the making of chariots. They did not speak of Aera, or of any other earthly thing.

Emry was living in Metos' world. It was a world of absolute focus, of pure will. He lived, ate, breathed chariots. When he slept, they filled his dreams. He would wake with a start, and it might be black night or full morning, but he would know, his hands would know, exactly what they must do.

He lost track of the days and nights. The moon waxed and waned. They were still in the camp of the gathering, but the tribes had begun to scatter. They would not be waging war this season. The new king would firm his rule before he began his first conquest.

But that was nothing to Emry. Emry was making a chariot.

Came a day when he stood under a sky heavy with cloud, and looked at the thing which he had made. It was a smaller chariot, not the two-man war-car but a lighter, whippier thing, meant to carry a single man behind a team of swift horses. He had left it plain except for copper sheathing on the end of the pole, and copper bells on the bridles, and bits cast in copper.

"It's not badly made," Metos said beside him.

"I suppose it could be prettier," Emry said.

"Pretty is for fools and children," said Metos. He inspected the pole, and peered beneath the car. "This is different. What did you do?"

"I made it lighter," Emry said, "but it should be stronger."

"We'll see the truth of that," said Metos. He had given no signal that Emry could see, but one of the younger makers led out a team of golden duns, and another brought up a chariot already harnessed, as plain and almost as light as the one that Emry had made.

Emry had to be a charioteer in truth: had to see the duns harnessed with his harness and bidden to draw his chariot. He stepped gingerly into it. The woven leather of the floor had a live feel under his feet. The chariot rode almost weightlessly light. The horses sprang forward rather too strongly, all but pitching him out before he had well begun.

He found his balance somehow. The horses settled. They were fine horses, well trained. They forgave his uncertain hand on the reins, and taught him to be less awkward.

As they found their stride, he began to find his. The chariot rolled smoothly over the new grass. It balanced well though it was so light. The horses could stop and turn with ease.

He tried their paces around the field, first slow and careful, then swifter. The chariot flew behind them.

If they had been even a fraction less perfect in their obedience, Emry's poor skill would have brought him to grief. These were wonders, marvels of their kind. And the chariot, he thought, was not too ill a thing, either.

He brought it to a halt from a full gallop. The horses' rumps tucked; they slid to a stop. He stared astonished at a crowd that he had not even known was there, men of the tribes whooping and cheering.

But only one man's praise mattered. Metos halted much more sedately than Emry had. "Let me," he said.

Emry was surprisingly reluctant to give up his chariot, but this was Metos. He stepped down, surrendered the reins.

Metos drove like a wild boy. The horses, the chariot were like parts of his body: swift feet, deft hands. It was pure beauty to watch him.

A long sigh escaped them all when at last he finished. The horses stood snorting, streaming sweat and foam, but their eyes were bright, their necks arched and proud. They would happily have run another race, if this man had asked it.

Metos tossed the reins to Emry. "It will do," he said. "For a first effort."

"You think I'll do it again?" Emry asked him.

"It's not in your blood now?"

Emry shrugged uncomfortably. "I still have no gift for it."

"A gift is very well," Metos said. "But without will and heart, it matters little."

That was praise. Emry ducked his head under it. The dun stallions tugged gently at the reins. Emry began to walk them out, lest they stiffen.

"Good," said Metos. "Care for them well. They belong to you."

Emry bowed. He could not quite keep the grin off his face; but he thought he managed a little dignity.

61

Aera knew what Emry was doing—she could hardly escape it. It was the talk of the gathering. She refused to watch him, or to approach him. Part of it was pride, and part was fear that if he failed, and she saw him do it, her heart would break.

On the day when he finished his chariot, she heard the roar, the shouts and cheers that told her he had won his wager. But she did not go out of her father's tent, nor did she stop what she was doing, though moments after she had done it, she did not remember what it was.

She was not waiting. Oh, no. But the cheering died down, and the sun touched noon and began its descent, and nothing changed. He did not come. No one came. She was alone, abandoned even by her sisters.

Well, she thought; he had done the thing for his own pride, and because no one believed he could do it. She had nothing to do with it, even as the prize he fought for.

She had no cause to be angry. She had laid the price on him herself, by demanding her due as a woman of good family. If he chose not to take what he had paid for, then that was his choice.

It was a long and lonely night. She heard the sounds of feasting and laughter, dancing, music, gladness.

She lay in the dark, listening to the breathing of her sisters. They slept the sleep of the blameless. She felt as if her skin were on fire; but her heart in her breast was cold.

She would not go to him. Oh, no. Even if he had told her that a woman could do that among his people. Even if he would be abed and not dancing round the king's fire. She was a woman of the People. She could not be other than she was.

She buried her face in the worn furs of her bed. If she wet them with tears, only she would know.

⇒ ⇐

She woke abruptly from a heavy doze. It was still dark, her sisters still sleeping, snoring softly.

A shadow bent over her. Her heart knew who it was, even as she caught the clean warm scent of him, and felt his arms closing about her, lifting her up. She was still a good part asleep: she nestled against that broad breast, wrapped in nothing but a blanket, content as a child with its mother.

He carried her out into starlight. It was late, not far from dawn. He trod softly through the sleeping camp.

She drowsed herself, altogether without apprehension. Part of her tried to declare that this was mad; that he could be carrying her off to a terrible fate. But this was Emry. She trusted him.

Past the king's tent, notable for its height and the bull's head and hide raised on spears in front of it, he paused. There was a new tent there, of respectable but not remarkable size.

A cluster of lamps burned within. Everything was in it that she had asked for, all the comforts, the necessities—all but the servants; but she was not going to insist on those tonight.

Emry set her down. The blanket slipped. She clutched it, but it had a will of its own. It pooled about her feet.

He, bless him, kept his eyes on his own feet. She fought the urge to cover herself with her hands, turning slowly, taking it in. This was a lord's tent. The bed was thickly covered with woven fabrics, riches from the traders' store. There was a carved chest and a nest of copper pots, and a splendid golden platter set to catch the lamps' light. Birds flew on it in graceful spirals, paying homage to the Goddess of the westerners.

"If you would prefer," he said as diffidently as she had ever heard him, "you can be brought here in daylight, in my chariot, so that the world knows—"

"Gods forbid," she said.

"Or," he said, "you needn't come at all. It was presumptuous of me to carry you off. I only wanted to talk to you, and there seemed no other way to do it."

"It was presumptuous," she agreed. Her lips kept wanting to twitch. He was blushing and shuffling his feet, awkward as a boy.

"I do mean what I say," he said. "This is yours to choose. You can simply go. I did this for you, but not to buy you. Not to make you my slave."

"Then why did you do it?"

"Because you asked it of me. Because . . . when I think of you, my heart sings."

"They're making songs of you," she said. "Did you know that?"

He shrugged. "I didn't do it for them."

"It gives you standing," she said. "Respect. Position in the tribe. They love audacity. A man who ventures the impossible—if he goes far enough and lasts long enough, they call him a god."

"That is not why I did it." He spoke through gritted teeth. "What is it? You want me to drive you off, because a woman doesn't refuse a man here? You have no need for that. Just go. I won't pursue you. I won't even keep this tent, if you want it. It belongs to you—it's your dowry. This is all yours, to accept or cast away."

"If I told you to go, would you go?"

"I would go," he said.

"And not come back?"

"If that was your wish."

She pondered that, standing in the lamplight, just close enough to him to touch. She stretched out a hand and laid it over his heart. It was beating hard, though his face wore no expression.

Such a strange man, she thought. To do so much to win her, and to give it all to her, freely—truly he was a marvel.

She moved closer, till her body was almost against his body. She was naked, as she had never been in front of a man. And yet she did not feel immodest at all. His eyes clothed her in beauty.

He made no move to seize her. It was she who stripped him of his tunic and loosed the lacing of his leggings. Then they were equals.

She closed the hand's breadth of distance between them. "Promise me something," she said.

"Yes," he said. He sounded dazed. Had he not dared after all to believe that he had won? Foolish child. There had never been a battle, not in truth. Not in her heart.

"Promise," she said, "that you will never betray me. Even if we become enemies. Even if one of us must kill the other."

"I will never betray you," he said steadily. "Nor shall I ever take your life."

"I will kill you," she said, "if I must. And if you betray me, I will do worse than that."

He bent his head. She drew it down a little further and kissed him. "I belong to you now," she said, "and you to me. You've won me full and fairly. Pray your Goddess that you don't regret the bargain."

"That I shall never do," he said. All his heart was in it, and his clean bright spirit.

"Nor I," she said after a pause. "Whatever comes of this, I'll never regret that I chose it."

Minas had never passed a winter in such comfort as that first winter he spent in Lir. These houses of wood and stone were wonderfully warm, and food was plentiful, kept in storehouses that silenced him in awe when first he saw them. No one here grew thin, and few sickened and died. Truly this country was blessed of the gods.

Every night he dreamed of the steppe. His days were occupied, and richly, with the makers and smiths who had gathered in the king's house. When cold and snow permitted, he could ride out with the chariots, both those that had been brought from the east and those that had been made here, and he could oversee the training of the horses. But these tamed fields were nothing like the sea of grass. The sky was walled in stone or wood, or hemmed in with trees. Sometimes he thought he would die for want of air, waste away like a wolf in a cage.

In Rhian's arms he found what rest he could. She was even less a part of this place than he was. Her office was a strange one, high and holy but rather formless. She served the mare wherever the mare chose to be, which this winter was in Lir. Herdsmen had come from afar, and silent weathered women, traveling one by one to impart to the mare's servant those rites and duties which she should know.

She was welcome in the king's council and, Minas gathered, should have been welcome among the priestesses, but they had declared themselves her enemies from the day of her birth. Although she was a priestess, she could not be one here, not without offending the temple. She could learn, but not practice what she had learned.

Most of her days she spent among the horses. She took to herself the choosing and training of the chariot-teams; and that, by none too subtle design, took her out and about a great deal. There were grasslands to the south, steppe less wild than that from which he had come, where great herds ran, and descendants of the horsemen whose forefathers had conquered, and been conquered by, the priestesses of the Goddess.

She was gone for a whole month in the spring, performing the mare's rite in the south, and gathering young horses to be trained to chariots. Minas should have barely noticed her absence: once winter's grip broke, the wagons began to come in, rolling down from the forests in the west and north. They carried a wealth of wood, such as Metos would have killed to get; and the makings of bronze for the smiths, and bales of tanned hides. Men and women came, too, to learn the making: a small army of them.

And yet however long he might stretch his labor, he had to sleep. His dreams were of the steppe, as always, but now Rhian was in them, riding with him, hunting, dancing, lying bare under the stars.

She came back just before the festival they called high summer. He had been hearing of that in the city, how wild it was, how wanton. Women chose new lovers then, and lay with them in the furrows, blessing the land with fruitfulness and gaining its blessing in return. It was even wilder, people assured him, than the rites of spring; and those had driven him into hiding, shocked out of all reason.

Rhian had brought a herd for the training, and a company of herdsmen. Those were mostly men, and all besotted with her. Minas had yet to see a man who was not.

But he had not, before this, seen her ride quite so close as she rode with one of the herdsmen—knee to knee and touching hands. And when the man looked at her, Minas saw a thing he could not mistake. Rhian had not slept alone while she traveled among the herds.

He was a slave. He was not allowed to care what a free woman did, or with whom she did it.

He fixed himself grimly on his work. There was a great deal of it, and the workers were sorely distracted by the coming of the festival. He dismissed them well before sundown, and ordered them not to come back before the festival was ended. They danced and sang at that, and proclaimed him the best of men.

He stayed after they had gone. He had learned to cast bronze: a wonder, a marvel, an art like no other. He was making fastenings for a harness, small work and delicate, and easily ruined. It was not perhaps the best task for his state of mind, but it kept him occupied.

When the light dimmed, he closed up the forge. He was careful about it, as he had been with the casting. Metos had taught him that care, that patience, even when he wanted to burst out in a temper and fling it all into the fire.

At the coming of dark, a clear call rang from the summit of the temple. That was the summons, the call to festival.

Minas retreated to the stable. The king's house would be full of revelry, and he was in no mood for it. The horses had been fed; their caretakers were gone, he could well imagine where. They had left behind a little dry bread and a jar of thin sour barley-beer. He dipped the bread in the beer, and it quieted his hunger well enough. His stomach yearned toward the feast in the king's house; but he stayed where he was, alone among the horses.

He made a bed of straw near the grey stallion. The sound of horses breathing, snorting, working their way through heaps of cut fodder, filled him with a kind of peace.

Warm arms slipped about him. Soft breasts pressed against his back. A gust of breath tickled his nape.

It was she. He would know her anywhere, with or without eyes.

He bit his tongue on bitter words. Silence was best, he thought as she drew him round. He buried his face in her hair, and let her take him where there was no thought, nor any words. Only pleasure.

⇒ ⇐

Rhian would not let Minas hide through this festival as he had through the last. She was up before him, dragging him to the bath, waking sleeping servants to attend them both. For the first time since he came to Lir, Minas wore the garments and ornaments of a prince.

She paraded him like a fine stallion. No doubt it delighted her fancy to boast of a bright chestnut amid all the blacks and bays. She kept him by her; when he tried to escape to the chariots, she said, "Let them rest. Honor the Goddess for a while."

No Goddess of his, he thought. But he kept on holding his tongue. He even smiled, if tightly, at women and girls and even a few men who admired him none too discreetly. He was surprised not to find people rutting in the streets. In daylight they ate and drank to glorious excess, danced in interweaving circles through the city and the fields about it, and sat to hear singers sing the whole Great Song of Lir from beginning to end. That was a three days' labor, from dawn to dusk, in rounds of singers who took turn and turn about.

He was adept enough now in the language of this country to understand most of the words. If the Song was to be believed, Lir had stood for thousands and thousands of years. At first it had been the domain only of Mothers, and horses were not known there. Then horsemen came off the steppe, came to conquer but made alliance, and there were kings in Lir. Those kings had defended the city for years out of count, while the Mothers ruled and judged and interceded with the Goddess.

There was no Mother now. Priestesses and king were at odds—they had quarreled often through the winter and spring. Lir was growing old, and weakening in its age.

That was not so evident in the king's house, where the lords and defenders had gathered, warriors male and female, and a scattering of guests and traders. The herdsmen from the south were there, wiry dark men who had not the bulk or height of the men of Lir. They greeted Rhian with wine-scented gladness.

She had in courtesy to pay her respects to the king. That was brief enough: he was deep in colloquy with some of his warleaders. He spared Rhian a smile and Minas a distracted glance.

Minas would have been content to find a place out of the way, but

Rhian would not let him go. She dragged him back to the herdsmen and pulled him down with her at their table. They were loudly delighted to see her, and openly fascinated by Minas.

As they plied both with food and drink, the one who had cast eyes on Rhian thrust himself in beside Minas, flung an arm about his neck, and grinned broadly at him. "You're beautiful. She told us that, but we thought—I don't know what we thought. Maybe that love is blind."

Minas felt the heat of mortification on his cheeks. They were all grinning like a pack of wolves. He hid as best he could in a cup of wine.

His tormentor laughed, embraced him and kissed him on both cheeks. "Why, you're shy! Who'd have thought it? See, he blushes!"

Minas began to see, through a red haze of rage, that this was a man who made free with every creature, male, female, human, animal, it did not matter. Among the People he would be dead. Warriors did not tolerate such liberties.

Minas took pleasure in contemplating that slow and painful death. He managed a smile—bland enough, he thought, until Rhian plucked him from the circle and dragged him out of the hall. He followed willingly, but even so, her grip was bruising-tight.

Outside the hall, in the shadow of a pillar, she stopped. She was breathing hard. He stood in silence until she composed herself. "You can't kill a man here," she said. "You shouldn't even think of it."

He raised his brows. "I didn't think I was that obvious."

"If looks alone could kill," she said, "that man's head would be on your spear."

"That," he said, "would be a pleasure."

"He means no harm," she said. "It's only his way."

"Did you bed him?"

She stared at him.

"Did you bed him?" he repeated. "While you were among the herds—did you find him charming?"

"I found him tedious," she said. "But he's very good with the horses."

"Then he should stay with the horses," Minas said.

She took his face in her hands and kissed him till he was dizzy. While he stood reeling, struggling to breathe, she slapped him lightly, first one cheek, then the other. "You don't own me," she said.

"No," he said. "You own me."

"You should remember that," she said.

"You did," he said. "You did bed him."

"If it had been you, and he had been she, and you had taken her as tribesmen do, would I be permitted to be jealous?"

"I'm not—"

"Don't lie," she said. "Don't be a fool, either. Consider where I am now, and where I was last night, and will be tonight, unless you annoy me excessively. I told you before—I've lost my taste for black-haired men."

"I pray you never get it back," he said.

She drew his plait over his shoulder and wrapped it about her hand. "I pray you never encourage me to get it back."

He bit his tongue. She nodded approval of his prudence, moving closer, opening her mouth to speak: something light, from her expression; something wicked.

She never said it. His back was to the pillar. She could see past him to the entrance of the hall. People were coming and going, a constant bustle and clamor, but just then it stopped. Just as Rhian did, they all stared.

Minas moved to see what so engrossed them. Rhian's arms tightened. He twisted in them, peering past the pillar.

His heart stilled.

Men of the People, warriors, charioteers. He knew them very well. They were his brothers, sons of his father. And in the midst of them, guarded like a treasure of great price, a woman in veils and gold. She had a shadow, a woman likewise veiled, but the maid's eyes were lowered. Hers stared boldly into the hall.

Westerners were with them. Priestesses. The one who walked foremost, he recognized: he had seen her in that same hall when he first came to Lir. She was one of those who had wanted to kill Rhian when she was born.

It must be a deep pleasure for her to bring the witch Etena into the king's hall. She made it seem that she honored the king with her presence, bringing this guest who had, she made it clear, insisted on being presented to the king of Lir.

Minas struggled against the arms that held him. They had had no warning. None at all. And she was walking through the unguarded gate, approaching the king, entering into this world that did not know what she was.

Rhian was stronger than a woman had a right to be. He fought her, but he was weak; he could not strike the blow that would set him free.

He lunged against her grip. It broke. He half-fell against the frame of the gate, and stood staring.

Etena and her escort had come to a halt in front of the king. The priestess was speaking. "Lord of warriors, I bring you a guest and an ambassador. She begs you to hear her, and to offer her sanctuary."

The king had risen at their coming. He looked strikingly like his son whom Etena had bought as a slave—who was not here with her. Minas would have given a hoard of bronze to see what expression she wore, looking up at that face.

The king's expression was unreadable at that distance, and with his face so thoroughly concealed by the thick greying beard. He looked down at the strangers. The priestess he did not acknowledge at all. "I will hear you," he said to Etena.

Etena said nothing. The priestess spoke for her again, as the Voice spoke for the Goddess. "I come from the east," she said, "from the sea of grass. I bring a gift to you: chariots, and charioteers. I ask your protection."

"Protection?" asked the king.

"Against my enemies," the priestess said. "They have murdered my husband, my king. They have driven me into exile."

Minas' knees buckled. He clung to the frame of the gate. Of course—of course she would be an exile, if she was here. But if she was—if the king was dead—then—

"You have come far," the king said, "to find sanctuary."

"I came to the Goddess, who protects all women." That was Etena herself, in the traders' tongue. She advanced from among the rest and flung herself at the king's feet. "My lord, I fled death and dark magic to seek the Goddess' aid. I was hounded across the steppe, and hunted to the river. Only when I had crossed it did I find myself safe."

"I see that you have found the Goddess' protection," the king said. "No tribes have crossed the river; the steppe is quiet. For what, lady, do you need me?"

"For your strong hand," Etena said, "and the defense of your name. I am an easterner, my lord. We trust in the protection of men, and in the strength of warriors."

"The Goddess protects you," said the king. "I serve the Goddess, as do all men and women in Lir." He beckoned to the servants. "Come, eat, drink. Share our festival."

63

Minas came out of darkness under a crushing weight. As light brightened about him and his wits recovered themselves, he realized that he was flat on the tiled floor. There was a brawny black-bearded man on his chest and another on his legs. Rhian was standing over them all, glaring at him.

"Let me—" Minas gasped. "Let me up."

She nodded to his captors. They hauled him to his feet, but kept a firm grip on him.

"You will not kill her," Rhian said. "You will not. Do you understand me?"

"I understand that that sorceress has somehow, by the will of the gods below, found her way to this country and set her claws in your king. I also understand that she has corrupted your priestesses. She breathes poison here as she did among the People. The sooner she is dead, the better for you all. Does it even occur to you to wonder how she came here? Who cast her down? And where your king's heir is?"

"If you kill her," Rhian pointed out, "we'll never know any of that."

"I'll ask, then kill."

"No killing."

To his astonishment, she bade his captors let him go. They grinned and petted him like a dog, and at the arch of Rhian's brow, wandered off in search of further amusement.

Minas was beyond anger, and almost beyond humiliation. "The gods are laughing at us," he said.

"Listen to me," said Rhian. "Listen very carefully. She knows you're here—the priestesses will have made sure of it. We are going to throw her into confusion. Can you master yourself? Can you follow my lead, and act exactly as I bid you act?"

Minas eyed her warily. "How shall I act? Groveling like a slave?"

"Like an honored guest and a prince in exile."

"Then I shall have to call for her death," he said, "because she is my enemy from life into life."

Rhian struck him hard, with none of his weakness that kept him from striking a woman. As he reeled under the blow, she hissed at him. "Stop that! Think—if you are capable of it. She expects to find a slave, beaten down, vanquished. If you give her the truth of you, and make it clear that you enjoy the king's favor, that will throw her off balance. Then," she said, "then, when we can, we'll warn the king. Though I think he sees her for what she is. Did you notice? He didn't welcome her to Lir. He'll feed her, because that is the law of the festival, but more than that he'll not give her."

Minas blinked. He was still dizzy.

She shook him, which did not help at all. "This is not your tribe. Our men are not like your men. They know how strong a woman can be. She could blind your king and seduce him and destroy him. But not ours."

"No," he said. "Only your priestesses."

Rhian did not hear him, or chose not to hear. "Follow," she said. "Remember. We will destroy her—but not now. Not today."

He set his teeth and lowered his eyes and hoped that she would take that for acceptance. It seemed she did. She turned on her heel and swept into the hall. He strode in her wake.

She did not reduce them all to silence as the others had. Rather the opposite in fact. Two who left as abruptly as they had were known to have left in honor of the Goddess, as people spoke of it here. Rhian encouraged them to think so by linking hands with Minas and drawing him to a place near the king.

As it happened, some of the chariotmakers were there, and some of the tamers of horses: a much more congenial gathering than the herdsmen from the south. They were drinking wine and telling tales.

Mabon the captain reeled into their orbit and dropped beside Minas. He was flying high with wine, or so it seemed; he challenged them to sing a song that had nigh as many verses as the Great Song of Lir.

Under cover of it, he leaned toward Minas and said distinctly in his ear, "Stables, later. Both of you."

Minas sketched a nod. From where he sat, he could see the king and his unexpected guests. They could hardly fail to see him, surrounded as he was by black-haired people.

As he had hoped, one of his brothers caught sight of him. It was gratifying to see how he started and suddenly paled. Minas smiled the sweetly terrible smile he had learned from Rhian, raised his cup and saluted with it.

Lycon looked ready to faint. Clion next to him turned from eyeing the full-breasted girl who served them, saw what he was staring at, and leaned toward Sardis on his other side, whispering rapidly.

Minas watched the whisper travel toward Etena. When it reached her she stiffened wonderfully. She was too wise to let Minas know she was aware of him, but he had no doubt of it. He let his smile linger, dreaming of sinking his dagger in her heart, and carving it living from her breast.

Rhian's substantial weight dropped into his lap. She linked arms about his neck and nibbled his ear. Just as he sighed, letting the pleasure wash through him, she nipped him hard enough to bleed. He bit back a yelp. "You look like a man in love," she said in the wounded ear: "ready to eat her alive."

"Heart first," he murmured. "Then liver. Liver is sweet, raw and warm—*ah!*"

She kissed the lip she had bitten. It was swelling already. "Curb your dreams, tribesman. Look as if it's me you lust after, and not her quivering vitals."

"I do lust after you," he said somewhat painfully. "But her I hate with a perfect passion."

She swooped toward him. He flinched, but this time she kept her teeth to herself. She kissed him long and deep. It was played grandly for Etena's sake, but she did nothing by halves. Her hand slid down between them, found his rampant rod, and did things to it that would have made him groan aloud if she had not held him captive with the kiss.

This was sacred, he told himself. Their Goddess accepted it as worship. And Etena would see, and that would be a beginning of revenge.

Just when he would happily have taken her then and there, and never mind how many watchers there were, she slid away from him. He followed half-blindly. There were others bent on the same errand, the woman leading as Rhian did, withdrawing to—where? The furrows of the fields?

She chose the stable, which had the advantage of being close by. The newcomers' chariots were there, and their horses, fretting in confinement. Minas was ready to fall with Rhian into the nearest heap of straw, but she had forgotten his existence.

Mabon was leaning on the barrier between stalls, nose to nose with a bay stallion who looked remarkably like Mabon himself: big, ruddy, with a glossy black mane and a wicked dark eye. The stallion snorted at the newcomers and retreated into the stall. Mabon turned to greet them.

Rhian's embrace was tight and rather long. Minas surprised himself with one as full of gladness. He had not seen Mabon since the autumn, when Mabon left Lir to oversee the building of fortresses between Larchwood and World's End. Mabon was a prince after all, kin to the king, and high in the king's favor.

"You didn't come here for the festival," Rhian said when the greetings were over, when they had settled together outside the bay's stall. "Did you come with the king's guests?"

"I graciously provided escort from World's End to Lir," Mabon said. He grinned at Minas. "I made sure that she was well guarded, and carefully—by a company of women. Her magic doesn't work with them, it seems—unless they're priestesses. It's very odd."

"Very," said Minas dryly. "Did you have anything to do with the priestesses' adoption of her?"

Mabon sighed. "No; and that's the Goddess' own truth."

"Tell it like a proper tale," Rhian said. "From the beginning."

He nodded. Minas bit his tongue. It was best this way; Rhian had the right of it. He unclenched his fists, which were aching, and set himself to listen.

Mabon wriggled till he was comfortable, stretched, yawned and rolled his head on his shoulders. When Minas was ready to beat the words out of him, he said, "I was in World's End after spring festival, bearing messages from the king to the commander there, and waiting for a new company of workers who had been promised for the fort above Whitewater. Word came down from the garrison across the river: a riding of chariots had come asking sanctuary. Of course I went to see—the message was

brief, but it was urgent, and my workers were delayed. And chariots—
that, my king would wish to know, and quickly.

"I found them as you saw: the king's wife and her women, and half a
dozen charioteers. She had told the story you heard her tell the king. I
got the rest of it from her men, with the help of a rainy evening and a
jar of wine." Mabon paused for breath. Minas resisted the urge to choke
it out of him.

"Your king took his own life—took poison. He was brave at the end,
and in possession of his wits. As soon as he was dead, the tribe turned
against his wife. The priests and shamans came back, and she was cast
out. They say . . . it was the gods' decision; no man made it. And so no
man can bear the blame, whatever comes of it."

Minas' throat locked shut. He forced out words in spite of it. "Who—
who is king now?"

"You are dead," Mabon said. "They mourned you for nine days, your
brothers said. It was a terrible, a grievous loss. Then when the time came,
the king named a new heir: her son, the prince Dias."

Minas slumped against the wall. Of course it would be Dias. "And he
is king."

"King," said Mabon, "and her most bitter enemy."

And the son of her body, so that it was the most terrible of sins to kill
her, even in the name of justice. She was alive and in exile, and in Lir,
because Dias and not Minas was king.

"Tell me the rest," Minas said harshly. "Tell it straight. No more questions."

Mabon looked at him a little oddly, but did as he bade. "She was
turned out on the steppe, but half a dozen of the king's sons, who may
have had reason not to want to stay under the new king, went after her
and found her. She convinced them to follow her westward. She was
looking for the country where women rule, where no woman is forced
to hide behind a man.

"Of course she found it—but from the first she insisted on being taken
to the king. Old habits die hard, I suppose.

"The priestesses were in World's End when I brought her back to it.
They had business in the temple, they said, but they were in the commander's house, with little enough reason for it, and not a great deal of
welcome, either. The house of war and the house of the Goddess are
much divided now.

"Yet there they were, as if they were waiting. When she came, they
took her to themselves, and swept her away to the temple before any of
us could stop her."

"She wants Lir," Minas said, "for vengeance, and because she thinks
she can rule it. Does she know that the king's wife has no power here?"

"There is no Mother in Lir," Rhian said slowly. "You don't think she means to—"

"She is capable of trying," said Minas.

"No," Mabon said. "Oh, no. The priestesses see in her something they can use, but they would never—"

"Would they not?" Rhian clasped her knees and rocked as she was fond of doing when she had a great deal to think about. It cleared her head, she had told Minas once. "She has power. She invokes spirits, and they come. She subdued a king to her will, and ruled a tribe from behind the shield of his name. And what do they have here? An empty place. A daughter whom they hate, who can't be Mother because the White Mare has claimed her. A king who defies their will, builds forts instead of temples, and fails to include them in his councils. What could be more perfect? Consecrate her priestess, claim a revelation, ordain her Mother— then trust her to seduce this king as she did the other. How can she fail, with the temple behind her?"

Mabon shuddered. "Goddess forbid. Surely they'll see what she is. The king does; that's as plain as the daylight."

"That won't matter," said Minas, "if the priestesses either fail to see it, or see it and don't care. She wants to destroy my people as much as they do—maybe more. They won't object if the king falls, either. It would be a great thing for them, surely, to cast down all men who would presume to rule." He glared at Mabon. "You saw all this, and yet you brought her here. Why?"

"Because," said Mabon, "if she's a danger to us, best we have her where we can see her. The priestesses claimed authority; they forbade me to send word to the king, and commanded me to provide escort. That's why there was no warning. I tried to send a man ahead, but he had a mishap on the way—fell in the river and drowned. The Goddess—"

"The priestesses did it," Minas said. "You should have cut her throat before she crossed the river—or drowned her in it as the priestesses drowned your messenger. They say they saw their world end when the Mother bore her daughter—and everything they've done from that day has brought that ending closer. Now they have the one who will end it for them, not here with us, but in the hall with them, eating the king's meat and drinking his wine. She is their destruction."

They were staring at him. He did not see why. He was speaking the clear and evident truth. They could see it; they were not blind.

To relieve the burden of their stares, he said sharply, "You didn't tell us—what of the king's heir of Lir? Is he dead?"

Mabon shook his head like a man fighting free of a dream. "They said he was alive. And well, they said. He was the new king's ally, his guard and protector."

Minas' sigh of relief echoed Rhian's. The man was his born enemy, that was true; but a king's son was a king's son. It was well that Emry had not died for Etena's sake.

"He was guarding Dias, you say?" Rhian asked.

Mabon nodded. "So I was told. There was some debate as to who laid it on him: the king's wife who owned him or the king's wife who fostered Dias."

Minas' teeth clicked together. "The king's wife who—my mother?"

"One of the king's sons kept insisting that they were lovers, but the others declared that she would never do such a thing."

"She would not," Minas said, snapping off the words. "That's baseless rumor. So Etena set him to spying on my brother—and he became my brother's man. Marvelous are the ways of the gods."

"Indeed," said Mabon. And after a pause: "There is . . . one more thing."

Minas waited. Rhian raised a brow. "And that is?"

"The woman is with child."

Minas burst out laughing. "Great gods of the air! Is there no lie she'll not stoop to?"

"It's true," Mabon said. "It seems to matter a great deal who fathered it—and they all agree that it could not have been their king."

"Gods," breathed Minas. "Oh, gods. So that was why she wanted him."

Neither of them seemed to understand. Very likely they did not care. But it was a great thing, a dangerous thing. "She bought your prince," he explained to them, "because he was a prince. She needed him for a purpose: to beget a child whom she could raise as her own and claim as the king's, to rule by her will. My father was no longer capable; that we suspected. But he died too soon, and she was cast out—her gamble failed. And so she gambled again. What would it be worth, for a woman to bear a child to the king's heir of Lir?"

"Why," said Mabon, "not a great deal. Except . . ."

"Except," said Rhian, "that the king's heir is also the eldest son of the Mother. If it's a daughter, the Mother has an heir of her blood, though not of her line. And if it's a son—"

"If it's a son, it's the son of the king's heir." Mabon whistled softly. "That woman will have power however she can find it."

"Now do you see why we should kill her now, tonight?" Minas demanded.

They both shook their heads—sorrowfully, even with anger, but there was no shaking the will of either. "No," Rhian said. "Not if she's with child. The child is an innocent, and it's Emry's. It would be a terrible sin against the Goddess to kill the woman who carries it."

"Even if letting her live will hasten the destruction of Lir?"

"They let me live," Rhian said, "and the omens about my birth were terrible."

"You are not what that woman is," Minas said through the bile in his throat.

"Certainly," said Rhian. "But the laws of the Goddess are clear. Every bearing woman is sacred, for the sake of her child. If anyone harms her, he invokes the Goddess' wrath."

"I would chance it," Minas said grimly.

"I will keep you in chains like the slave she imagines you to be," said Rhian, "or you can swear to me solemnly by all you hold holy, that you will do nothing to harm that woman's child."

Chains, thought Minas. Captivity was terrible enough. If he was bound, he would die.

And yet, to let that woman live . . .

He covered his face with his hands. "I will not harm the child," he said.

He had said nothing of Etena—but Rhian had not asked him for that. Did she, perhaps—?

It did not matter. She accepted his word as it was, nor demanded that he change it.

64

Rhian lay with Minas in the dark before dawn. The sounds of revelry in the king's hall had muted somewhat. The lamp flickered low. The room in which Minas slept was dim and cool, with a glimmer of bronze: he had been learning to forge it, and bringing his efforts here. He had a passion for the metal; it surprised her that he did not decorate himself with it as he had the room. But he only ever wore the bell that she had braided into his hair.

She raised herself on her elbows. Minas' eyes were shut, but he did not breathe like a sleeping man. She kissed him softly. He did not respond.

He was beautiful in that faint golden light. Her eyes loved his narrow, high-cheeked face with its noble arch of nose.

"Are you grieving?" she asked him gently. "Is the pain too great to bear?"

His breath shuddered as he drew it in. "What? That you won't let me dine on Etena's liver?"

"No," she said. "That your father is dead. That someone else is king."

He rolled onto his face. His shoulders were knotted tight. When she reached to smooth out the knots, he thrust himself away from her.

She let him be. After a while he spoke. The burr of the tribes was thick in his voice. "Nine days they mourned me. That's a king's rite; princes merit three days at most, or four. I'm an ancestor now, enrolled among the gods. When the People pray, they pray to me."

"Well," she said. "You crossed the river of souls. Your grandfather is a god. Is he dead, too?"

"You know he's not."

"There, you see. A living god."

"I'm dead," he said. "They mourned me. They propitiated my spirit. And a living man is king over the People."

Words alone would not console him. She laid her body against his and held him. He did not push her away. Maybe her presence was a comfort; she chose to believe it was.

→ ←

The king was always glad to see Rhian, even when she caught him in a moment of quiet before the daymeal. His youngest son was with him, and a servant who was plaiting strings of golden beads into his hair. It was the last night of festival, and the king's house had been made splendid with bright banners and garlands of flowers. All the high ones who were in Lir would dine here today. There would be dancers and singers and tellers of tales, and when night fell, the long dance out into the fields for the great blessing.

But in this hour the king was as much alone as a king could be. He smiled his sudden smile at Rhian's coming, embraced and kissed her, and set her beside him on the carved bench. "I'm glad you came," he said. "It's been lonely without you. All went well in the south?"

"Very well," she said.

She rested for a while in his warmth. Her youngest brother had curled like a puppy on the floor and gone to sleep: exhausted, she could well guess, from the rigors of the festival. He was just old enough for the women to notice him, and a goodly number had. He had the family beauty, after all, and a sweetness about him that could melt a woman's heart.

How strange to have found these kin so late, and to be so perfectly at ease with them. Bran was in Larchwood teaching the smiths there to forge fittings for chariots. The rest of Long Ford was a fading memory.

She had grown far away from it. She could have been dead and been closer to it, if her spirit chose to linger where it had been in life.

But she was not here to muse on her own sorrows. "The woman from the east," she said. "Will she be in the hall tonight?"

"There's a great rite in the temple," he said. "The priestesses let it be known that she would be attending it with them."

"Did they?" Rhian said—without expression, she thought.

But he saw beneath her pretense of calm. "Should I press the invitation more strongly?"

"Minas would like to see her dead," Rhian said.

"So that is the one who traded him for gold. She would have done better simply to bury him on the steppe."

"They would all have done better to slaughter her with the rest of her tribe," said Rhian. "But since they did not, and since the one killing they truly shrink from is the killing of a man's mother, she lives to plague Lir. Do you think the priestesses see what she is?"

"I think," said the king, "that they see a woman after their own hearts."

"They want to be rid of you and of any man who rules. They freed themselves from the Mother. Would you like to wager that she's promised them full rule of the tribes when they come?"

"Can she give them that?"

The king was not an innocent, to ask such a question. He was testing her, a little; asking her to judge. "With the man who is king now, no. But men are mortal, and her will is strong. She's very dangerous."

"Yes," said the king. He frowned, stroking his beard. "I can't in law or in justice have her put to death without clear cause. She killed no one that we know of. The king killed himself. The king's son, whom she could have killed, she let live."

"She doesn't kill bodies," Rhian said. "She kills souls."

"Not mine," he said, with a growl in it. "We are wise to her. That may defend us. I'll send a messenger to the priestesses, to warn them. It's not likely they'll listen, still less be grateful, but for Lir's sake I must do it. And maybe," he said, "they can teach her the ways of the Goddess, and gentle her so that she's no danger to Lir—only to the tribes."

"We can pray for that," Rhian said. She embraced him and kissed his cheek. "And thank the Goddess that she blessed Lir with a wise king."

⇢ ⇠

Minas stood in front of the temple gate, looking up at the elaborate carving of its posts and lintel. He shifted uncomfortably. His clothes were new, the coat stiff with embroidery. It was a gift from the king, to make him seem more princely before the priestesses of the city.

He was not the most likely messenger, but the king had insisted that he was the best choice. "You know her," he said when he summoned Minas to him, "and know what she is capable of."

"I also hate her," Minas pointed out, "and will slit her throat if I can get near enough to her. Won't that make me worthless as a messenger?"

"Not at all," the king said. "You're an honest enemy. If you speak simply and without deception, they'll trust what you say."

Therefore Minas was here, two days after the end of the festival, with Lir still a little lazy and a little drunken, but returned to most of its proper self. It was a fair morning, rather cool after a day of rain, but the sun was warm on his head. Passersby smiled at him, recognizing him; some gave him greeting with the gentle courtesy of these people.

He straightened the coat one last time, drew a deep and steadying breath, and walked through the gate. Men, he had been assured, were not banned here, only in the temple itself. Even so, he was the only man within sight, though his brothers must be somewhere about.

The king had told him where to go: toward one of the houses near the temple, not the highest or most ornately carved, but distinguished by a frieze of birds above the door. There were birds everywhere, both living and carved in wood, but the house he had been sent to was difficult to mistake. A whole flock of birds flew above its door, a long winding skein of doves, white and grey and brown. Not all of them were the work of hands: many lived and breathed and cooed softly to one another, fluttering amid the images of their kin.

Priestesses were coming and going. They eyed him curiously, but maybe took him for one of his brothers; one rangy redheaded tribesman was very like another. No one was openly hostile, though not all glances were friendly, either.

He knocked at the door of the house as the king had instructed him. It took its time in opening, but he had been instructed to be patient. The woman who peered out at him was naked but for a thickly embroidered apron, and distinctly with child. That, he had not been taught to expect. It was a long moment before he could master himself to speak, and longer still before he could remember the words in the language of this place. "I—I would speak with the Voice of the Goddess," he said.

"The Voice is occupied," said the priestess.

Minas suppressed a sigh. Of this too he had been warned, and told how to respond. "I will wait for her," Minas said, "in your courtyard, by your grace and leave."

The priestess looked him up and down. Her eyes sharpened. "You're not one of hers. They don't speak proper language, or show proper manners, either. Who sent you?"

"The king," Minas answered. "Lady."

"So," the priestess said as if to herself. "You're *that* one. Come in, then. What are you gaping for? Come into the house!"

Minas obeyed as meekly as he was capable of. Now that she recognized him, she was—not more friendly, no. But less stiffly suspicious. That was interesting. The priestesses were not all of one mind, then, and maybe less so since Etena came than before.

The priestess led him to a lovely court, a green space thick with flowers, and gave him a cup that proved to be full of clear water, and left him to wait in the scented shade. He sipped the water because a good guest did such a thing, then put the cup aside and wandered a bit. From here he could come up close to the wall of the house, and see exactly how it was made. It was masterful work, even without the carving and painting that made it remarkable.

He took no notice of the passing of time, with so much to look at and decipher. When at last he turned and found himself watched, the sun was notably closer to its zenith.

This watcher was older than the woman who had let him in, perhaps by a great deal, and somewhat nearer to being clothed: her heavy sagging breasts were bare, but she wore a skirt of many overlapping panels, that fell to her sturdy ankles. She was amused as people often were, by Minas' fascination with the way things were made. It was only when he approached to speak to her that he realized she must be blind, or nearly so. She seemed to see, even with those clouded eyes.

"Good morning, maker of chariots," she said. Her voice was deep for a woman's, and a little harsh, and yet it had a smoky sweetness. It was quite beautiful in its way.

"Good morning, lady of the temple," Minas said in return. "Would you be the Goddess' Voice, then?"

She inclined her head. "I am the Goddess' Voice in Lir. You I remember: you were with the mare's servant when she first came to the city."

"I remember you," he admitted, "lady. But not—no one told me who was who. And I didn't understand your language so well then."

"You speak it very well," said the Voice. "Indeed you look, and sound, quite civilized."

He bridled at that, but kept his temper. "Why, lady, have no doubt, I'm still a wild beast of the plains. But even a beast may stand on its hindlegs on occasion and speak like a man."

"Particularly if that beast is a shaman?"

Minas started as if she had struck him. "I am not—"

She laughed, rich and warm. "No. You never had the training. But the power is there. It shimmers in you." She took him by the hand, with no more shyness than if he had been one of her kin, and led him to a chair that was set in the shade, and made him sit in it. She squatted on a stool in front of him, like a servant, and smiled up at him. She still had his hand in hers. "Child, you are as beautiful as a red-gold stallion, and well you know it, too. Now tell me what brings you here."

She had meant to take him off guard, and indeed she had. But he was quick-witted. He answered her bluntly. "The king sent me. I'm to warn you—your new guest: she's deadly dangerous."

"Indeed she is," said the Voice with no sign of surprise. "Particularly to men who can fall prey to her power."

"Women, too," he said. "Maybe, here, especially women—because they don't expect that anyone can be stronger or more devious than they. She's a witch, lady, of an old and terrible line. Blackroot shamans, we call them—born and bred to serve the gods below. We killed them all and broke their power, but my father took the daughter of the clan to be his concubine. She was young and beautiful, and he was strong. He thought that he could master her. She mastered him instead. In the end she destroyed him. His own hand wrought his death—that I was told, and I do believe it. But it was her doing that he died."

"Wasn't it fair, after all? He slaughtered all her kin, and left only her alive. Can you blame her for taking vengeance?"

"No," he said. "In truth I don't. I don't even greatly blame her for the manner of it—it was all she knew. But I hate her no less for that. Do your people know evil, lady? Do you know the dark behind the light?"

"We do know it," the Voice said.

"And yet you took her into your temple. You can't cure her, or redeem her—any more than you can stop a lioness from being what she is. She will twist you if you let her, and shape you to her ends. She is not able to do, or be, anything else."

"Is the king afraid that we will name her Mother?" the Voice asked. "Tell him to have no fear of that."

"Even if she bears in her womb the Mother's grandchild?"

"Through a son," said the Voice. "And if it is a son, there is no danger at all."

"But if it is a daughter?"

"If it is a daughter, we will take the omens; then we will do as we judge best. We are not men of the tribes who see no strength in a woman. We know what a woman can be. All of it. For good or ill."

"It is true," Minas said. "Even your Mother's child, when the omens were bad—you cast her out. Has it struck you that she wasn't the cause of any of this? That you caused it by your actions then?"

"Often," said the Voice. "Some of us are without doubts, but most wonder, always, whether we chose rightly."

"I pray you remember that, lady," he said, "when you face the Blackroot witch."

"Tell your king," said the Voice, "that we will take his warning to heart; and we are grateful for the spirit in which he sent it."

That was a dismissal. Minas bristled a little at it—he was not accustomed even yet to bowing to the will of a woman—but he was learning, slowly. He bowed to her and let himself be sent back to the world of men and war and horses.

65

Etena delivered a daughter in the mellow gold of autumn, a dark-haired, dark-eyed child who was, Rhian heard, the living image of the Mother who was dead. That the priestesses fostered this rumor, she could well believe; but she found it interesting that nothing was said of the omens that had attended the child's birth.

"There were none," her brother Gerent said.

They were out with chariots, Rhian and Minas, Gerent and his friend Bronwy, trying a new team in company with Minas' seasoned duns. A long race by the riverbank had ended in a victory for the young bays, who had Minas' skilled hand to guide them, and a near-plunge into the river for the duns. Rhian had taken them in hand then, exiling the very contrite Bronwy to Minas' chariot, and walked the duns till they were dry and calm.

They paused in the heat of noon, drew off the road and let the horses graze by the river. Rhian had brought honey mead and brown bread and cheese and a sackful of apples. They all ate hungrily, calling greetings to passersby on the road, talking lazily of this and that.

Of course the boys spoke of the child in the temple: the city was buzzing with it. "There were no omens," Gerent said, "or none that meant anything. As far as anyone could tell, this is a perfectly ordinary child who will live a perfectly ordinary life."

"Or," said Bronwy, "she won't live long at all. She'll die in war, and no one will know if she would have grown up to be Mother."

"I think I prefer the other," Minas said. He was lying in the grass, fingers laced behind his head, watching the play of sun and cloud above them. "To have borne a child without distinction—there could be no greater horror. She means to be mother to the Mother of Lir."

"She has no milk," Bronwy said. "My sister in the temple told me they had to find a priestess to nurse the baby, because the mother can't. That's great grief to her."

"But she never lets the baby out of her sight," said Gerent. "Even when it nurses, she's there; she snatches it as soon as it's done."

"She's taking no chances," Minas said. "This one she'll be sure to raise as her creature—since she failed so notably with the last."

"It won't matter," said Gerent. "It's only the daughter of a son, and if the omens are lacking, it can't be Mother."

"Can you be sure of that?" Rhian drew up her knees and clasped them. There was an odd deep warmth in her middle. It was not rounding yet, and yet she knew what was there, what grew in her day by day, till in the spring it would be seeking its own omens.

None of these men knew, not even Minas. She would tell him—soon. But he would fret, because she rode out and about, and drove chariots, and tamed horses. He would want her shut in walls and protected from every ill of the world; and she could not bear that, or the battle it would be to convince him of the fact.

Gerent answered her question. "They didn't invent omens," he said. "If they meant to do what she wants of them, they would have done that."

"I wouldn't put it past them," Minas said.

"But they didn't," said Gerent. "They gave us silence. She may not know what that means—she's a foreigner, after all. She can go on dreaming, and by the time she learns what they've failed to tell her, it will be too late to change it."

"That is devious," said Minas with approval.

Rhian let her eyes linger on him. The charioteers, that summer, had taken to wearing a light kilt for comfort in the heat. It had become a fashion, and a mark of honor, that simple garment of plain linen, broadbelted with leather and bronze.

He was well suited to the fashion, with his smooth fair skin and his lean grace. She would have loved to touch him, and more than that, but he was horribly shy about such things where anyone could see. She settled for the lesser pleasure of the eyes, and for reflecting on what they would do later, in the king's house, when the lamps were lit and the rest of the world had gone to its rest.

⇨ ⇦

This was a well-traveled road, the road that ran southward from Lir. Many of those who passed, paused to stare at the chariots, though by now the sight of them was familiar to people from the city and the towns about it. They were still a curiosity, and charioteers were the envy of every headstrong child. Companies of them had taken to appearing in Lir, begging for a place among the chariots. Those that were willing, the king took on as servants; those that were talented, Minas set to work among the makers.

The road was full of wagons today, rolling slowly toward the autumn festival in Lir. A year ago, Rhian thought, they had been in Larchwood, guests of its Mother; and the king's urgency had brought her, with Minas, headlong to the city. But that urgency had dissipated. No war had come. The steppe was quiet. The king built his forts in peace, troubled only by the temple's disapproval. Now autumn was on them, and winter would follow, with a good harvest and storehouses full.

One wagon slowed to a crawl as it approached them. It was not like others that Rhian had seen. It was elaborately painted in a strange fashion, with a tasseled canopy and gilded wheels. The oxen that drew it were the color of cream, and their horns, like the wheels, gleamed with gold.

People walked with it—all men, dressed in heavy, strange garments, wrappings and swathings of thick fabric. They were dark men, not as tall as the people here, but thickset, with thick black hair, and beards to the breast, but their upper lips were shaved: an odd thing, and very foreign. They were armed with spears and swords and heavy curved bows. None of them rode on horses.

Rhian understood from that what these men must be. Men of the cities far to the south, cities of mud and water as the traders called them. They were strange but very rich, and they wrought fine things in gold.

The wagon was the first of several. The others were laden with bundles—baggage, Rhian supposed, or trade-goods. That in the lead carried a man who must be a lord: he was weighed down with ornaments of gold, and he had no weapon about him. He rode with his hands folded in his lap: plump soft hands, ringed with gold.

The caravan halted. Bronwy sat up, staring. The others stayed deliberately where they were. Gerent looked merely lazy. Minas, without moving a muscle, looked profoundly insolent.

Rhian smiled at the foreigner. "I welcome you to Lir," she said in the traders' speech.

The foreigner answered smile with smile. His eyes admired her without shyness, but without giving offense, either. That was an art she had thought unknown outside of the Goddess' country.

He stepped down from the wagon to stand on sturdy feet. He was very thick and short, but surprisingly graceful. He bowed to Rhian with elaborate ceremony, and to the others with a fine edge of mirth, and inspected the chariots in open fascination. "So this is the great thing we heard of, even we in the cities by the two rivers," he said.

Minas roused at that. "Two rivers? Where are they?"

"Far to the south," the stranger answered, "beyond the lesser sea of grass."

"You have no horses?"

"They are rare in my country," the stranger said. "And you—would you be a tribesman from the east? A charioteer?"

Minas inclined his head slightly. He never admitted it, but it pleased him to see awe in people's faces when they realized what he was. This stranger's response must have been gratifying: wide eyes, slight gasp, and markedly greater interest.

"Even from so far away," said the stranger, "we have heard of you and your terrible new thing, your weapon of war. Many said it was legend or myth, a tale to frighten children, but I reckoned it true. I came to see— to know if it could be so."

"It is so," Minas said.

The stranger might not understand the odd tilt of his smile, but Rhian understood it very well. Wherever chariots were, the curious came—and spies, too. This pleasant man had not come on a whim, any more than she or Emry had gone to the steppe.

She smiled at him and said, "Come, sir. We'll take you to our king."

"Not to your Mother?"

She met his eyes. The question seemed innocent, but in these matters she trusted nothing and no one. "The king is the master of all that has to do with war," she said, still smiling. She held out her hand. "Come with us."

He looked from her to Bronwy, who had brought up the duns with their chariot. His expression was comical in its astonishment. Terror warred with childlike eagerness. He flushed and then paled. "In—in— that?"

"In this," she said, as sweetly as ever.

He was a brave man, for all his seeming softness. When she had as- cended and taken the reins, he climbed up behind her, catching his breath and clutching the sides as the chariot rocked under his weight. She half expected him to retreat then, but he was stronger of spirit than that. He held his ground.

She did not spare him. The horses were refreshed and ready to run, and their stable was waiting. She let them choose their own pace. The stranger clung for dear life, but made no sound. Perhaps he could not. A glance back showed her a stark white face and open mouth and eyes perfectly round.

Minas was following with Gerent. Bronwy, still in disgrace after his mishap with the duns, would be condemned to walk with the stranger's escort, to guide them to the city. He was a better guide than charioteer, that was certain.

She smiled to herself. Her mood was bright today, barely shadowed by the child in the temple, or by the quiet but continual war between the priestesses and the king. Once she had settled the stranger in the king's house, she would take the mare, and ride out for a day or a hand of days. The horse-herds needed settling for the winter, and the new chariot-teams needed testing, to see which of them should come to Lir before the snow fell. There were rites, too, and festivals of the mare, to which she should devote herself.

Maybe Minas would come with her. His chariotmakers were quite able to work without him now, and he had a look about him that spoke of too much confinement. He was a wild thing; he could survive for a while in a cage, but then he needed to run free.

"Stranger," she said over her shoulder as they flew down the side of the road, scattering passersby too startled to understand that they were in no danger, "what name may we call you?"

At first she thought him incapable of answering. Then, faintly, he said, "My name is long and difficult for your people to pronounce. Most often they call me by part of it: Eresh."

"Eresh," she said. "I am Rhian, and yonder redhead is Minas, and that is Gerent the king's son riding behind him."

"Are you the king's daughter?" he asked.

She raised a brow, though not so that he could see. Nor did she answer him. The Goddess provided a convenient distraction: a wagonload of cut and bound fodder for the horses in the city, that barred the road and part of the verge. The chariot could scrape past, but had to slow greatly to do it.

Thereafter the road widened and its verge narrowed on the way to the city. They had to proceed at a much more stately pace, at which the horses fretted, but Eresh the foreigner was visibly glad. He began to breathe again, though he barely loosened his deathgrip on the chariot's rim.

It was market-day in Lir, the last of the autumn. In the lowing of cattle and the bleating of goats and sheep and the babble of bargaining, Rhian brought Eresh to the king's house. Truly he was a man of cities: the more crowded and noisy the street was, the greater his ease.

He had to be helped down in the court of the king's house. And yet he was smiling, an almost hectic grin. "That," he said, "will be the dream of every wild youth between the rivers. To race the wind—to fly. But I," he admitted ruefully, "am incurably earthbound. I thank you for this, with all my heart, but I think I'll keep to my oxcart hereafter."

Rhian grinned back at him. "An honest man is a delight to the Goddess," she said.

She heard a soft snort behind her that might be one of the horses, or might be Minas. She kindly ignored it. "Come to the king," she said, "and again, be welcome in Lir."

"And someday maybe," he said, as if on impulse, "you may be welcome between the rivers."

She paused. His smile had changed. He was thinking, she could see, of what his world and people could do with this terrible and wonderful thing. Just as she had done on the steppe, he was seeing what could be.

The world was a much wider place than she had ever imagined when she was a potter's child in Long Ford. In these bright dark eyes she saw how wide it truly was — wider than any single spirit. It frightened her. And yet it struck her with a strange wild joy.

66

The king was in a rage. It was not obvious. He was shooting at targets with some of the warband; he greeted the arrivals with courtesy, even smiled, and was gracious in escorting Eresh back to his house. But Rhian saw the tightness in him, a whitening of the nostrils, a quickening of the step as he left the field.

Eresh offered no more of his purpose in Lir than he had given Rhian, though he did it in many more words. He had come to trade and to see chariots. To spy, as the boys had thought — there could be little doubt of that.

Lir had nothing to hide. Eresh, and his following when at last they made their slow way to the city, was given a house near the king's house, and servants, and whatever else they had need of. That day they feasted with the king, sharing the fruits of the harvest: richness that widened their eyes, though Rhian could see that they too came from a rich city.

"You are a legend to us," Eresh told her over wine, as the lamps grew bright in the dusk. "The land of women, where goddesses walk living on the earth. And now there is this engine of war, but the legend proclaims that you never wage war — that when war comes to you, you fight it, but you do not ride out to conquer."

"That is true," Rhian said. "We defend. We protect. We worship our Goddess. We need no more than we have, nor want more. It is enough."

"It is said in our country that for men, nothing is ever enough."

"For men," she said with a tilt of the brow.

He bowed slightly. "That is so. And yet you have a king. It's clear that he rules; that he fights and leads fighters. Has none of them ever pressed for more — more land, more wealth, more power?"

"I don't doubt it," she said. "There will be fools in every part of the world. But sometimes there is enough wisdom to keep the fools in check."

"Your country is fortunate," said Eresh.

⇒ ⇐

Often when Rhian was in the city, she rose at dawn and went out to the mare, and rode wherever fancy took them. The morning after Eresh came to Lir, Rhian came down in the grey light. Minas was still asleep. So should the rest of the king's people have been, but as she crossed the hall, a stirring by the hearth brought her up short.

The king sat in his tall carved chair, long legs stretched out, beard on breast, glowering at the embers. He looked as if he had been all night there: he was still in the fine coat that he had worn at dinner, now worn and rumpled.

Between Eresh and later, more delightful distractions with Minas, Rhian had forgotten the anger she had seen in the king's face when she brought the stranger to him. The ashes of it were still there, the fire all but cold.

Rhian sat at his feet and looked into his eyes. "Tell me," she said.

He started slightly, as if he had been sleeping awake and had just now roused to her presence. His smile was quick, almost too quick to see before it vanished into the rich curls of his beard. "You think there's something to tell?"

"You've been in a banked rage since yesterday," she said. "I've never even seen you in a temper before."

"I am usually better at hiding it," he granted her. He sighed heavily. "For the first time since I was a child, a woman asked for me, and I refused her."

Rhian blinked once, slowly. "Etena?"

"Yes."

"That made you angry?"

"No." He all but spat the word.

She waited.

He thrust himself upright. "One would expect her to have little skill in the art of asking a man—after all, where she comes from, men take women and never ask their leave. She summoned me, which a woman may do, and received me in a house in the city—a rich house; two of its daughters have gone into the temple. She was alone there, waiting in the bedchamber, and what she wanted of me was clear to see.

"But her eyes—those eyes were starving. Not for me; for my soul. For the power that I carry, as king, as the father of kings. A daughter was not enough, though she be Mother of Lir. It must be a son, too, to be king; so that she can rule the world.

"I turned my back on her. I left her there. She cursed me, but I cared nothing for that. Better her curse than my soul sucked out of me."

"And anger makes you strong," Rhian said, "and lets you battle the memory of her."

He raked hands through his hair. It was all out of its plait, tangling on his shoulders. "She has a power," he said roughly. "Oh, Goddess, such a power! I hate her; I shudder at her. But I hunger for her. And that, I cannot endure."

"If I were not your child," said Rhian, "I could make you forget her."

A gust of laughter shook him—took him by surprise. "So you could," he said. "But—"

"But you are my father," she said regretfully. "Still . . . surely there is a woman in this city, one who would come willingly, and share your bed, and keep the spell at bay till she wearies of casting it?"

She had shocked him. "I would never be so importunate as to—"

"I would," she said, "and could. Tell me who, and I'll speak to her. Once she understands, surely she'll be glad to be your protector."

Why, she thought, he was blushing. This was nothing a man of good breeding would think of, but Rhian, for all her lineage, had been raised in a simple village. People were blunt-spoken there, and yes, men even asked women to bed them, now and then, when the women were slow to speak.

And here was the king in Lir, blushing like an unbedded boy, too tongue-tied to speak.

"What," Rhian said to him, "shall I find you a guardian myself? That won't be difficult. I've seen how they all look at you." She searched his face; and understood, all at once, why he was so very shaken. "You haven't—not since—but surely Etena is not the only one who—"

"I was soulbound to the Mother," he said. "No one dared."

"Now someone will," said Rhian, "for that same soul's sake. And if you won't find her, then I will."

"No," he said. "No, child. What I had with the Mother, it gave me all my strength, but it laid me open to this woman. No woman but the Mother can protect me as you think to do. That is the truth, child. There is no changing it."

"But—"

"Child," he said, "your care for me is more than I deserve. Let be; trust such strength as I have, or if not that, then the strength of my people who love me. I'm forewarned, as that other king was not. I'll be safe from her."

"Goddess grant," said Rhian.

He did not need to know everything she did to protect him. She made certain that servants were with him when she went out, and that his sons would be up soon to keep him company. Then she sent a message.

⇒ ⇐

"So," said the Goddess' Voice. "You too warn me against her."

They met in a corner of the market, where the joining of stalls made a tiny courtyard, and no one could see them. The Voice had a basket over her arm like a simple woman, and a staff in her hand to support her steps. Her eyes could see shadows in this bright sunlight, Rhian suspected. They regarded her steadily.

"When Minas warned you before," Rhian said, "you did nothing. Now she moves to do what he warned of: to destroy the king. It's a sickness in her, a desire without reason or measure. She simply must do what she does."

"And you think none of us encouraged her to work her spells on the king?"

Rhian set her teeth. "I'm not that much a fool. But be certain: the more rein you give her, the freer she is to do as she pleases—even when it pleases the temple—the closer she brings this country to the end that you foresee."

"The same could be said of you," the Voice said without expression.

"Oh," said Rhian, "but you know how dangerous I am. I don't think, even yet, that you understand what she is. You think none but one of your own can be truly deadly."

"We thank you for the warning," the Voice said. Her tone was a dismissal.

But Rhian was not to be dismissed. "Tell me. It's true, isn't it? There were no omens of note for the foreigner's child."

"Rumors are always rampant," the Voice said.

"So it is true." Rhian tilted her head. "No child that woman bears will come to anything. Only the one she rejected—and he is the king of the charioteers. When they come, priestess, you should be very wary. He won't kill his own mother—that ban runs deep in his blood—but his followers are not so bound."

"We do know that," said the Voice.

"She has you, too," Rhian said in sudden understanding. "All of you—she has you. She's a slow poison. Wherever she settles, ruin follows."

The Voice said nothing. She had nothing to say. Rhian left her, not without pity, but there was nothing she could do for these priestesses who had rejected her.

But for the king there was a little she could do, and she was doing it. She hoped that it would be enough.

V

WORLD'S END

THE TRIBES HAD come to the river. Word came to Lir by swift messengers, relays of riders that began beyond World's End. They had known that the steppe was stirring; that after a hand of years— more time than they had ever hoped to be given, and the Goddess be thanked—the young king of the charioteers had brought his many quarrelsome tribes and clans together, and secured the steppe, and turned his eyes toward the west.

Rhian was with the king of Lir when the message came that they had all been waiting for. He had asked to see his daughter's daughter; Ariana, having been occupied for the past day and more with a new foal, was most insistent that she visit the king. She seized possession of his lap while her mother was still passing the door of the king's workroom.

Rhian smiled to see them. Ariana had been born four springs past, in no little pain, but she was worth every stroke of it. She was dark like her mother, tall like her father, and her eyes were green. She could ride anything on feet, and had been doing it since before she could walk. She was no mean charioteer, either, when she was allowed to try, which was never often enough in her estimation.

By the time Rhian had settled on a stool across the table from the king, Ariana was deep in praises of the new filly—not the white mare's own, this year, but a daughter of the mare's sister, elegant and tall and fiercely determined to rule the world. "She is mine," Ariana declared. "Father said so."

The king's brows rose. "Did he? And what was it he said? That you deserve one another?"

"You were listening!" she accused him.

"Maybe I was," he said. "Maybe I know your father. And you."

"She *is* mine," Ariana said. "She kicked Father. She'll never kick me."

"May that be so," the king said, gravely amused.

The messenger came then, brought direct to the king as all messengers from the east were. She was caked with mud, and she was limping: she had not even paused to wash before she came. "They've come," she said. "They're at the river. Hordes of them—numbers beyond counting."

They had been waiting for this, all of them, and the king more than any. And yet it struck with the force of a blow.

The king broke the silence first. "Gerent," he said to his youngest son, "call the servants. Have them ready a bath, food, a bed."

"It's done," Gerent said.

He had grown up well, Rhian thought. He looked, in fact, much as his brother Emry had when she first met him. But there was a lightness about him that Emry had not had—because he was the youngest, maybe. Because he was Gerent.

The messenger resisted his hand that would have led her away. "No, not yet, by your leave, sirs and lady. I'm to tell you that their king is the one we expected. And that he has a thousand chariots."

"You counted them?" Rhian asked.

The woman—girl, truly; her breasts were barely budded—answered solemnly. "Britta the commander did, and her reckoner of troops. Britta said ten hundreds. The reckoner said ten hundreds and twenty and three."

"Close enough," said the king.

"That's what Britta said," said the messenger. "She told me to tell you that she'll guard the river-crossings as long as she can, but you know they'll win through. Be ready, she said. Be as strong as you know how to be."

The king's smile was faint, nearly hidden in the greying black of his beard. "That is her very voice and her living self. Go now, rest, be at ease. Your duty is done, and well done."

She stiffened. "I will rest, my lord, because my body is weak. But then I beg you, send me back. None of us can be idle now, not with what is coming."

"Nor can any of us afford to waste our strength before the battle comes," said the king. "Rest well. Be certain that when the time comes, I will use you to the utmost."

That pleased her. She was content then to let Gerent take her away.

Rhian sat with the king in silence. Ariana played on the floor, making finger-shadows in a patch of sunlight from the high window.

At length the king said, "The whole city will know by sundown."

"I'll wager the temple knows already."

"No wager," said the king. His voice was flat.

He never spoke Etena's name, nor would he suffer a priestess' presence in his house while Etena inhabited the temple. Her daughter, no one outside those walls had seen. She was a meek little thing, Rhian had heard, as little like Ariana as it was possible to be.

Ariana had lived her first year under guard. She had been watched day and night, so that not even a mouse could escape her guards' vigilance. Twice Etena's young men had tried to creep in upon her and been driven back. Minas had killed the second—sinking his bronze dagger in his own brother's heart, and singing a fierce keening song after, half of exultation, half of grief.

After the prince's death, Etena seemed to have grown weary of the game, perhaps even afraid. She contented herself with ruling inside the temple and raising her daughter to be her creature. She waited as they all waited, for the chariots to come to the river.

It was like waking from a long and turbulent sleep. Rhian rose. "I'll summon the warleaders," she said, "and the elders of the city."

The king bowed to her presence of mind. "I'll see that the house is ready for them. The king's messengers—send someone to fetch them. I'll see them here, before the warleaders come."

Rhian was already in motion. She knew what to do—they all did. They were as ready for this as they could be; as anyone could be, against a thousand chariots and warriors without number.

⇒ ⇐

Minas had gone to the far field that morning to gather the colts for training. They had come up from the south not long before, and been settled here while the horse-tamers saw to other things; today he had decided that it was time to bring them in.

Most of them had been obedient to the herdsmen and gathered at the field's edge near the road to Lir. But one small herd of bays and greys, no more than a dozen, had proved recalcitrant. Ifon thought he had them, but they eluded him and bolted for the wood that edged the field to the east. Ifon would have gone after them, but Minas was nearer, and his dun was swifter than Ifon's stocky bay. Minas called him off with a shout and a sweep of the arm, and went after the strays himself.

The wood was a thicket. The herdsmen had encouraged brambles to grow just inside it, till they made a wall higher than a man; in summer they were laden with ripe berries, but it was still spring. The berries would be hard and green, the thorns impenetrable.

Minas sent the dun in an arc, aiming to head off the strays before they came to the wood. They were the wild ones, the young hellions, and worst was the thickly dappled grey who drove them from behind. Now and then he rolled an eye at Minas, as if to be sure that he was properly infuriated.

Minas laughed at him, which made him pin ears and fling a kick, but he was fast and he was unburdened by a rider, and his fellows were utterly in his power. He could lead a merry chase.

Suddenly, violently, he shied. An instant later, Minas' dun veered, snorting. Minas held on with knees and hands. The renegade herd wheeled and bolted away from the wood, toward the safety of numbers. Even the dapple had forgotten his defiance.

The dun would have been more than glad to follow, but Minas held him, though he bucked and plunged. His ears fixed quivering on the shadows of the wood. His back was like a strung bow.

A wolf sat under an arch of new leaves, red tongue lolling, yellow eyes laughing. He yawned and stretched and stood up a man, lean and supple, with a twisted foot and a crooked grin.

He had gone as grey as a wolf, though he was no older than Minas. His face was still young, and his quickness as he moved. His teeth were whiter and sharper than Minas remembered, more like a wolf's than a man's.

"The beast and the man become one," said the shaman whose name once had been Phaiston.

"You crossed the river," said Minas.

"She opened the way," Phaiston said. "When she came, the souls fled."

"Or she ate them."

"Only the kings."

Minas' lips stretched back from his teeth. "Not here. Not in this country."

"She must be starving," Phaiston said.

"Not she," said Minas. "She dines on priestesses and their acolytes."

"Thin fare, if she needs so much of it."

"But steady, and always more to be had."

Phaiston did not seem to move, but all at once he was by the dun stallion's shoulder. The dun snorted and cocked a wary ear, but did not shy away.

"It's time," Phaiston said.

At first Minas did not dare to believe he understood. It had been so long, his captivity so complete. He had a woman here, or she had him. He had a child. He had standing—not as a slave, but as a prince. A captive prince, but a prince nonetheless, and a lord of charioteers.

And yet, after all, he was still of the People.

"They're at the river," the shaman said. "All the People—all the tribes and clans, the allies, the vassals, the whole world; and a thousand chariots."

"A thousand . . ." Minas laughed. "You're joking."

"By the gods, I am not. All the makers your grandfather was training, he sent to the tribes. There they took apprentices, just as you did here. And they made chariots. Hundreds of them."

"But with what?" Minas demanded. "There's not enough wood on the steppe to—"

"There are forests to the north and the east. With men enough, wagons enough, courage enough, anything is possible. And once the king knew where *she* had gone—"

"The king? Dias?"

"The great king, the king of kings, the conqueror of worlds, Dias son of Adas son of Kronos of the People."

Minas son of Adas son of Kronos, who should have been king, discovered that his fists were knotted tight in the stallion's mane. With care he worked them free. "Dias," he said. "Dias whom his mother despised, calling him a feeble shadow of a man. How it must gnaw at her liver!"

"And at yours?"

Minas looked down into those wicked yellow eyes. He could break the man's neck, he thought coldly. No one would know, nor would anyone care.

Maybe Phaiston knew how close he was to death. It did not seem to trouble him.

"I am a dead man," Minas said. "I have no liver to gnaw."

"The dead have great power," Phaiston said.

"But they cannot be kings." Minas drew a shuddering breath. "Enough. I am what fate has made me—what *she* has made me. Are not we all? And now he comes to take vengeance."

"You know," said Phaiston, "that if you went back, he would give up his kingship for you."

"Would he?"

Phaiston did not hesitate. "He has grown into it, and some say into greatness, but he never wanted it. It was always yours."

Minas laughed harshly. "Oh, it was mine! But no longer. Leave off tormenting me, and tell me. Have they crossed the river?"

"Not yet," said Phaiston, "but soon. The defenses have given them pause, but will never stop them."

"They're not meant to. They're meant to bring the enemy into a trap, to surround and crush them."

"A chain of forts," Phaiston said. "But the cities and towns are seldom walled, and they're full of innocents. What will they all do, run and hide? Where will they go? The forts can't hold them all."

Minas shrugged. "I'm not privy to those councils."

"No. You only make chariots to fight chariots."

"Ten score against a thousand," Minas said. "And I reckoned that it would be an even match."

"Did you hope for that?"

"What is hope to the dead?"

"So young, and yet so bitter." Phaiston eluded a half-hearted blow, dancing his mockery. "You can wager that the temple knows of this, and therefore *she* does. What do you think she'll do, now she knows the reckoning has come?"

"Panic," said Minas.

Phaiston whooped and yipped. "Oho! Ohai! Oh, won't she! And what will she do when she panics, O prince of slaves? Whom will she seize as a hostage, on pretext that after all there might be danger of betrayal?"

"There *is* danger of—" Minas broke off. "She can't. She does nothing outside the temple. The king's power protects me."

"For once, the king will agree with her," Phaiston said. "You are a threat. You know everything that matters, of the defenses, of the people who man them—councils or no councils. The chariots are your chariots. The horses you trained, or you saw to their training. Take all that to your brother in the east, and you give him the gift of this country."

Minas' heart swelled till it was like to burst. To see his people again, his brother, his kin—to be alive and no longer dead—

Rhian. Ariana. He gasped with the shock of memory, the pain he had known would come, and he thought prepared for. But nothing could prepare him for this.

A man should not be so bound to a woman, still less to a daughter. The tribe was his heart and soul. He lived for the tribe, died for the tribe.

They would be safe. The king protected them here. When the People came, Minas would protect them.

"The dead have great power," he said aloud. He glanced about quickly. The herdsmen seemed to have forgotten him. They had the herd together and were driving it down the road to Lir.

He had no food with him, and only the clothes on his back. He had a bottle of water, a sword and a dagger, his bow and a quiver of arrows. He had a good horse, born on the steppe and bred to travel far on short commons.

He needed no more thought than that. There was a way through the thicket—he had found it once, searching for a strayed colt. He turned the dun toward what seemed to be the thorniest part of the wall, found the all but invisible gap, and slipped within. Thorns clawed at him, but he made himself small, and kept the dun on the straight track. Eastward. Away from Lir. Toward the river and the horde of the People.

68

Minas did not come back with the herd from the far pasture. That was not uncommon; sometimes he went hunting, sometimes he lingered among the horses. But today Rhian's nerves were strung tight. If he had had the news—if he had heard that his people were coming—she knew beyond doubt what he would have done. He was a tribesman; it was bred in him. He would have no choice but to escape.

She knew his honor, as peculiar as it was. He had stayed while his people were still on the steppe, had served as he reckoned a slave should. But their coming set him free.

Ariana insisted that she must spend the night with the king. That suited Rhian splendidly. There was no safer place to be than in those strong arms, deeply and obliviously asleep while he held his war-council far into the night.

Rhian slipped away not long after dark. She would not be missed for a while; there were numerous others coming and going, and the king's house was in tumult. Lir was no more subdued, though like the king's house it had forborne to give way to panic. Rhian was proud of her people then, of their courage in the face of war.

The mare was waiting for her. The stable was dim, with only moonlight to illumine it. The mare's coat glowed, white as the moon. Rhian wrapped arms about the silken neck and leaned there for a while, simply breathing. She was not brave, not like the people of this city. She was stark with terror—not of war or death, no. But of losing him.

She had taken Minas to use and cast away. But since she first lay with him, she had not wanted any other man. Nor it seemed did he want another woman, though many had asked. He was not a man to open his heart easily, and more so now than when he was free among the tribe. And yet she had seen how he was when she bore Ariana, the fear in him, the crazy courage as he held her through the two days' battle. He went to the gates of death with her, and never left her until she was firm again among the living.

He was the other half of her. Whether she was the same to him, she did not know. It was not a thing he would speak of.

She mounted the mare in the moonlight, and rode her out of Lir. There were guards and walls, but Rhian knew other ways, and the mare could melt into the night when she chose.

The mare tracked Minas. When daylight came, Rhian recognized the print of his horse: narrower, more oval than horses' feet here. He would be riding one of his duns, she thought, and most likely the stallion whom the mare favored.

He was keeping to the uplands, to the woods and the edges of fields, staying as far away from the towns as he could. He had begun half a day ahead of her, but she had brought provisions, and she could see that he had not: he had to stop to hunt, and to graze his horse.

She caught him in the evening of that first day, camped in a clearing deep in a copse. He had hidden his traces well, but the mare was not a mortal creature, to be so easily deceived.

He was roasting a brace of rabbits over a fire, its smoke shielded by the branches of a tree. He started a little as the mare came out of the trees, but his eyes when he lifted them to Rhian held no surprise. No hatred, either. She remembered to breathe then, swinging her leg over the white neck, sliding to the ground.

"I'm not going back," he said.

"I didn't think you would." She opened her traveling-pack and brought out fruit, cheese, cakes from the king's kitchen in Lir.

"Ariana?"

"With the king."

He sighed softly, and the tautness in his shoulders eased. "She'll be safe there."

Rhian nodded.

"So will you be."

"I'm going with you."

"You are not."

She was silent.

The rabbits were cooked, spitting savory grease into the fire, making it flare. Minas lifted the spits and handed one to Rhian. They ate without speaking. He was hungry: he had devoured his share before she was half done with hers.

She wanted to touch him, but she knew better than to try. He lay back while she finished eating, sprawled in the grass. She thought he would insist that she speak first, but he surprised her. He said, "If you go with me, you are a traitor to your people."

"If you're caught without me, you could be killed."

"I don't intend to be caught."

"Can you be sure of that?"

"Will you betray me?"

"No," said Rhian. "I will not."

"Why?"

"Because I love you."

That word had never been spoken between them. It slipped out of its own accord.

"I will not stay for love of you," he said.

"Ah," she said, "but you are a tribesman, and I belong to the mare. I go where she goes. She brought me here."

"Against your will?"

"Hardly."

He frowned. "I don't understand you."

"Did you ever?"

"No!"

That was pure temper. She laughed at it. He snarled, but his lips began to twitch. He never had been able to stay angry for long, not when she smiled as she did now.

→ ←

Minas tried to slip away in the night. But Rhian had expected that. She was close behind him as he rode out. The moon caught the flash of his glance. She thought he might turn back, but he was as stubborn as she was. Once he had begun, he would go on.

In any event it was better that they travel by night. The king's messengers had gone out. The fortresses were armed, and all roads guarded. It did not seem that anyone should be searching for a lone rider or two—the enemy would come in a wall like a storm, without need of stealth—and yet there were armed parties traveling the roads and roving the hills.

Rhian knew the country well for two days' journey about Lir, but past that she knew only the roads. Minas knew less than she: he had been kept close to the city, and when he left it, he had gone by river or with chariots. If they followed the river, they would meet guards; but if they took to the country, they must go blind, aim as nearly in the direction of the river as they could, and hope that the land would protect them.

It failed them on the fourth day. They had taken a narrow pass over a steep ridge to avoid a cluster of villages, and found the going terribly slow: the valley was thickly wooded in parts, and in parts slippery with stones and scree. Worse, it narrowed as it went up, until it ended in a meeting of steep walls; and no way up unless they had wings.

They camped there, as it was nearly dawn. When night came again would turn back, and hope that they could find a way around the villages—or through them, as Minas proposed.

"You're mad," Rhian said to him.

"Am I? I'll cover my hair. We're armed, mounted. If we ride boldly in the open, and look suitably grim, they'll take us for soldiers, and hardly give us a second glance."

"And the mare?" Rhian asked. "Do you think she'll go unrecognized?"

"Turn her loose. She'll find her own way. We'll go together."

"On a single horse?"

"I'll walk," he said—and that was a princely sacrifice, for a tribesman to surrender his horse to a woman.

They argued for some little time longer, but there was no other way that either of them could see. They slept then in the grey morning, first she and then he. When her watch ended, the rain that had threatened began to fall. Mist closed in. It would be a black night.

She called Minas' name, softly. He woke all at once as he always did, upright even as his eyes opened, flashing a glance that recalled where he was and why.

"I think we should go now," she said. "Come nightfall, we'll be blind. And if you cover your head and face, it won't be as suspicious in the rain as it would be on a starlit night."

He nodded. They broke camp quickly, in amity that belied the heat of their dissension before. The mare was already gone, vanished in the mist. Rhian had not even heard her go. The dun was uneasy, ears flicking, nostrils flaring. He disliked to be alone, apart from his mare.

She would happily have walked, but as Minas pointed out, his legs were longer. He could go faster. With him afoot and her astride, they made their careful way back down through the narrow cleft of the valley. The mist was thick. They could barely see the ground in front of them.

The dun grew more uneasy rather than less, the farther they went. Even Minas' hand on his bridle did not comfort him. Rhian crooned to him, stroking his neck. He was sweating and trembling.

Minas stopped abruptly. "Wolf-shaman," he said in his own language. "Come out; you're upsetting the horse."

Nothing came, neither wolf nor man. Rhian held her tongue. She knew Phaiston had come back—Minas had told her. But she had not seen him or found trace of him, only Minas and the dun. Maybe his spirit had come to Minas, and his body was still with the tribe.

Still there was no denying that something in the mist greatly troubled the dun. They advanced slowly. Minas drew his sword. Rhian strung her bow, though the damp made it harder to keep the string taut.

Even as wary as they were, alert and on guard, they walked straight into the trap. It had closed about them before they were fully aware it was there.

Shapes loomed out of the mist. Horses; riders. Dull gleam of weapons.

All the riders were women. They were armed and armored. Their helmets were high, ornamented with wings of birds. Their eyes were clear and hard.

Rhian put on her most innocent face. "Not so fair a day," she said, "but a fair meeting."

"Indeed," said the woman who must be the leader: her helmet was highest, and she wore an armlet of gold.

Rhian kept a smile on her face, urging the dun toward the circle's edge. "You'll pardon us if we don't tarry," she said, "but we're on the king's business. We—"

The circle closed about her. Swords and bows were trained on her, and on Minas standing motionless at the dun's shoulder.

"You may go," the captain said to her. "But him we will take."

"He is the king's man," Rhian said.

The captain swooped and plucked the mantle from Minas' head and shoulders. His hair was fire-bright in the grey light. He showed her his teeth.

"Indeed," said the captain. "Which king?"

"King of kings, lord of chariots, conqueror of the world," Minas answered her, sweetly.

Rhian kicked him. He grunted, but took no other notice. He was in one of his wild moods, when he was as near a madman as made no difference.

"You will come," the captain said.

"Not," said Rhian, "until I know whose warriors you are. I don't recognize your fashion. What are you and by what right do you take us prisoner?"

"We serve the Lady of the Birds," the captain said. "We have no quarrel with the Lady of Horses. But with this man, we do."

She said the word *man* as if it had a sour taste in her mouth.

Rhian looked at her in dawning comprehension. There had been rumors, whispers, but no surety, until now. "You belong to her. To Etena."

"To the Lady of the Birds."

"This man belongs to the king in Lir," Rhian said. "Without his leave, you cannot touch him."

"We have his leave," the captain said.

"You do not."

The captain set her lips together. "We will take you to him. We must bind this one—we are so ordered."

"The king would never order that," Rhian said sharply.

"We are ordered," the captain said.

Minas held up his hands. His grin was wilder than ever. The captain nodded to one of her women. The priestess—for she must be that—advanced warily, but Minas offered no resistance. She bound him tightly.

He looked happy. It was not the hectic fever of despair. Rhian looked for that. It was . . . relief, almost. As if he had expected this, and was glad to be done with it.

She understood him no better than he understood her.

But this much she did understand. The king and the temple for once had joined forces. They could not let Minas go, either of them. It was wise. It was heartening in a strange way: because if they were to win this war, they must fight together, not against one another.

Maybe that was why Minas laughed, though he was truly a captive now, truly a prisoner. Because he had done the impossible: he had brought them to the same side. Minas had a fine appreciation for the gods' humor.

69

The People swept like a storm across the river. There was fighting, and plenty of it. These people were ready, armed and honed for war. Warriors young and not so young welcomed it with howls of glee. Many sought it out, luring the Goddess' people into spats and skirmishes while behind them, boats and rafts ferried the chariots and horses across the water. There the enemy's inexperience in war showed itself: they were easily distracted. But they learned quickly. Later waves of the People did not cross as easily as those that had gone before.

The sound of the war-drums and the skirling of the pipes throbbed in Aera's blood. She was with the horde, riding among the warriors—a change that Dias had made. Most of the women and children rode behind in wagons, and would camp on the far side of the river until this country was made safe for them. But a few were suffered in the king's company, women of wisdom and standing, the chief of his wives and the wives of his vassal kings. And Aera, because she was Metos' daughter and Dias' foster-mother, and because her husband was the king's charioteer.

There was no mistaking that one of all the lords of chariots. He was taller than many and broader than most, and his black beard was striking among so many fair-bearded or shaven faces. Not a few of the vassals persisted in thinking that he and Dias were brothers, because they were both dark broad-shouldered men; no matter how well it was known that Emry was a prince of the west. If they two were kin, that kinship went back to the dawn time.

Truly they seemed brothers in spirit. And that was well for Dias. Dias needed to be one of two. That was Etena in him, maybe: his soul was not complete. As if, Aera often thought, he was the moon, and he needed a sun to grant him its light. Etena devoured souls to feed her hunger. Dias only needed one, and that he bound with the love of brothers. Etena was the dark of the moon. He was the full, shining with white light.

The night before the whole of the horde crossed the river, the king camped on the eastern bank. He had been across more than once already, leading assaults against the defenses, but for this one last night he would sleep on the shore of the sea of grass. His men were not feasting yet, but there was celebration in plenty, small victories won and the great victory ahead of them, and a splendid war to revel in.

Emry ate with the king, because it was expected of him, but he came early to the tent. Aera might not have known that he was troubled; he smiled, he spoke lightly, he kissed her with a hunger that had not abated in a hand of years. But he did not bear her backward into the sleeping-furs, and he stood quietly while she undressed him. That was not like him at all.

When she sat him down in the furs to comb out his thick black hair, he said, "It's too quiet here. No magpies chattering. No baby crying."

Aera's breasts ached, but no more than her heart. She had weaned the baby when they came to the river. He was with Dias' lesser wives, being spoiled shamelessly, and being kept safe until the war was over. His sisters were with him; his protests had been vociferous enough, but theirs had been loud and long.

It was only Aera and Emry tonight, for the first time since the twins came. She felt the same odd emptiness as he did, the same excess of stillness. But more than that, she felt a stillness in him.

She knelt behind him, clasping arms about him, resting her head against his back. He sighed, a gust of wind in her ear. His voice was a rumble of thunder. "Dias gave me leave not to cross the river," he said.

Her breath caught, then resumed its rhythm. "Will you accept it?"

"No," he said.

"Then you will fight your own people."

"No," he said again. "Aias will drive the king's chariot. I'll ride with your father and the rest of the makers. I won't be bound, unless I give cause."

He was very calm. This was expected, planned for. His word was long since given. On the sea of grass, he was Dias' man, his brother and friend. Past the river, he was a prince of Lir.

Aera held him tightly. His ribs creaked, but he made no sound of protest. "I don't think I can bear to lose you," she said.

He shuddered within himself, but did not speak.

Wind cooled their faces, sudden and briefly blessed. The one who had brought it stood in the flickering lamplight. His eyes were wild. "He lives. He is alive!"

Aera frowned at Dias. He was acting no more like himself than Emry was. Dias never burst in upon anyone, never blurted out words as if he had no power over his own tongue.

He was utterly beside himself. Both Aera and Emry rose, took him in hand, sat him down and poured kumiss into him until he gasped and spluttered and flung the skin across the tent. "Gods below take you! Are you trying to drown me?"

"Ah, good," Aera said, squatting in front of him. "That's better. Now tell us what brings you here. Who is alive?"

"Minas," Dias said. "Minas lives. He's here—there. With the Goddess-worshippers."

Aera sat heavily on her heels. Emry, she noticed distantly, was not even feigning surprise.

"Who told you this?" Emry asked.

Dias raked fingers through his hair. It was snarled out of its plait, tangled on his shoulders. "A shaman. He went spiritwalking, he said. He found my brother alive, in the city called Lir. And—he found—" He shuddered. "He found *her*."

"Etena?" Now that did surprise Emry, profoundly. "Etena in Lir?"

"In the temple of Lir." Dias' lips curled back from his teeth. "With the Goddess' servants."

"The king?" Emry demanded. "Does he live? Is he safe?"

"The shaman didn't say," Dias said indifferently. "Probably he's dead. Or his soul is. But my brother—he is alive. His soul is alive. The shaman swore it. My brother is alive!"

Aera could not breathe. She could barely think. She knew she must, but she could not find the way to do it.

Minas alive. He was dead, mourned, elevated among the ancestors. He was a prince of the gods below, a great lord of the dead.

She began to laugh. Once she had begun, she could not stop, even with three of them—three?—shaking and slapping her and calling her name.

It was the third man who recalled her to herself. She did not remember him at all. His hair was wolf-grey but his face was young, thin and sharp-boned. His eyes were pale brown, almost yellow. As laughter shrank to giggles and faded away, she began to understand who he must be. The necklaces of bones and shells and feathers, the amulets woven in his hair—a shaman. He must be—

"You saw him," she said. "You saw my son. Among the dead."

"I suppose," the shaman said, "that you could say that. He is across the river, where the gods live. He is a prince among them. He makes chariots for them, and tames horses."

Was that satisfaction in Emry's eyes? Dias was rapt, hearing only that Minas lived. Nothing else mattered to him.

But Aera was not as simple a soul as that. "You knew," she said to Emry.

He met her stare steadily. "I knew," he said.

Her heart went cold. "Tell me."

"She traded him," Emry said. "Etena. For me. They wanted—needed chariots. She wanted to be rid of him, but hated him too well to give him the gift of death. We had come to learn what we could and take what we could. He was a gift of the Goddess, through that unlikely instrument."

"They traded you—for—"

"She needed one of royal blood to do what she had in mind. And we needed one to teach us the ways of chariots."

Aera looked at him as if she had never seen him before. This man who had shared her bed and made children with her and kept her heart warm for this past hand of years, was altogether a stranger. "Do I know you?" she asked him. "Did I ever know you?"

His face went white above the shadow of his beard. "I gave you everything but that. That was I sworn to; I could not tell you."

"I don't know you," she said. It was not meant to wound or cut. It was simply the truth. She searched his face, that was as familiar, as beloved as any in the world. Its lines were still the same. His eyes—his beautiful eyes, the color of the sky at twilight, that deep and supernal blue. Their son had those eyes.

He had not lied to her, no. Not except by silence. She could understand that. He was what he was, a stranger in the camp of an enemy. And yet she could not say, any longer, that her spirit and his spirit were one. He had kept himself back. He had let her grieve for the first of her sons, had stood without speaking while her heart was torn in two.

She could understand. But she could not forgive. "Go," she said to all of them. "Let me be."

Dias protested. The shaman looked troubled. Emry bowed as if to a king, and did as she bade.

The tears came when they had all gone. She was alone as she had never been in all her years. Her firstborn was alive, but she knew no joy.

A wise woman would have gone after Emry, called him back, made what peace she could. Aera could not move. It was a warm spring night, yet she sat frozen as if she had been naked on the steppe, whipped with icy wind, lashed with snow.

She heard Dias outside, babbling with excitement. "We'll go direct to the city. We'll rescue my brother. We'll destroy her at last."

"Oh, you will," the shaman said. "She's taken him prisoner—he tried to escape, but she's too strong for him. He had the king to protect him before, but once he ran, he lost that. He's in great danger, lord."

Tempter, Aera thought. Trickster, troublemaker. This was the wolf-shaman—he lived for mischief. But she could not go out, could not warn Dias. The young king was ripe for temptation. His brother alive, his mother laired where he had meant to go—it was a trap, as neat as any she had seen.

Emry would see it. But would he speak of it? He was the enemy. Even love could not change that.

She sat unmoving, and maybe she betrayed her king, too, with her silence. She had no power to move or speak.

She was still there come morning, when the horde of the People surged across the river. Then she could rise. Then, stiffly, she could go out. She moved like one in a dream. She had put on garments that came to hand, and taken what went with them: bow, spear, battleaxe. Chariots rumbled past, toward the boats and rafts. One swept her up, its charioteer still yawning, bleared with sleep.

She rode across the river as a warrior, crowded in with a boatload of charioteers and fighting men. The chariots rode behind, and the horses preternaturally still in the barges. The priests and the shamans chanted ceaselessly, sustaining the force of the spell.

She could die. Or she could live, and see her elder son again. It did not matter which the gods intended for her. Not without Emry. Not without the half of her spirit.

70

Emry left the camp of the People in the deep night before the horde crossed the river into the Goddess' country. He could not take a chariot— not from this side of the river. He took the sturdiest of the teams that Dias had given him, a pair of strong-bodied bays, and riding one and leading the other, crossed the river under the stars.

The Goddess was with him. An eddy of the river caught him just before he stumbled into a company of guards, and swept the horses downstream to a jut of bank that no one had thought to watch. His mount and his remount scrambled out of the water, paused to shake away the wet, and with no urging from him, set off westward.

He was empty of words. His heart felt nothing. When he looked within, he saw Aera's face, the cold lack of recognition, the words that damned him. *I don't know you.* So simply, so completely she had cast him away.

She had set him free. He was going home. What he went to, he did not know, nor care. His father dead, the kingship gone, Etena set up as Mother—it did not matter. It was home.

He put aside memory of Aera's face, the children's faces, the tent that had housed them, the belongings they had gathered—all the home that he had made in his captivity. He was going back to Lir. He was going where he belonged, whether he lived or died.

✦✦

The king of Lir inspected the prisoners. His eyes were cold, but Minas saw no hatred there. No death, either, though he would not have been surprised to find it.

The priestess-warriors had brought them in, but his own people guarded them now. "I hope you understand," he said to them, "how fierce a battle I fought to gain possession of you. The temple wanted you—both of you—and badly."

"What did it cost you?" Rhian asked him. Minas wondered if she meant to sound so impudent.

The king kept his temper. "A little gold and a great deal of pride. And a promise. You're bound in this city until the war is over."

Minas' teeth ached with clenching. It was no more than he had expected, but it was not an easy sentence.

"You'll need me beyond these walls," Rhian said, "and the mare, to give heart to the people."

"Did you think of that before you ran westward?" the king asked.

Minas, watching him, reflected that betrayal cut deeper and festered longer between kin who loved one another. But that was not just; it was not necessary. "She did not run," he said. "I ran. She pursued me. Punish me, but let her go. She did nothing that she should not have done."

"Don't believe him," Rhian said. "I made no effort to bring him back."

"Except with guilt," Minas said, "and the constant reminder of what fate I was forcing on you." He turned to the king. "Keep me captive, yes, because if I see even the hint of an opening, I will bolt. But spare her. This is none of her doing."

"You love me too much," Rhian said. "Stop it. Let him punish me as I deserve. Let him—"

"Enough."

The king did not raise his voice, but the slap of it silenced them both. "I am going to punish you. You, prince of chariots, will not leave this house unless bound and under guard. You may make chariots. You may ride horses within the walls. You may instruct recruits under the eye of such captains as I may choose. One word, one hint of corruption, and you will be shut in your chamber until this war is ended.

"And you," he said to Rhian, "are free of the city, but nowhere beyond it. You will not speak with this man, except under guard. You will not be alone with him. You will do nothing to further his cause in this war."

"Or?" Rhian asked.

"Or you die." The king's voice was perfectly flat. "She wanted you dead when you were captured. It's your good fortune that the women who caught you were not entirely her creatures. There is still reverence for the White Mare, even in the temple. The captain will live, I hear, though she was flogged with canes until the darkness took her."

Rhian stiffened. Minas liked it little, either. The woman had been as kind as her orders would allow, and only as implacable as she had to be.

"Have you considered," he asked the king, "that that one's death now might save us all?"

"It was too late when she came to Lir," the king said. "Some say it was too late when the Mother's daughter was let live in spite of the omens." He sighed and rubbed his eyes. He had not slept in much too long. None of them had. "There is truce now between this house and the temple. I will do whatever I must to sustain it, within the bounds of law and justice. If that is to execute you—both of you—then I will do it."

Rhian took his hands in hers. He had melted her heart, as no doubt he meant to do. "I'll stay in Lir, if that will keep peace with the temple. But let me help with the war."

"Dare I trust you?"

"This time," she said, "yes."

He paused for a long while. Then he nodded slowly. "I have captains enough, and soldiers, and the people know what to do. But one thing I need. You spoke of it—and it's true. Heart. Someone to keep up their spirits and bolster their strength and see that no one breaks for fear or exhaustion. Can you do that inside of the city? Are you strong enough?"

Of course she was, Minas thought. It was the very nature of her.

Was he strong enough to endure captivity, shut in the king's house without her and never left alone? If the People were coming, if there was hope of freedom, maybe. Maybe he would not wither and die.

He would never let anyone see him quail, even Rhian. His hands were unbound, at least, and his guards were as congenial as guards could be. "We don't blame you for bolting," Huon told him—having taken a place in Minas' guard since, as he said, he had been doing it since Larchwood; he had grown accustomed to the duty. "We'd do it, too, if we were prisoners in a foreign country."

They were vigilant, and there were always at least two of them. They followed him everywhere, even to the privies. When he occupied himself with the chariots, they idled about the edges, just happening to guard every path of escape. They were king's guards: princes of their kind.

They were all men. Large men, larger than Minas, and strong. They were very well armed.

He did not see Rhian all that day, nor know if she was guarded as he was. He threw himself into the making of a chariot, even knowing that it would be sent against his own people. It kept him from dashing himself against the walls.

And this was only the first day.

He was the only one there, that day. The others would come back, the guards promised him. They were out preparing for the war.

As the day stretched, someone else appeared in the broad high workroom. He darkened the light, rousing Minas from a near-trance of weaving strips of leather to be the chariot's floor.

Minas looked up into a face that had become familiar over the years. It was a broader, thicker, darker face than most of those he saw here, with a beard crimped into waves, and the upper lip shaven. It was smiling, round brown eyes crinkling at the corners.

Minas warmed in spite of himself, almost into a smile of his own. "Eresh," he said.

The foreigner swept a low bow. "At your service, O maker of chariots. You didn't expect me? It's spring. The roads are open. The river of trade flows free. Where else would I be but in the land of gold and beautiful women?"

"Somewhere where there is no war?"

Eresh threw back his head and laughed. "Oh yes, that would have been wise, wouldn't it? But the astrologers, you see — they said that this was a year of peace and plenty, and trading would be profitable. So we went out. Now it seems I should have consulted the soothsayers instead."

"Or the gossips in the markets," Minas said. He straightened, flexing his shoulders, stretching the knots out of his back. "There's still time to escape."

"Not in oxcarts." Eresh did not seem dismayed. Either he knew little of war, or he had more courage than his soft body might have indicated. He perched on a stool, his ample rump and tiered kilt overflowing it, and watched with his perpetual bright interest as Minas went back to his weaving.

He was good company, better than the guards. He told stories of his country, his king and gods, and gossip from the lands to the south.

There were many of those — as many as there were tribes on the steppe. They all built cities, beside which this city of Lir was a simple village, and houses as high as mountains. "They even build mountains," he said, "in a country very far away, and bury kings beneath them."

"Like barrows?" Minas asked as he cut new strips from the tanned bullhide. When Eresh looked blank, he said, "Hills on the steppe, made by men's hands, for the burial of kings."

"Are they as tall as mountains," Eresh asked, "and built entirely of stone?"

"They're dug in the earth," said Minas, "and heaped with turves. Sometimes they're shored with wood, sometimes with stone."

"These are all stone," Eresh said. "The building of them is years long.

Kings begin them in youth, as a vaunt and a promise. Houses of ever-lasting, some people call them, for the dead to live in until the world's end."

"Our dead go to the otherworld," Minas said, "and become gods."

"There too," said Eresh, "but these people must keep their bodies whole, or their spirits die."

"Then if you take a head or burn a body, the spirit is dead? Don't their bodies rot?"

"Their sorcerers have great arts to keep them whole."

"So only kings can live forever." Minas shook his head. "That's not a world for me. I'd be terrified to die."

"They do love the world of the living," Eresh said. "Why, do you have no fear of death?"

"Death is a passage," said Minas. "Some of us stay, and are gods. Some come back. For need or desire, love or vengeance, or because we haven't earned godhood—we live again, until we win our freedom."

"That is . . . an unusual world to be living in," said Eresh. "But comforting. It must be that."

"And you? What is death to you?"

"Darkness," said Eresh, "in the Great Below. Our dead don't come back—except for one. He was a goddess' lover. She went down and down and down, through the realms of shadow, and won him back with the beauty of her body. Even the gods below were no proof against that."

"No god is," Minas said. "Did you know, to the tribes on the steppe, this country we sit in is the otherworld, and the river between is the river of souls. I am dead to my people, dead and a god."

"Can gods go back?"

"Not the gods of the dead."

"And yet you tried."

Minas bent to his cutting. "I had to try. Even knowing . . ."

He could not finish. Eresh was kind enough not to do it for him.

But there was no turning his heart away from it. Etena had killed him, just as surely as she had destroyed his father.

⇒ ⇐

Rhian was not in the room when the guards brought Minas to it. Her belongings were still there, but the air felt strangely empty.

Although there was no sleep in him, he undressed and lay on the bed. The guards took positions: one by the door, one by the window. His lip curled at that, but he kept his thoughts to himself. He closed his eyes.

When he opened them again, the night had advanced very little. Warmth stirred against him. He looked down at his daughter's tumbled hair and bare cream-brown shoulder.

She looked up, wide green eyes in a tangle of black curls. Her expression was by no means tender. "You ran away and left me," she said.

He could not deny that.

"Now they're punishing you." Her satisfaction was palpable. "*She* wanted you whipped. She wanted to watch. The king threw a bag of gold at her and told her to keep her poison to herself."

"He really said that?" Minas asked.

"Do I tell lies?"

"You do not," he said gravely.

"I think a whipping would do you good," his daughter said. "Next time you run away, you'll take me with you."

"If I run away again," he said, "I'll be killed."

"Not if I'm with you." She sat on his chest, as bare as she was born except for the image of the Goddess that hung on a cord about her neck. "I hate you," she informed him.

"I do deserve that," he said.

"Huon says you were trying to get killed. That's why you ran. You are not allowed to get killed. I need you alive."

"I was not trying to get killed," he said.

"Don't lie." She glared down at him. "Don't ever leave me again, either. Promise!"

"I can't do that," he said.

"Promise."

"What if I die before you? Will you curse me for an oathbreaker?"

"Promise you won't leave me."

She was as stubborn as her mother. "I promise," he said, "that as long as I'm alive, I won't abandon you."

"You won't leave me."

"I won't leave you alone," he said.

He held his breath. But she was very young. The subtleties of words were new to her. She accepted his oath.

He did not like this taste of guilt, this mingling of sour and bitter that burned in his throat. She slid back down to his side, sighed and wriggled and went to sleep, abruptly, as children could. He cradled her in his arms, stroking her hair till it was smooth. "I'll try not to die," he said softly. "For your sake, I will try."

71

A handful of days after Minas was brought back to Lir, a rider came down the eastward road. He was riding a sturdy bay horse and leading another. People greeted him as he rode past, taking him for one of the king's sons; they were all as like to one another as pups in a litter. Only a few paused to wonder why a king's son would be dressed in a fashion that not been seen in Lir since—

Since the princes of chariots came in their leather coats and their trousers and their high soft boots, their beads and braids and ornaments of gold and copper and shell and bone. There were strings of amber braided in his hair, and bands of gold about his arms, and the mantle that protected him from spits of cold rain was the hide of a lion.

Rhian was on the wall that surrounded the city's heart, seeing to the disposition of a wagonload of arrows, when she caught sight of him on the road. The usual crowds were thin today, between the rain and the dread of war; people were keeping to their towns and villages, and traveling as little as they could.

The captain of the city guard leaned on the parapet beside her. "Who's that? Conory? I thought I just saw him in the market square."

"No," said Rhian as the truth dawned on her. "No, that's not Conory." She had turned already, running toward the ladder, barely touching the rungs as she flew down.

Mabon was still on the wall, calling out to her—then he saw what she had seen. His great voice lifted in a bellow. "Emry! *Emry!*"

He swung right down off the wall, rolling as he landed, running headlong toward the rider on the road. But Rhian was ahead of him. She was lighter and quicker, and she had recognized Emry first.

He had stopped his horse and dismounted before either of them reached him. Rhian knocked him flat. Mabon hauled him up and hugged the breath out of him, babbling his name.

Rhian was hardly more coherent, but she had enough wits left to pry Mabon loose before he killed Emry with gladness. Emry stood swaying. His face was blank.

Slowly it came alive. "Mabon," he said, as if the name had come to him out of old memory. "Rhian." He paused. "Rhian?"

"Yes," she said. "Yes. Come, you look as if you haven't eaten or slept in days. Your father will be—"

"My father is alive?"

"And as well as he ever was," Mabon said.

"I thought—" Emry swayed again. "I heard—*she*—"

"He is safe from her," Rhian said grimly.

As if that had cut the cord that was holding him up, Emry collapsed. Mabon caught him, grunting as he steadied his feet: Emry was not a small man.

But as Mabon braced to lift him, Emry fought free. "I will not," he said fiercely, "I will *not* go to my father like a child in arms. Let me walk!"

"Better than that," Rhian said. "You'll ride. Up with you, and come."

Even after a hand of years as a tribesman, Emry was obedient to a woman's voice. He mounted like a rider of the steppe, with ease that was altogether unconscious.

People were gathering. They had heard Mabon's bellow—that must have been audible in World's End.

With the courtesy of Lir, they did not crowd or clamor, but the murmur of their excitement followed him to the king's house. Some recognized him. Others insisted that it must be one of his brothers; but they could hardly deny that his fashion was not the fashion of Lir.

Rumor had wings. The king met them outside his house, all dignity forgotten, and all sense that might have bidden him mistrust anything less than the sight of his eyes. But for Emry he would even forget that he was king.

They were so very like, the two of them: big beautiful men. The king did not speak his son's name, not aloud. Nor did Emry say a word to his father. They closed in a long embrace. Maybe they wept. Not even Rhian, who was closest, could see. They might have been alone in the world, for all the notice they took of the crowd about them.

They went arm in arm into the king's house. The people loosed a long sigh. There was still no Mother in Lir, but with the king's heir returned, some of the heart had come back into the city.

⇢ ⇠

Emry ate ravenously and drank watered wine to bolster his strength, but he would not rest. "I need to see—I need to know—everything. Some things I heard as I came here, and many things I saw, but there's still so much—"

"Tomorrow," his father said. "Today is for joy. Tomorrow we'll think again of war."

Emry might have defied his father, but he was both too wise and too weary to venture it. His brothers were all there, his friends, his kin, as many of the king's council and his warleaders as were in Lir or able to come there. They filled the hall, all watching him, all hungry for the sight of him.

Whatever he had expected to feel when he came home again, it was not what he felt, which was nothing. Somewhere, dim and far away, he knew that he should be singing with joy. The Goddess had brought him home safe, unwounded, uncaptured, and no more hungry or tired or filthy than he should be after riding straight from World's End. His father was alive. There was no taste or smell of Etena here, no taint of her in anything that he saw. And the war—they were ready; splendidly so.

He had come looking for death and disaster, and found life and strength. He should be profoundly happy. He was only empty.

People were talking, laughing, easing into the pleasure of his presence. When silence fell, it fell slowly, until it was complete.

Emry followed their eyes—but Rhian's most of all, a stare as fierce and swift as the stoop of a hawk. Someone new had come to the hall, and paused in the doorway, as if taken aback by the crowd within. It was a man with a child in his arms.

He had changed very little. Except about the eyes. Those were old in the young face, as old as the world.

Emry was a little dizzy, looking at him. A prince of the People held a child—girlchild, no less—as if he had been a man of Lir. She looked like him, but her hair was dark, her skin cream instead of milk. Emry did not need to ask who her mother was.

She wriggled until Minas set her down, and trotted into the hall, altogether unperturbed by the crowd that filled it.

She stopped in front of Emry and looked him up and down. "You look just like all your brothers," she said. "But I like your clothes better. May I sit in your lap?"

Emry opened his arms. She clambered up, made herself comfortable. "You smell different."

"That's the air of the tribes," Emry said. And after a moment: "You have a name, I suppose?"

"Ariana," she said.

"Ariana," he said, inclining his head. "And I am Emry."

"I like your name," she said. She nestled against him, as comfortable as a young thing could be, tucked her thumb into her mouth and seemed well content.

He was . . . almost content. With a child's warmth in his arms, he was closer to the world of the living.

Her father wavered transparently between advance and retreat. But he was a warrior of the steppe; he had to conquer whatever troubled him. He strode into the hall, putting a swagger in it. The seat he chose was near the king and the king's son. People granted him respect; some smiled.

He had done well for himself, for a prisoner and a slave. But there were those eyes, and a bitter set to the mouth as he refrained from looking at Rhian.

Emry knew that bitterness, oh yes. The pain beneath it, too. His clasped Minas' child—his sister-daughter, his wife's grandchild—in his arms and rocked, as he would have done with one of his own. Both his daughters were very like her.

He gave in not long after to his father's urging that he rest. He did not need to feign the weariness, either. Exhaustion dragged at his bones.

But it was not to his own chamber that he went, that they had kept ready for him. One of the servants was pleased enough to tell him where the tribesman slept—"Lord Minas," she called him, with the same air of respect that he had received in the hall. That was a feat for a foreigner, to win not only courtesy in Lir, but also the goodwill of its people.

Was Minas not Aera's son? She was lady and queen wherever she was.

The room was empty. The shutters were fastened open, letting in light and air. There were few furnishings, but a mingling of belongings. The walls glowed with bronze: bits, bridles, blades and hilts and spearheads, and a sunburst of ornaments, some of remarkable delicacy.

Emry was examining these when Minas came into the room. Two burly men loomed behind him, dressed in the manner of the king's guard. One stayed by the door; the other settled by the window.

Emry raised his brows at them. "You've lived so for five years?"

"Five days," Minas said. "Since I ran for the river."

"Ah," said Emry. Carefully he lifted a brooch from the wall, turning it in his fingers. It was intricately, beautifully inlaid with bits of colored stone, all shades of green like a field in summer. "You do wonderful work."

"*That* is work," Minas said, tilting his head at a row of spearheads. "This is play."

"It's a joyous thing."

Minas folded his arms and propped himself against the wall, as insolent a young buck as had ever strutted through a war-camp. "They let you go," he said.

He was keeping the grievance out of his voice, but Emry caught the hint of it nonetheless. "No," Emry said. "I ran, too. They were busy crossing the river; no one hunted me once I reached the western bank. Not with a whole kingdom to conquer."

Minas' glance raked him. "You've done well. For a slave."

"King's charioteer," Emry said.

Minas laughed, a sharp bark. "Oh, indeed!"

"Truth," said Emry.

"Remarkable," Minas said. "But then I build chariots for your king. I'm sure the gods are amused."

"The Goddess finds balance in all things."

"So they say." Minas rubbed his chin, which he still kept shaven in this land of bearded men. "Are you here for a reason? Do you have messages?"

"Not exactly," Emry said. "Your brother is well. He knows you live. He's glad beyond measure, and determined to win you back."

"Is he?"

"To the very heart of him," said Emry.

"*You* never told him."

"I never knew for certain. They found ashes and ruin, and no trace of any living thing."

Minas grunted. "You stayed. Why? The bargain was a mockery. I was presumed dead. You could have run home again."

"Yes," Emry said.

Minas' eyes narrowed. "What are you afraid to tell me? Is it my mother? Is she dead?"

"Dear Goddess, no." It was as much a prayer as a denial. "She was well when I left the camp."

Minas' relief was palpable. "Good. Good, then. She's looking after Dias' tent, I suppose, and ruling his wives. That would suit her very well."

"No," Emry said. "She has a tent of her own."

"Metos? She looks after Metos?"

"Not she," said Emry.

"She married again?" Minas' voice was incredulous. Angry? Emry could not tell.

Emry answered with a nod.

"King? Warleader? Clan-chieftain?"

"King's charioteer," Emry said.

The silence was enormous. Minas was not a fool, and he was not at all slow in the wits. "*You—*"

He laughed loud and long. He fell down doing it, clutching his middle, rolling and kicking. He howled like a mad thing.

Emry waited him out. It was better than what he had expected, which was a knife in the gut.

When he surged up, still howling, Emry was ready for him. So was the guard by the window. Between them they wrestled him to a standstill; and a fierce battle it was, too. The years in Lir had done nothing to lessen Minas' skill or his strength.

When at last he lay flat, breathing hard, Emry said mildly, "Yes, I. I earned the right to ask for her. They made songs of it. You have sisters, prince, and a brother."

"Don't lie to me," Minas said, flat and hard. "She was barren after she bore me."

"The Goddess blessed her," Emry said, "and made her fruitful."

"She is old enough to be your mother!"

"So she used to say," Emry said, "until she saw how little it mattered."

"You stayed for her." Minas had gone limp, but neither Emry nor the bull of a guard trusted that. He ignored them both. "You—stayed—"

"For her," said Emry, "and for Dias."

"For her." Minas gasped. It might have been laughter again. It might have been a sob. "Gods. My sides hurt. Maybe I am dead, and this is a particularly clever torment."

Emry nodded to the guard. The man rose reluctantly, but stayed close.

Minas made no effort to renew his attack on either of them. He lay where they had left him, sprawled on the floor. "You left her," he said.

"She sent me away. Because," said Emry out of all the pain in his heart, "I knew you lived, and I let her grieve for you."

Minas grinned with utter lack of mirth. "Serves you right," he said.

Emry bent his head to the justice of that.

"I do not accept you as my father," Minas said. "If you demand it, I will challenge you. I will probably win. Your people are very brave, but none of them teethed on the bones of an enemy."

"No," Emry granted him. "I'm not your father, or stepfather either. But we are kin. You are my sister's man, and I am your mother's. Our children share the same blood."

"We are enemies," Minas said flatly.

"Kin can be the worst enemies of all," said Emry.

"My brother loves you," Minas said. It seemed he had to say it, to begin to understand it. "My mother . . . loves you. She would never take a foreign husband else. Is it a spell? Do you have your mother's powers after all? Did you think you could destroy us?"

"I am not Etena," Emry said.

"No," said Minas. "You are not. Your people have more strength to resist her than mine do. You submit to women as if it were a natural thing. Her greatest power is to take men by surprise, and rule them who never expected to be ruled by a woman. Those who expect it seem proof against her spell."

"I hear that she has taken the temple and set it against my father."

"The temple was set against your father before she ever came to plague it."

"Poor Etena," Emry said. "She'll never rule the world."

"You think so?"

"I pray so."

"We can all pray," Minas said. He yawned and stretched. "Will you take the bed? I'll sleep on the floor."

Emry grinned. "I have a bed of my own. And five years' absence to make up for."

"Then you had better make up for it."

Emry was still smiling as he sought his own place. The familiar passage, the door, the room with its treasures of a life he had almost forgotten, struck him strangely after the lash of Minas' wit.

It was only when he had shut the door that it struck him. He was feeling again. Aera's son had opened his heart that she had closed so deathly tight.

72

This was not such a country as the People had conquered before. Instead of camps of tribes and clans, they faced chains of cities, and forts of wood or stone perched like eagles on crags.

But Dias was possessed. He would, he must, find his brother in the great city. Instead of taking the towns, he took the river and the road beside it.

The enemy had never thought that the charioteers would sail up the river in boats, or take nothing but the riverbank and leave the towns untouched unless they had need of provisions. Then raiders would swoop down, seize what they needed, and take to the river again.

The People were as disconcerted as the enemy. "We are not boatmen!" they had cried when he gave them their orders.

But his will was firm, and he would hear nothing that stood against it. He mounted a hill above them and called to them in a great voice. "Come with me! Do what the People have never done before. This country is prepared for us—for what we've always been. Let us astonish them. Let us ambush them. Let us conquer them as they never looked to be conquered."

He won them. Quiet Dias had lit with a fire that swept them all before him.

They passed by the citadel of World's End on its crag, took the boats on the quays below, and the boatmen with them, and thrust toward less strongly defended cities. Wherever they could take boats, they took them, and shipped warriors in them, and chariots, and even horses.

Two days past World's End, having driven back a force that rode out from the stronghold to harry them, they found what they needed: a city on a level of the river, and a crowded mass of boats in its quays. Many had fled from downstream; more seemed to have sought refuge there. There were enough to make a great army on the water; and Dias meant to take them.

First they took the walled city by storm, broke down its walls by sheer force of numbers. Against arrows from above they had shields that Metos had shown them how to make, hide stretched over woven withies and sealed tight and hard. From beneath these they shot arrows tipped with fire. The city's wall was wood; for all its people could do, it burned.

Aera was among the chariots that drove through the burned and broken wall, close behind the mass of mounted warriors who had done the breaking. In the confusion of war, she had found it remarkably easy to vanish among the warriors. She was tall for a woman, and spare; with her breasts bound tight and her hair braided like a man's, she roused no one's suspicions. There were so many men here, of so many tribes; so many of them now followed Dias' fashion of shaving the beard. Who, after all, would look for a woman among the fighting men of the People?

She rode in the warrior's place behind a young man of the Red Falcon clan, whose name was Vatis. Vatis had a gift with horses, and could get his chariot and his team of red mares in where no one else could go. Aera was no great warrior, but spear and war-club took little enough skill. She could leave the finer arts to the bowmen and swordsmen, keep her charioteer alive and beat back enemies who rode or ran howling toward the chariot. It was all any warrior needed to do.

It was remarkably satisfying. The men with their black beards reminded her vividly of Emry—she took a grim pleasure in overwhelming them. The women, who were as likely to be armed and in armor as the men, fought much more viciously. Against them she was fighting for her life.

And yet it was clear to her that most of the enemy were not fighters. Those that were, were spread thin. The rest fought as they could, with little skill. Soft people, gentle people, not only unused to killing, but often incapable of doing it. The blows they struck swung wide or came down feebly. They were striking to wound or maim. They were not striking to kill.

Emry could kill, and had. He was a warrior, a king's son. But he had never danced with the others about the heaps of slain, nor would he drink from a skull-cup, though he had earned a king's treasury of them.

He was a gentle man. Soft? Yes. But hard too, and cruel in ways that she had never understood until that last day.

These people were simply soft. They had courage, but not enough to sustain them against the People. The People truly did not care if they died. These people did, profoundly. They loved life too much to be eager to leave it.

She had been striking blindly. Now she struck with intent, to kill, and kill quickly. The chariot lurched and rolled over bits of wall and fallen bodies. The mounted men were piling to a halt, as herdsmen will when the flock was driven tight together. Arrows rained down from rooftops. Flames leaped up: part of the city was burning.

A city was too close, too crowded for chariots. They needed open land, and room to move, to turn. They drew back while they still had room, leaving horsemen to finish taking the city, and came together on the field. Dias was there, grinning a wild battle-grin. Aera could see what anyone with eyes could see: that the enemy had taken the bait. All their fighters were trapped in the city. The road by the river was clear, and the way open to the boats.

They thundered down the road or on the grassy verge, whooping, yelling, singing. There was a guard on the boats, but it was a pitiful few. Could they truly not understand what Dias was doing? Could they not turn their minds from defense of their cities, and move to defend the river?

A woman launched herself at the chariot, shrieking something in her own language. She had a spear with a long bronze head. She stabbed with it, aiming at Vatis, at his hands that held the reins. Aera raised a sharp light lance, sighting along it, measuring the distance to the woman's heart. Time slowed. Her thoughts were clear. Bronze was deadly, but fire-hardened wood, sharpened to a needle's edge and aimed by a cold eye, was just as dangerous. She thrust the lance home.

The woman died in a state of perfect astonishment. Aera met her eyes as the life poured out of her. She was no killer, no more than the rest of her people. It seemed almost an affront to her, that Aera was.

⇒ ⇐

They found not only boats in that place, but a vast store of provisions in wooden houses that some of the young warriors nearly burned, but wiser eyes stopped them. They took the provisions — much of which consisted of fodder for horses: truly a gift of the gods — and burned the storehouses after, loaded the boats and pressed the boatmen into service and went on up the river.

Some of the People were beginning to understand about boats. Young charioteers, riders and warriors, took to the smooth flow of the water, and the art of skimming over it, even in boats laden down with horses and cargo. They made a contest of rowing against the current, testing strength against strength, and learning quickly that if they did not all pull together, they tangled their oars and overset the boat.

Aera would have preferred to stay on land. But after they had taken that trove of boats, Dias divided the horde. More than half it, he set free to raid and pillage wherever they pleased, as long as they kept moving toward Lir. The rest, all that could ride in boats, aimed straight for the city.

The river that had been such a terror for so long, was now their best friend and ally. The land was in turmoil; riders and chariots swarming over it, attacking in a score of different places at once. The defenders could not gather, could not focus in a single battle. There were too many tribes and clans, too many raids, too many towns to protect.

There was little enough fighting on the river. When they passed forts on the crags, arrows would rain down, or flights of stones, but never enough, and seldom along the farther bank. Sometimes boats would come at them, full of armed fighters. None of those had shields. Archers could pick them off at will, or if they eluded those, men in smaller, lighter boats would surround them and overwhelm them and take their boat.

Dias loved the river. He rode in a boat that was narrower than most, with a higher prow, graceful on the water like a swan. Aera found ways to be on that boat, even as perilous as it could be if he or one of his warband recognized her. But no one was looking for the king's foster-mother in the company of his warriors.

She kept to the stern, crowded in with boys who would never have known her face, and watched him. He smiled often. She had not seen him do that since Minas lived among the People. Even when his men grumbled, complaining that all the fighting was on land and there was nothing for them here, he only laughed. "You'll have all the fighting you could wish for, once you come to Lir. That I promise you."

Lir was coming closer. There were more forts, more strongly guarded. There were archers on the banks, and once a fleet of boats moored together from bank to bank. That was a strange battle, rocking and swaying, fighting as much against the water as against the enemy.

As the fight engaged, an army swarmed out of the wood along the bank, aiming for the first of the boats. Aera raised her voice in a shrill of warning, a fierce ululating cry that stopped every man of them cold.

Aias was riding in a boat like Dias', a little apart from the rest of them. He snapped an order to his men. They dug in oars, beating toward the bank. Their boat wallowed for long enough that Aera's heart was in her throat; then suddenly it leaped across the water. Aias and a handful of others in the bow drew swords and knives. Under cover of archers from behind, they fell on the third or fourth boat from the bank, hacking at the ropes that bound it to its fellows.

There were only a few men in it. The army was still running toward the bank. Aias hurled two of the defenders into the water in one great heave. His fellows disposed of the rest, sometimes bloodily.

The boat broke free. The current caught it and whirled it about. The boats on either side, no longer anchored, fell prey to the current.

The army had lost its bridge. The chain of boats was easy enough prey, as lightly manned as it was; and the bindings that had made it so dangerous, now were its downfall. Boats bound together could not maneuver, could not escape the swarm of attackers.

⇥ ⇤

"A dozen new boats," Dias said in satisfaction. They rowed by night, choosing not to camp as they had before. The bank was too thick now with towns and forts. They stayed on the river, rowing more slowly, taking shifts so that everyone could rest.

Dias was well pleased with the day's work. His hands were still wet from washing; he had addressed a captive just now, learned what the man knew, then cut his throat and flung him overboard. The man had bled a great deal. Dias had washed off most of the blood; one or two of his warband were still scrubbing it from the boat.

He perched on a heap of baggage almost on top of Aera, and smiled at the moon. "Three days," he said, "and we come to Lir."

"Three days if no one stops us." Aias' boat came up beside Dias', matching pace with it. They had all learned to do that without fouling oars or capsizing boats.

Dias folded his arms on the rim of his own boat and grinned at his friend. "You think anyone will?"

"I think there may be other traps upstream," Aias said. "A scout came in—hailed us from the bank, and we pulled him aboard. Sirtis' clan is dead. They ran into an ambush, took a town that seemed to have no defenders—but there was an army hiding in the hills. They're all gone, to the last man."

"All of them? The scout?"

"Died telling it."

Dias gave that a moment's silence. But the loss only fed his wild humor. "So: the women can fight after all. Good! I was afraid this would be too easy."

Aias grinned back at him. "We've lopped off a limb or two, but now we're coming to the heart. They'll fight for that. I let off a handful of riders, sent them to see what they can see. They're all from White Horse country: dark-haired men with beards. With luck they won't be suspected before they come back to us."

"Wise man," Dias said. And then: "We'll stay on the river as long as we can. There's a place a day's ride from the city—a ford; the western goddess came from there. It has a landing, and open fields. Maybe a fort, but not likely a large one. We'll land there, most of us, but send the rest onward, to let the enemy think that's all of us."

"They can count horses," Aias pointed out.

"Can they? Do they know we brought them—or that we even could?"

They both looked back down the line of the fleet to the barges in which the horses rode. The shamans were with them. The drone of chanting was fainter than it had been when they began. Most of the horses had grown resigned to their fate; those that had proved intractable were long since killed and eaten.

"Those who go up the river will need horses when they land," Dias said. "We'll be sure those are clear to see."

"Wise king." Aias was mocking him, but gently. Dias aimed a cuff at him, which he eluded with ease.

The boats drifted apart. Dias returned to his favored place in the bow, face uplifted to the moon, as if he drank strength from it. He was smiling still. Nothing could sadden him, not now, not since he knew that Minas lived.

Aera curled in the stern and shut her eyes. Her back was against Vatis', her knees propped against the hull of the boat. It was not particularly comfortable, but she had slept in worse places.

But sleep did not come at once. Her mind was too wide awake. She knew where Dias had learned of the ford—Long Ford; she remembered the name of it rather more clearly than he did. But then she had heard all of Emry's stories, some over and over.

No one had spoken of Emry since the People crossed the river. Not a word, though anyone who knew him would know where he had gone. If he lived, if he had not been killed on the journey, he was in Lir. As Minas was. Both of them in one city. Both waiting for the war to fall upon them.

Emry could tell his people much. But everything Dias had done after he left—could he have predicted that? Not even Aera had expected them to take to the river. Dias was less simple a man than anyone had thought, and more distinctly a king.

73

"They've taken to the river."

The king was not as appalled as the rest of his council. He could admire a truly clever mind, even if it belonged to an enemy. He bent his glance on Emry, who sat beside him. "Did you know he would do that?"

"I'm not even sure he did, until he'd done it." Emry shook his head. "Who'd have thought it?"

"Certainly not I," the king said ruefully. "We built all our defenses on land, against an enemy who has never been seen on water."

"We do need those defenses," said Mabon. "He's unleashed the tribes; they're raiding wherever they will, from World's End to Larchwood. There's rumor of raiders closer even than that, but nothing certain yet. We can't gather forces for any single battle. There are too many, in too many places, too far apart."

"He's coming here," Emry said.

Nobody seemed to hear him. The council had erupted at Mabon's words. The whole country was overrun; they were on the knife-edge of panic. There had never been a war like this. There had been no war at all here since before their grandfathers were born.

Amid the overlapping voices, one spoke for them all. "How can we fight this? They're on us like a swarm of bees."

"Kill the king."

That caught their attention. The babble of confusion stopped.

Emry faced them all. "Bees swarm at the command of their king. Their king is coming to Lir. His brother is here; likewise his mother, who is the cause of all his sorrows."

"And his good fortune, too," Mabon observed. "If not for her and her trading, he'd never have been king."

"So," said the king of Lir. "He's coming here. We're ready for him. With his horde divided, our cities are endangered—but we're also safer than we would be if the whole of them came on together. We don't have to face the whole horde; the army he brings here may be no larger than ours."

"If he's wise, he'll call them back in before he reaches us," Emry said. "But these are wild tribes, some so barely tamed that they still fight with clubs and stones. Now they've had the taste of blood, they may not obey the call to muster."

"Let's give them more blood," said a woman in a long kilt like a priestess'; but she spoke and carried herself like a soldier. "Give them as many diversions as they can swallow—order all towns and forts that can to mount attacks against the raiders. Keep them busy, so that when the summons comes, even if they want to answer it, they can't."

"That's well thought of," said the king. "Do you see to it, then. We'll scatter the swarm till there's no hope of its coming together again."

The heart had come back into the council. Amid the hum of their interwoven conversations, settling this and that, Emry heard a sound that raised his hackles.

There was buzz and bustle enough in Lir, these days, with the city full of fighters and preparations for fighting. But this was a different sound. Many feet coming on swiftly. Clash of metal. A cry, abruptly cut off.

He was out of his seat and halfway to the door when the invaders burst through it. They were all women, and armed. There was blood on some of the swords. Servants' blood, he could suppose. Guards' blood.

He stopped short. An arrow was aimed straight at his heart, and a pair of cold black eyes behind it.

The council had gone absolutely still. None of them was armed. Their weapons were laid outside. There was not even a knife for cutting meat.

The king's voice spoke behind him, deceptively soft. "What is the meaning of this?"

His answer came from behind the warrior priestesses. She was dressed in black, and veiled. She led a small veiled figure by the hand. Priestesses followed her, elders whom Emry knew well. "Take him," she said to the armed women on either side of her.

Emry heard the rustle and scrape as the king rose. "I will not be—"

A bowstring sang. Emry whipped about—no matter if he took an arrow in the back. His father's eyes were wide. An arrow sprouted from his heart. It pulsed once, hard, as he toppled across the council-table.

Councilors scrambled back in horror, all but Mabon and one or two of the captains. It was Emry who cradled him in his arms, and Emry whom he saw as the life ebbed from him. He reached up, groping as if in the dark, and laid his hand against Emry's cheek. Emry held it there long after the warmth had gone out of it.

That warmth, that fire of spirit, had entered into Emry. The last breath his father drew, Emry drew with him. King to prince. Prince to king.

He looked up in the terrible silence. Somewhat to his surprise, no arrow flew. When the invaders moved, they did not move to slay him. They took his father from his arms. He fought—but they were many and he was one, and those who would have helped him had swords at their throats.

Him, for whatever reason, they needed alive. They bound and gagged him and held him still struggling, while Etena sat in the king's place. Her daughter perched on the arm of the tall chair, as small and big-eyed as a bird.

"My lords and ladies and captains," Etena said when she was settled in comfort, "you have a choice. You may go as your king has gone, or you may accept the will of the Goddess. We need you and the forces you command, but we can manage without you. Which will it be? Life and acceptance? Or a quick death?"

"What will you do with him?" Mabon demanded, tilting his head at Emry.

"He will live," Etena answered.

"As your creature?"

"As whatever he elects to be. Our ally or our enemy. He has wife and kin among the tribes. That will serve our purpose. And you? Will you live or die?"

Emry willed him to live. He was a stubborn, headstrong, unshakably loyal man, and he wept freely and unconsciously for his king. But thank the Goddess, he had a little sense. He said, "I live for Lir, and for my young king."

Emry's knees tried to buckle with relief. He stiffened them. They all took Mabon's example, however grudgingly they did it. They chose life.

Etena was well pleased. "Even men may be wise," she said. "Listen now. Your fealty is to the Goddess, and to the Goddess' servants. You will do as we bid, exactly, without objection, without question. Now go. One of mine will go with each of you. She speaks my will; she carries out my orders. Obey and all will be well. Disobey, and you die."

The councilors glanced at one another. There was great shame in them, to be conquered without a battle, and bound in service to a stranger.

They were alive. That for now was all that mattered. Emry tried to reassure them with his eyes, since his mouth was bound shut. None of them would look at him, except Mabon; and Mabon's despair was so deep that Emry doubted he saw anything beyond it.

They left—fled, some of them. Only Emry remained, and the company of priestesses, and what clearly was the new council of Lir.

Etena looked long at him, taking great pleasure in the fact that she could do such a thing. Emry stood as much at ease as he could, gagged and with his hands bound tight behind him; yet he was poised, light, ready to leap. Such a leap would be his death, but he would do it if he must.

Maybe she hoped that he would. Lir would not lack for a king. He had six brothers, and a son among the tribes.

She smiled in her veils and said, "Oh no, young king. Don't do that. We want you alive. You're wonderfully useful: king's heir, king of Lir, king's charioteer of the People. If you'll be reasonable, we'll stand at your back when you take your kingship before the people. If not . . . what would Dias give, I wonder, for the man who was friend and brother, who abandoned him at the border of this country?"

Emry, gagged, could not answer. But she was not looking for conversation. She flicked a hand. "Take him away."

⇒ ⇐

They locked him in his own chamber, bound but freed of the gag. He had half a dozen guards to the two that his father had set on Minas. He supposed he should be flattered—and concerned for the prince of chariots, who might not live long now that Etena ruled in Lir.

Emry lay on his bed. The coldness that had been on him since Aera cast him out was his protection now. Far beneath it he howled with grief for his father. His father, his brothers, his people—all of Lir. Fools, every one of them, for letting her live, for dreaming that she would keep quietly to the temple.

Anger flared and faded. He would wait, he thought, until dark; he would sleep. He would let his captors think him resigned to his fate. And then . . .

What? Something mad or stupid, that would get him conveniently killed?

He groaned and rolled onto his face. Maybe he wept. He took no particular notice. Nor did he care if his guards saw. The weaker he seemed, the better.

⇒ ⇐

Minas was in the workroom with a handful of the makers when the warrior-priestesses came, finishing the last chariot that he intended to build in Lir. He had been rather surprised not to find Eresh perched on the stool in the corner, telling stories, as he invariably did when he was in the city. Maybe he had found people willing to trade even with the People so close.

The priestesses burst in as if charging into battle, swords drawn, arrows nocked to string. They bowled over Lathan, who was nearest the door, and hacked at him when he protested. He lay twitching, head half severed from neck, bleeding out his life on the floor.

The rest of the makers retreated, drawing back behind Minas. Wise fools. These women had come for him, he had no doubt of that. Their leader was the same who had taken him in flight. He could suppose that his guards were dead, since she was here, with blood on her blade; and she had not been the one to kill poor Lathan.

He smiled at her with all the charm at his disposal, and held out his hands for her to bind. She gripped them tightly. One of her women, thick-armed and cold-eyed, lifted a war-club with a bronze head. He sighed faintly. Death, then; and quick. That was well.

The club lashed out. He felt no pain, not then. But his legs no longer held him up.

A slow death, after all, he thought distantly. His legs were broken. One knee, he thought, was shattered. When the pain came, it would be exquisite, a thousand splintered shards of it.

Two of the priestesses heaved him up. He made himself as heavy as a stone. They grunted at the weight of him, but forbore to drop him. Neither they nor their captain granted him the mercy-stroke. The woman with the club had put it away, perhaps with some regret.

"I would have preferred to give you death," the captain said. "But those are not my orders."

"The king," said Minas. "Dead?"

"By now, yes."

Minas let his head roll on his neck. The pain was coming like a storm across the steppe, a black cloud of it, shot with lightnings. *Ariana,* he thought. Dear gods. She was the daughter of the daughter of a Mother.

If he did not name her, maybe they would not think of her. Maybe she was safe.

He was losing his wits. It was pain. He knew how to endure it: he was a warrior of the People. But it clouded his thoughts; it reduced him to silence.

Better silence than shrieking and begging for mercy.

They carried him to the small room that opened off the workroom. It was meant for storing the makers' tools. There was a pallet in it, for when one of them—often Minas—labored through the night.

They laid him on the pallet, not too roughly. What could he do? their manner said. He was crippled.

He showed them. He drooped and dragged and let them struggle with the dead weight of him. And while he did that, he slipped a dagger from its sheath, concealing it against his arm. The cold bite of it was welcome.

They arranged him on the pallet as if he had been a stiffened corpse. One bent just a little too close. The bronze blade slipped sweetly home in her heart. The other was not even aware that she had died, until she crumpled on top of Minas. Even then the second was not sensible enough to stay out of reach. She tugged at her sister-priestess, freeing Minas' hand.

This blow was not so sure, nor so strong. It struck low and jerked upward, ragged, catching on bone. She, fool to the last, started and twisted, driving the dagger into her own heart.

She fell across Minas' legs. He keened with pain. The knife was caught between them, lodged in her breastbone.

Through the red darkness of agony, he saw a shadow that was the captain, and other shadows behind her. They lifted the terrible weight from his legs. They bound his hands and jerked them sharply above his head, a punishment so petty that he would have laughed, if there had been any laughter in him. They tied him to the post that held up the roof. And they left him, as if they no longer cared whether he lived or died.

Death would be a pleasant thing. Etena would not like it. She wanted him alive and maimed. A maimed man could not be king.

Would she break Dias' legs, too, when he came? Or cut off his manly parts? Minas was rather surprised to have kept his. Maybe she had a use for them.

Etena. Slayer of kings, destroyer of worlds. There was a god from long and long ago, a name Minas had forgotten. He had a consort, lady of blood and slaughter.

Minas drifted inside the shell of his body, in a fiery ring of pain. Darkness was in the heart of it, and coolness. And eyes. Glowing beast-eyes. Wolf-eyes.

Phaiston the shaman looked at him out of the center of his self. For once the wolf was not laughing. Was it even possible that he wept? He did not say anything. After a while he stood up on four legs and flicked his tail and went away. Then the darkness was complete, except for the black-red glow of pain.

74

Gerent found Rhian at the farthest edge of Lir, down by the river, overseeing the breaking of piers and the scuttling of boats. She had made a contest of it, with the party that scuttled their boat the fastest to win a skin of southern wine. They went at it with a grand good will, and no cringing of fear; in laughter and singing, and a bright air of defiance.

She saw her brother running down the road, darting past a company of soldiers, hurdling a heap of fishing-nets. It was not unusual for Gerent to run; Gerent was swift-footed and proud of it, and he often ran messages from the king's house.

But as he came closer, the look on his face made her stand up slowly, rising from the bollard from which she had been overseeing the contest. He was stark white, and his eyes were as black as his hair. She had never seen such an expression on a human face.

He might have run right into the river, if she had not caught him. The force of his speed spun them both about.

For a long while he could only stand there, stiff in her hands, breathing hard. Then she said, "Tell me."

He blinked. A little life came back into his eyes. "The king is dead," he said.

Rhian gasped as if he had struck a blow to her middle.

"*She* sits in the king's place," Gerent said. "Priestesses hold the king's house."

Rhian found a word to speak. Only one, but it was a very important word. "Emry?"

"Alive. Imprisoned. The others were out in the city, thank the Goddess. Except me; somehow they overlooked me. I got out. The council— they're alive. He wanted that. Emry. Father—Father would have—if—"

He was close to breaking, but he held himself together. Rhian gripped his shoulders. "Ariana?"

"I don't know. I didn't see her."

Rhian could not break, either. There was one last name she must speak. "Minas?"

Again Gerent said, "I don't know. I came from the hall. He was with the chariots, I know that; I saw him there before council."

She could hardly fault him for his failures. He was in shock. He had thought to come to her, at least. "Gerent," she said carefully, and for his ear alone. "Find Mabon. Be careful; don't let anyone catch you. Find him and bring him to me. I'll be with the mare's herd, up in the north pasture. Be sure that no one sees either of you, either going or coming. Can you do that?"

Gerent nodded jerkily. As she had hoped, her orders steadied him. He had a task; a purpose. He could focus on that. Maybe it would keep the horror at bay.

She turned to the people who watched. They all stood staring, struck dumb. "Finish it," she said to them. "For the king's sake, for the love you bore him, for any hope you have for this city—finish what you've begun."

She did not wait to see if they obeyed. Gerent was already gone. She set off at the run, letting them see her go toward the king's house; but when she was out of sight, she turned toward the north, out of the city and toward the high pastures.

The mare was there, grazing with her sisters, looking as if she had been there since the world began. Rhian had not seen her since that day in the mist, four days' ride to the eastward. For a long while it was enough just to cling to that sleek white neck and smell the familiar smell of grass and wind and horse. Then the mare stamped at a fly, and one of her sisters squealed at the stallion, and the world was back again, black-edged with grief.

Her father was dead. Etena had killed him. What fools they all had been, dreaming that because that daughter of the dark gods had done nothing for a handful of years, she would continue to do nothing. She had been biding her time. She was a great master of that. Had she not proved it among the tribes?

It was a long while before Mabon came climbing up the steep slope. Rhian had dried her tears. She was sitting on a stone in the sun, just beyond the mare, listening to the wind. It had no gossip in it today; its song was a keen.

Mabon's face was as blankly shocked as her own must be. But he had Ariana in his arms, and she was quiet but her eyes were clear. He came up beside Rhian and sat in the grass. Ariana slid from his lap to Rhian's, clasped arms about her mother's neck and held tight.

It was all Rhian could do not to crush the breath out of her. She was safe, whole—alive.

Mabon's voice startled her; for a moment she had forgotten he was there. "I can't stay long," he said. "It was all I could do to get out unseen. They're hunting for her—for you both."

"Where was she?" asked Rhian.

"I was with Eresh," Ariana answered for herself. "He was telling me stories. When the priestesses came, he helped me hide. I hid for a long time, even after he went away. Then Mabon came and got me."

"And glad I was to find you, little bird," he said, ruffling her tumbled curls. To Rhian he said, "There's no safe place for you anywhere in Lir. I've left a pack down below, with everything in it that you're likely to need."

"Where will we go?" Rhian demanded of him. "And what of our kin, our friends? Her father?"

A catch in Mabon's breath made Rhian go still, except for the tightening of her arms about Ariana. The child squawked in protest. Rhian barely heard. "Minas is dead," she said.

"No," said Mabon. But his voice was strange. He would not look at her.

Rhian drew a steady breath, and then another. "What has she done to him?"

Mabon's eyes closed. His back was rigid. "He's still alive. He's still a man."

"*What did she do to him?*"

Mabon told her, very simply, very starkly. "Eresh the foreigner found him. Thank the Goddess, the man has sense. He sent for a bonesetter in the city, and for a miracle she was willing to come — and for a greater miracle, none of *her* servants was there to stop her. She did what she could. Is still doing it, I suppose."

"How bad?" Rhian could hardly say the words, but say them she must. "How badly broken is he?"

"Badly," Mabon said. "But the bonesetter is the best in Lir. If anyone can heal him, she can."

"He'll want to die," Rhian said. "He's not a tame thing. He endures this cage because of me — because I'm here. He — "

"And me!" Ariana broke in. "He stays for me. He told me."

"And you," her mother agreed. "You set his heart free. But if we go — wherever in the world we can go — he won't want to live."

"You'll die if you go back," Mabon said. "You may matter little to her, but your daughter is the Mother's heir."

"She is not — " But Rhian stopped. Ariana was, as far as anyone could be, heir to the Mother who was dead. And Etena knew it. The whole temple would know.

"I'll do what I can for Minas," Mabon promised her. "I'll keep him alive for you. Now go. They'll be looking here soon; they know as well as anyone, where you're likely to be."

Rhian made up her mind all at once. What she would do; where she would go. It was a terrible thing she would do, but do it she must. Etena and the temple had made sure of that.

Mabon brought the pack up from the lower field. The mare was waiting, conspicuously patient. Rhian settled the pack on her back and mounted the mare. Mabon lifted Ariana up in front of her. "Go with the Goddess," he said.

Rhian stooped and kissed his forehead. "Stay alive for me," she said. "And keep that fool of a man alive. Sane, I won't ask for. Just keep the soul in his body."

"I give you my word," he said.

As the mare began to move, one by one her kin lifted their heads. The stallion pawed extravagantly and shook his mane on his heavy neck. The chief of the mares, as white and old and massive as a mountain under the moon, heaved herself up from where she had been basking in the sun, and called to her children. They came across the field, from coal-black foal to moon-white matron, and took their places ahead of her. With the stallion as outrider and the queen mare to drive them and the living goddess pacing before, the Goddess' hooved children turned their backs on Lir.

Rhian had no part in it. The mare carried her, that was all, and her daughter still and silent in front of her. She willed nothing, commanded nothing. It was all the mare's doing.

The Goddess was with her. What she did, as appalling as it was, she did with the whole of the White Mare's kin behind her.

She closed her eyes and buried her face in her daughter's hair, inhaling the sweet familiar scent. When she lifted her head again, the rise of the hill lay between the herd and the city. What Mabon thought, what expression he had worn as Horse Goddess declared her will, Rhian might never know.

Her heart was burdened down with grief and a terrible anger, but looking back at the herd that followed, Rhian knew a glimmer of hope. If Horse Goddess was with her, then maybe, just maybe, some good would come of this.

75

The village called Long Ford was empty when the People came to it, its inhabitants fled into the hills. There was a fort above it, but no one had troubled to raise it up out of ruin.

There was nothing whatever in the houses, not even a basket of grain. Some of the young men, furious at the lack of plunder, set fire to the village. They burned it to the ground and trampled the ashes underfoot, and rampaged through the fields, beating down such crops as there were, green and small and months from the harvest.

Dias made no move to stop them. He had ordered a camp in the fields upriver of the village, and sent out scouts to reconnoiter between there and Lir. As eager as he was to find his brother again, he had a king's gift of patience.

The day after Long Ford burned, before the scouts had come back, Dias was in among Black Deer clan, which had brought in a trove of grain and cattle from a cluster of villages to the south. They had taken heads, too, twoscore of them, and leather armor and bronze weapons. It was poor plunder, for there was little gold and only a dozen horses, but Dias was glad to have the weapons, and even more than those, the grain and cattle.

Aera had been as close to him as she dared come, among a crowd of hangers-on, but an eddy had caught her and thrust her out toward the edge. There was a hill, a long slope up to the ruined fort. On a whim she climbed to the top. No one else seemed drawn to that vantage. She could see the whole of the camp below, and the long bend of the river, and the boats moored in multitudes. There were villages up and down the river, but from here they were hidden by an arm of forest or a rise of the land.

To the north was another long hill. The scouts had gone over it, spying out the land toward Lir. A hawk was circling above it, lazily, turning on the point of a wing.

She looked where the hawk was looking. At first there was only the curve of the hilltop and the cloud-shot blue of the sky. Then they came up over the hill.

Horses. Grey horses, dark or dappled or white. They had the look of a wild herd from the steppe: tangled manes, long unkempt tails, patches of winter coat still dropping from some of the elders. And yet they gleamed in the sun, moon-silver or white as snow.

So strange was the sight of them, so alien to this settled country, that at first Aera did not even see the riders. The mare who led the rest, a white mare, carried two figures, one larger, one smaller: a woman of this country, black-haired, rich-bodied, and a dark-haired child riding at ease in front of her.

Aera, perched on the height in the sun and the wind, knew in her heart that the Goddess of this country had come riding over the hill from Lir. The mare shone like the moon. The woman's beauty was not mortal. Together they were more real than the world they walked in.

The People had caught sight of them: faces turned, fingers pointed. Men began to run toward the northward end of the camp; but the nearer they came, the slower they ran. The herd came on without pause, in no particular haste, at the pace of the foals and the gravid mares.

There was something about them that made even the wildest of the young men forget his courage. Some remembered, then, the woman and the mare. "The goddess. The western goddess. She came with the traders. She—"

Dias had recognized her before any other. He was on horseback, galloping headlong toward the grey herd and the woman who led it.

Aera had only her feet, but those were swift enough when they had to be. She ran as he rode, with as little conscious thought.

Whether she would kill Rhian or embrace her, she did not know. The child who rode with Rhian was dark like a child of this country, but her face was of the People—was Minas' face, the very lines and shape of it, and his eyes in it, clear green, looking gravely at Aera as she halted in front of the mare.

The child held out her arms. With no more thought than had brought her here, Aera reached for her. Rhian made no effort to stop her. Rhian knew who Aera was; in a country where women wore armor and fought in battle, clothes alone were not enough to hide behind. And Rhian had seen Aera's face before.

Dias pounded to a halt. Aera turned. He did not see her at all, only the child in her arms and the woman on the white mare. "Don't tell me he's dead," he said. "Don't you dare tell me that."

"He's not dead," Rhian said.

There was a stillness in her, an enormous silence beneath the simplicity of her words. She was beyond anger, Aera thought; beyond anything so feeble.

"The White Mare has come to the People of the Wind," Rhian said in their language, clear enough for everyone to hear. "I am her servant. Will you receive me, king of chariots?"

This was a very great thing. How great, Aera did not yet know. Nor Dias, she thought, but he too understood that something profound had changed. "I will receive you, lady of horses," he said.

A horse had come up beside the mare: still young, still dappled, with the high crest and strong jaw of a stallion. His nostrils fluttered, but he offered the mare no other impertinence.

Rhian's glance was unmistakable. Dias was to mount and ride.

No bridle. No saddle. If the stallion had in mind to run away with him or kill him, there would be little he could do.

He laughed and sprang onto the broad moon-colored back. The stallion danced a little and tossed his elegant head. Then, calmly, he stood still.

As if that had been a signal, the herd scattered over the hillside. Mares settled to graze, foals to nurse. The grey herd had come where it wished to go.

Rhian rode with Dias to his tent through the rising excitement of the camp. Word was spreading. "The Goddess has come to us. She gave the king a horse. The Goddess has claimed *us!*"

⇥ ⇤

"Is it true?" Dias asked.

They were in his tent, with its front wall rolled up to let in the sun and to let the People see them, but except for a chieftain or two and a handful of men from the warband, no one could hear what they said. Aera was there because the child insisted on it, and still apparently invisible: she was a pair of arms about the child with Minas' face. People were spreading rumors that this was the lost prince's son, but Aera knew a girlchild when she saw one. Most of the men likely would not: how often after all did they see a female of any age, except in veils or in the shadow of a tent?

Dias asked his question again. "Is it true? Has your Goddess come to us?"

"Horse Goddess has," Rhian said. "This is her doing, not mine."

"You came to me," Dias said. "Why? Because if you are a trap, and this is meant to destroy me, you will die before you leave my presence."

She regarded him without visible fear. "Etena rules in Lir," she said. "The king of Lir is dead. The king's heir of Lir is bound and confined and no doubt will die when it suits her pleasure. Your brother lies broken in the king's house. The Goddess has withdrawn her blessing."

"My brother," said Dias with a swift intake of breath. "Broken?"

"He'll not run again," Rhian said. "He may never walk, either, or ride. But she keeps him alive. He can, after all, build chariots."

Aera watched the same stillness fall across Dias that lay on Rhian. It was the same absolute rage, the same perfect hate. "So that is why you came," he said. To one who did not know him, it might have seemed that he was calm. "You want me to kill her."

"I want Lir to be free of her," Rhian said. "I brought you our daughter. She's heir to the Mother of Lir, and royal blood of the People. She needs your protection."

"You're going to kill that one whom we do not name." Aera did not know she was going to speak until she did it. Her voice was rough with grief and soul-deep anger.

Rhian kept her eyes on Dias, but answered Aera. "Who else can do it? She's no kin of mine. She killed my father. I have blood-right."

A low growl ran round the circle. The People understood blood-right, oh, well indeed.

"And when she is dead," said Aera, "what will you do? Arm your people against us?"

"Conquerors have come before," Rhian said, "and become kin. One such is in your arms. Are there not more in safety beyond the river?"

Aera's throat closed. "So. He did come home."

"His father died in his arms," Rhian said. "He has no more cause to love her than any of the rest of us."

Did he love any of the People? Even Aera?

That was an unworthy thought. He had lied; he had hidden a truth that would have healed her heart. But that he believed he loved her—yes, she could admit that.

"I propose an alliance," Rhian said, "between the White Mare and the People. Do you take Lir, overcome those who defend it at her orders, and clear the way to her. I will do what kin-bond bars you from doing, and do it gladly, for all our sake."

"We'll need your knowledge of the city and its defenses," Dias said, "and of the country between. How hard must we fight even to come there? How many traps are laid for us? Tell us everything. Do that, and you have my word: she is yours to do with as you will."

Rhian smiled. It was a sweet smile, and terrible. "I will tell you," she said.

⇒ ⇐

Aera caught the rest of the council in snatches. The child Ariana was hungry and thirsty and needed the privies. She was tired, too, though she was fierce in her insistence that she was not. When she had eaten and drunk and had her needs tended, Aera made a bed for her in the inner room of Dias' tent. There were no women there: Dias had left the last of them behind when he took to the boats. The servant, a yellow-haired boy, refused to burden himself with a child. It was a simple matter to put him to flight.

Ariana had taken in everything about the camp with open curiosity, and the king's tent no less than the rest. She did not like to lie down, "like a baby" as she put it, but when Aera lay down with her, she consented grudgingly to do as she was told.

It was pleasant to lie in the dimness beside that small warm body, and to hear the light voice speaking with determined alertness. "Why does everybody think you're a man?"

"Because I'm wearing a man's clothes," Aera answered her, "and I'm in the men's camp, and there's no veil over my face."

"They think I'm a boy, too. Is that why? They're silly. Anybody can see we're not men."

"Anybody who knows what a woman looks like in the daylight and on a horse," Aera said.

"You're my grandmother, aren't you? Father told me about you. And Emry—he told me everything. He said you're beautiful, and you look like Father."

"I do look like your father," Aera said.

"And you're beautiful. Father is, too. Even if he's broken now. He's going to mend. I asked the Goddess. I made her promise. He won't always be broken."

Aera's eyes stung. She never wept; it was a moment before she recognized tears. "Does the Goddess talk to you?" she asked.

"All the time," said Ariana. "She talks to Mother, too, but Mother calls it the wind."

Aera smoothed black curls away from the eyes that were so like Minas'. Sleep was making them heavy, for all her efforts to keep them open. "Tell your Goddess," Aera said, "that if she heals my son, I will give myself to her as a servant."

"You can tell her yourself," Ariana said sleepily. "She's always listening."

"Will she listen to the likes of me?"

A soft deep breath was her only answer.

Aera lay listening to the child's breathing. She was wide awake. The council was all but done: men were stirring without, rising, going to do the things that they had agreed upon. Most of that was to prepare their men to march in the morning. Dias no longer had to wait for his scouts. Rhian had brought him everything he needed.

If she could be trusted.

Aera cast down the thought and set her foot on it. Rhian had given her child to Dias as a hostage. She would do nothing to harm her. If Aera knew anything of these people, she knew how sacred a child was— and a girlchild most of all.

76

The People began their march in a clear warm morning. They formed their ranks by tribe and clan. Mounted men led and followed. Chariots took the center. Baggage and herds followed behind, and among them, but set subtly apart, the grey herd—all but the mare who was a goddess, and the young stallion who had been given, or had given himself, to Dias.

Dias rode in the van, leaving Aias alone in his chariot. Aera would have taken her place with Vatis, for Ariana was riding again with her mother, but Rhian had met her on her way to the chariots. Rhian was riding the living goddess. A second mare followed, bridled, with a saddle-fleece on her back. It was a handsome mare, silver-white but dark of mane and tail, with a bright imperious eye and a haughty air. Clearly, if Aera refused her, she would be royally insulted.

Aera was of the People, woman or no. She could no more resist a horse of such quality than she could forgive Etena for the things she had done to Minas. She bowed to the mare as if she had been a prince of the People, and mounted by her gracious leave.

It was a seduction: tempting the high ones of the People with these children of gods. But it was a wonderful temptation, well worth whatever danger it might bring.

⇾ ⇽

Past Long Ford the cities came closer together. Every one was shut behind walls. They saw no human creature on the road or in the fields or copses, nor were there men in boats upon the river.

"This was planned," Rhian said when the king rode back, troubled by this stillness, and made restless by it. "It leaves the way clear to Lir, where the trap will close."

"We have our own trap," said Dias. "But I don't like this. It's too quiet."

"You'll have a battle," Rhian said. "Have no doubt of that."

His eyes rolled like a skittish stallion's. He rode away down the line, taking refuge in comforting his people.

"He knows who you are," Rhian observed when he was well away from them.

"How can you tell?" Aera asked her.

"He's too careful about ignoring you. If he notices you, I suppose he has to send you away."

"It would be the most honorable thing," said Aera.

"I should hate to be a woman in the tribes," Rhian said.

"If we win this war, that is what you'll be."

Rhian slid a glance at her. "Oh, no. Not I. The mare has no use for a veiled woman in a tent."

"Yet you condemn your people to this."

"Only those who have earned it." Rhian shut her mouth with a snap.

She was on a thin edge. They all were. Aera had dreamed of Minas in the night, seen him lying broken on a cot, his face blank, his spirit crushed and dying. Her beautiful son, her young king. Rhian had claimed the life of the one who did this to him, but Aera wanted part of her. The black heart. The liver full of hate.

Where the river's valley narrowed and its banks rose again in steep crags, a party of the scouts met them. The army had paused to water the horses; those who could rest were doing it, as wise soldiers learned to do.

The scouts had a stranger with them, guest or captive: a woman in armor with a white oxtail on a staff. That was the sign of truce, and of an embassy.

Dias received her on the field. "She has an escort," said the captain of scouts. "It's waiting for us past the wood yonder. She came alone to prove her trust in you, and to offer herself as a hostage."

Dias bent his eyes on the messenger. She was pale with fear, but her gaze was steady. "Lord king," she said in the traders' speech, "I come bearing word from the lady of Lir."

Dias' growl was clearly audible. "I will hear no word from that one. If you would please me, you would bring me her head."

"Hers," said the messenger, "I do not have. But I do come bearing a gift." She lifted a bag from her horse's shoulder, unbinding it, casting its contents at the feet of Dias' lordly grey. The stallion snorted and struck at it.

Aera gasped and clutched the mare's mane. It was a head, long sundered from its body, and somewhat worn with travel.

It was not Emry. This had been an older man, grey-bearded, his black hair shot with grey. But the likeness was striking.

"The king of Lir," said the messenger. "She offers him as a token of her good faith, and proposes a bargain."

"Does she take me for a merchant?" Dias demanded. "I do not bargain with that one."

The messenger swallowed visibly, but went on as she must have been instructed. "She holds your brother, lord king. She will give him back to you, and the whole of this country with it, if only you will give her Lir and the lands about it. One city, lord king, in return for all you desire."

Dias sat motionless on the grey stallion's back. He had been struck dumb, Aera thought. The men nearest him seemed no more able to speak.

Was she the only one in the army with any wits left? Whatever it cost her, whether she was sent away in bonds or even struck down, she could not keep silent. She rode forward to Dias' side, so bold that no man raised hand against her, and faced the messenger of Lir. "Why? Why give us everything and only keep one city?"

The woman blinked at her. Like Rhian she knew a woman in the warrior's dress; it seemed to take a little of the edge off her terror. Her speech was less tight, her words easier and quicker off her tongue. "Lir is the Goddess' city. The temple is there. It is very holy, very much beloved. While it stands, the Goddess is blessed in all this world that she made."

"Ah," said Aera. "So you preserve the temple, and destroy your country."

"While the temple stands, the Goddess lives."

That, thought Aera, was Etena's own blindness, her spell laid on these priestesses of Lir. "This bargain serves us well—except that you require the king to come all but unattended to your city. You'll pardon us if we scent a trap."

"He may bring half a hundred warriors. We will swear oaths if you wish, that he will be safe; that he will come unharmed before our rulers, and fetch his brother with his own hands. Or would it suit him better to send another?"

"No!" Dias thrust past Aera. The messenger recoiled. He took no notice. "I will go. My army will camp outside the city, but only my warband will go within. If all is as you promise, and my brother is surrendered to me, the bargain will hold. You keep Lir. We take the rest."

The messenger bowed to him—a sag of relief, perhaps. "That is well," she said. "You are but half a day's journey from the city. If you press the pace with your smaller company, and leave the army to follow, you will be in Lir by sunset."

"We will find your escort," Aera said, "and make camp. In the morning we will ride to the city."

Neither Dias nor the messenger gainsaid her, though both seemed inclined to do so. Only after the words were spoken did it strike her what she had done: she had spoken aloud before the king and his warband, and given them orders, and not one of them had stopped her.

This country was working its spell on the People. Aera moved to efface herself, but Dias caught her hand. "You stay with me," he said.

She bent her head to him. She would have given much just then for a veil, but there was nothing of the sort within reach. She had to ride with her face bare and brazen, and the king beside her, so that no one could fail to see her.

He had nothing to say to her. As they resumed the march, Dias took the lead, with only the vanguard of the warband in front of him. The rest of the People followed, passing through the narrow valley and out upon a green river-plain jeweled with cities.

The messenger's escort was waiting for them there, a dozen tall women in armor, with spears and bows and long swords. They were not at ease before the massed power of the royal tribe, but they had courage. They fell in about their captain, meeting men's stares with cold eyes. It said much for the strength of their will that no warrior ventured an insolence. Even the words muttered from man to man were more admiring than not.

✥ ✥

They camped on the long green hill above the cities. Lir lay in the distance, largest of them all, ringed with white walls: stone, those would be, but the city inside them seemed a city of wood, green with trees.

Aera faced her reckoning in the king's tent that night, after the daymeal had been eaten and the warriors had gone to their rest. She waited in the inner room with Ariana and Rhian; they were asleep in the corner, the child in her mother's arms.

Dias came in to find her waiting for him, sitting cross-legged, hands on knees. She had been dreaming awake, of Minas again, and of Emry—in the dream he was dead, and that was his head in the messenger's bag, and she was trying to sew it back onto his body.

For a moment as she stared at Dias, she saw Emry instead. But Dias was a smaller man, and his eyes were brown, and he did not grow his beard.

He sat as she was sitting—as warriors sat, or kings, cross-legged in front of her. He had become a king since it was forced on him: the strength of his presence swayed her, the clear and imperious power of him. But he was still the child she had nursed beside her own son, and the boy she had raised and taught the wisdom of the People.

"You know that I should send you back to the river," he said.

She nodded. "And I know that we've come too far; you'd need a war-clan to take me back safely."

"Or I could kill you," he said, "for the dishonor you've cast on the king's house, wearing the weapons and semblance of a warrior."

"You could do that," she said levelly. "After all I'm not your mother by blood."

That stung him. "Then what am I to do with you? You'll be a scandal from here to the eastern horizon."

"Give me to the mare's servant," she said. The words came to her as she spoke them. "Let her command me; let her honor be my honor."

"Not Metos?"

"My father cares little for anything but the work of his hands."

Dias did not mention her husband. That was kind of him. She folded her hands and waited while he pondered what she had said. At length he said, "She's already claimed you, I think. She gave you a horse, yes?"

"It would seem so," Aera said.

"Then let it be so," said Dias.

He was relieved, she thought. Dias had no difficulty passing judgment as king, but women's matters made him desperately uneasy. Yet he was no more a coward in that than any other man of the People.

The sun came through the window of Emry's prison at a slightly different angle each day. He liked to lie in it, basking; for when he woke after the first sleep of his captivity, he found that they had removed his bindings — but they had also taken all his clothing, and emptied his storage-chest of anything that could be fashioned into a garment.

It was meant for a mockery, he supposed, and a humiliation. In the nights he shivered: they had not even left him a blanket for the bed. In the day he let the sun bathe him, since he was given nothing else for the purpose. He was fed when the first light came into the sky, but only then, and poorly enough: bread and sour ale, and once a rind of cheese.

After the first day, there was only one guard on his door. The guard changed in the night; the first night he heard them talking desultorily, less than delighted with the duty. In that way he learned what had become of Minas, and that Rhian was nowhere to be found. The night guard supposed that she been quietly disposed of, but the morning guard begged to differ: "She's still in the city, I'll wager, biding her time."

He would have burst through the door if he could, and overpowered the guards, but they had barred it from the outside. When the morning guard fed him, she did it with drawn sword. She was not fool enough to treat him with contempt.

No one came to gloat over him or threaten him. He had been laid away like a garment in a chest. Clearly he had value as a living man, or he would be as dead as his father. But just as clearly, he was to be given nothing that was not strictly necessary. She wanted him weak, body and spirit. Then — what? A public execution? Sale to the highest bidder? A bargain: his soul for his body's freedom?

By the third night, Emry was ready to throw the whole of his weight against the door, until the bolt was broken, or he was. When the guard changed, he pressed his ear to the door, straining to hear what they said. It was only gossip tonight, except for a tidbit or two: the hunt still had not found Rhian, and the tribes had come almost to Long Ford. Etena had a plan, but what that was, no one seemed to know.

He would wait for the deep night, when the house was asleep and the guard, he hoped, was nearly so. Then he would break free. He cared little what happened after that — escape, he could hope, or at least a little freedom before he was caught and killed. Whatever became of him, it was better than lying trapped within these walls.

He slid down in the corner, knees clasped tight to keep in what warmth there was. It was not as cold tonight, or else he was growing accustomed to it. He drowsed a little, keeping a thread of wakefulness.

The sound was small, like the scraping of a rat in the wall; then a scuffle and a soft thump. It came from outside the door.

Emry was on his feet, poised, when the bolt slid. The door opened.

Emry crouched to spring. Shadows filled the room. Only slowly did he see that there were but two shadows of big broad men: his brother Gerent, and Mabon flexing his fingers with an air of great, if pained, satisfaction. "Jaw like granite," he said in his rumble of a voice.

Emry shifted until he could see the huddled shape of the guard. She was stirring already. He was on her before the others could move. The sound of her neck snapping was loud in the silence.

His rescuers gaped at him. Even Mabon, who had gone to the steppe with him, stared speechless.

There was no time to explain all that needed explaining. Emry dragged the guard into the room and arranged her on the bed. She was as tall as he was, and almost as wide in the shoulders. Her armor did not fit him, but her shirt and trousers were close enough. Her weapons were light for his strength but very comforting.

His brother and his friend were still staring. "I suppose you have a plan," he said. "Or shall we simply run, and hope for the best?"

Mabon recovered first. He swallowed hard and said, "There's a way out. Conory and Davin are keeping it clear."

Emry's brothers. "And the other three?"

"Waiting in the city."

"Good," said Emry. "Go on."

They obeyed him. Gerent kept shooting glances at him. Emry caught the last one and held it, and willed him to stop. It was too dangerous.

Gerent kept his eyes to himself after that, scouting ahead on soft feet, leading them through darkened corridors. The king's house was full of priestesses and their servants. It was telling, thought Emry, that Etena had laid claim to this house and not the Mother's. When Etena thought of power, she thought of kings.

Nearly everyone was asleep. They met one late wanderer, a young priestess with a child-swollen belly, coming back from the kitchen with a laden basket. The room into which they retreated was mercifully empty. Once she had passed, they moved more quickly.

Conory and Davin were waiting for them beyond the kitchens, keeping watch over a door that Emry knew well. They had all crept out through it when they were boys.

Guards were waiting for them outside, a company of a dozen, armed with spears and bows. They were smiling.

Emry swept out his sword and sprang. The taste of blood was in his mouth, the dizziness of it in his spirit. He would not be shut in prison again. He would *not*.

He was in the midst of them, where bows were of no use, and spears were too clumsy. He fought with cold skill, all fear, all anger shut away. The heart was *here*. The lifeblood flowed *there*. He struck to kill. Wounded could name the ones who came with him, and send out hunters to seize them. The dead could speak, after their fashion, but neither so quickly nor so clearly.

He was aware in his skin that Mabon had found some semblance of wits, and had flung himself into the fight. His brothers came in last, but not in vain: Conory hacked down a woman who was about to spit Mabon on her spear.

It was a fierce fight, but short. Emry felt the sting of small wounds, but nothing mortal. The others were unharmed. All the guards were dead. As he had done with the guard on his door, he dragged them out of sight, so that they would not be so quick to betray him.

The sky was lightening as Mabon helped him conceal the last of the dead. Reinforcements had not come, nor, so far, had anyone come to see what had become of the company.

But someone would, and soon. Emry herded his brothers and Mabon away from the king's house, aiming for the depths of the city, where the streets tangled one upon another, and a hunt would not easily find them.

Mabon took the lead once they were out of sight of the king's house. There was refuge waiting, or so he said. Emry would be certain of it when he was in it, unharmed and uncaught.

They kept to the shadows. People were beginning to stir, to go about the day's duties. For all the confusion in the king's house, the city was much as always. Either Etena had not yet managed to interfere with it, or she was too wise to try.

The place to which Mabon led them was in the southern quarter of the city, not far from the river. It was a house of good size, well kept, with a sturdy gate and, as Emry discovered, a great deal more space inside than he would have thought from the outside. The rear wall of its garden opened upon that of a second house, so that in truth it was two large houses and a garden large enough to pasture horses in.

There were in fact horses there, a grey and a bay, grazing in a pen near a little orchard. The mistress of the conjoined houses was leaning on the fence as the sun came up, tempting the horses with a handful of sweet cake. She turned as her doorkeeper brought the arrivals to her, smiling as much with relief as with welcome.

Emry knew her rather well. Mabon's mother had been an elder of the

Mother's council, and was still a power in the city. She looked like her son: tall, broad, with fine brown eyes under a strong arch of brows.

"Thank the Goddess," she said, holding out her hands to them. "You're all safe."

"Not for long," said Emry, "if anyone thinks to look here."

That was abrupt, and rude, but Modron seemed inclined to forgive it. "You have time to rest and eat and be in comfort," she said. "I think our enemy may find herself hard pressed to keep her own affairs in order, let alone go looking for escaped prisoners."

"Pray the Goddess it be so," Emry said.

⇒ ⇐

To be bathed, fed, dressed in clean clothes—Emry had dreamed of this. And to go out of the room, that was beyond blessed; to walk where he pleased within that house, and out into the garden again, and no walls to close him in.

He could not rest. He had had nothing to do but rest for three days and three nights. He found a servant who would fetch the others, and waited for them in the orchard by the horses' pen. While he waited, he prowled among the trees, inspecting the green fruit and regretting, a little, that none of it was ripe enough to eat.

Only his brother Gerent came, of all of them, and Modron, whom he had not presumed to summon. "They have duties, which they must be seen to do," she said. "They'll come when they can."

"And you have none?" Emry asked them both.

"Ours is to look after this house," she said smiling, though Gerent looked as if he might have silenced her, had he dared. "And, of course, you. At nightfall there will be horses ready. You'll go to Larchwood. The defense of this country can continue there. The Mother has already asked for you—for the young king of Lir."

"And Lir itself?" Emry demanded.

"That one is trading the rest of our country for it," Modron said; for the first time there was no warmth in her voice. "She has sent an embassy to the king of chariots, to bring him here, and give him his brother and all our people, so that she may keep Lir."

"I don't suppose she was planning to trade me as well?" asked Emry. He was not shocked, at all, nor surprised. He knew Etena well enough to have expected this of her; Goddess knew, the temple would stand with her. Even before the Mother died, it had concerned itself with nothing but its own preservation.

"You were to be traded in whatever manner was most useful," said Modron. "The king of chariots might want his charioteer back, after all, if only to make an example of him."

Emry regarded her with newborn respect. "You do understand her," he said.

"One does not need to be a thing in order to comprehend it," she said: gentle, but unquestionably a rebuke. "We are not all fools, my young lord, though it may have seemed so."

"Not fools," Emry said. "Innocents. Strangers to the kind of war that these people fight—in spirit as well as body."

"It has been difficult," she admitted.

"Well then," he said. "What's being done? Once the king is in the city, if we hold him hostage we may win a little time, but his tribes will fight. Even she may fondly imagine that she has preserved Lir; but she only postpones the inevitable."

"Yes," said Modron. "Therefore we continue to arm the defenses. Once you're safe in Larchwood, the army can rally to you there, and the cities look to you for leadership. Lir is our sacrifice, if there must be one."

Emry nodded slowly. "Yes. Yes, that's wise. But I'm not leaving Lir tonight. Send Conory—I'll name him my heir, king by right if I don't come out of this alive. Let him take the rest of our brothers and go."

"And you?"

"I am warbrother to the king of chariots," Emry said. "I was his charioteer. And . . . by the law of the tribes, I am father-by-right of the king's best-loved brother. The ties of kin are strong among the tribesmen. I may be able to strike a bargain that will save Lir."

"Or he'll put you to death as a traitor."

"That is possible," he said calmly. "But if Lir can be freed of her, that's worth the price."

She bent her head. "You will do as you see fit. You are king, after all."

Emry's stomach tightened. He had not been thinking of that, of how it had happened, or of what it meant past the most obvious. He had deliberately and cravenly turned his back on it. A king could command even women, even elders, save only the Mother and the highest of the priestesses.

If he went to Larchwood, all that power would be his. If he stayed in Lir, it was considerably more likely that he would be killed before he could be of any use. And yet he could not change the words he had said, now that they were spoken. "It would be safer for you," he said, "if I hid elsewhere."

"And unsafe for someone else," she said. "These houses are large and full of hiding places. The river is close; we have boats, if any or all of us needs to escape. Rest assured, young king, when I chose myself to be your protector, I thought long and hard on all that that would entail. I'm content with the choice. So therefore let you be."

"Very well," Emry said. He spread his hands. "Who am I to gainsay a woman of such rank and wisdom?"

She smiled at that and took her leave. But Gerent stayed. He had been sitting on his heels, listening like the child he still nearly was, while his brother and Modron spoke. Once she had gone, he went on sitting, staring hard at the ground. His shoulders were tight. His jaw was set.

"Well, puppy," Emry said. "What is it?"

"I'm not going to Larchwood," Gerent said to his fists.

"Of course you are," said Emry.

"What will you do if I don't go? Kill me?"

Ah, thought Emry. "It's not just that I'm sending you away," he said. "Is it?"

"Isn't that enough?"

"It would seem not," Emry said.

Gerent shuddered so hard that he nearly fell over. "That guard. She wasn't even awake. And you snapped her neck like—like—a rabbit you'd trapped."

"She could tell the others who was with me," Emry said as gently as he could. "They'll hunt me—that's expected. It's fair. But I won't have them hunt you and Mabon."

"You committed murder!" Gerent cried. "Cold-blooded, hardhearted, ice-eyed—"

"This is war," Emry said. "What, did you think it was just like arms-practice? Hacking at one another with wooden swords, and pretending to be dead, and getting up at the end and clasping hands and going in to dinner? People die in war, puppy. That's what war is."

"I don't know you," Gerent said—if he had known it, just as Dias had, and Aera. "The brother I knew, the one I loved—he would never have said such things."

"I am what the Goddess has made me," Emry said. "May she preserve you from any such thing. You will go to Larchwood, my brother, and you will do as Conory tells you, until I come there."

"Yes, I'll go," Gerent said angrily. "I hope I never see you again!"

He did not mean it, Emry thought as he fled. Gerent was wounded, and striking at the one who had hurt him. But it was necessary. Emry could not bear to lose any of his brothers—and that one least of all, whom he had always loved best.

78

Dias brought his army within sight of Lir and arrayed it on the broad green field between the river and the hills. While he rode under the sign of truce, none of the towns had come against him. He stood safe before the heart of this country, the city that ruled all the rest.

When his warband mounted to ride into Lir, Aera was with it. That was not Dias' will. When it came time to ride to the city, Rhian said to Aera in his hearing, "You go. Find your son. Bring him out if you can. No matter what else happens—keep him safe."

That was Aera's intention exactly, but when Dias turned to expostulate, both Rhian and the white mare had vanished.

He had given her to Rhian; therefore he could not in honor forbid her to do this. He kept her by him. "At least then I can keep my eye on you," he muttered. When they rode out, they rode so, with Aera at Dias' side.

They had not taken chariots. Ridden horses were better for cities, quicker and lighter, and better able to fend for themselves than pairs in harness. Aera could not tell if the messenger was disappointed. These people had chariots; Rhian had said so. But none of the People had yet seen them. They were being kept in reserve, Aera supposed. She would have done that, if she had been the ruler of Lir.

The city was open to them, waiting for them. There were figures in armor on the walls, standing still, spears at rest. Many of those were men, though there were a fair few women. People lined the streets: children, unarmed women, men with infants in their arms. No one of age or condition to fight. Was that a sign of trust, or a sign of contempt?

None of the people made a sound. Even the infants were silent. They watched the riders, staring blandly at their armor, their ornaments, their horse-trappings. They showed more interest in the horses that Aera and Dias were riding: widened eyes, a murmur of voices.

Greys were sacred here. But it was more than that. Had they not known that the grey herd had come to the People?

Etena would hardly lower herself to meet them at the gate, still less to wait for them outside the house she had claimed for her own. That was a king's courtesy. Etena, in her mind, was higher than a king. They were received at the gate of the city by a woman in armor, to whom the envoy bent her head in respect, and at the gate of a tall house—taller than most of those near it—by one dressed with shocking immodesty in a skirt or kilt of scarlet cords, and a mask without nose or mouth, only the slits of eyes. The hair that flowed loose to her massive buttocks was threaded with grey. Her belly was heavy, and her breasts, as if she had borne many children. But she was light on her feet as she turned without a word and entered the house.

"You are to follow," the armored captain said as the warband sat motionless on their horses, the eyes of even the veterans nigh starting out of their heads.

"That is a priestess," Aera said so that they all could hear. "We're being honored, I think. Come, my lord. Let's see what further delights our host has prepared for us."

As she spoke she dismounted. The grey mare stood where Aera had left her, beside the likewise motionless stallion. When one of the warriors ventured to take their bridles, they pinned ears and snapped. The rest, wiser, let them be.

Most of the warband stayed outside, by Dias' command. A dozen went in with him, all those he most trusted, with Aias looming behind his king. They entered the hall of the fallen king of Lir.

They had prepared with great care for this, and Rhian had warned them what to expect. But these walls, this place loftier than any temple, the way echoes played among the beams of the hall, were like nothing they had ever known.

They were brave men. They kept their heads up, their backs straight. They fixed on the one who sat in the tall chair by the hearth, in which a fire burned even in the warmth of the day.

She was tiny in that chair, hardly larger than a child, wrapped and veiled in black. She had not taken to the fashion of the women who served her, all of whom, ranked behind her, were dressed as their guide into the hall had been.

It was meant to shock. Aera leveled a glance at Dias, and at Aias beyond him. Both of them steadied under it. They kept their eyes on Etena. Cold eyes, with a fire of hate beneath. It burned deep and it burned strong.

She did not flinch from it. This was her place, the lift of her head said. She ruled in it. She needed no man to rule for her. Everyone, man or woman, did her bidding.

"I accept your bargain," Dias said abruptly. "Keep the city; I will take the rest. Give my brother to me and I go."

"You shall have him," she said. "But first, break bread with me. Seal the pact with the wine of the south."

Dias growled in his throat. "I will not break bread with you. Where is my brother?"

"First we seal the pact," she said.

"And sup poison?"

"By the womb that bore you," she said, "there is no poison here. Shall I be your taster? Will you trust me so far?"

"I trust nothing," Dias said, "that is not purely of my People."

"Then you do not even trust yourself. For," she said, "you are half of Blackroot tribe, and only half of the People you rule."

Dias stood rigid. Aera bent toward his ear. "Do as she bids. Pretend to endure it. I'll see to the rest."

She had attracted Etena's notice, but that was a risk she had taken. That one could hardly have failed to see her: a woman in armor among the king's warband. But Etena did not speak as Aera had expected. The hate in her glance was strong enough to rock Aera where she stood.

Aera had known herself hated. But this was like a blast of icy wind.

She held her ground for pure pride, and for love of the young king who so mastered himself as to say, "Let it be done, and quickly over."

Which of course it was not. Servants had to come, to raise tables and spread them with a feast. There was bread and wine, of course. A dozen kinds of each, and meat and fish and cheese and herbs and green things and cakes both savory and sweet, early fruit of the meadows and the last of the winter's store. It was outrageous, extravagant. It was meant to mock Dias with the wealth that he was bargaining away.

Tribesmen learned from their mother's breast never to refuse a feast. Dias would not sit beside Etena, nor at the same table, but she, expecting as much, had ordered a table set in front of hers. They were face to face across a brief expanse of floor.

Aera took a place at the end of the warriors' table, close by the door, and kept quiet and kept her head down. Rhian had taught her how this place was made, and where a prisoner was likely to be. Aera told over the lesson in her head, while eating what she needed for strength: bread, meat, a little cheese. No wine. When she was sure of herself, and reasonably sure that she was not watched, she slipped away.

There were servants in the passage, men as well as women, trotting back and forth with platters and jars and bowls. They eyed her curiously but said nothing.

Except one. It was a man, and rather an odd one at that. He wore a servant's tunic, but with an air of one playing a part. He was plump, and smaller than many of the men here, but broad and sturdy. The men here all wore their beards cut to the shape of their faces, but his was long, all the way to his breast, and meticulously curled; and his upper lip was shaved clean.

He took her in with round brown eyes and nodded to himself. "Your name is Aera?" he asked her in the traders' tongue, with an accent she had not heard before: thick and guttural.

"My name is Aera," she said. "And you are what kind of creature?"

He laughed like a boy, though he was clearly a man of middle age. "You may call me Eresh. I come from far away from here. The lady of horses, she told me to look for you. Will you come with me?"

Aera did not move. "Who is the lady of horses?"

"Rhian," said Eresh. "The potter's child from Long Ford. The Mother's daughter."

Aera frowned. "*She* knows that. Tell me what she might not know."

"Your son's name is Eros," he said, "and you do not understand his father."

She started as if he had struck her. It was all she could do not to wrap her hands about that plump throat.

He drew back a prudent step, but his smile barely faded. "Will you come?" he asked her.

She would come, if only to have the satisfaction of throttling him once his errand was done. He turned his back on her, which showed either great courage or great foolhardiness, and led her not toward the upper rooms as she had expected, but onward and outward—toward the stable, she thought. Or toward the place where the chariotmakers were.

She did not let herself hope. If she went to her death, so be it. She might be a fool for trusting this foreigner, but that Rhian had sent him, she no longer doubted. Did she trust Rhian? Not in most things. But in this . . . yes. She did.

The place of the makers was a broad open room. Shorn trunks of trees held up its roof. Long windows were cut in its sides to let in the light. It was like a vast round tent on enormous poles.

It was empty but for the fading scents of the making: heat of the forge, new-planed wood, leather and paint. Eresh led her through it to the far end, where a room was closed off from the rest. It had a door, with a bar on it, and two guards in front of it. They eyed Aera suspiciously, but Eresh spoke to them in the language of this place, too rapid for Aera to understand. She caught words that Emry had taught her: *prince, mother, healer*. But what they meant all together, she did not know. Maybe she was afraid to know.

At length one of the guards exchanged glances with the other, shrugged, unbarred the door. They ushered her in with drawn swords.

It was lighter in the room than she had expected. It had a window, high and narrow, and there were lamps, a whole bank of them, though not all were lit. A bed lay under the window, a wooden frame raised up on legs in the fashion of this country.

She saw the long still figure, the tail of bright hair, and thought, *He is dead. After all, he is dead.*

But her heart refused the thought. He was asleep or unconscious, but dead, no. His breast rose and fell. He stirred under the woven coverlet. His face twisted in pain or anger.

She looked down into eyes as green as the night-glare of an animal's. That was fury so pure that it had gone perfectly calm.

He spoke, but not to her. "Take her away. Or I will kill you."

"You will not," Eresh said. "Sit up now. Be polite. You'll be out of here by evening."

"I will not," Minas said. He closed his eyes. "Go away."

"He will not," Aera briskly. "And neither will I." She plucked away the coverlet before he could stop her, and considered what was there to see. It gave her time to steady herself.

"The bonesetter says he may ride again," Eresh told her. "She's not so sure of the walking—that left knee, it took the brunt of the first blow. She's been pulling out the bits of bone. The other breaks, they're clean, mostly. He's healing well. She has a poultice, you don't want to know what's in it, but it keeps wounds from festering."

Aera did want to know what was in it, but not this moment. The bonesetting was well done: tidy splints, taut bandages, very clean. Her heart was wailing: *My child! O my beautiful child!* But her spirit was coldly calm. "We would have brought a wagon or a litter, but we judged it best that she not know we knew."

"Oh yes," said Eresh. "Yes, that was wise."

In the same instant Minas said, "How did you—"

His mouth snapped shut, but he had betrayed himself quite sufficiently. Aera smoothed a tangle of hair away from his face, catching her fingers in something that was braided into it: a bronze bell. "The lady of horses," she answered him, not wanting to speak a name where the guards could hear. "They all came to us, all the grey ones, and she, and your daughter."

"My—"

"She is safe in the camp," Aera said.

He turned his face away from her. "Everybody knows."

"Everybody does not. Only your brother and I and one or two of the warband, who have been sworn to silence. Do you think the People would have let us play her game, if they had known? They'd have taken this city with fire and sword."

"Why didn't they?" he demanded of the wall.

"Because they would have burned you with it."

"Yes."

"My child," she said with hard-fought patience, "you may be as insufferable as you please elsewhere, but with me you will remember your manners. We will bring you out of here. Then she'll be paid as she deserves."

He thrust himself up. His lips were white with pain, but he beat away their hands that would have helped him. When he was sitting against the wall, breathing hard, shaking with effort, he managed to say, "Who will give it to her? You?"

"One not bound to her by kin and clan."

"Coward."

Aera struck him. He gaped at her, startled green eyes above the livid print of her hand. He would bruise, she observed coolly. To Eresh she said, "Send someone to our king, and someone else for a litter. It might be well to send an armed man or two, if the guards should offer objections."

"Or if someone else should do so?" Eresh inquired, sliding a glance at Minas.

"Indeed," said Aera dryly.

He did her bidding as a good servant should: quickly, quietly, and without troubling her with further questions. After he had gone, Minas said, "That is a lord of a city whose name none of us can pronounce. We think he may be quite a high lord. Possibly a king's kin."

"I'm sure he trains his servants wonderfully," Aera said. She looked about for a garment to clothe her son in, but there was none. The coverlet would have to do.

He was scowling at her. The fury had turned aside from her; the scowl was his wonted expression when he was baffled by something or someone. He had stopped feeling quite so sorry for himself.

"They kept you clean," she said. "Good. You should be presentable."

"Why?"

She did not dignify that with an answer.

And after a while he said, as if he had just noticed: "You're dressed like a man. You're carrying weapons."

She did not answer that, either.

He seized her hands. His own were cold, and stronger than she had expected. "Leave me here," he said. "Tell my brother I'm dead after all. That will be true soon enough. Do this for me, if you ever loved me."

"I mourned you once," she said. "I refuse to do it again. The bonesetter says you'll be able to ride. You'll walk lame, but I trust in the Goddess of this country that you will walk. Now scrape yourself together and stop this nonsense. Coward, you called me. And what are you?"

"Crippled," he said.

"Never," she said. "Never speak that word to me again."

Her face must have been terrible. He blanched as he had when he was a child, when he had done something to raise her wrath.

"We are going out there," she said, "and you are going to face your people. Then let the gods do what they will—and truly, O my son, I do believe that they will avenge you."

79

Mabon was still captain of the guard on the wall, as Rhian had hardly dared to hope. Better yet: he had Emry with him, dressed as a guardsman. It was a bold thing to set him out in plain sight, and yet it might have been the wisest choice. Who after all would expect him to be walking the wall with a spear in his hand?

They were properly startled to find her sitting up against the rim of the wall. She could see the warband waiting in front of the king's house, and if she lifted her head, she could see the tribe drawn up in the field beyond the city.

She rose as they came. Emry had a dark look about him, as if he did not care if he lived or died, but still he managed to smile at her.

"Tell me where the chariots are," she said.

They glanced at one another.

"If there's going to be a battle," she said, "they'll be needed here. Tell me you didn't send them somewhere else."

"They're scattered through the cities," Mabon said after a pause.

"And none here?"

"A few," said Mabon, "that the temple has taken."

"Sweet Goddess," said Rhian. "What were you thinking, that you suffered that to happen?"

Mabon stiffened, and for once she saw a spark of temper in his eye. "This was not my thinking. This was the temple—assuring a quick escape for the priestesses of the cities."

"You made no effort to stop it?"

"There was nothing I could do," Mabon said.

"Too late now," said Emry. He was leaning against the wall's edge, looking out at the massed power of the tribe, and the long line of its chariots. "We'll have to trust to walls after all."

"These have been breached," Rhian said, "thanks to *her*."

"You went to the enemy," said Mabon with great gentleness. "The grey herd went with you. Do we trust you, lady of horses? What do you want with us now?"

"I want watchfulness," she said. "And defense of this city—to protect it, not destroy it."

Mabon's eyes sharpened. "Tell me what you are saying."

Good, thought Rhian. He was thinking. Emry she could not read: the helmet shadowed his eyes. "Remember. Defense only. And whatever happens in the king's house or the temple, do nothing, unless it threatens the rest of the city."

"I'm coming with you," Emry said.

"No," said Rhian.

He stood straight and set himself beside her. The tribes had taught him something: he could be a threat simply by being large and male.

Mabon's lips twitched. Rhian glared at them both. "You will only be in my way," she said to Emry. "Stay here. They need you."

"You need me more," he said.

She considered the wisdom of striking him, and the possibility of knocking him flat. But before she could move, he had caught her and trapped her, gripping her tight against his body. She struggled fiercely. He hissed in her ear. "*Stop* that! Look!"

Her eye caught what he had seen first, because it was behind her: an armed company trotting along the wall. Warriors of the temple. Their faces had a look of grim purpose. Their swords were drawn, their spears leveled.

"Now, now," said Mabon easily as they came on, ambling out in front of them, blocking their way to the others. "No need for that. We've got her. We'll take her where she's wanted, if you'll just—"

The company did not slow its advance. Mabon stood his ground. He lifted his spear in one hand; the other went to his lips. He loosed a piercing whistle. The priestesses wavered but did not stop. Farther down the wall and in the guardhouses, figures sprang into motion: seizing weapons, pulling on helmets. Guards ran round the wall from the rest of the gates.

Rhian sank teeth into Emry's arm. He gasped but did not cry out, nor did he let her go. He heaved her up over his shoulder and began to run.

Mabon shouted. Metal clashed.

It was battle up there. Rhian, helpless and near mad with fury, beat on Emry's unyielding back. She only gained bruised fists for it.

People were running in the streets—armed people. She groaned aloud. Lir was fighting Lir, temple against city guard. In front of the king's house, Dias' warband was stirring, drawn by the sounds of fighting.

Emry had enough sense at least not to run into the midst of those. He skirted the edge of the broad open space. His breath was coming a little quick: Rhian was not a small woman, nor a light one.

He stopped by the wall of the Mother's house and set her down, but kept a grip on her wrists. "I will not run away," she snarled at him. "Now let me go."

He hesitated long enough to fan the fires of her temper, but he did as she bade.

The warband had drawn together. The man in charge of them—whom Rhian did not recognize but Emry likely did—snapped out an order. They formed in a circle, weapons drawn or held at the ready.

"Battle order." Emry spoke as if to himself. "What are you proposing to do? Walk into the king's house and slit her throat?"

"Not till Minas is out of there," she said. "If you would help me, go and see that all the servants and the king's people are elsewhere. When we go in, there should be none but women of the temple."

She was asking him to go back where he had been a prisoner, where he was still being hunted. She watched him consider that. He liked it: it was mad enough to suit his mood. "Don't get killed," he said. "Promise me that."

"I'll try," she said.

He hugged her tight, squeezing the breath out of her, and slipped away round the Mother's house.

Rhian paused before she followed. The sounds of fighting had grown louder. And something else, something that raised her hackles: a long deep rumble. The sound of many hundred hooves on living earth, and of chariot-wheels rolling over it.

The warband had heard it, too. Their captain snapped an order. One of the young men sprang down from his horse and ran toward the king's house. The guards at the gate barred him with spears.

It was like a slow crumbling of earth on a mountainside, seeing how it all fell apart, every plan and scheme. Rhian strode up to the gate with the young messenger still standing in it, about to draw his sword, and smiled into the eyes of the guards. "Let us in," she said. "We have messages for the one who rules you."

She had gambled well. They recognized her. She drew the startled tribesman with her, past the motionless guards, across the court and into the king's hall.

The feast was still going on, but not only Dias' men were uneasy. The sounds of fighting were audible even here. Only Etena seemed in comfort. She had not touched the food set in front of her. All her hunger was satisfied by the sight of her son sitting before her, subject to her will.

Rhian and the tribesman entered just as the truce broke. An uproar erupted through the inner door. Priestesses, armed, driven back by servants with no weapons but the weight of their numbers. Behind them came a cluster of bearers, and a litter, with Minas on it.

He was sitting upright. His mother was with him, and Eresh the foreigner.

Dias surged to his feet. So did the rest of his men, oversetting tables, flinging benches aside. The sound that came out of them was even more terrible than the sound of chariots rolling to battle.

The priestesses were not fools, not when it came to saving their skins. They saw the look in the tribesmen's eyes, and bolted. Even Etena in her arrogance was borne along with them. She had a fair turn of speed for so small and so heavily swathed a person.

Rhian sprang after them. A wall of guards rose up before her. She recoiled from it. Her mind was clear, and running swift.

She whirled. Minas' litter was laid in the middle of the hall, and his people crowded about it, with Dias innermost. But Aera stood apart.

Rhian's heart knew where it wanted to be, and that was not here, beyond the circle, face to face with Aera. "She's headed for the temple," Rhian said. "I'm going after her. There's fighting on the walls. The tribe is moving. They'll be thinking it's an attack on their king. If he can go out there, stop it before it reaches the city—"

"I doubt that he will want to," Aera said.

Rhian met those cool green eyes. There was no help in them, no mercy for Lir. And did Rhian want any?

Maybe a little. "The city guard is fighting priestesses," she said. "Your people might be made aware of this. Priestesses are hers. They broke your prince. The others are simply defending what is theirs."

"You had better go," said Aera, "if you would catch her."

That was manifestly true, and Rhian would gain nothing else from her—not in this. Rhian turned and ran.

She knew all the ways of this house, better, she was sure, than Etena's women did. But they were well ahead of her, and there were many of them. No servants barred their way. Emry had got them out, then, if there had been any left.

Rhian knew as she ran that she was perfectly foolhardy, running alone against a hundred armed warriors.

Feet pounded behind her. She glanced back. Tribesmen, armed. And— Emry?

Not only tribesmen. Men of Lir, too, running together, as if they were allies. The huge red-headed man beside Emry was the chieftain Aias. He had been in the hall but a moment ago.

They all owed Etena a debt that she would be forced to pay. With half of Dias' warband at her back, and a company of the city guard, Rhian tracked the priestesses through the king's house and out into the glare of the day.

The rest of the warband was waiting for them, a line of feral grins and bristling weapons. On its edges stood the chariots of Lir: teams a little raw, a little new to this face of battle, but willing and strong of heart.

The priestesses were not cowards. They measured the forces against them, before and behind. With Etena and the elder priestesses protected in their midst, they drew together, lowered spears, and charged toward the temple.

The warriors who had followed Rhian streamed past her, yelling war-cries. The mounted fighters stood their ground, but the chariots rolled inward, falling on the priestesses from either side.

More were coming down the streets from the city: armored women, and some of those were mounted. It was full-fledged battle, growing fiercer the longer it went on.

Rhian, outside of it, knew a thing that had to be impossible. It could not have happened, not in her full sight. And yet her bones were sure of it.

She turned back into the king's house. The passage the priestesses had taken was straight, but others opened off it, winding away to the servants' quarters, the kitchens, the storehouses.

Rhian followed the aching in her bones. The city was breaking apart beyond these walls, three sides of battle, and confusion wherever her heart turned. But here, in the dimness of the king's house, it was all very simple. Etena had slipped away from her guards and her allies. By sleight or sorcery, she had hidden herself.

But Rhian was sworn to hunt and take her. The kitchens were in disarray, with signs of hasty departure everywhere: an ox still on the spit, half-baked loaves spilling from a basket by the oven, a scatter of spices and sweetness across a table. Rhian took up a lamp, saw that it was filled, lit it at the hearth. With its flickering light to guide her, she ventured into the storerooms.

Etena had hidden herself well. Rhian would never have found her but for that niggle in her bones, which might be the Goddess' voice, and might only be the purity of her hate. Deep amid the jars of grain and oil and wine, behind a barrel of last year's apples, was a space as large as a small room. Whether it had always been a bolthole or whether Etena had prepared it for herself, it was a remarkably comfortable lair for a serpent. Food and drink were to hand, and a soft bed, and lamps, and even a chest for belongings.

At first Rhian thought Etena was alone. She had been lying on the bed; at Rhian's coming she sat up, blinking at the light, hand lifted to shield her eyes. Then from the shadows beyond her crept a small figure, staring at Rhian with great round eyes.

Rhian could feel the weakening of her will, the spell sapping her strength. Pity, she thought. Compunction. Separated from her loyal guards, shut in this cupboard of a place, surely Etena posed no danger. She was defeated, hunted and hated. She would not rule again in this world. And see—here was her child, Emry's child, Rhian's own brother's daughter, stretching out small trusting hands to the one who had come to kill her mother.

Fiercely Rhian shook off the spell. As long as this creature drew breath, she was deadly. She fixed Rhian with melting eyes and pitiable expression. "Please," she said in a soft trembling voice. "Don't let me die here. Let me die in the light. And my child—my poor child—"

That too was a spell. Rhian snatched knife from sheath and sprang.

She stopped cold, a hair short of sinking the keen bronze blade in the child's heart.

The creature was simple, or else she was drugged. She stared at Rhian without fear. Her mother's face beyond her was a mask of triumphant hate—briefly, before she concealed it again behind the semblance of help-lessness.

"Take me out," said Etena. "Let me see the sun again. Then you may do with me as you will."

Rhian measured the distance between them, and the woman's grip on her daughter. It must be painful: her fingers were sunk like claws in the thin arms. But the child showed no sign that she felt anything.

Drugged, for a certainty.

Rhian darted round her, striking at her mother. The blade met flesh, bone; caught, slid.

Etena screeched like a cat, dropped her shield and went straight for the eyes, stabbing with long nails, snapping at the throat.

Rhian stabbed blindly, fending off teeth and nails. White pain raked her arm again and again. A vise clamped about her throat, sharp-needled with claws. The world began to go dark.

She slashed with the blade. Hot wetness sprayed her face. Through the scarlet haze she saw her target, the twisting dark-clothed body; heard a heartbeat like thunder in her ears. She struck at that sound with all the strength that was left in her. To pierce it deep. To make it stop.

Etena wrenched away. The dagger's hilt tore from Rhian's fingers. Etena clawed at it. Rhian, unarmed, cast her eyes about wildly for a weapon.

A soft sound brought her wheeling about. Etena smiled at her. The child lay limp in her lap. The blood on her was not wholly her mother's. Her eyes were open, hardly less empty than they had been before, but there could be no doubt that she was dead.

"She was mine," Etena said. "You will never have her. Never corrupt her. Never—" She coughed. Whatever else she might have said was lost, drowning in blood.

She died upright, eyes fixed on Rhian. The hate lingered in them even after the breath left her body, as if after all it was stronger than death.

Rhian straightened slowly. Her arms, her face stung. Her throat was red agony.

What she had to do, she could not ponder too deeply, or her spirit would revolt. Gently she lifted the child's body and laid it in the bed.

She was not so gentle with the mother. She laid the dead woman on the packed earth of the floor, taking no such care as she had with the child. Then with her dagger she cut the head from the neck, severed the spine, and pierced the heart with a wooden spit from the kitchens. She spoke words that she had learned in the service of the mare, words of binding and of cleansing. Her voice was a rasp, and each word was pain, but she spoke as best she could.

She wrapped the head in a sack, and again in another lest it drip blood on the floor, and hung it from her belt. She took up the child, still careful, gentle as if she had been alive, and walked out of that place, into the roar of battle.

80

The world had gone mad. Emry fought side by side with warriors of the People as he had so often before — against the priestesses of the Goddess, in his own city of Lir. The city guard, and what had once been the king's own guard, fought with him. There was fighting all over the city, on the walls, in the streets. Beyond the walls, the massed horde of the People came on with chariots.

He did not know when he was sure that the woman the priestesses were protecting was not Etena. Certainly it was after he saw a wounded charioteer carried off to the healers, and took the chariot for himself.

A chariot was not the best weapon for hand-to-hand fighting, but for breaking away from the skirmish and hurtling through the gate into the hall, it had no match.

They were fighting in there, too, Dias and his dozen defending Minas against a mass of women in armor. Minas had a short horseman's bow — Goddess knew where he had found it, or the filled quivers, either — and was shooting when he could, with excellent aim.

He nigh shot Emry in the heart, but in the last instant his eyes flickered with recognition. The arrow flew wide.

The horses were young and fractious. Emry could not both drive them and fight. But he could send them full into the crowd of attackers and scatter them. The most fortunate fled. One or two fell and rolled sickeningly under the wheels, like his dream of battle years ago. But in that dream, he had not been the charioteer; he had been among the slain.

This was not the world, or the war, that he had expected. He brought the horses to a clattering halt in front of Dias' defenders. They stared at him as if they could not decide whether he was friend or enemy.

One appeared to have no doubts as to which he was. She was dressed as a man. Her spear had seen use. She regarded him with a flat inimical stare, mantling like a falcon over the body of her son.

Emry turned his eyes from her to Dias, nor need she ever know how great an effort that was. "The priestesses have attacked the city guard on the walls," he said, "and my people are fighting side by side with yours inside the city—but your army doesn't know that. It's riding to the attack. Will you send a messenger to call it off, or shall I?"

"Should I wish to stop it?" Dias asked.

"Yes," said a raw shadow of a voice. "You should."

Rhian was standing in the doorway to the kitchens. She had been in a fight, and not a clean one: her face and throat were torn, her arms and hands bleeding. She held a black-wrapped bundle in her arms. She laid it down, uncovering it carefully, with visible grief. Then beside it she laid the thing that had hung in a sack at her belt.

Emry gagged on bile. The child—the dead child—had the face of his kin; was his kin, his daughter whom he had never known. Her mother's head stared lifelessly from beside her. Blood pooled on the tiles beneath the severed neck.

"It is done," Rhian said, "as I swore to do. Now keep your own oath, lord of chariots."

Dias was staring as if he could not stop. "But she was out—I saw her—"

"A ruse," said Rhian. "Her last one. And her last murder: the murder of her own child."

Emry unclenched his fists, if not his heart. What he had been thinking was unworthy of his sister and of himself. With an effort that grated in his bones, he turned his gaze on Dias. "It's over, lord king. She's dead. Your army is still riding against the city. Will you come?"

Perhaps it was the title, perhaps Emry's voice, but Dias closed his eyes; he shuddered. When he opened them, he was the Dias whom Emry knew. He too, Emry noticed, was no longer looking at what lay at Rhian's feet. "King of Lir," he said. "Whose victory is it, then?"

"One would think hers," Emry said.

"I will stop my army," Dias said, "but there is a price."

Emry tensed.

"We can fight the war to a standstill and burn this country to the ground. Or we can end it now."

"You'll leave?" Emry asked with a touch of incredulity. "You'll go back to the steppe?"

Dias snorted—not quite laughter, but close enough. "I'll give you Lir," he said, "as I would have given it to her. The rest is mine."

"No bargain," Emry said. "You have safe-conduct back to your army. After that, it's war."

"Enough," Rhian said. She stood between them, glaring from one to the other. "I am the Mother's daughter of Lir. This once, and only once, I claim the authority of that office. The temple is yours, king of chariots. Do with it as you will. Lir is yours, my brother. Be wise in disposing of it."

"And the rest?" They spoke together, Dias and Emry, startling one another.

"That you will settle between you," she said, "by single combat if you must. But settle it before the sun sets—and after you have stopped the army."

Emry looked at Dias, and found him looking back. His brows rose. Dias' mouth quirked. "Single combat," Dias said. "Winner take all. Are you man enough for that, king of Lir?"

"Are you, king of chariots?"

They clasped hands, a brief struggle, quickly over: Dias leaped; Emry pulled him into the chariot. People were grinning or scowling. It did not matter. They had a battle to stop, and a battle of their own to fight.

⇒ ⇐

The fighting in the city was fierce. But the sight of two kings in a chariot stopped all but the most determined and left them staring.

The great gate was shut. Mabon, limping but alive, stood guard above it. His warriors with sword and spear beat off the warrior women from the city. His archers stood along the wall, bows strung, arrows nocked.

"Open the gate!" Emry bellowed as he drove the chariot toward it. "Mabon! Open the gate!"

Mabon, bless his wise heart, did not waste time in gawping. He sent a man to do as Emry bade. "The Goddess' blessing on you!" Emry called to them both.

The chariot thundered through the gate and out onto the plain. The massed power of Dias' people descended upon him, horsemen and chariots. The sound was indescribable. The earth shook with it. It was terrible, glorious.

Emry laughed as a man may when he looks death in the face. Kings he and Dias might be, but they could not stop this. Nothing could do that but the walls themselves; when they had done it, they would tumble down.

A horn rang. Emry's hands clenched on the reins. The horses jibbed, half-rearing.

Mabon had lied. Or someone had. The chariots of Lir were coming, nigh tenscore of them. A prince of the city led them, his brother Davin. They were a brave sight with their fine trappings and their armor of leather and bronze. They fell on the flank of the horde with such force that it buckled, horses and chariots reeling back, careening into one another.

A cry of pure joy went up from the mass of the People. Battle—glory and splendor. And chariots to fight against. No enemy had ever had them, and here were nigh as many as they themselves had in this place. A grander game had never been, nor a better fight.

Emry forgot who was in the chariot with him, forgot everything but the battle in front of him. The horses barely needed his urging. They flew into a gallop.

Davin's charioteers had driven deep into the army of the People. Too deep. The enemy closed behind them. Emry roared at them, bellowing like a bull: "Back! *Back!*" But they did not hear, or did not choose to hear.

Chariots thrust together lost their advantage. That lesson Emry had learned over and over in battle with the People. They needed an open plain, and a long span to run in, and room to wheel and turn. The People had kept the bulk of their chariots free, but Davin's people were trapped, locked together, wheels tangled, teams clambering over one another, doing worse damage to their allies than their enemies.

Emry struck like a dart at the front of the horde. Riders and chariots, startled, seeing their king, gave way.

Davin was surrounded by men on horseback, blocked to the sides and rear by his own chariots, fighting for his life. Emry flung the reins at Dias and vaulted into his brother's chariot, and loosed a shrilling, ululating cry.

It surged outward in a wave, stilling the battle. "Dias!" he cried. "Lord of chariots! I propose a match. On the open field—a hundred of yours, a hundred of mine, and all power to the victor."

Dias grinned, wide and white. "Ah! I do like that. It's better, much, than hammering at each other until one of us is tired."

"Yes: now we do it a hundredfold."

Dias saluted him, laughing, and called off his men, choosing out his hundred.

While he did that, Emry considered the force that had appeared all unlooked for. There were a hundred chariots and teams intact, easily, and charioteers for them, and warriors to fight. Most of the charioteers were women, lighter and quicker of hand and eye if not as strong as the men. That would disconcert the enemy, which was well.

The two forces drew up facing one another on the open field below the wall. The horde had drawn back to give them room. The wall was thick with people: wide eyes, startled faces staring down.

Emry raked his glance down the line of his people. Some he recognized. Most he did not. Of his brothers, only Davin was there—and that was a relief.

"Remember," he said. "Give yourselves room to maneuver. Don't be trapped again. And aim for the charioteers."

They all knew him, knew what he was. None moved to gainsay him. To Davin he said, "You drive the chariot. I'll fight. Drive straight and choose targets carefully. Let me deal with them when we come to them."

Davin nodded shortly. He was not happy, but he would be obedient.

Emry, in the center of his line, faced Dias in the center of his. Their eyes met. They loved one another as brothers, as heart's friends. That they were kings at war mattered very little in that moment; though in the next, it was everything.

There was nothing in the world like the charge of chariots. The long line gathering, poising, surging forward. The rumble of wheels. The snorting of horses. The sheer inexorable force of them.

The two lines met with a ringing crash. Swords, spears, warclubs, axes, met, collided, swept past one another.

Davin checked his team of blacks, rocked them back on their haunches, turned them in a tight arc, almost spinning on a single wheel. Then they were at the charge again, closer together now, wielding weight as well as speed against the enemy's line.

Wheels ground together and locked. Stallions screamed. Men shouted and howled and sang. Emry was singing. It was wonderful to let the song pour out of him, to feel the wind on his face and the sun on his helmet, and know the bruising shock of his sword meeting sword in the line of battle. It was not Dias whom he fought. The king of chariots was farther down the line, locked in combat with a warrior whom Emry did not know.

It was life for life, blood for blood, and no quarter given. Davin was good with the horses, always had been. He kept them alive, moving, and the traces uncut.

Others were not so fortunate. It was the difficulty that all his people had: to kill with the true joy of killing, and not to flinch or to pull back just short of the stroke.

Emry had been a tribesman long enough to become a slayer of men. He did not do it gladly, but he did it.

The line of his people had grown terribly thin. Empty chariots ran round the field, tangling with one another, throwing knots of fighters into confusion. Emry rallied those that were left, formed them into a charge, and flung them against the broader, deeper line of the enemy.

He would do it, and do it again, until there was only himself left, and however many of the tribe as were still alive. Dias, he hoped. Dias his warbrother, his friend, his implacable enemy.

At last they came face to face. Dias had lost his helmet; his temple was cut, and had bled appallingly as head wounds did. He grinned through the blood. Emry grinned back. They knew one another's strengths and weaknesses, all the ways in which they preferred to fight, from many a battle against each other and against the enemies of the People.

There was a lovely inevitability in it. Emry was taller, stronger, but Dias was lighter and quicker and had grown up from childhood fighting in chariots. His team was better trained, his charioteer more skilled. It would have to be quick.

He pressed hard, hammering at Dias' blade, driving him back and down. The chariots veered about one another, swinging wide, crashing together with a splintering of wood and a grinding of wheels. The horses strained to pull them apart again.

Dias came up from the floor of the chariot, whirling his sword about his head. Emry caught it in mid-whirl, bracing against the shock of the two blades' meeting. It rocked him on his heels. The chariots lurched, wheels screeching as they tore free. He staggered.

He saw the blow coming. He scrambled to beat it aside, but his counterstroke flew wide. He went down in a whirl of darkness and stars.

81

They brought Emry in on a litter of spears. He was alive. So were a handful of those who had fought with him, led behind him in bonds, captives but proud of it. The dead stayed on the field, would be buried there in honor.

Aera had not meant to trouble herself with him. He had left her; he had become the enemy. Now he was conquered, as they all were, sooner or later.

But as night came down on a city that had fallen in large part to the People, Aera found herself standing over the bed in which Emry was lying.

He had always come back from battle covered in wounds that he had not even noticed until it was time to stitch and tend them. She counted them as she had so often before.

They had had to clip his beard to stitch the worst of them: the long deep slash that ran from brow to chin. The stitching was tidy. It would scar, she thought, but not so badly as to ruin his beauty.

He opened his eyes. They were dark and soft with sleep. He smiled, seeing her, and drew a small sigh, as if he had been wandering far and had come home.

Enemy, she thought. Conquered king. And he had let her believe her son was dead.

Her son of his begetting was living, and would come here when the country was settled. Her elder son slept in a room near this one, broken but mending, and alive in spite of himself.

Dias had said nothing of what he meant to do with Emry, had simply brought him back and sent for healers and ordered them to tend him. Then Dias went back to the battle. He had won Emry's part of Lir, to be sure, but there were still the priestesses; they were intractable.

Emry reached for her hand and pressed it to his unwounded cheek and slid into sleep again. Had he even remembered where he was, or what had brought him there?

She had intended to slip free and escape. Instead she lay beside him, her body against his warm familiar body. She buried her face in his hair and wept a little. He never stirred.

She woke when Dias came back. He regarded her with an arch of the brow that said a great deal without uttering a word. She met it with a flat cold stare.

"Give him to me," she said. His brow arched even further. "He's yours now. Let me have him."

"For what? So that you can make a cup of his skull?"

"Wasn't that what you were going to do with him?"

"No," Dias said. "I was going to keep him alive."

"As your dog?"

"Why not? He was that before. He's a better charioteer than most men of the People."

"He was a slave then. He's a king now. He might prefer to be dead."

"I can give him the choice," said Dias. "Will you?"

"Of course not."

"You can have him," Dias said. "But you can't kill him until I'm done with him."

She assented to that.

Dias hung on his heel, but she had said all she intended to say. After a while he obliged her by leaving.

Aera stayed where she was. She felt rather than heard the change in Emry's breathing. He was awake, aware. He said, "I lost the fight."

"And the city," she said, "and everything else you fought for."

"Did I?"

It was hard to stay angry, with him lying so close. "It's not defeat to you, is it?" she said. "As long as the city stands, whoever rules it, you don't truly care."

"I do care," he said. "I'd rather Dias than Etena. I'd rather myself most of all, of course, or better yet my father, but that was not the Goddess' will."

She would never understand him. But neither, it seemed, could she live without him. She had tried, and found nothing there but emptiness.

"You belong to me now," she said. "The king has said it."

"I've always belonged to you," he said.

"And I belong to the mare," said Aera. "Your sister claimed me, so that I could ride with the men."

"So I belong to the mare," he said. His grin was crooked, misshapen with stitches, but it was as wicked as ever. "And you said I lost everything. It seems I gained a great deal in return."

"No man of the People would say such a thing."

"But," he said, "I'm not a man of the People. I'm the mare's servant. As are you."

"Maybe we shall all be, in the end," she said. An unwilling smile tugged at the corners of her mouth. "By the gods and your Goddess, I missed you."

"And I you," he said softly.

He closed his arms about her, stroking her back in the way that she loved best, so that she arched and purred. He winced with all his aches and twinges, but she knew how to soothe those. She was hungry for him—starving. And he, it seemed, for her. They made their own feast there, a feast of victory after all, and in its way a promise. That whatever became of the rest of the world, they would not be parted again.

⇾ ⇽

Minas did not see the battle of chariots, but he heard the tale of it over and over from the warband as they came back to the king's house at evening. He was still in the hall. He even still had the bow that he had browbeaten a servant into bringing him, unstrung and laid beside him. He had used it to good advantage against Etena's women.

Now Etena was dead at Rhian's hand. The child whom she had killed had been taken away for burial, with such mourning as any of them could spare. Etena's head was set on a spear outside the king's house; her body had been flung to the dogs. The people of Lir found that appalling. The People reckoned it just.

They were not making a festival of his return to the land of the living. That was their courtesy. Nor did they look on him in pity, as the broken thing he was. They treated him—why, he thought, as they treated Metos: as one of them, and yet not. Almost as if he were a god himself.

Had he not come back from the dead? He lay and listened to their stories, and to the news of the battle as it came with newcomers. There was an odd feeling to it, clear and yet remote.

Some of the king's guard of Lir came, after Emry was brought in but before the sun went down. To them Minas was alive and no god. They were glad to surround him, and maybe to use him as a shield against the men of the warband.

It was a strange war, and an uneasy peace. There was still fighting in the city, although the horde was camped quietly without. Dias had brought in the rest of his own clan, and Mabon's men and women were with them.

"Most of the priestesses are in the temple now," said Huon. His lips were white with pain and loss of blood: he had taken leave from Minas' guard to fight in the city, and lost his sword-hand to the stroke of an axe. But he would not go among the wounded. He drank wine with strong spices, and propped himself up against the side of Minas' litter, telling him the latest news of the fight. "The city's mostly quiet. They're not sacking it, though some of them wanted to." He stopped, flushed. "Ah! Your pardon. You're one of them, too."

"Not any longer," Minas said. "Not really. And the temple?"

"It's surrounded. They'll break in come morning." Huon shivered. "Is it an awful thing that I'm glad? The temple was the heart of Lir for so long, but they ate away at it till there was nothing left."

"And now there are wild horsemen in our king's hall," said a woman whom Minas did not know.

"We were wild horsemen once," Huon said. "Or our fathers' fathers' greatest great-grandfathers were."

"We didn't even have fathers before they came," someone else said. "It was all mothers, and mothers' brothers bringing up the children."

"My mother's brother brought me up," said Huon. He yawned, and belched. "Who's for more wine?"

No one else was. He had the jar to himself, and would drain it, Minas was sure, before the night grew too much older.

He could understand. Huon was dulling pain, and trying to forget what he had lost. Wine did no such thing for Minas. It only made him stupid.

He looked up from the circle about him, drawn by the shift of a shadow. Dias was standing at the edge of the light, watching. He looked as if he had been there for a while.

Minas could not read his expression. For a moment Minas saw what he must be seeing: the brother returned from the dead, sitting in a circle of foreigners, speaking in their language and acting as if he were one of them.

They melted away before Dias, all but Huon, who had fallen asleep with the winejar in his hand. Dias sat on the other side of the litter, perched on a stool. He did not say anything.

Minas studied him in the silence. He had grown up. The boy's softness was gone from his face. He was a man now, a man who was a king. He had scars seaming his face, the backs of his hands, and no doubt the rest of him as well. He carried himself differently: taller, straighter. He was no one's shadow now, least of all Minas'.

It hurt, very much. But not as much as Minas had thought it would. The edge of it was dulled. "It must have been a grand war," he said, "when you made yourself king of all the tribes."

"If I'd known you were alive," Dias said, "it would have been shorter."

"I'm quite dead," said Minas.

Dias gasped as if at a blow.

"There now," Minas said. "It really is simpler this way. I couldn't challenge you even if I would, and you can't give it all away like the fool you were planning to be."

"It should have been yours," Dias said.

Minas shrugged. "It seems the gods willed otherwise."

"They did not. *She* did."

"She is dead in every possible way, soul and body. Her debt is paid."

"And what of mine? She was my mother."

Minas gripped Dias' hands. "She gave you nothing but the use of her womb. Everything else was my mother's, and mine. You owe us nothing."

Dias shook his head, but he did not try to break free. His eyes were full of tears. "Though I live a hundred years, I will never forgive her."

"I can forgive her for one thing," Minas said. "You."

"I would rather never have been, than see what she has done to you."

"Brother," said Minas, "I will mend. I may mend crooked, but I'm not broken. I'm going to ride. I'll walk, too, for all that the old crone says. That I promise you."

Dias' tears overflowed. Minas pulled him in and held him, and let him weep himself out.

There were no tears in Minas. The fire on the steppe had burned them all away.

When at last Dias' shoulders stopped shaking, Minas held him at arm's length and looked him in the face. "Good," he said. "You can feel. A king should be heart-whole. That way he understands his people better and tempers his justice with mercy."

"What, you're an elder now?"

Even better: Dias' dry humor was coming back. "I'm more than that," Minas said. "I'm an ancestor."

"Some ancestor," Dias said, tugging at Minas' coppery plait. "You still look like a yearling cub."

"That's my curse," sighed Minas. "Should I grow a beard, do you think?"

"Can you?" Dias asked, rubbing his own dark-shadowed chin.

Minas bared teeth at him. "More than I could before."

They sat with hand locked in hand, gripping hard enough to bruise, grinning at one another. There was a strong tang of grief beneath, but joy, for the moment, was uppermost. Minas had his brother back again, and Dias his. Day and night, sundered for so long, were together at last.

⇀ ↽

"I heard your promise," Rhian said.

Dias had gone out again, with tearing reluctance, but there was still a battle to finish. Minas would have given heart's blood to be striding beside him. But that was not the gods' will. He slid into a doze, aware of people passing in the hall, but resting on the edge of a dream.

Her voice pulled him back into the waking world. She sat at the foot of his litter, feet tucked up, eyes fixed on his face.

"I'm going to hold you to it," she said. "You will walk."

"Yes," he said. "I will."

"You'll have to be alive to do it," she pointed out. "Or no more undead than you already are."

"I know that," he said.

"Good."

The silence had edges, like a bronze blade. And yet it was oddly comfortable. Sparks were interesting, Rhian liked to say. They kept the heart from growing dull.

But this was worse than a simple quarrel. Minas was not the man he had been before. Nor would he be again, for all his proud promises. If— when—he walked, he would walk lame.

She rose to her knees and walked on them up the length of his body, taking care not to jar his splinted legs. Halfway to the top of him, she stopped. His blanket was no barrier, nor the trousers she had been wearing. Nor, to his abiding shock, was the fact that they were in the hall, and it was full of people coming and going, and though they were set apart near a corner, anyone could look and see.

One part of him was everything it had been before. She made sure of that. She lowered herself onto it and began the slow rocking rhythm that he loved best, like a long easy gallop over rolling country. She smiled down at him, rich and sweet as cream.

She was the most beautiful woman in Lir. The young men of the city had decreed that soon after she came there. They were terribly jealous of Minas.

He looked in that face for pity. He saw only beauty and strength, and deep contentment.

She stooped. Her lips brushed his. Her rhythm quickened, and his breathing with it. She had said no word, and yet he never felt more a man, or more beloved. Her kiss was as certain a promise as his words to Dias. He would walk. And she would walk beside him.

82

Dias stormed the temple in the morning, broke down its walls and rode over the rubble, and let in the horde of his People where no man of foreign nation had ever walked. While they hunted the last of the priestesses, he took a torch, and with his own hand set fire to the innermost shrine.

Its wood was ancient beyond reckoning. It burned like a torch itself, flames leaping up through the elaborate carvings and roaring to the sky. The birds that for long ages had nested in its eves flew up in a torrent of wings.

Emry saw the burning from the roof of the king's house. He was imprisoned there under heavy guard; every door and window was barred to him. Did they not think that he could leap from the roof?

It seemed they did not. He clung to the wall that rimmed the edge. If he had had wings he would have beat toward heaven like the Goddess' birds. His wounded cheek stung with tears.

All the priestesses that were still alive, that could walk or run, came together toward the pyre of the shrine. They had forgotten the men who hunted them, forgotten any fear of death. They flew like moths to the fire, flung themselves into it before the eyes of the tribesmen, and vanished in smoke and flame.

Last of all came the Goddess' Voice, preserved surely by her will. She was dressed in the garb of the most sacred of rites, in the scarlet kilt, the collar of gold, the blank shield of the mask. Emry knew her by her gait and by the blindness of the mask, which had not even slits for eyes. She was stiff and slow in her age, but none of the horsemen could come near her.

She paused only once, as she passed Dias. What she said, Emry could not hear, not from so far away. Dias offered no response. She turned from him, bowed low to the flames, and gave herself into their embrace.

With her passing, the earth seemed to draw a great sigh. The fire of the temple roared up anew, reached for the trees of the grove, leaped from bough to ancient bough, swifter than a man could run.

The tribesmen recoiled from the heat, drawing back in a long ragged line. The fire pursued them as they had pursued the priestesses, with the same deadly purpose. First one and then another, and then the whole tribe of them, wheeled and abandoned dignity and ran.

→ ←

The temple burned all that day and into the night. Tribesmen and people of the city labored side by side to keep it away from the king's house and the Mother's house and the rest of Lir.

For that, Emry was allowed out of the king's house. They needed every willing pair of hands, and every bucket and basin and waterskin. But Dias would not suffer them to pass beyond the line of the broken walls, even if the heat of the flames had permitted. The temple would burn, and burn to the ground. That was his will, as conqueror king.

They stood leaning on one another in the firelit night, Emry and Dias, and watched the flames at last die down. The skeletons of trees, the charred remnants of the temple, glowed ember-red. The pall of smoke burned their eyes and clawed at their throats.

Dias' face was black with soot. Emry supposed his own was, too. All his wounds ached. He was beyond exhaustion.

It dawned on him, slowly, that the person leaning on his other side was Aera. He had not even recognized her among all the shadowy figures struggling to keep the fire at bay.

They held one another up, the three of them. When Dias spoke, his voice was a rasp. "I think it's dying now."

Emry nodded, though his head felt as if it would fall from his shoulders. "There must be someone who's fresh enough to keep watch while the rest of us collapse."

"I'll see to it," Dias said.

"You'll sleep," said Aera. "I'll call in one of the clans from the camp. They've been idling about long enough. It's time they made themselves useful."

Dias opened his mouth at the same time as Emry. She silenced them both with a firm word. "Go! Sleep. I'll see to it."

Emry was raised to obedience, but so it seemed was Dias. Still arm in arm, staggering with exhaustion, they retreated to the king's house.

→ ←

Emry knew where there was a jar of wine from the southlands, strong and sweet. Dias was still awake to help him drink it: like him, too tired to sleep. They drank in the room that was Emry's, sprawled on the broad bed, passing a cup back and forth.

They had stripped off their filthy clothes and washed away the worst of the smoke and soot. There was still a reek of fire on them, sunk deep in skin and hair, but the fumes of the wine lessened that.

Dias dipped the cup in the jar, drank a draught, passed it to Emry. "I'll make you a cup of her skull," he said.

"I think that belongs to my sister," said Emry. His tongue was pleasantly numb, his mind limpidly clear.

"She doesn't want it. She said when she needs a snake's head for anything, she'll find one with less poison in it."

Emry laughed. It hurt less than smiling, after the sword-stroke he had taken in the face.

"You people are soft," said Dias.

"So is water," said Emry, "and yet it wears away stone."

Dias peered at him through the haze of wine. "What will you do, wear away at us?"

"Unless you dispose of me before I can begin," Emry said, "yes."

"I'm not going to dispose of you. I'm going to let you live."

"As what?"

"As . . ." Dias drew out the word till Emry was ready to hit him. "What would you like to be?"

"What will you let me be?"

"King in Lir," said Dias. "The bargain I gave her. Lir and the lands about it. The rest is mine."

"What bargain did you give my wife?"

"I gave her you," Dias said.

"If she agrees to it," said Emry, "I'll take what you offer. The rest you'll have to win for yourself."

"Are you not king of this country?"

"I'm not king of anything," he said, "in strict point of fact—I've not been raised or consecrated. But if and when I should be, I take only the kingship of this city. I won't command any other. What you want, you win for yourself. I'll have no part of it."

"That's a bargain?"

"It's the best you'll get."

"It means the war will go on. You could stop it if you would."

"Would your young men thank you for that?"

"No," said Dias. "Would yours?"

"Probably not. Young men are fools everywhere. But the Mothers, the elders, the rulers of cities, they'd not thank me for giving them up in their absence. They'll fight you, my brother. Some may even win."

"That's the splendor of war," Dias said. "I'll take your bargain. With one condition."

Emry waited.

"That you do nothing to help the cities. No armies. No chariots. They'll fight on their own, and win or lose without you. Your war is fought. You lost. This is the price you pay for it."

Emry lay on his face. The wine dulled grief and pain, of the spirit as of the body.

He turned onto his side, propped on his elbow. Dias lay flat, eyes on him, silent. "I accept your condition," he said.

"Good," said Dias.

"Lir is mine, then? Truly mine?"

"Yes."

"Then when morning comes, you will leave it. You will not come again except as I bid. Beyond the borders I am your man as I ever was. Here, I am lord and king."

Dias' expression was pure delight. "You are insolent! You're splendid. Is it true that there are no kings in this country but you? That all the rest are women—Mothers?"

"It is true," said Emry.

"Do you know what I'll do when I conquer them?"

Emry shook his head.

"Marry them!"

Emry's mouth was open. He shut it.

Dias grinned and hugged himself. "I'll make them all wives. They'll learn to be modest; they'll discover obedience. I'll tame them, every one."

"Or they'll tame you."

"Not in this world," said that king of men.

He could dream, Emry thought. Waking would come soon enough, when he met the Mothers of cities.

83

Emry rode out with Dias, riding as charioteer behind a team of greys. The rest of Dias' men who had been in the city rode behind, mounted or in chariots. The people of Lir watched them from the walls. The People of the Wind watched them from the field.

As they came, the tribes began to beat on drums and shields and the sides of chariots, a steady, rolling sound that resonated in the earth. A name was woven in it. It was not Dias'. It was Emry's. They were giving him the accolade of a king.

Emry glanced over his shoulder. Dias was grinning from ear to ear.

And there with the royal tribe, closely surrounded but free, clean, and dressed as lords and warriors—even to the women—were Emry's charioteers whom he had thought dead. Most were wounded, but all were able to stand. Davin stood foremost, head up, living, breathing, and doing his best not to disgrace himself or his kin in front of all these wild tribesmen.

"These are yours," Dias said. "We kept them for you."

"Were you treated well?" Emry asked them.

They all nodded, some stiffly, some unhappily, but none of them could deny it. Davin spoke for the rest of them. "So. It was all for nothing."

"Hardly," said Emry. "You won the respect of the tribes. They'll call us brave now, and reckon us equals, rather than slaves."

"We're still conquered," muttered Davin.

"So have we been before," Emry said, "and won in the end. Come here. Keep your head up. Smile. We're guests; I'd thank you to act like it."

Some of them barely managed as much, but Emry's will held them. They were like the rest of Lir: fractious, but at heart obedient.

They would do. It was good to have them there. And it was good to be with the People, eating their food, even drinking their hideous kumiss, side by side with Dias and Aias and Borias and the rest.

When Emry rode back to Lir, not only his own people came with him. Metos the maker of chariots rode beside him, bringing Rhian's daughter to her mother. Emry's daughters and his son were coming, riding on the river from the sea of grass. It was time they were safe with their father again, and with their mother.

She was in the city, but she was hardly idling about, waiting for him. There was a great deal to do to clear away the wrack of war and prepare for Emry's kingmaking. That would come with the full moon, the first moon of summer, which was a festival in every country that any of them knew.

⇒ ⇐

It was a strange kingmaking. There were no priestesses. The White Mare's servant was there to say the words that should be said, to speak the blessings in all their richness; the mare herself stood with her.

In older days the king had been made in the enclosure of the temple. But that was burned to ash. Emry chose instead the field where chariots had first met chariots in open battle. The horde of the People stretched down along the river, and the people of Lir filled the field from the hill to the walls.

Emry came out in a chariot. This time Dias was his charioteer. It would tell the People a thing that they needed to know, and assure the people of Lir that they were more than slaves or captives.

There were chariots all round the circle of the kingmaking, and charioteers both of Lir and of the People. In one, Aera was standing, still dressed as a warrior, with their two dark-haired daughters, as like as cubs of the same litter. In the chariot beside hers, their son bounced and gurgled in Metos' arms—a sight to widen eyes among the tribes, but in Lir it was a perfectly common thing. Metos at heart, Emry had been thinking, was remarkably like the men of Lir.

Emry turned his eyes away from them, if not the whole of his mind. Rhian waited for him on the hilltop, all alone, mounted on the White Mare. For the first time he saw her in the garments that were proper to her office: tunic and leggings of moon-white doeskin, embroidered with signs that were older than Lir. There were river-pearls and white doves' feathers braided in her hair, and silver about her neck and wrists and waist. She held a cup in her hands, a skull-cup bound with silver and studded with blue stones. It was very old and very powerful, and had come from the treasury of Lir.

Emry was resplendent in crimson and gold, the sun to her moon. But it was he who blinked, dazzled, and she who regarded him steadily. He descended from the chariot and knelt on the grass of the hill, at the White Mare's feet.

The words she spoke over him were as old as the cup in her hands, so old that their meaning was forgotten. He felt them as a wash of wind over him, a rush of warmth like the flare of a fire.

She poured water from the cup on his bowed head. It was cool and clean, little like the heavy scented oil with which his father had been anointed in his day. Her hands rested briefly where the water had fallen, blessing him. She crowned him with gold, a narrow fillet that Minas had made, binding his brows like the clasp of strong cool hands.

She raised him up. The roar of acclamation rocked him on his feet. As when he brought Dias to the tribes, they began their accolade, beating swords on shields and spears on earth, pounding on drums, chanting his name. His own people took it up, caught up in it, till the great roll of sound shook the sky.

⇒ ⇐

Minas and Metos between them had contrived a means for him to get about while his legs healed: a cart on the wheels and axle of a chariot, shaped for him to sit in with his splinted legs stretched out. With his beloved duns in the traces, he had a fair turn of speed, and he could go almost anywhere out of doors that a man could go on foot or horseback.

He was at the kingmaking, though he took his place neither with the People nor with the folk of Lir. He sat in his cart somewhat apart from both, with his daughter perched beside him. He was content, he told himself. When he looked at Rhian, he was a great deal more than that. She kept so little state; it was wonderful to see her as she was meant to be, a person of power in the world.

He left after Emry was crowned, but before the crush of people and chariots could bar his escape. As he reached the open field north of the city and let the duns choose their own speed, Ariana stood behind him and clasped arms about his neck and whooped like the wild thing she was.

They ran till the duns were tired, which was a gratifyingly long way. Minas was not greatly inclined to turn back; but he should be seen at the feast, to honor Emry and to reassure his brother. Dias would not believe even yet that Minas intended to keep on living.

Maybe it was cowardice, but Minas had no intention of dying. He would live, if only to spite Etena.

He drove back slowly. Ariana had curled up beside him and gone to sleep. The warm weight of her against him was remarkably comforting. His legs ached deep in the broken bones; his shattered knee throbbed, with flashes of sharper, fiercer pain: pain that had become so familiar he barely noticed it, except when he had nothing else to think of.

On a whim he took the long way back, winding through fields and copses, round a handful of villages. The people there went about their tasks as they had before war came to their country. It mattered little to them who was king in the city; their world was the turning of the seasons and the tilling of the fields and the tending of their own, both the beasts in the byres and the children in the huts and houses.

Farther away, down the river toward World's End, the war went on. Larchwood was besieged. Towns and villages fought fiercely against parties of raiders. Many had fallen, been sacked and burned, its people killed or taken captive. A few had surrendered. None had chosen Emry's way. But then, thought Minas, Emry was different. He was a man, a king. He had ridden with the People. These Mothers and ruling women neither understood nor wished to understand the People's ways.

Minas wondered how long Emry would hold to his promise that he would do nothing to help or harm anyone but Lir. His brothers were in Larchwood. Rumor was that the second son, next eldest after Emry, would declare himself king of Lir, and condemn Emry for a coward and a traitor. But Minas suspected that that was merely rumor. It was more likely that the Mother would name herself Mother over all her people, and undertake to rally them against the enemy.

Or maybe she would submit to marriage with Dias after all, and persuade the rest of the Mothers to do as she did. Those that did not would die. Dias would not again suffer a woman to seize power as Etena had, nor let her live to destroy him.

Minas could already see how this country had changed the People. His own mother riding as a warrior, driving a chariot, standing unveiled beside her husband, would have been unthinkable in the world he had been born to. Men who ventured to ravish women here were as likely to be gutted or gelded as to gain what they were after. These people were gentle, but they were not weak. And the women fought as strongly as the men.

Just before the last rise of the road, from which he would be able to see Lir, he paused to water the horses. There had been few travelers on the road; war kept people at home, and anyone who would be out and about was at the kingmaking. And yet a rider came toward him on a short thick-bodied horse. The man was well matched to his mount, riding without elegance but skillfully enough.

Ariana leaped out of the cart and ran laughing toward the rider. Eresh the foreigner laughed and swung her up in front of him. "Good day, little warrior," he said. "Where have you been keeping yourself?"

"Riding with Father," she said. "Did Mother send you to bring us back?"

"I'm sure she would have, if she'd thought of it," Eresh said. He smiled at Minas. "The feasting's begun. They'll be looking for you."

"Yes," said Minas.

Eresh brought his gelding up beside the cart, loosed rein and let the beast graze beside Minas' stallions. The duns ignored him. "You're healing well, they say," said Eresh. "You do look more alive than you did. Are you still dead?"

"To the People I am," Minas said.

"And in Lir?"

Minas shrugged, one-sided. "I'm the one who makes chariots, who belongs to the mare's servant."

"Is that enough for you?"

Minas frowned. "What else is there?"

"Certainly," said Eresh, "the making of chariots is a great thing. But will you live your life in this city? Or will you go with your tribe after all, and make chariots for them, as your grandfather does? He's dead to them, too, yes? Or can a man be living and still be a god?"

Minas pondered the man and his words. They opened wounds he had been trying to ignore until they healed. But wounds of the spirit festered deeper than any other.

He belonged nowhere but in Rhian's arms. That was the truth. The People were no longer his people. When he rode among them or feasted with them, he was welcome, he was beloved, but he was not part of them. It was the same in Lir, though he was not so well loved there. He had no home, no tribe, except Rhian and the daughter who regarded him gravely from the back of Eresh's horse.

He was the one who made chariots. That was what he had become. Everything else had dropped away. King's heir, warrior—he would not be either of those again. Etena had made sure of that.

"I'll stay in this country till autumn," Eresh said. "By then it should be safe enough to go back to my people—or I'll beg your brother to make it so. You'll be riding by then, I hear. Would you be pleased to ride with me?"

"To your country?"

Eresh nodded. "To the land of the two rivers, to the blessed cities. We have no chariots there. A man who can make them would be honored as a king, or as a living god."

"Do you think I want to be a god?"

"Do you?"

Minas' lips tightened. "No. No, I don't."

"Then you want to stay here?"

"No," Minas said again.

"No need to choose now," said Eresh. "But think on it. There's a world beyond this world of steppe and cities, and peoples varied and wonderful, and sights—such sights!"

"Mountains," said Minas, "made by men's hands."

Eresh nodded, delighted. "Just so. Wouldn't you like to see the truth of all the tales I've told you?"

"*I* would," Ariana declared.

Minas found that he was smiling. He never could keep a grim mood where she was—or Eresh either, for the matter of that. But he only said, "Come. They'll be looking for us at the kingmaking."

······· 84 ·······

"Do you want to go?"

Emry was king now, and lord in Lir. Dias had gone to Larchwood and taken it, and slain Emry's brother Conory in the battle. The Mother had consented then to be wife to a foreign king, a surrender that was, Minas thought, anything but absolute.

And he had told Rhian at last what had been in his heart since Emry's kingmaking. They lay together in the early morning, warm in one another's arms. The sounds of Lir came softly into this room in the king's house, song of birds, people waking, a dog's bark.

Rhian had not been angry or even shocked when he told her what Eresh had said. She only asked the question that brought it all to a single point.

"Do I want to go?" Minas ran his hand down the smooth line of her back. "Yes. Yes, I want to."

"Then go."

He drew back. Her face betrayed nothing, even when he laid his palm against her cheek. "And leave you here?"

"Would you do that?"

His heart clenched. But he said, "I would come back."

"Would you?"

"Yes. Even," he said, "from the dead."

She shivered. "Don't say that! If I went with you, would you try to stop me?"

The leap of joy was so sudden, so strong, that for a long moment he could not speak. He had to choke out the words. "You would do that? You would come?"

"I should like to see mountains that men have made."

His blinked at her. Then he glared. "Eresh told you! You knew. You let me—"

She kissed him into silence. "Of course he told me. I was almost out of patience, waiting for you to scrape together your courage. Will you tell the kings at all? Or will they wake one morning and find us gone?"

"Emry I can tell. Dias . . ." Minas traced slow spirals on her breast while he thought about it. Not that he had failed to think before, but her presence cleared his mind somehow. "Dias might object. A slave forced to labor for his masters, that's one thing. A man of his free will, making weapons for people not of the People—that's called treason."

"This country is very far away," Rhian said, "and there are many tribes and cities between. Nor do these cities look toward us for enemies. They look south and west. We're on the edge of their world—some would say we're beyond it."

"What, I'm going beyond the world's end again?"

She laughed softly, caught his hand and held it against her breast. That was fuller, he thought, than it had been—when? A month ago? The year before?

His rod was rising between them. She took it inside her. "We," she said. "We are going."

"The mare? The grey herd?"

"If they will. And if not," she said, "not."

"They'll let you go?"

"I won't let them stop me."

A gust of laughter escaped him. "We'll have to run away in the night. You from the horses. I from my brother."

"Far and far away," she said. She gasped as he surged up and round, braced on hands and knee. "What—"

But her body was thinking for her. She locked ankles about his middle and drove him deep.

It was quick, but strong. He dropped, catching his breath at the grinding of shards in his knee. But the rest was only ache. He was healing. By the gods, he was healing at last.

⇒ ⇐

Minas sat in his cart in the north pasture, glowering at the herds of horses. One, with bridle and saddle-fleece, stood hipshot beside him. It seemed hardly a worthy mount for a lord and warrior: an elderly white mare with sagging belly and slack lip, sleeping in the sun.

But he was not glowering at the chief and queen of the grey herd, who had let it be known that she would consent to carry the broken man. He was glowering mostly at himself, for the flutter in his belly and the clenching of something that, he had begun to suspect, must be fear.

Was his spirit broken, too, that he should be afraid to mount and ride an ancient mare?

There was no crowd here, at least, to watch and jeer. It was only his kin: Rhian and Emry, Metos and Aera. Metos was paying no attention to him at all. He was inspecting one of the cart's wheels, muttering to himself.

Minas swallowed. His throat burned with bile. His hands were cold. "Now," he said to Emry: crisply, he hoped, and not in a dying fall.

Emry did not laugh at him. The strong arms lifted him. He reached almost blindly for the mare's mane, catching hold, pulling himself up. His muscles were as weak as an infant's. Emry had to raise him like one, and settle him on the broad back. The mare sighed vastly but made no other move.

Minas shifted very carefully. His knee was throbbing; but then it always did.

He was tall again. He was a rider, however feeble. He straightened his back and breathed deep. His head, his shoulders came up. He turned his face to the sun. Its light poured into him. He had not drunk sunlight since—gods, since he was a prince on the steppe. He gave it a scrap of the sunrise song, though it was nearly noon. The sun did not seem to care.

He was grinning so broadly his cheeks hurt. The mare was signally unimpressed, but she consented to amble down the field.

It was small, a child's step, but it was a beginning. He barely even minded that Emry had to help him off as well as on, and carry him to the cart, and lay him in it as if he were an infant. He had been less than that before. And now that he had begun, he would be a great deal more.

⇒ ⇐

Minas told Dias after much thought, and in a way that might have been foolhardy, but it proved that he was a man again. Dias had been in Larchwood, making it and its Mother his own, but he had come back to Lir on his way toward the southern cities. Minas met him on the road, riding one of his own duns—a much less quiet mount than the old mare who had been carrying him. But he would not ride before his brother's war-band on a mare, even the queen of the Goddess' greys.

The dun was a sensible enough soul, for a stallion, but Minas' weakness made him uneasy. He was difficult to settle; he danced and snorted, shy-ing at shadows. At sight of Dias' warband, he reared and struck the air.

Minas clung grimly to the stallion's mane, and prayed that his balance would not fail; for he could not grip with his knees. *Fool,* a small voice sang in his head. *Fool, fool, fool.*

The gods were kind. He did not tumble ignominiously to the ground in front of his brother. The dun came to a snorting, head-tossing halt, glaring challenge at Dias' grey.

Dias' glare was hardly less ferocious. "What in the gods' name are you doing?"

"Meeting you," said Minas, not too breathlessly. "Welcome again to Lir, my brother."

Dias took him in, from unraveling plait to thickly bandaged knee, and shook his head. "Even for a dead man, you're mad."

They paused by the roadside, ostensibly to make themselves beautiful for the entry into the city. But Dias had set Minas a test. "Come down and sit," he said, "and we'll make you fit to be seen."

Minas eyed the ground. It was grass, and soft enough, but he had yet to dismount without hands to catch him. No one here was going to do it, that was obvious.

He gritted his teeth. The dun for a miracle was steady. Somehow he got his leg over and slid. His good knee held for a moment as his foot touched the grass, then buckled. He sat rather more abruptly than he had meant to.

"Idiot," said Dias. He sat on the grass beside Minas. "You'll break yourself again."

"I will not."

"You will."

Men of the warband—not the boys who served them, but the warriors themselves—brought gifts: a comb, a coat, a pair of leggings. They laid each gift at Minas' feet, not speaking, but offering a smile or the warmth of a glance.

Dias began to work the knots and snarls out of Minas' ruddy mane. "Don't you ever comb it?" he asked.

"There's never time," said Minas.

"Never inclination, you mean to say."

Minas smiled, then yelped as Dias resorted to force.

There was a sort of peace in this comfortable bickering of brothers. Minas had not had it in far too long.

And he was about to give it up again.

He said it straight, as a warrior did. "When the moon comes to the full, I'm leaving Lir."

Dias' hands paused, a brief mercy. "We're wintering in Larchwood," he said. "But we'll ride a fair quarter of the earth before we stop there."

"The young men will be glad of that," Minas said.

"That sitting chariot of yours," said Dias, "would be better than the back of a horse. Though if you want to ride—"

"I'm not riding with the People," Minas said.

There was a silence. Dias' fingers went on with his tangles, blindly maybe, and none too gently.

"I'm going with the foreigner," said Minas. "He asked me to ride with him to his own city, far away in the south."

"Because you can make chariots."

Minas shrugged.

"That's all anyone wants you for. Except us. You're our kin, our brother."

"I'm dead." Minas shifted, careful of his mending body. "I've promised Emry I'll come back. I make you the same promise. But, brother, there's a whole world I haven't seen. I can't be a warrior now; I can't conquer it. But I can ride in it, and in time I'll walk."

"You told Emry? You waited to tell me?"

Minas twisted until he could see his brother's face. "That's why," he said. "You're angry."

"Because you didn't tell me," snapped Dias, "not because you're going. Damn your eyes, brother! Don't you know me better than that? I can see your spirit dying in the city, shriveling little by little. Thank the gods you're getting out of it."

Minas gaped at him.

"We can't live in cages," said that astonishing man. "Nor in cities, either, unless we're of a mind to kill our souls. These cities, they'll feed us and defend us and make us unimaginably rich, but we won't live in them, not for any longer than we absolutely must. We're Windriders, brother. Even you, who call yourself a dead man."

Minas closed his mouth. "Rhian is coming with me. And Ariana. And . . . she's not telling me, but I think—there will be another in the spring. I suppose she's afraid I'll forbid her to go."

"Will you try?"

"No more than you will."

Dias' smile was not as steady as it might have been. "I know better.

Stay alive, will you? Or no more dead than you are now. I've mourned you once. I don't intend to do it again until we're both appallingly old."

"We'll die together," Minas said, "with a skin of kumiss between us, and a chariot under us, and the wind of the morning in our faces."

"May the gods make it so," said the king of chariots.

MORNING SONG

ON THE DAY that Minas left Lir, he went out in the dawn with his brother Dias beside him, his arm about those broad shoulders, hobbling painfully—but walking, after a fashion. They went to the place where the temple had been, and stood on the hill amid the ashes of the women's world. This was their world's end, Minas thought. He sang the morning song of his People, calling the sun into the sky and the light to the earth, and the gods' blessing on every living thing. It was Dias' gift to him, to perform the king's office at his last sunrise in this city.

Dias carried him away from the fallen temple—much against his will, but he was a weak thing still. They went not to the king's house but to that in which Eresh had spent his days in the city, down toward the southern wall. The caravan was forming already. Men were hitching oxen to the slow heavy carts, heaping them with baggage.

Minas' cart was there, and his duns, and the White Mare; and a pair of greys tethered behind—mares, the pick of the Goddess' herd. A dark grey foal ran at the heel of one, with a bright imperious eye and a look about her that reminded him vividly of his daughter.

Dias moved to lower Minas into the cart, but a large grey body intervened. A fourth mare stood there, white as the moon. She was not the old queen, but one of her daughters. Her neck was nigh as lofty as a stallion's, and her eye was royally proud. She would carry him, it said, and he would endure it, mere mare though she might be.

He flushed. Her rebuke had a sting like the lash of a whip. He bent his head as humbly as a prince of the People could manage, and let himself be lifted onto her back.

She had soft paces, that one, but with a hint of fire in them. If he laid too firm a leg against her, she snapped at it. He would ride her subtly, or he would suffer her wrath.

While he made the mare's acquaintance, people had been coming to
surround the caravan. There seemed an uncommon number of them.
Rhian of course, with Ariana in her arms, and Eresh, and Aera and Emry,
and Metos, but with them a mingled crowd from Lir and of the People.
Men of the warband. Men and women of the city guard. Makers and
smiths. Servants. Tamers of horses.

They had come for him as well as for Rhian. He was glad to be
mounted, to be a rider and not a cripple in a cart. He could leave them
proudly, as a prince of the People should.

No one wept or wailed, which was well. This should be joyous, this
parting. Minas eyes only brimmed once, when his mother came and took
his hands and looked long into his face. "Go with the gods," she said.

He stooped to kiss her. "May the Goddess of this place keep you," he
said.

That startled a laugh out of her, even through tears. She kissed his
hands and held them to her cheeks, then turned away.

The caravan was moving—so soon?

The White Mare came up beside him. Ariana stretched out her arms.
Minas took her, to her manifest satisfaction, with a smile over her head
for Rhian. Rhian's cheeks were wet, but her smile was bright, and growing brighter.

"Adventures," their daughter said, clapping her hands. "We're going
to have adventures!"

"Many and many of them," Minas agreed. "You and I and your mother
and—your brother?"

Rhian was properly taken aback. "How did you—"

He smiled with perfect sweetness—a smile, he knew well, precisely like
the one for which she was notorious. "I may be halt, my lady of horses,
but I'm hardly blind."

"I was going to tell you," she said.

"Yes: when we were too far to turn back." He settled their daughter
more comfortably in front of him. "Well? Is it a son?"

She nodded.

This new smile filled the whole of him from the soles of his feet to the
crown of his head. By the gods and the Goddess, he was happy. He would
not have given this up for the world—no, not even to be king of the
People.

✢ ✤

Aera and Emry and the rest followed the caravan to the gate and out
upon the road. There they stopped, and the caravan went on.

Aera slipped her arms about Emry's waist and leaned against him,
watching them go. Her son rode straight and tall. The long bright tail of

his hair swung, brushing the mare's broad white rump. In coat and leggings, he showed nothing of the strokes that had maimed him. He was as beautiful as he had ever been.

He was whole in spirit. And so, she thought, was she. Her king in her arms, their children in the king's house, the youngest in her belly, had healed the wounds in her heart.

She looked up just as Emry looked down. She smiled through the last of her tears.

"Are you sorry," he asked her, "that you didn't go with them?"

"A little," she admitted. "But only a very little."

"I, too," he said. He tilted up her chin and kissed her, and no matter that the whole world could see. "Come, lady," he said. "Come rule with me in Lir."

They walked back hand in hand, as lovers walk: back to the city; back to the world that they and their kin had made.